THE
SHE

ALSO BY CAROL PLUM-UCCI

The Body of Christopher Creed

What Happened to Lani Garver

Greek Painted Pottery

Greek Painted Pottery

R. M. COOK

LONDON

Methuen & Co Ltd

First Published in 1960
Reprinted with corrections 1966
Second edition 1972
by Methuen & Co. Ltd.
11 New Fetter Lane, London EC4P 4EE
Reprinted 1977

© 1960 and 1972 R. M. Cook

Printed in Great Britain
by J. W. Arrowsmith Ltd

ISBN 0 416 76170 4

Distributed in the USA by
HARPER & ROW PUBLISHERS, INC.
BARNES & NOBLE IMPORT DIVISION

to
Kathleen Cook

Contents

Illustrations

Numbers in square brackets after the descriptions of the plates indicate the pages on which the plate in question is discussed.

xi

c Ripe Corinthian alabastron: ht 9·7 cm. *c.* 625–600 B.C. (EC). Cambridge G.28. [55, 56, 232]
Photo: R. Johnson.

11 A Transitional Corinthian olpe: ht 27·5 cm. Perhaps by the Sphinx painter: *c.* 640–625 B.C. (Tr.) Oxford 1879.100. [55, 226]
Photo: Ashmolean Museum, Oxford.
B Ripe Corinthian oinochoe (some repainting): ht 38 cm. *c.* 625–600 B.C. (EC). Paris, Bibliothèque Nationale 4756. [55, 56, 224]
Photo: Bibliothèque Nationale.

12 A Ripe Corinthian kotyle (detail): ht of field 6 cm. By the Samos painter: *c.* 580 B.C. (MC). Boston 95.14. [60]
Photo: Museum of Fine Arts, Boston.
B Ripe Corinthian kotyle (detail): ht of field *c.* 6·5 cm. *c.* 580 B.C. Louvre CA.3044. [59, 60]
Photo: Louvre Museum.
c Ripe Corinthian column-krater: ht 46 cm. *c.* 600 B.C. (EC). Louvre E.635 (Camp. 33). [59, 60, 119, 128]
Photo: Louvre Museum.

13 Ripe Corinthian red-ground column-krater (detail): combined ht of fields *c.* 20 cm. By the Cavalcade painter: *c.* 570 B.C. (LCI). Vatican 126. [61]
Photo: Alinari.

14 A Protoattic hydria: ht 52·5 cm. By the Analatos painter: *c.*700 B.C. Athens, N.M. 2696. [65–7, 223]
Photo: J. M. Cook.
B Protoattic krater: ht 39 cm. By the Analatos painter: *c.* 690 B.C. Munich 6077. [67]
Photo: Antikensammlungen, Munich.

15 A Protoattic amphora: scale *c.* 1 : 4, By the Ram Jug painter: *c.* 660–650 B.C. Berlin A.9. (70)
After *CVA Berlin* I, pl. 5 (C. H. Beck'sche Verlagsbuchhandlung).
B Attic Bf dinos? (fragment): scale *c.* 1 : 1. By Sophilos: *c.* 580–570 B.C. Istanbul 4574. [75]
From C. Blinkenberg, *Lindos* I, pl. 127.2629 (Verlag Walter de Gruyter & Co.).

16 Protoattic amphora: ht 108·5 cm. *c.* 660 B.C. New York 11.210.1. [69–70]
Photo: Metropolitan Museum, New York.

17 Protoattic amphora: ht 122 cm. By the Nessos painter: *c.* 615 B.C. Athens, N.M. 1002. [71–3]
Photo: National Museum, Athens.

18 Attic Bf dinos and stand: total ht 93 cm. By the Gorgon painter:
   c. 590 B.C. Louvre E.874 (Camp. 30).   [74, 230]
   Photo: Giraudon.

19 A Attic Bf volute-krater: ht 66 cm. The François vase. By Clitias:
   c. 570 B.C. Florence 4209.   [76–7, 228]
   Photo: Soprintendenza Antichità, Florence.
   B Detail of lip from the other side: ht of upper field 5·6 cm.
   Photo: Soprintendenza Antichità, Florence.

20 A Attic Bf hydria: ht *c.* 25 cm. By the Polos painter: *c.* 600–570
   B.C.   [79–80]
   Photo: National Museum, Athens.
   B Attic Bf amphora: ht 38·8 cm. Tyrrhenian group, by the Timiades
   painter: *c.* 570–560 B.C. British Museum 97.7–27.2.   [78–9, 220]
   Photo: British Museum.

21 A Attic Bf one-piece amphora: ht 54 cm. *c.* 600 B.C. Munich 1360.
                                                             [73, 80, 221]
   Photo: Antikensammlungen, Munich.
   B Attic Bf Panathenaic amphora: ht 61·2 cm. The Burgon amphora.
   c. 560 B.C. British Museum, uninventoried (B.130). [84, 91, 221, 264]
   Photo: British Museum.

22 Attic Bf one-piece amphora: ht 80·5 cm. By Exekias: *c.* 530 B.C.
   Vatican 344.   [80, 86, 221]
   Photo: Alinari.

23 Attic Bf amphora: ht 33 cm. By the Amasis painter: *c.* 530 B.C.
   Paris, Bibliothèque Nationale 678 (Cat. 222).   [85, 88, 220]
   Photo: Giraudon.

24 A Attic Bf cup: ht 9·5 cm. Comast group, manner of the KX painter:
   c. 580–570 B.C. New York 22.139.22.   [77–8, 234]
   Photo: Metropolitan Museum, New York.
   B Attic Bf Siana cup: ht 13 cm. By the C painter: *c.* 570–560 B.C.
   British Museum 67.5–8.940 (B.382).   [78, 234]
   Photo: British Museum.

25 A Attic Bf lip cup: ht 12·4 cm. *c.* 550–530 B.C. Manchester Mus.
   iii. H. 45.   [81, 82, 234, 252]
   Photo: H. Spencer.
   B Attic Bf band cup: ht 13·3 cm. *c.* 550–530 B.C. Manchester Mus.
   iii. H.39.   [81, 82, 234]
   Photo: H. Spencer.

26 A Laconian cup: diam. (without handles) *c.* 21 cm. Early 6th cent.
   B.C. Taranto.   [95]
   Photo: National Museum, Taranto.
   B Laconian cup: ht 9·5 cm. Early 6th cent. B.C. Taranto. [95]
   Photo: National Museum, Taranto.

27 A–B Laconian cup: diam. (without handles) 17·8 cm. By the Rider painter: c. 550–540 B.C. British Museum 42.4–7.7 (B.1). [96–7]
Photos: British Museum.

28 A Boeotian Bird cup: ht 21 cm. Mid 6th cent. B.C. Munich 2238.
[101–2]
Photo: Antikensammlungen, Munich.
B Eretrian amphora: ht 75 cm. c. 625–600 B.C. Athens, N.M. 12077.
[104]
Photo: J. Boardman.

29 A–C Linear Island amphora: ht 43·5 cm. Early 7th cent. B.C. Thera.
[106, 220]
Photos: German Archaeological Institute, Athens.
D East Greek Bird bowl: ht 5 cm. c. 675–650 B.C. Oxford 1928.313.
[116–17, 234]
Photo: Ashmolean Museum, Oxford.

30 A Wild Goat style oinochoe: ht 30 cm. c. 630 B.C. Berlin F.295.
[118, 119, 225]
Photo: Staatliche, Museen, Berlin.
B Wild Goat style oinochoe: ht 36 cm. c. 625–600 B.C. British Museum 67.5–8.928. [118, 119, 225]
Photo: British Museum.

31 A Wild Goat style oinochoe (detail): ht of field c. 6·5 cm. c. 625 B.C. Zurich, Technische Hochschule. [121]
Photo: F. Brommer.
B Wild Goat style krater (detail): ht of field c. 3·7 cm. c. 600–575 B.C. Tübingen 1473. [121]
Photo: Archaeological Institute, Tübingen University.
C Chiot Wild Goat style bowl (fragment): ht of field 7·8 cm. c. 615–600 B.C. British Museum 1924.12–1.84. [123, 125]
D Clazomenian sarcophagus (detail): ht of field c. 17 cm. c. 515–500 B.C. Vienna IV. 1865. [137]
From *Antike Denkmäler* I, pl. 45.

32 A Fikellura amphora: ht 30·5 cm. By the Running Man painter: c. 540–520 B.C. Birmingham University V. 58. [131–2]
Photo: Department of Ancient History and Archaeology, Birmingham University.
B Clazomenian Bf amphora: ht (as preserved) 31 cm. By the Petrie painter: c. 540–530 B.C. British Museum 88.2–8.69. [135–6]
Photo: British Museum.

33 A East Greek situla: ht (as restored) 47·6 cm. c. 575–550 B.C. Philadelphia 29.71.189. [138]
Photo: University Museum, Philadelphia.

45 Attic Rf pelike: ht 41 cm. By the Chicago painter: 460–450 B.C. Lecce 570. [173, 177, 178, 222]
Photo: G. Guido.

46 A Attic Rf amphora: ht 58·1 cm. By the Peleus painter: *c.* 440 B.C. British Museum 47.9–9.7 (E.271). [179, 180, 181, 220]
Photo: British Museum.
B Attic Rf squat lekythos: ht 19·4 cm. By the Midias painter: 410–400 B.C. British Museum 56.5–12.15 (E.697). [182, 183, 231]
Photo: British Museum.

47 Attic Rf squat lekythos (detail): ht of field 9·2 cm. By the Eretria painter: 430–420 B.C. Berlin F.2471. [180]
From Furtwängler, *la Collection Sabouroff*, pl. 55.

48 A Attic Rf bell-krater: ht 31·5 cm. By the Dinos painter: 420–410 B.C. Philadelphia MS. 5682. [180, 182, 229]
Photo: University Museum, Philadelphia.
B Attic Rf bell-krater (detail): ht of second figure 15·4 cm. By the Lycaon painter: *c.* 440 B.C. Goluchow, Czartoryski 43. [179]
From J. D. Beazley, *Greek Vases in Poland*, pl. 25 (Clarendon Press).

49 A Attic Wg lekythos: ht 38·7 cm. By the Achilles painter: 450–440 B.C. British Museum 91.8–6.85 (D.51). [176, 180, 231]
Photo: British Museum.
B Attic Wg lekythos: ht 31·5 cm. By the Reed painter: 420–410 B.C. British Museum 73.8–20.303 (D.73). [182, 231]
Photo: British Museum.

50 Attic Rf pelike: ht (as made up) 28·7 cm. By the Jena painter: *c.* 380 B.C. Exeter University. [184]
Photo: B. B. Shefton.

51 Attic Rf pelike: ht 42·5 cm. By the Marsyas painter: *c.* 350 B.C. British Museum 62·5–30.1 (E.424). [185, 222]
Photo: British Museum.

52 A Early Apulian Rf volute-krater (detail): combined ht of fields *c.* 29 cm. By the Sisyphus painter: 430–420 B.C. Munich 3268. [195]
Photo: Antikensammlungen, Munich.
B Early Lucanian Rf bell-krater (detail): ht of field *c.* 17 cm. By the Amykos painter: 440–430 B.C. Denver, Colorado. [197]
Photo: Hesperia Art, Baltimore.

53 Apulian Rf calyx-krater (detail): ht of field 28·5 cm. By the Lycurgus painter: 360–350 B.C. British Museum 49.6–23.48 (F.271). [196]
Photo: British Museum.

54 Lucanian Rf amphora of Panathenaic shape: ht 81 cm. By the Primato painter: *c.* 340 B.C. Ipswich 1921/120. [197, 231]
Photo: Ipswich Museum.

GPP—B

FIGURES

Acknowledgements

It is impossible to assess and acknowledge all debts to the work and assistance of others. Here I mention by name only those who have been so kind as to read and criticize my text. Professor J. M. Cook and Mrs K. Cook have been through most of it, and I thank them first. Next and no less sincerely I thank those who have looked at one part or another – Sir John Beazley, Mr J. C. Belshé, Miss M. Bimson, Mr J. Boardman, Mr J. K. Brock, Mr P. E. Corbett, Professor J. A. Davison, Mr V. R. d'A. Desborough, Dr M. I. Finley, Dr J. M. Hemelrijk, Dr L. H. Jeffery, Professor A. W. Lawrence, Dr S. R. Nockolds, Mr A. Purves, Dr F. H. Stubbings, Professor A. D. Trendall, Mrs A. D. Ure, Professor A. J. B. Wace, Professor T. B. L. Webster and Mr A. G. Woodhead. If more often than not I have rejected their advice, I hope that they will set it down to obstinacy and not to ingratitude.

The help I have had with the illustrations is more easily summarized. For advice and the loan or procuring of photographs I am obliged to Professor A. D. Trendall, Mr P. E. Corbett, and Mr E. A. Lane; to Sir John Beazley, Professor J. M. Cook, Mr R. A. Higgins, Mrs S. Karouzou, Dr L. Talcott; to Professor P. Amandry, Dr M. Bernardini, Mr J. Boardman, Dr D. von Bothmer, Mr J. K. Brock, Dr G. Buchner, Professor F. Brommer, Mr T. Burton Brown, Dr A. Cambitoglou, Dr G. Caputo, Mr V. R. Desborough, Mr P. Devambez, Dr N. Himmelmann, Dr R. Lullies, Professor H. Möbius, Mr R. Oddy, Dr C. N. Schmalz, Mr B. B. Shefton, Dr F. J. Tritsch, Mrs A. D. Ure, Dr C. C. Vermeule, Mr J. B. Ward Perkins, Dr R. S. Young: and not least to Mr R. Johnson and Mr S. C. Collard. Permission to reproduce photographs and drawings has been given courteously by the authorities of museums and by other institutions and persons: the names may be found at the beginning and end of many entries in the list of illustrations. Some plates and figures are taken from other works by the generosity of publishers and authors. It is a pleasure to record my debt for these and other kindnesses.

Lastly I thank Mr Peter Wait for his patience.

FURTHER ACKNOWLEDGEMENTS

In revising this book for its corrected first edition and still more for the second I have been aided by many colleagues. Of those who have read and criticized various passages I am indebted most to Mr J. N. Coldstream, next to Professor A. D. Trendall, Professor F. Villard, Dr J. V. Noble and Dr J. W. Hayes, and further to Mr B. F. Cook and Dr B. A. Sparkes. For help over photographs I add the name of Dr D. Willers, and for much practical assistance those of Mr B. D. Thompson, Mr E. E. Jones and Mrs G. J. Blake. To them and many others I offer my honest thanks.

Note on Orthography

The rendering of Greek names and words into English is difficult. For a long time Classical scholars have tended to reject more and more of the Latin forms that are naturalized and familiar. 'Pheidias', for instance, is now almost regular in learned works, and 'Thoukydides' has made his appearance. Such innovations are pedantic and often objectionable. First, the Greek alphabet is not the same as the English, so that any system of transliteration must be arbitrary. Secondly, English spelling has its own patterns, which decency should respect. The Greek name ʿΗρακλῆς may serve as an example. Most students of the Classics now render it 'Herakles', though English usage prefers a 'c' rather than a 'k' in such a position and there is the compelling analogy of 'Heraclea', 'Heraclitus' and 'Pericles'. So I have kept to 'Heracles'. But in the names of shapes I have (as I see) been timid, writing 'krater' where Payne wrote 'crater', and repeating learned plurals like 'amphorae' instead of risking 'amphoras'. The French do these things better.

1   *Introduction*

Greek pottery differs in character from the pottery of other civilizations, and those who have formed their tastes on porcelain may at first sight find it surprising. Though they liked a shiny surface, the Greeks did not use a high glaze. Their shapes, designed to be useful, are constructed with a clean and vigorous precision of contour. The decoration, which is arranged in a band round the pot to confine or emphasize its structure, in appearance as well as in fact keeps to the plane of the surface. Of the decorative motives the human figure becomes the most important; it is drawn with a neat economy of line, and though in time the roundness of the body is suggested, movement and grouping usually avoid the implication of depth. The whole effect shows a considered and logical planning, which imposed a strict discipline on artists and left little room for virtuosity.

Besides a sound artistic tradition Greek potters had other advantages. During much of the period covered in this survey there was a large class of customers of moderate wealth for whom painted pots were near the limit of luxury. So fine pottery was a profitable industry and offered not only employment but opportunity to artists even of the first rank. In the Protogeometric and Geometric periods it was one of the few forms of art generally practised. In the seventh century sculpture and free painting appeared; but statues had the special difficulty of being in three dimensions, and reliefs and pictures differed from vase-paintings in little more than a larger scale and a wider choice of colours. It was not till the fifth century that free painting began to draw away, and vase-painting at last declined to a minor art.

In the Late Bronze Age the Mycenaean style of pottery became universal throughout the Greek world and beyond. It was based on a Cretan model, which, with its flowing shapes and freely spreading decoration of plants and sea creatures, appeals immediately to modern taste. But the Mycenaean potters did not have a genuine understanding of the subtleties of curve and spacing, and the history of their pottery is one of steady decline into rigid composition and stiffer and clumsier forms. By the mid eleventh century, when the Bronze Age was in Greece passing into the Iron Age, all that remained was a lifeless and limited repertory of simple ornaments generally arranged in bands. At this point a revival began. The new Protogeometric style [PLATES 1 and 2B] remodelled the shapes and decoration it inherited and gave them precision and dignity; the weary spiral for instance was converted into neat sets of compass-drawn concentric circles, and the sagging shapes were tautened and defined. What caused this artistic revolution is unknown, for Attica where it flourished most strongly was according to tradition the only major province of Greece to escape the invasions of the Dorians and other tribes; its originators may even have believed that they were doing no more than restore the decadent Mycenaean style to its ancient vigour. The effects however are clear. By its strong sense of logical order, which is the antithesis of the spontaneity of the models that inspired Mycenaean, the new spirit determined the course of Greek art till its decay.

The Protogeometric style succeeded Mycenaean throughout Greek lands and in time evolved into what is defined as Geometric. But parochialism was growing and some local schools lagged behind others or strayed off on their own. At Athens, which led the development, a climax was reached in the ninth century in such harmonious exercises as the pot illustrated on PLATE 3B, where the abstract decoration (notably the hatched meander) with its nice balance of dark and light is economically but lucidly disposed to emphasize the strongly articulated shape. Further development led some Attic workshops to a vulgar profusion of ornament that obscured the shape [PLATE 4B], and Corinth to a neat and delicate mannerism [PLATE 8B]. As the eighth century advanced, Greek vase-painting was ready for a change and Oriental art, with which the Greeks were already acquainted, showed that other styles than the Geometric were possible.

The Oriental examples – metalwork, ivories and textiles – came chiefly from Syria, where there flourished a competent and tasteless hotch-potch of the artistic achievements of Nearer Asia and Egypt. Fortunately the Greeks were not overwhelmed by its sophisticated senility – good sense or the strength of tradition saved them – and instead they selected suitable motives and adapted them. Without the Oriental influence Greek vase-painting of the seventh century would have had a smaller fauna and a floral ornament that was rarer or at least more abstract. But even if the black-figure technique, unknown to the pottery of the Orient, was derived from Oriental metalwork or inlays, the evolution of the human figure from the austerely stylized silhouette of Geometric would have been similar, though perhaps slower. The new style widened the divisions between local schools. Corinth, which now took the lead, developed the black-figure technique, in which the figure is drawn in silhouette but enlivened by incised – that is engraved – detail and touches of added colour, and with it created an elegant miniature style [PLATE 9B]. At Athens there were two generations of ambitious exuberance which preferred to draw in outline [PLATE 16]. The cities of Asiatic Greece were content with unadventurous mediocrity [PLATE 31]. Other schools in their own time and way followed or defied their betters, and gradually the smaller and less successful faded away.

In the later seventh century Corinth forced the pace by switching to a cheap and showy style which greatly increased her production [PLATE 11B], and this example was uncritically and sometimes disastrously imitated by her competitors [PLATE 20A and FIG. 18]. So the black-figure technique became almost ubiquitous. But the Corinthian staple was an animal style, and during the early sixth century Athens created a new artistic standard based partly on improved technique and partly on the more regular use of human figures [PLATES 19, 22 and 23]. About the middle of the century Corinth was in turn eliminated and such other local schools as were left did not survive much longer. Once again there was a single style of vase-painting among the Greeks, with the difference that it was no longer universal but the monopoly of a dominant local school.

The black-figure style was well fitted for the representation of action, but Attic vase-painters were now ambitious to express mood and to experiment in anatomy. This was made possible by the red-figure technique, which replaced the convention of silhouette and engraving by the freer method of outline drawing with painted linear detail [PLATES 38–39]. The red-figure style, the first manifestation of the Classical spirit, was established in the late sixth century and by the middle of the fifth had driven out its older rival: its achievement during this time was extraordinary [PLATES 37–45]. Meanwhile free painting was adventuring towards perspective, modelling and subtler expressions of human feeling, and soon the painters of pottery were faced with a dangerous choice, to stand still and stagnate or to advance out of their depth. Though a respectable compromise was contrived, vase-painting in the later fifth century was no longer a creative art, and during the fourth century at Athens and soon after in South Italy (where new red-figure schools had sprouted) the long tradition withered away. Hellenistic vase-painters, if they can be called that, mostly made do with a few tatty ornaments from the conventional stock.

Greek art is the source of most Western art, and no branch of it has survived in such quantity as the painted pottery. But there is no need for historical reasons to justify the study of this pottery. It is one of the few subjects of archaeology that can give aesthetic enjoyment.

2   *The Protogeometric Style*

1. Introduction

The first monumental achievement of Hellenic art was the Geometric style. It is best represented by the painted pottery, of which much has survived. A glance at PLATE 3B shows its character. The decoration, in dark paint on a lighter surface, is carefully planned in bands of simple ornament which emphasize the shape of the pot. The individual elements of the ornament are unimportant, it is their cumulative effect that concerns the artist. To an unusual degree the style depends on composition without regard to the detail.

There is an essential contrast between the Geometric style and the Mycenaean style of the Late Bronze Age which preceded it. A typical sample of each is illustrated in PLATE 2A and PLATE 3B. The Mycenaean artist conceived his pot as a single whole; the contour has a flowing continuous curve, the painted decoration may embrace the full field in freehand balance. His Geometric successor observes a more orderly system: his pot is composed of clearly articulated parts, and the pattern is plotted exactly in bands of linear regularity. The intermediate stage, which was late in receiving its recognition, bears the cumbrous name of Protogeometric. This Protogeometric style [see PLATES 1 and 2B] is not simply the transition from Mycenaean to Geometric proper, but a separate entity with its own standards. It has a sober easy discipline, firm but not finicky, with a conscious preference for definition of shape and ornament and for mechanical rather than individual forms. The shapes are solid and neat, and the articulation of the parts is clear without being punctilious. The decoration depends on broad contrasts of dark and light with a modicum of simple balanced ornament. The effect, as is evident in the amphora of PLATE 2B, is direct, bold and harmonious, thoroughly satisfactory if not inspiring. In its own limited way it cannot be bettered, and by its standard the Geometric style – and much of later Greek pottery – is fussy and pedantic.

The creation of the Protogeometric style marks a new era in the art of the Greek lands. Its trend towards geometrical precision has evoked comparisons with Middle Helladic vases some five hundred years earlier: a natural taste for Geometric forms in art, it has been suggested,

4

was inherent in the early population of Greece, had been suppressed by the creators of the Mycenaean culture, and now on its collapse re-emerged. A safer statement is that the ultimately Cretan characteristics of Mycenaean art had now been bred out, and for the evolution of a fresh style the Geometric method was as obvious and handy as any other. In fact it had been preparing since the fourteenth century, when the Cretan culture broke down and Mycenaean artists were left to their own limited resources. The freshly sketched forms of plants and marine animals which distinguished Cretan vase-painting become in Mycenaean more and more conventional, their disposition more and more stereotyped. Technically Mycenaean pottery maintained its high standard, but its artistic ability contracted: shapes became clumsier, decorative motives fewer and more abstract, and particularly in the 'Close style' a growing tendency towards banded decoration was reinforced by the use of such compact linear motives as sets of concentric arcs and fine scale pattern. The last phase, the Submycenaean, was current in the earlier eleventh century; even technical quality is declining. Here bottom is reached: recovery, when it comes, is in a new direction. Submycenaean and Protogeometric have much in common, but in one vestiges of the old naturalistic forms are visible, the other is purely abstract. In other words the one looks backwards, the other has hope for the future.

Another theory sees in the geometrical impulse the effect of a new people. Ancient Greek tradition makes much of the Dorian invasion of southern Greece, which it dated about the same time that archaeologists now date the end of the Mycenaean period. The proposition that the Dorians brought the Geometric or the Protogeometric style with them from Macedonia or the Danube has therefore been attractive. But first, the centre of both these styles was in Attica, the one important district of Old Greece that according to tradition was not touched by the Dorians – a difficulty which one or two scholars have resolved by assuming some unremembered invasion of Attica. The second and graver objection is that there is a satisfactorily continuous evolution from Mycenaean to Geometric art.

The Mycenaean style, centred in the Argolid, had been widely spread and remarkably uniform, though towards its end local variations became more evident and Attica was gaining importance. With Protogeometric Attic took the lead, but again the new style had an extensive popularity. Mycenaean had been made in the Peloponnese, Attica and Boeotia, probably in the major Ionian islands other than Corcyra, in Euboea and Thessaly, in Rhodes and Cos and perhaps

Samos and Miletus. In Crete Mycenaean had affected but not ousted
the old Minoan tradition. Here Protogeometric too met with opposition, while in Laconia and Western Greece development was now largely
independent. Elsewhere a Protogeometric of Attic character was
adopted; and this also established itself, though feebly and belatedly,
in Macedonia, which had imported but not imitated Mycenaean pottery, and – in a purer form – in the new Greek settlements in Ionia.
Further east in Cyprus, Cilicia and Syria the Levanto-Helladic style,
which is Mycenaean in a mixed local idiom, was beyond the range of
Protogeometric influence, unless perhaps some details of the early
Cypro-Geometric style are to be explained by contact with Crete and
the Dodecanese. In general there was still a considerable uniformity,
but provincialism was growing during the early Iron Age and some
areas lagged behind. So, though in Attica and the Argolid the period
of the Protogeometric style runs – to use a very rough chronology –
from about 1050 to 900 B.C., the same dates cannot be assumed further
afield. Certainly in some areas it lasted on for another generation or
longer.

2. Athens

It is only at Athens – thanks to the excavations of the Germans in the
Ceramicus and the Americans in the Agora – that there is evidence
enough to trace in detail the history of the Protogeometric style. Fortunately, the Attic school is of primary importance, since it both introduced and continued to set the standard for the new style, and so anyhow it deserves much fuller treatment.

The Attic pioneers of Protogeometric pottery were evidently determined that the decoration should harmonize with and be generally
subsidiary to clear well-designed shapes. Two principles were in use,
both inherited from Mycenaean, light-ground and dark-ground. The
amphora of PLATE 2B is a fair specimen of the light-ground manner,
which sometimes invades the neck also: it is used mainly on large
vases, and becomes less popular towards the end of the style. The sparse
ornaments and bands of dark paint only emphasize the prevailing light
tone. PLATE 1 illustrates the complementary dark-ground manner, which
on the oinochoe D is carried to an extreme that might be called the
black style. It is no accident that such ornaments as concentric circles
and chequers and even cross-hatching are composed equivalently of
dark and light, and so can be interpreted according to their context
either as light ornaments on a dark ground or as dark ornaments on a

light ground. The normal decoration emphasizes the shoulder of closed
vases, the field between the handles of open vases; large closed pots
may have a second decorative field round the middle of the belly – so
some amphorae have concentric circles where that of PLATE 2B has its
wavy lines. Towards the end the black style shifts the main field to
mid-belly, and in anticipation of Geometric makes experiments with
ornament on the neck [so on PLATE 1D].

   The ornaments, few and simple, are derived from Mycenaean. Typical are sets of concentric circles and semicircles, drawn with a compass
and multiple brush in contrast to the freehand spirals and arcs of

FIG. 1. *Late Mycenaean cup*
Ht 9 cm. *c.* 1150 B.C. (LH IIIc)

Mycenaean which they replace [cf. PLATE 2A and FIG. 1 with PLATES 2B
and 1A]: at the centre of these circles is a dot or a solid core – this
usually early – or an hour-glass ornament as on PLATE 2B, and the sets
are sometimes divided by pendent groups of tongues. Cross-hatched
triangles, lozenges and panels are common, and small chequers [see
PLATE 1A–B]. Besides these are lesser ornaments – solid triangles set in
a row like teeth or alternate and separated by oblique strokes (or
'opposed diagonals'), zigzags, and the wavy lines popular on the bellies
of amphorae. It is a simple repertory, and simply and sensibly used:
thus of the major motives semicircles and cross-hatched triangles belong
to the strongly curving shoulders of closed vases, full circles to more
rectangular fields. The composition is symmetrically balanced. Either
there is a continuous row of – say – semicircles [so on PLATE 2B, and

divided by dots on PLATE IC]; or a central panel is flanked by free ornaments [PLATE IA] or by other panels [PLATE IB]. Occasionally the field is divided into an upper and a lower register. The more elaborate products, with several panels or the alternation of semicircles and cross-hatched triangles, are generally later. Protogeometric is a severely abstract style, direct and calculated, and the extremely rare organic forms are introduced in unusual places or without conviction: so on an amphora from the Ceramicus a little silhouette horse stands shyly under the wavy lines to one side of the handle frieze, amusing but irrelevant.

The commonest shapes are neck-amphorae with vertical or horizontal handles (now the standard container of the ashes in Attic graves), krater, trefoil-mouthed oinochoe, lekythos (which already in Submycenaean was superseding the stirrup vase), cup, 'tea-cup', spherical pyxis and kalathos (sometimes provided with a handle). Most of these shapes are inherited from Mycenaean, though modified and remodelled as can be seen by the comparison of PLATE 2B with PLATE 2A or PLATE IA with FIG. I. In general contours are tauter and more clearly, if not yet sharply, defined; and there is a tendency from globular to ovoid forms with a higher belly. Necks are now larger and stronger, and feet more firmly marked and even – on cups, kraters and many 'tea-cups' – boldly conical: high incurving feet, found in some Protogeometric schools, are alien to Attica. The pots illustrated on PLATES I and 2B show the clean vigour of the new profiles; there is nothing niggling about them.

The technique is similar to Mycenaean, though not as good as the best work in that style. The clay, sometimes gritty, varies from a pale to a mid brown: the larger light-ground pots, which are generally pale, seem often to have a thin coating of a finer yellowish slip. The paint ranges from dark brown to near black, sometimes accidentally fired to red. In ornaments a variation in its density often shows the brush running dry; but there was some deliberate dilution, notably in the zigzag that frequently runs above a row of concentric circles or round a lip [as on PLATE IB]. Both paint and unpainted surface have a sheen, now often worn off. Generally the later vases, particularly of the black style, are the most careful, and their darker clay, blackish paint and strong sheen are indistinguishable from much Early Geometric work.

The Attic Protogeometric style began about 1050 B.C., and after a short spell of experiment established its canon. The mature style is powerful and deserved its acceptance in other Greek areas. In the tenth century the elongation of shapes led to a shift of decorative emphasis from shoulder to neck, and there appears some effort for elegance in the now popular black style and the elaborate panel decoration; but since each shape had its own system or systems of decoration, this evolution was not uniform. The end of the style, which came about 900 B.C., was as rapid as its beginning. Attic influence on other Greek schools was wide, and occasional exports have been noticed.

3. Protogeometric outside Attica

Finds have mostly been too few for much knowledge of Protogeometric outside Attica. What is clear is that the other Greek schools, apart from those of Crete and Laconia and Western Greece, were derived from Attic and followed Attic developments more or less closely. It is not always so clear whether the connection was direct or indirect, when it began, and what other influences – such as the survival of a local Submycenaean style – may have been effective. At present it seems safer to suppose that generally these schools, except the Macedonian, knew Attic models at first hand; that, except in the Argolid, this knowledge did not come or at least was not used till Attic had reached its mature stage; and that, except in Thessaly, older traditions did not intrude. There was, of course, some give and take among neighbours, and one must allow too for local originality and incompetence.

The *Argolid*, which had been the dominant artistic region of the Late Bronze Age, produced the only Protogeometric school comparable with Attic, to which it remained close; generally this must have been due to imitation by Argive. From *Corinth* there are so far only a few modest dark-ground pieces, related to Attic or Argive, and the apparent survival of Protogeometric for a generation or so longer suggests that its school was a minor one. This connection of the North-East Peloponnese with Attica may seem curious to believers in ethnic solutions. Even more curious is its severance from the rest of the Peloponnese.

Thessaly was for long on the border of the Greek world. In the Late Bronze Age Mycenaean pottery had been made there, but the Protogeometric that followed owes much to Attic models. It is a provincial and not very ambitious school, notable for cut-away necks and spurred (or trigger) handles, both inherited from the old native tradition. Some Protogeometric pots akin to Thessalian have been found in *Skyros*, and during the tenth century connections appear in *Euboea*,

Andros, *Tenos* and even *Boeotia*, though in these places the Protogeometric style of Attica was followed more sedulously, as long as there was an Attic Protogeometric style to follow. Afterwards, and especially in Euboea, there developed a manner that has been called with more accuracy than elegance Subprotogeometric. Its most notable and enduring products were the cups with low foot, inturned rim and usually two intersecting sets of pendent semicircles on the body: FIG. 2 shows an unusually fine specimen. These cups, sometimes called Thessalo-Cycladic but more conveniently PS cups, seem to have been made from the beginning of the ninth century to the middle of the eighth and were exported widely: some have been found at Delphi and Thasos, and others reached Cyprus and the Levant, where they are generally interpreted as evidence of Euboean enterprise. We have little information about the Protogeometric of the *Southern Cyclades*

FIG. 2. *Cup with pendent semicircles*
Ht 8 cm. Probably Cycladic or Euboean: 9th or early 8th cent. B.C.

(including Naxos), but what there is suggests an Atticizing style free of Thessalo-Cycladic vagaries.

Macedonia, not yet reckoned Greek, had imported Mycenaean but retained its native tradition. That tradition continued in the Iron Age, but at some time a Protogeometric style took root beside it. The quality varies, perhaps according to remoteness. Some examples are respectable enough, but others are barbaric with their impoverished decoration and clumsy shapes. Typical are cups with deep bowl and high lip, decorated with sets of pendent semicircles or three-quarter circles; and the set consists sometimes of only two arcs. Such influences as can be detected suggest that Macedonian derived from Thessalian. On some sites at least it lasted till about 600 B.C. when Corinthian imports became numerous.

Much Protogeometric has been found in *Rhodes* and *Cos*. Once again the style is modelled on Attic (and possibly Argive), and there are some admirable pieces. Gradually local variations appeared, for instance an excess of latticing and (as in some of the Cyclades) the linking of grouped circles by bands of zigzag or straight lines. This Dodecanesian school seems to have received some new influences when Geometric was beginning at Athens, though a proper Geometric style did not succeed for another fifty years. At *Smyrna*, *Samos* and *Miletus* and also in *Caria* the earliest Protogeometric was very like Attic. Finds elsewhere in *Ionia* and *Aeolis* are too few for useful conclusions, whether because the early levels have not been explored or because Greek settlement in those parts had hardly begun. Imports and local imitations are reported – perhaps too hopefully – at Sardis in Lydia.

For *Laconia* we have a fair number of sherds, but few complete pots. The decoration is clumsy and crowded, with frequent cross-hatching on the lip of cups (the commonest shape among the finds), sets of squarish panels between the handles, and dark paint below. The motives are mostly rectilinear, the favourite being the cross-hatched triangle. Horizontal grooving of the body is a peculiarity of this school, the clay is darker than usual elsewhere, and the deep brown to blackish paint often has a metallic sheen. There may be Attic influence, perhaps through Argive, in the occasional use of circles, but generally this looks a conservative style of separate origin, whatever that origin may be. The closest connections in system of decoration and motives are with Western Greek workshops of the time – or so it is suggested by the rare finds of pottery in *Messenia*, *Elis*, *Aetolia* and *Acarnania* and the more comprehensible material of *Ithaca* and *Achaea*. In these schools too Attic influence appears slight, but there is evidence for independent, if parochial, emergence out of Mycenaean. In both Laconia and the Western region the local Protogeometric (which might be more accurately described as Pregeometric) seems to have lasted without much change till round the middle of the eighth century.

In *Crete* the material is embarrassingly numerous and obscure, and may represent more than one local school. Here the antecedents were different. In other parts of the Greek world the style of the Late Bronze Age had been uniformly Mycenaean, but in Crete the older Minoan tradition was tenacious and had partially resisted the mainland style. Now in turn there was resistance to Protogeometric. So we still find the stirrup vase, kalathos, pyxis with high steep sides, duck vases, and the deep cup which turns into a kind of bell-krater. Other common shapes are squat trefoil-mouthed oinochoe, amphora with very short neck or collar, and a footless amphora which tends to acquire a long inward curve towards its flat base. The decoration, in light or dark style, is lax. The commonest ornaments are concentric circles, often floating loosely in the field and filled with an oblique hour-glass, and thick bands of paint to separate zones are used more freely than elsewhere. Other characteristic motives are double horizontal zigzags and even (so it seems) the cable pattern. Clearly the Protogeometric style did not originate in Crete, but evident signs of foreign influence are few though there are some imported Attic pots. It lasted at Cnossus till the middle of the ninth century and in remoter places probably longer.

3   *The Geometric Style*

1. Introduction

A conscious insistence that shape should be clearly defined and decoration have an abstract regularity distinguishes the Protogeometric from the Mycenaean style. Geometric takes these tendencies a stage further: contrast the two amphorae of PLATES 2B and 3B. Geometric ornament has recurred again and again throughout the history of art, but the almost mathematical logic of the Greeks makes theirs the preeminent if not the only Geometric style. The shape of the pot, analysed into its component parts, is carefully balanced. The decoration is placed and designed to emphasize the shape. Here is a style so self-disciplined that it can be monumental.

The Protogeometric amphora of PLATE 2B is a sober but easygoing work, plump in shape and ingenuous in decoration. Its Geometric counterpart [PLATE 3B] has drawn itself in and the band of meander, compact and rigid, advertises the restriction. To suit the new shape and the new feeling for shape the decorative emphasis is shifted from shoulder to belly and neck – Protogeometric groping towards this is shown on the late oinochoe of PLATE 1D, and a transitional stage on PLATE 3A. The ornaments change in sympathy. The groundling semicircles vanish; the loosely spaced rows of full circles survive only in backward schools; and the firm, continuous meander becomes the characteristic Geometric motive. The difference between Protogeometric and Geometric is sharp, but the transition though rapid was evolutionary and there is no sign of artistic prompting from outside. Older theories that the Dorians brought in the new style and particularly the meander were still ignorant of the nature or even the existence of Protogeometric and of the foreshadowing in it of Geometric.

The strict Geometric formula was simple and its ideal easily and quickly reached. Further development in the eighth century tried to complicate the decoration. The ornamental fields were multiplied till sometimes they covered almost the whole surface of the pot, panels and vertical strips interrupted the horizontal rhythm, and some new ornaments, though still regular and abstract, were invented. In the hands of a master this development allowed a subtler and mellow

13

grandeur, as on the amphora of PLATE 4A. Here the principal field, set in its proper structural place, still dominates the decoration of the pot, though the shape has lost much of its primary importance. But more mediocre pieces, such as those of PLATE 6 and even of PLATE 4B, are restless displays of decoration. The strength of the Geometric conventions is becoming a weakness, since painters rigidly limited in their repertory of ornament let themselves indulge in new and ostentatious arrangements which often ignore or contradict the shape. But progress was made with the figures, human and animal, which first appear regularly in the eighth century. These figures, drawn in silhouette, were quickly geometricized into abstract types, but the problems of pictorial composition set a satisfying task to the more ambitious artists who gradually lost interest in enriching the subsidiary decoration. In Attica their austerer models educated the pioneers of the new art of the seventh century.

No style of pottery has been more successful than mature Greek Geometric in adjusting decoration to the shape of the pot. It achieves its aim by precise planning, assisted by quite simple, almost mechanical ornament. The recipe is easy and calls for no special artistic ability, and for that reason there is till near the end little bad Geometric pottery. This impersonal self-sufficient style flourished for about two centuries, and its end when it came was due less to the impact of outside forces than to its own internal exhaustion. On the artists of the next stage of Greek vase-painting – except in the Subgeometric schools which in most areas continued a watered Geometric tradition for another generation or so – its chief influence lies in the discipline and sense of order which it had implanted in Greek art.

The home of the Geometric style was Athens, and till the middle of the eighth century all the important advances were made there. Because of this dominance it is useful to apply to other Geometric schools the stylistic divisions invented for Attic, so that for instance the earliest Geometric of Laconia may be described as Late (or perhaps late Middle), though consistency is perhaps impracticable.

Very roughly, Attic influence on other schools was proportionate to geographical distance, by sea rather than by land, till in the later eighth century most of them found Corinthian novelties more congenial or experimented on their own. At Corinth an unassuming Geometric developed in the mid eighth century a delicate mannerism which easily admitted Orientalizing motives and ideas and was widely imitated. Laconia was coarse and backward; Tegea, probably no better, combined impartially Argive and Laconian elements; Achaea, the western mainland of Greece and Ithaca, came under Corinthian tutelage when at last they tried to modernize their sluggish Protogeometric tradition. The Boeotians were heavily provincial. In Thessaly a grudging Geometric became established in the eighth century, but Macedonia seems not to have progressed beyond its Protogeometric. The Cyclades and Euboea generally reflected the easier forms of Attic, till at last they went their own ways, some contrary to Geometric principles. Of the East Greek schools Rhodes and Cos show an evolution from their local Protogeometric, which remained a recognizable constituent of their Geometric styles; what is known of Ionia shows as well as connections with Rhodian a deeper Attic influence. Cretan vase-painters for long continued with their abnormal Protogeometric, then turned to a still more abnormal and partly Orientalizing experiment, and did not accept a properly Geometric standard till the end of the ninth century. Finally, in the early eighth century a simple Geometric style was adopted in Etruria and later by some of the native peoples of Italy and Sicily. This incidence of the Geometric style corresponds pretty closely to that of the 'polis' or city-state: Geometric was an urban, not a peasant style.

The date when the Geometric style began can be only vaguely conjectured. In Attica it may have been about 900 B.C., and it was not much later in Argos nor in Corinth and Boeotia. In Euboea, the Cyclades and the East Greek cities it seems to have been adopted around 850. In Thessaly and Crete a definitely Geometric school appears about the beginning of the eighth century and Laconia and Western Greece were later still. As for the end of the style, Orientalizing became established in Corinth about 720 B.C. and in Athens, some of the Cyclades and Crete around 700. Elsewhere there was more laggardness and, particularly when no strong Orientalizing style developed, the old tradition persisted in an enfeebled manner, often differentiated by the title Subgeometric.

Technical competence is generally no higher than in Protogeometric. The clay, aiming at a clear medium brown, is fairly fine. A paler slip was used occasionally in Early Geometric, at least in Attic, and more regularly in some Late Geometric schools. The dark paint has some sheen. It is often deliberately diluted for hatching. Towards the end white is sometimes applied over dark paint, but normally (except in Crete) only for small or subordinate ornament. Very rarely a linear pattern, such as a zigzag, is incised on a dark band. The throwing and the trimming of pots are accurate and assured. The control of firing is still erratic.

In painted pottery Greek Geometric art expressed itself most fully. There was no sculpture or architecture worth the name, and free painting – if it existed – can hardly have been more distinguished. The bronze and still more the terracotta figurines, which were numerous, have not the same concentration of purpose. Metalwork with decoration in relief or engraved, though in the eighth century attracting some competent artists, did not offer enough scope in its small fields. Textiles have naturally perished, but it is hard to believe that their decoration had the tectonic quality that characterizes much of the pottery. Geometric art was in its way a perfection of the potter's craft.

2. Athens

Of the various Geometric styles that of Athens is both the best-known and the best. Its evolution, which covers the two centuries from roughly 900 to 700 B.C., may be divided into three stages. The divisions, though conventional, are convenient and can be further subdivided. The number of specimens is large. Graves and stratified deposits have been recorded, notably in the Ceramicus cemetery and the Agora at Athens and also at Eleusis.

Early Geometric (c. 900–c. 850 B.C.)

About the end of the tenth century the Protogeometric style passed into the Geometric style proper. As usually happens, progress was not uniform; and pots in the older style were made at the same time as pieces of more distinctly Geometric quality. But the trend is to shapes with less swelling curves, and on the flatter fields that result the decoration, now regularly in the dark-ground scheme, becomes a little bolder. Circular motives give way to rectilinear, particularly the meander, which is used both as a short strip in a panel and repeated to form a continuous band. It appears first in the battlement form and built of parallel strands [PLATE 3A] – conceivably an angular version of the wavy lines of Protogeometric [PLATE 2B] – or else stuffed with dots; but soon it is regularly involuted and hatched [as on PLATE 3B], and this form becomes the characteristic ornament of Attic Geometric. Attempts have been made to derive the meander from contemporary cultures outside Greece, but the parallels suggested are both unsatisfactory and unnecessary. An ornament of such simple form could have been thought out independently by Greek artists, and the general aspect of the earlier Geometric period suggests a style developing in thoughtful isolation.

The shapes too change. Amphorae grow slimmer and stiffer and – partly by lengthening the neck – rather taller. The oinochoe in contrast becomes squatter and more solid in the body, and its neck is more emphatic. The pedestalled krater continues. The cup, which at first falls behind the kantharos in popularity, gives up the Protogeometric high foot for an abrupt broad base as if the pot had been sawn off a little way up the body [compare for the effect PLATES 1A and 8A]. Among new shapes the most curious is an ovoid pyxis with pointed base, in defiance of the general trend towards stability. The lekythos is replaced by a squat narrow-necked oinochoe. The decoration is re-arranged in rough correspondence to the shape. Thus on the three forms of the amphora the position of the handles determines that of the main decorative field. Where – on the survivors of the Protogeometric favourite – the handles cling to the belly, the emphasis is now regularly on a panel stretching between them. The more modern amphorae with handles either set on the shoulder or reaching up to the neck have panels respectively on shoulder or neck, at first smallish and starkly framed. An example of the latter type, which soon became canonical, is shown on PLATE 3A. Here the panel on the neck is wider than usual and the ornament round the belly has become of equal importance: the Early Geometric painter was tiring of austerity. For the same reason the reserved bands which complete the decoration become finer and more numerous. The repertory of ornaments is still small – the meander of both types and the set of horizontal zigzags, which soon take the principal places, the row of solid triangles, and for a time the triangles between oblique strokes; concentric circles remain fashionable only on kraters and belly-handled amphorae. The arrangement, loosely spaced in Protogeometric, becomes neater and more compact. The total effect, simple as it is, shows a clear and firm artistic conception.

Middle Geometric (c. 850–c. 760 B.C.)

The trends just described are logically fulfilled about the middle of the ninth century. The amphora on PLATE 3B has already been mentioned as typical of the Geometric style in general. Here the forms inherited from earlier phases have been refined, the composition is more precise. The neck, because of the position of the handles, carries the principal decoration: note how the top of the panel is exactly level with the upper junction of the handles. To balance the decorative effect a second field is reserved on the belly, and filled with the same ornaments. Below come neat groups of reserved bands. The dark ground still covers most of the surface of the pot, but is no longer oppressive. There is a similar refinement of the shape. The transition from body to neck, which before was slurred, is now sharply articulated; the proportions are carefully harmonized; and the whole has a more architectural quality. There is little room in this style for original invention and less for virtuosity. For his effects the artist depends on logical planning and the careful repetition of simple ornament. In consequence the general level of attainment was remarkably uniform.

This solution, admirable in its way, had narrow limits. Further development took two courses. One continued to lighten the dark tone of the pot by inserting more bands of ornament and reserved stripes. The other revived the system of dividing a large field into panels [a later and more thorough-going version is presented by PLATE 4B, on the shoulder]: such panelling had been current in Protogeometric [PLATE 1A–B], but in earlier Geometric was more or less restricted to narrow strips of chevrons acting as side frames. Both changes weakened the connection of shape and decoration; the pot tends to be regarded as a surface to be covered rather than a shape to be accentuated. This effect is more evident in Late Geometric, as on PLATE 6A; here the vertical stress of the panels has no structural relevance, though excusable because of the formlessness of this pyxis. But change was gradual, and particularly on less ambitious pieces the severer style was never wholly superseded.

The repertory of ornament grows richer during this stage. Among early novelties are opposed triangles between vertical strokes [illustrated in a coarse version on PLATE 7A] and in the eighth century there are added small circles linked tangentially [as on PLATE 6B] and the string of lozenges with a central dot [PLATE 5, in the next field to the bottom]. More important was the introduction of animate figures. These had appeared even before Middle Geometric, though very rarely and unobtrusively. But with the eighth century the horses, birds and human figures are displayed more boldly, first in subsidiary and then in major panels. Such organic forms do not naturally belong to the severe and abstract Geometric environment, and some time was needed to adapt them. So the earlier representations have a greater freedom than is permitted later [as for instance on PLATE 5].

The shapes generally become more clearly articulated and the greatest diameter of the body tends to be higher. There are also changes in types. The flat pyxis, later often embellished with horses on the lid [PLATE 6A], is popular from the beginning of Middle Geometric, and subsequent innovations include the mug and the kantharos with high handles.

Production was increasing in the eighth century, to judge by the number of surviving pots, and there is some decline in the quality of technique and draughtsmanship; but judged by purely abstract standards Attic Geometric comes to its perfection in the Middle phase.

Late Geometric (c. 760–c. 700 B.C.)

In Late Geometric the enrichment of decoration goes still further so that almost the whole surface of the pot may be covered [PLATE 4B], and the division of fields becomes more popular, now often in a series of squarish panels [PLATE 6A] which usually are filled with a hatched swastika or quatrefoil. Meanders may be more complex, justifiably where they give extra height to a principal field [as on the neck of the oinochoe of PLATE 4B]; the tapestry design is invented for the same purpose [PLATE 4B, on the belly]; the row of hatched leaves is frequent [PLATE 4A, near the bottom]; and other common innovations are chequers, too strident for the half-tone principles of Geometric decoration, cross-hatched batons, derived from the plastic ribbing of the walls of pots, and snakes, which are drawn in regular undulation and more often without head or tail. Some of the earlier works of this phase still have a disciplined assurance and even grandeur [PLATE 4A and to some degree 4B], in others the style is overblown and soon both invention and diligence decay. Painters, especially on smaller pots, lost interest in the old Geometric tradition and the style breaks up.

Ambitious artists turned increasingly to human figures and actions. The standards were set with uncompromising assurance by the painter of the so-called Dipylon amphora in Athens [PLATE 4A], made about the middle of the eighth century. Its full height is over five feet. The dark areas are limited to the underside of the moulded lip, the junction of neck and body, and the base, though here broken by reserved bands. The rest of the surface is covered with broad and narrow bands of ornament, which except between the handles run continuously round the pot. This field between the handles [PLATE 5] gets further emphasis from its subject, a scene of human figures, which have now been reduced to the canonical Geometric form, inorganic and abstract and still in silhouette. Silhouettes to be intelligible must have intelligible outlines and this, rather than incompetence of draughtsmanship or some primitive vision, determined the conventions which govern figure scenes. Here we have a scene of lamentation round the bier, on which the dead man or more probably woman lies covered by a pall, but for clarity the pall is lifted and cut away in steps – rectangular of course – to reveal the corpse. Around are the mourners, careful not to overlap. Their structure consists, again for clarity, of profile head and legs and frontal thorax, and each shows both arms and normally both legs. Even the corpse conforms to this scheme, with the addition of limp fingers set like the teeth of a comb. Here there are no signs of sex, except for the swords of the two men on the far left, though elsewhere women were sometimes distinguished by their breasts – little projections below the armpits – and later still by cross-hatched skirts. The technique of full silhouette (soon enlivened by a circular eye) is in uneasy contrast to the half-tones of the hatched meanders, though the filling ornaments between and around the figures give some relief. For figures Geometric perspective is satisfactory, but such objects as chariots raise difficulties of logic: sometimes one wheel is shown, sometimes both but side by side, and the front rail though viewed in profile is drawn as a wide loop. At first these figure scenes occur most commonly on large amphorae and stemmed kraters, which were set upright over the grave as markers and possibly also as chutes for food and drink, but later they appear on smaller shapes too, some perhaps intended for the use of the living. Besides the mourning at the bier the favourite subjects are processions of chariots and fighting by land and sea. In a few instances students have tried to demonstrate that some legendary or mythological scene is depicted, but all in all Geometric subjects appear to be of a general character and indeed paucity of detail would have made it difficult to indicate a particular incident. Even so, the attendance of chariots at battles, not a military practice of the time, shows that the painters sometimes added a heroic flavour.

Animals appear as well as men but except for the horse not normally in human company. The favourites are deer, goats, and birds. Towards the end of the century Orientalizing creatures occasionally stray in. On the neck of the Dipylon amphora [PLATE 4A] are deer grazing and recumbent goats with heads turned back and legs tucked under. These are the two usual postures, of which the second may be an early import from the East. But the animals are repeated as a pattern and do not detract from the main scene, which lies between the handles and is heavily framed by vertical strips of meander – an untectonic use of this ornament which becomes commoner as Geometric principles fail.

The Dipylon painter, who is the first recognizable personality in Greek art, left little or nothing to improve on within the conventions he set, and his rivals and successors, much less sensitive, might give their women skirts and strands of hair but tended to clumsiness and such mannerisms as swaying buttocks. In compensation they gradually reduced the importance of the subsidiary decoration. The ordinary amphora, for instance, which becomes the principal vehicle of the figure style, often has a relatively deeper main field on the body and for the rest plain stripes enlivened with a few narrow rows of zigzags and chevrons. This trend, which shows the influence of Corinthian ornament, leads to the new style of the seventh century and the abandonment of geometry for an organic approach to human anatomy.

The big grave amphorae [PLATE 4A] and kraters are the spectacular Late Geometric shapes. The commonest, though, are the ordinary amphora (which tends to grow narrower), the oinochoe with trefoil mouth, the bell-mouthed oinochoe (or pitcher) often with a fancy knob to its saucer-like lid [PLATE 4B], the mug, cups of various types, the kantharos with high handles, the kotyle, the cup or bowl with high lip and sometimes a tall stand, and the plate. Bell-mouthed oinochoe, bowl, plate and kotyle (which imitates Corinthian in decoration as well as shape) are novelties. On the whole the shapes in Late Geometric are treated with less respect than before, and it is not surprising that plastic snakes are soon permitted to crawl up the handles or round the shoulder or the lip. The snake is one of many creatures that have been associated with cults of the dead, but it is rash to make much of this ceramic fashion, prevalent perhaps through two generations, for serpents plastic and painted. Often they have become no more than abstract decoration, though of course protrusions on the lip must have made some pots impracticable for household use.

Technique declines after the Early stage, but even then firing or painting was often uneven, as is shown by the reddening of the dark paint. On the whole Attic Geometric clay is a little browner than Protogeometric, at least till its Late stage. The use of a yellowish slip persisted, though infrequently, into Early Geometric. Towards the end of Late Geometric there is an occasional use of added white for detail.

Of all the Geometric schools that of Athens was the most powerful and till near its end the most admired. Attic exports are fairly frequent in Aegina and Boeotia, and they occur also in the Cyclades, Thessaly and Crete, and during the eighth century even in Cyprus, Syria, Macedonia, South Italy and Sicily. Attic influence is strong in Boeotian and Cycladic, and affects Argive, Corinthian, East Greek, Cretan and Thessalian. It is not till the third quarter of the eighth century that the tide set the other way, and Corinthian imports and imitations became frequent. But already the Orientalizing style was imminent. In Attica, which was no longer the pioneer, this new style emerges about 700 B.C.; and though conservative painters clung to the old tradition, their Subgeometric – that is, belated, or mannered Geometric – did not survive more than ten or twenty years.

3. The Argolid

Argive Geometric

The plain of Argos was the centre of the Mycenaean culture and it remained important during the early Iron Age. Much pottery has been found at Argos, Mycenae and Tiryns, and some at Asine and the Argive Heraeum (between two and three miles south-east of Mycenae). Argos, the principal city of the area, was evidently the metropolis of the school, though in the Late stage there are some signs of independence at Asine.

This Argive Geometric, which follows a respectable Protogeometric style, begins about the same time as Attic. Judged by pretensions, it is the second most important Geometric school. Its Early and Middle stages follow Attic, though showing less enterprise. The Late stage, roughly from 750 to 690 B.C., develops on its own. Here the division of fields into panels is often excessive, anyhow at first. In the many figure scenes horses are common, sometimes paired and with a man or manger between them and large fishes floating in the field. Women often have two or three long strings dangling in front of their skirts. Meanders are plentiful, a favourite variety being the step meander, which by its diagonal slant tends to unbalance the composition, and hatching comes to be at right angles instead of oblique. Of the subsidiary ornaments the increasingly popular rows of massed zigzags, horizontal or vertical, deserve notice. The effect tends to be heavy, if not lumpish. The final phase admits a few Orientalizing motives and sometimes gives its figures more solidly constructed heads and even outlined faces. A less ambitious style without figures but adding a few simple Orientalizing motives to the traditional stock continues into the second quarter of the seventh century; but it is best called Subgeometric.

Of the shapes the most important are amphora, krater (rarely with a high stem), cup, pyxis and oinochoe: in the Late stage and in Subgeometric the krater predominates. The technique is competent. The clay sometimes has a greenish tinge and is rather coarser than Attic. The Argive school was evidently influenced by Attic and later by Corinthian. In turn it had some influence on Tegea and Sparta and perhaps at an early stage on Corinth. There was a little export to neighbouring districts and a few fragments have been recognized at Megara Hyblaea in Sicily.

'Argive Monochrome'

A pale unpainted ware has also been assigned to the Argolid and called 'Argive Monochrome'. The commonest shapes are the conical oinochoe (generally with arching body) and a small jug. The decoration is rarely more than incised or pricked zigzags and wavy lines. The clay is about the colour of putty. Most of these pots are shaped by hand, not on the wheel. This simple ware is found in the Argolid, but also in other parts of Greece and the West. Distribution suggests that Corinth has as good claims as the Argolid for its manufacture, and it may have been made elsewhere too. Its main period is the seventh century, but a similar monochrome was being made much earlier and it is found as late as the sixth century.

4. Corinth

We still know very little of Mycenaean and early Iron Age Corinth. A few Protogeometric pots have been found, akin to Attic and Argive but apparently local. The Geometric style is clearer, especially towards its end. It is a simple and neat school, which may be divided into three phases – Early (*c.* 875–*c.* 825 B.C.), Middle (*c.* 825–*c.* 750 B.C.), and Late (*c.* 750–*c.* 720 B.C.).

Of the *Early Geometric* not much has survived. The commonest shapes seem to be trefoil-mouthed oinochoai and cups. A peculiar variety of the oinochoe has a globular body and a small neck – Corinthian Geometric potters always liked plump shapes. The cup, at first deep, grows shallower. The decoration is usually confined to a single reserved field – on the neck of oinochoai and on the shoulder of cups – and the rest of the pot is painted dark except for narrow groups of reserved bands. The characteristic ornament is a set of three or four horizontal zigzags, often connected to the frame of the field by short strokes from their apices: a rather clumsy and later example is shown on PLATE 8A. The meander is rare.

In *Middle Geometric* the decoration is a little more complex. The single field, which remains normal, is more often stopped at each end by a narrow panel and may be underlined by a subsidiary horizontal strip. On cups and kraters the decorated area, as in contemporary Attic, continues round the pot under the handles. The main field is often filled by the hatched meander and sometimes by cross-hatched triangles. But even there, as well as in the minor horizontal and vertical strips, the favourite ornaments are groups of neat chevrons and zigzags or wavy lines, upright or lying on their sides. Curvilinear ornaments and human or animal figures are not admitted into this simple style.

The *Late Geometric*, in older works sometimes called Linear Geometric or Protocorinthian Geometric, continues the tradition of sober neatness but accelerates the trend to lightness of tone. The main decoration is, as before, at the level of the handles; but below it narrow stripes, alternately painted and reserved, spread well down the vase, and the neck (if the pot has a neck) is similarly striped. A few new ornaments and arrangements are added to the repertory, for instance opposed triangles [as on PLATE 7A], the false spiral, and – more significant in that the Geometric tradition of continuous ornament is broken – intermittent groups of zigzag or wavy strokes spaced, sometimes alternately, in a narrow band round the pot. The hatched meander soon proves too cumbrous for the new environment, except in the Thapsos class, which also has a fondness for the running spiral. Of the shapes the ordinary oinochoe remains popular [for the shape only see PLATE 8C], the conical oinochoe – like a narrow-necked version of the last sawn off at the shoulder – becomes more frequent, and the kotyle is invented. The kotyle [see PLATE 8B] is the most characteristic product of Corinthian Late Geometric, and shows the new style to best advantage. Its popularity was immediate and enduring. The shape, delicate and thin-walled to match the decoration, is derived from the Geometric cup by removing the lip and lifting the body and conformably the earlier examples are more spreading than the later. In contemporary Athens, where the Geometric tradition could not be so boldly denied, there occurs an opposite development of the cup, in which the body becomes shallower and the rim shoots up to equal it in height. Other common shapes are krater, round pyxis, plate and especially in the Thapsos class (where the kotyle is neglected) kantharos and cup. This Thapsos class, which has a distinct but not alien character within the Corinthian Late Geometric style, also tends to a greener tone of clay and a darker colour of paint. It is generally and reasonably considered to be the product of a more conservative workshop or group of workshops in Corinth; but if another home should be wanted, Megara has the advantage of being geographically convenient and ceramically still unknown.

Corinth was the first city to advance beyond Geometric principles. Its own Geometric school had been modest, so that tradition was not too strong to hamper innovation, as happened at Argos and even at Athens, and its characteristic virtue of neatness, as opposed to grandeur, was well suited to the new style that was forming. About this time Corinth's commercial importance seems to have been increasing, at least in the pottery trade, but whether that immediately influenced the style of Corinthian pottery (as some claim) is very doubtful. During the last quarter of the century Orientalizing motives entered Corinth, and though much of the Late Geometric style persisted and indeed continued to develop, it is more conveniently classed with Protocorinthian.

Technically the quality of Corinthian Geometric is good, more so at the end. The clay is fine and in colour lightish brown with a tendency towards pink or green. The surface is well finished and shiny. The paint is at first generally dark brown, but in the later eighth century a red tone comes to be preferred. In the earlier stages it is not always easy to distinguish Corinthian clay from Attic, but they gradually diverge – Attic towards orange, Corinthian towards yellow. Sometimes, in the later stages, an orange-red paint is used for ornament alongside the usual brown or red, of which perhaps it is a more dilute solution; and occasionally at the end white paint (or rather a solution of the pale clay) is used over the dark paint for an ornament normally painted dark on a reserved ground.

The export of Corinthian Geometric was negligible before the eighth century. Then there was progressive expansion. Middle Geometric is fairly frequent at Delphi and in Ithaca and occurs in Aegina, Thera, Cnossus, Smyrna and Thessaly. Late Geometric and its Early Protocorinthian successor appear, often in quantity, throughout the Greek world, from Al Mina in Syria to Etruria. The stylistic relation between the Corinthian and other Geometric schools corresponds. Till the early eighth century some mild influence of Attic and perhaps Argive is visible in Corinthian. In the later eighth century Corinthian Geometric was imitated in varying degrees by most of the other Greek schools, even by Attic.

5. Laconia

Knowledge of Laconian Geometric, as of Protogeometric, depends mainly on finds from sanctuaries in Sparta itself and at Amyklae a few miles south. These are generally unstratified, very fragmentary and probably deficient in some of the ordinary shapes. So, apart from the observed testimony that Protogeometric precedes Geometric, classification is by style. The account that follows is tentative.

Since there is very little in the decoration that would not or could not be considered of the Late stage elsewhere nor is there much sign of a transition from Protogeometric, it seems that Laconian Geometric appeared fairly suddenly about 750 B.C. At first, perhaps, a band of continuous decoration was regular and the typical ornament was concentric circles, the sets often carelessly spaced and sometimes intersecting. Later, richer decoration and panelling were preferred and the influences of Argos and Corinth are visible, even on the same pot. The step meander, other meanders with hatching at right angles, the big hatched zigzag, the quatrefoil and the occasional human figures are taken from the grandiose Argive style. The contribution of Corinth, increasing during the Early Protocorinthian period, is evident not only in a neat system of narrow fields and fine striping, but also in some linear ornaments and the little silhouette birds. Concentric circles, triangles and lozenges are Protogeometric survivals, and gridded hatching of meanders is a local aberration. The shapes generally lack the logic of the best Geometric schools. Those recovered include cups, a big stemmed bowl (perhaps a local equivalent of the krater), a small bowl, low flat dishes with incurved rim, tall pyxis with doubly curved wall, oinochoai (some with high narrow neck and strutted handle) and the lakaina (a derivative of the cup that remains popular in Laconia but is very rare elsewhere). Fairly soon slip was introduced, but did not drive out the older technique. In the slipped ware the clay is coarser and pink, the slip itself is thin, greyish and friable, and the paint is duller.

Till more is discovered it is impracticable to define the end of Geometric in Laconia. It seems that from the end of the eighth century onwards there was a gradual infiltration of Orientalizing motives (such as the broken cable, small solid meander, rays and chequers) but no consistent style was formed for another generation or more. If dates however arbitrary are wanted, then the Laconian Geometric style may be said to finish about 690 B.C. and Subgeometric (or Transitional) to continue till about 650 B.C.

This is a clumsy school. A few pieces have turned up in neighbouring districts, a couple of latish plates in Taranto and one cup (so it is said) in Cyrene. From the late eighth century on Corinthian imports appear, though not frequently, in Sparta.

6. Western Greece

Excavation in *Ithaca* has produced a fair quantity of imported Corinthian from the end of Middle Geometric onwards and also of a ware found nowhere else and presumably local. This Ithacan pottery is a mixture of Protogeometric legacies and Corinthian loans, the loans steadily becoming more dominant; some minor influences of Euboean and other schools have been detected, perhaps too hopefully. The typical ornaments, derived from the Protogeometric of the island, are sets of concentric arcs and large pothooks. The commonest shapes are krater, various types of oinochoe, kantharos, deep cups and globular pyxis. The clay is usually reddish to brown or occasionally pale. The paint is dark brown with a violet tinge. Dating, which depends through stylistic comparisons and contexts on Corinthian, is fairly safe. Ithacan Geometric begins little if at all before 750 B.C. and continues well down the first quarter of the seventh century, till it shades into what may be called Subgeometric or perhaps rudimentary Orientalizing.

Finds of Geometric have been increasing in *Achaea*, but there is much less from *Acarnania*, *Aetolia*, *Elis* and *Messenia*. Again some groups are datable by the import or imitation of Corinthian. Direct connection with Ithaca is no longer apparent, though the looseness of decorative composition is similar. Nor is there any evident connection with Laconian. The chronology seems to be more or less as that of Ithacan.

7. Boeotia

Boeotia is rich in cemeteries, as the peasants know; but archaeologists, contemptuous of its art, prefer to excavate elsewhere. So though there are many Boeotian Geometric pots in museums, of few is the place of finding recorded, let alone the context. It is lucky for classifiers that their style is imitative.

Very few graves of the Early or Middle Geometric phases have been recorded in Boeotia. They contain imported Attic and fairly close Boeotian imitations of Attic. It is not always easy to distinguish the simpler or rougher examples, and perhaps among better Geometric pots some which pass as Attic were made in Boeotia. Attic influence was still dominant in the second half of the eighth century, when the finds become more plentiful. The local painters even attempted ambitious scenes of human figures, but the drawing is usually clumsy and the composition often chaotic. There are also some characteristic ornaments. The Attic band of circles joined by tangents is developed into a high wavy line of thin up-strokes and very thick down-strokes. A spidery swastika with more than four arms appears among the filling motives. Rows of large concentric circles, a form of decoration too loose for Attic taste, are or become common. Towards the end of the eighth century Corinth was in the ascendant and Corinthian influence is to be seen, especially in alternating groups of upright straight and zigzag lines and in strips or narrow bands of zigzags, horizontal or vertical, which are sometimes joined to the frame by short strokes [as on PLATE 8A]. This Late Geometric, with or without Orientalizing intrusions and often affected, persists into the seventh century. The important shapes are the tall neck-amphora, the big oinochoe, and towards the end a simple kantharos with high vertical handles. An amphora of Linear Island type, with high foot and broad neck, appears towards the end (see p. 106–7). The clay resembles Attic, though rather coarser and darker. The paint tends to be duller and less even. There is not the evidence to decide in which of the cities of Boeotia Geometric pottery was made, or whether there were local schools. Export was negligible.

8. Euboea

Euboean Geometric is important more for its distribution than its artistic merit. At home the main finds – mostly of unstratified sherds – are from Eretria and Lefkandi, but there is little yet from Chalcis. The clay, which has no mica, is much like Attic, though often finer and harder. Slip, when used, is creamy in colour and thick. During the first half of the ninth century it seems that a sort of Protogeometric was still prevalent, shared with Thessaly and the northern Cyclades (see p. 10), and there is no trace, anyhow yet, of a true Geometric. Then, though the cups with pendent semicircles were still made, Attic Middle Geometric was imitated as in the Cyclades and indeed the Euboean products often cannot be distinguished by style alone. In the Late Geometric stage, which seems to have begun about 750 B.C., there is some Corinthian influence too, mainly on kotylai, but no coherent local style emerged. Still Euboea has some conveniently recognizable mannerisms. Among these are rows of small concentric circles or crosshatching round the vertical lips of Atticizing cups, and the careless lozenges with a dot in each quarter that serve as a main or subsidiary ornament in the panels; on Corinthianizing kotylai, besides clumsiness of composition and the coarser drawing of silhouette birds, fine striping is sometimes done in white paint instead of by reservation; and, more originally, slip may be used as a stuffing for the meanders, lozenges and fat crosses which decorate a class of late cups. The Late Geometric shapes – not in order of first appearance – include amphora of Linear Island type [cf. PLATE 29A], deep krater with flaring pedestal, oinochoe of normal type, oinochoe with cut-away neck, conical oinochoe, a slim jug with tall narrow neck and round mouth, aryballos, cup, kantharos and kotyle. Of these the amphora probably comes from Cycladic, the jug with cut-away neck is derived from Thessalian, the slim jug has no obvious Greek ancestry, and the others are taken from the Attic and Corinthian repertories. By the early seventh century Euboean Late Geometric is decadent, enough so to be classed as Sub-geometric, and in this form it lingered on for another generation.

At Al Mina Geometric from Euboea is notably frequent during the eighth century and towards its end there was even some local manufacture in a partly Euboean manner. Elsewhere in the Levant it seems to be less common. Nor are the cups with pendent semicircles numerous, though – whether significantly or not – their distribution is wider. In the West some Euboean Geometric pottery appears with Corinthian in the early finds at Ischia and Cumae and, to judge by clay, was also imitated there. Elsewhere in South Italy and Sicily a few pieces have been recognized as Euboean, of the time when Greek colonization had begun. There are also imports in Etruria (especially at Veii) which look Euboean – some still Middle Geometric in style – and the local Geometric style which developed there is considered to show specifically Euboean traits. In the older Greek lands imported Euboean Geometric is very rare.

9. The Cyclades

Travel in the Cyclades has usually been inconvenient, and so students have rather neglected the archaeology of these charming islands. Many Geometric pots have been found in the cemeteries of Thera, Melos and Kimolos and in the Purification enclosure on Rheneia, to which the Athenians transported the contents of graves from nearby Delos. There are also a few pots and some assorted sherds from Naxos, Paros, Delos, Tenos, Andros, Keos, Siphnos, Melos and elsewhere. But most of this material is Late Geometric, stratification and context have been unhelpful – least so in Thera – and Delos, a religious centre, imported catholically.

The Cyclades were not a political unity and it was only natural for particular islands or groups of islands to develop their own schools. For the earlier ninth century finds are still few, but it seems that in the northern chain the strongest connections were with Euboea and Thessaly (see p. 10) and that in the south Attic influence was dominant.

The Middle Geometric style, which began about 850 B.C. and became normal everywhere, was (as clay shows) practised in several places but without much local variation. This is because there was a common dependence on Attic models, from which the Cycladic imitations are often stylistically indistinguishable. Still there are some peculiarities – a preference, for instance, in shapes for the amphora with handles on the belly and in decoration for putting circles in each panel of important tripartite fields. With Late Geometric the material becomes much more varied, so that it has been possible to isolate four main schools and to locate them more or less convincingly according to their frequency in one island or another.

Naxian has a clay which fires from brick red to dark brown and contains specks of golden mica. Most often there is a creamy slip. In style it at first leans heavily on Attic and then repeats itself with complacent care. The grander products show an unusual understanding of the Attic system of decoration and generally Naxian is well-mannered. Of the shapes the most typical are neck-handled amphora and oinochoe, both of them narrow and becoming still narrower, till they reach proportions comparable to those of the Protoattic hydria of PLATE 14A. This school begins about 750 and ends about 700 B.C.

'*Parian*', found also in Siphnos and Tenos but more credibly at home in the more important island of Paros, shows a wayward initiative. The clay is brownish tending often to orange and again has golden mica; on exposed surfaces there may be a thin wash of finer quality. The style starts strongly Atticizing, but gradually emancipates itself. In decoration the trend is to looser and sparser composition, with minor ornaments enlarged and promoted to major positions. The most characteristic motives, all drawn thickly and used in rows, are tall blobs (or billets), short vertical zigzags and later the broken cable – perhaps here a simplification of the circles joined by tangents [as on PLATE 6B]; there is also the thick wavy line, again in a band of its own, and circles become commoner. The consummation of 'Parian' Geometric is in the fat, wide-necked amphorae of the Wheel group [FIG. 3], where the shoulder has three equal panels, each exhibiting a heavy spoked circle and obliquely across the corners a row of short zigzags or chevrons. Here by orthodox standards the effect is no longer properly Geometric. Favourite 'Parian' shapes are amphorae with vertical or horizontal handles and the hydria – all (in contrast to Naxian) abnormally plump – the krater, the cup, the kantharos and the plate. 'Parian' Late Geometric too seems to have been current from about 750 to about 700 B.C.

The *Melian* school, known from finds in Melos and Kimolos, has silver mica and black grit in its clay, which is a little darker than Attic. The style forms under Attic influence, but without ambition or exertion, and then quietly declines into a tame Subgeometric. Figures occur, often ingenuous and sometimes grotesque. On large pots the style is passable, but lesser work tends to be mean. Among shapes

FIG. 3. *Cycladic Geometric amphora*
Ht 42 cm. Wheel group: *c.* 725–700 B.C.

the fenestrated stand shows some inept originality. Stylistic evidence suggests that this school began about 750 B.C., and it may have lasted well into the seventh century.

Theran clay is reddish with coarse volcanic particles of various colours, and needs the yellowish slip that is regular in the Late Geometric school. Once more the origin of the style is in Attic, much transmuted, and though later a few Corinthian and East Greek elements are incorporated development proceeds in sluggish isolation. The characteristic shape is a big funerary amphora with broad flat lip and handles set horizontally on the shoulder, wider in the neck than the normal Geometric types and often about two feet high. Development is towards a slimmer body and a narrower foot. The front of the neck and of the shoulder carries the main decoration, which is arranged in broad and narrow bands, on the shoulder usually complicated by panelling; the rest of the body has spare groups of stripes. As can be seen on the smaller and simpler amphora of PLATE 6B, the result is affected and arid, partly from loose spacing and partly because the decoration of the main field has a routine precision. The most important ornaments are the meander, heavy zigzags, big circles containing an eight-leaved star or four disks, cross-hatched lozenges and triangles, the quatrefoil, and for minor bands the false spiral (or row of small concentric circles joined by tangents). At first the centre of the main field is occupied by a meander; but later the big circles replace them, the true spiral appears besides the false, and composition tends to be fussier. Of the other frequent shapes a squat pithos (or stamnos), darkground in its lower part, is an early alternative to the big amphora, and there are kraters, cups, kantharoi and plates. The Theran school looks as if it began later than other Cycladic schools of Geometric, perhaps about 720. The introduction of big circles into main panels early in the seventh century has been taken as marking its passage into Subgeometric, though stylistically there seems no sufficient change till rather later, and the tradition – reinforced by such simple Orientalizing motives as tongues and a primitive floral chain, and once even by incised figures – still persists in the middle of the seventh century.

Cycladic Geometric, of the Middle as well as the Late stage, has turned up occasionally in Crete and in respectable quantity at Al Mina; there both Naxian and 'Parian' products have been recognized. There are also Late pieces, certainly including 'Parian', from Cyprus. Elsewhere exports outside the Cyclades are rare and negligible, unless some pots from Veii and Cumae in Italy, of the first half of the eighth century, are Cycladic rather than Euboean. The distribution of cups with pendent semicircles, some of which might be North Cycladic, has been given already (p. 10). There was a modest import of Attic till the third quarter of the eighth century, when Corinthian began to come in, and less often East Greek.

10. Thessaly

Thessaly does not deserve much notice. Here the local Protogeometric style was tenacious, though some pots add on their necks rectilinear decoration apparently derived from the earliest Attic Geometric. This amalgam, which according to taste may be called Early Geometric or Subprotogeometric, lasted roughly through the ninth century. Around 800 B.C. Attic influence became much stronger, in shapes as well as decoration, though complex ornaments were avoided. How long this Geometric continued is not known, but so far there is nothing demonstrably later than the eighth century.

11. The East Greek Cities

At the beginning of historical times Greeks had settled the west coast of Asia Minor and the islands offshore. Politically – to use the term loosely – this region was divided into the Dorian South, Ionia, and to the north Aeolis, but since in art it is more conveniently treated as a whole it has received the general name of East Greek. In the Roman period many of the East Greek cities were very prosperous and in modern times they were within the empire of the Turkish sultans; but neither of these difficulties, the heavy deposits overlying early remains and official obstruction, excuse the excavators of several important sites for their reluctance to let others know what they found. In Rhodes, after consuls and local inhabitants had looted for half a century, the Danes and Italians have made available a mass of material. The Italians again, during their occupation of the Dodecanese, published a cemetery in Nisyros but have not yet fully published a cemetery in Cos. In Samos the Germans keep excavating methodically and have issued some comprehensive accounts. In Chios and Lesbos small sites have been dug and reported, and the pottery and other finds from the Aeolian site misnamed Larisa have eventually been revealed. For Old Smyrna parts of the publication have appeared. A few sherds are illustrated from Miletus, Ephesus, Clazomenae, Phocaea, Pitane and Lydian Sardis, and there are other sites of which even less is known. So knowledge of East Greek vase-painting is more or less hazy. For Geometric the only fairly complete series is from Rhodes; at Cos the finds stop early in the Late phase; elsewhere what can be studied is mostly or wholly Late.

Even so, though local distinctions should become clearer, the Geometric pottery of the Dorian and Ionian settlements has enough common characteristics to be regarded as a loose unity, and this unity continued into the sixth century. There was a radically different standard in Lesbos, which preferred a *Grey ware* (often called *Bucchero*) derived from a tradition already old when the Greeks arrived. Its shapes are sometimes Greek, sometimes Anatolian; the decoration, if there is any, consists of ridges and impressed or incised patterns of which the most elaborate, borrowed probably from the East Greek painted style, are hatched triangles and meanders. Presumably Grey ware was normal or common at other Aeolian sites in the Geometric period, as it was later – in some places at least down to the Hellenistic period.

It is in *Rhodes* and *Cos*, as has been explained, that the painted style can be examined best. Here during the first half of the ninth century, that is while the Early Geometric style was current at Athens, the local workshops accepted some of the new developments in shapes, but not in decoration. The emphasis continued to be on the shoulder of closed pots, though occasionally the neck is allowed a thick zigzag. Concentric circles and even semicircles continue in use, if more coarsely drawn, but the linking of circles is abandoned. As before, cross-hatched triangles, often opposed, and lozenges are quite as frequent. Strictly this stage is a decadent Protogeometric, even if – for convenience – it is described as Early Geometric. A properly Geometric style, the so-called Middle Geometric stage, begins around 850 B.C. Though for closed shapes the decoration is still concentrated on the shoulder, the meander appears, both in its simple and battlement form, with hatching (as usually in East Greek) in one direction only. Later, other varieties of meander develop and new ways of stuffing the members. A novelty of local origin is the triangle filled with hatched lozenges. The commonest shapes are oinochoai, the lekythos with a protruding ring where the handle joins the long neck, krater with pedestal, kantharos with high handles and cups of various types. The lekythos is the most significant, since though the shape came from Cyprus it was the first recipient of the new decoration and on it – not altogether conveniently – the new style was formed. The Middle Geometric of Rhodes and Cos is unusually composite; it absorbed much from Attic, perhaps indirectly through the Cyclades, but retained much of the older tradition and added a Cypriot ingredient. In the Late Geometric stage, which seems to begin rather after 750 B.C., the Rhodian material is richer in both quality and quantity. The dark-ground system continues and the field on the shoulder remains important, but close panelling partly replaces the old system of continuous bands. Of the ornaments the square hooks, which had been invented before the end of Middle Geometric, become very popular: they are used to embellish the free angles of lozenges as well as triangles [PLATE 7A] or are joined four together into a cross. Birds, often cross-hatched, are frequent, other figures rare. Some Orientalizing motives too occur, notably a stylized palm tree and the cable. The shapes include oinochoai of various types [of which that of PLATE 7A is a late but long-lived byform], lekythos, pedestalled krater, kantharos, cups and kotyle – this sometimes imitating Corinthian in decoration also. Besides the orthodox style there are various minor but distinct classes of Rhodian pottery that imitate Cypriot or Levantine models: some of them continue well into the seventh century. Generally Rhodian Late Geometric seems independent of other schools; at its best it has a dry competence, but its composition is often inconsequent, even on so careful a piece as the oinochoe of PLATE 7A. In Cos the local Late Geometric is, anyhow at first, more conservative and seems not to have taken to panelling. Rhodian clay, darkish brown with occasionally some silver mica, is considered distinctive. Exports – mostly Late – have been recognized in Ionia, the Cyclades, Euboea, Aegina and Asine and further afield at Al Mina, Tarsus, Ischia, Megara Hyblaea and Gela. There was some import into Rhodes of Cypriot. The end of the Late Geometric style, partly determined by context with Protocorinthian pottery, may be put about 680 B.C., though some Orientalizing experiments are probably earlier. A Subgeometric style lasted rather longer and in one special class – the Bird bowls – till the end of the seventh century.

In *Ionia* the course of development seems generally to have been similar. In the Early stage, which remains basically Protogeometric, circles are more and rectilinear ornaments less common than in Rhodes. In Middle Geometric and at the beginning of Late Geometric Attic influence is evident here too, but goes deeper. In Late Geometric, if not before, some Rhodian peculiarities were adopted – the square hooks, for example, though not the lekythos – and Rhodian products were copied, particularly the kotylai with birds. Of local trends within Ionia not much can yet be said. *Samos* shows some sophistication, especially in the Late stage, when even human figures are attempted, if without much comprehension. A minor idiosyncrasy, shared with Chios, is the stuffing of the meander with dots. Sometimes in the Late Geometric and more often in the Subgeometric stage there is a whitish slip. For *Miletus* the special characteristics of the local Geometric cannot be deduced from finds so far published. In *Chios* the Late Geometric usually has a thick whitish slip, sometimes used inside open shapes as an undercoat to the dark paint. In decoration the panel system is not adopted, and the arrangement tends to be in rows of shallow horizontal strips. The occasional human figures show more spirit than skill. From *Smyrna* only a few Geometric pieces have been made known. What there is suggests a sense of composition much like that of Chios, but a more ornate taste. There was little or no export of Ionian Geometric, except perhaps inland to Lydia. The chronology is presumably much as that of Rhodian.

In native Anatolia – at Sardis in *Lydia* and at various sites in *Caria* and *Lycia* – there are traces of local wares imitating Greek Geometric. Of these very little is known, but one would expect the more northerly to be derived from Ionian and the more southerly from Rhodian models.

12. Crete

The pottery of Crete does not fit comfortably into the regular classifications of Greek Geometric. Still there is plenty of it, especially in the museum of Heraklion, and the general development is clear, anyhow in Central Crete. West Crete seems to have had a local version of Protogeometric, but almost nothing is known of what came after it. At the other end of the island East Cretan – or, more tendentiously, Etocretan – workshops show peculiarities that may be as much independent as provincial. The account which follows is concerned with the products of Central Crete.

Protogeometric B

The nonconformist Protogeometric style, which lasts well down the ninth century, is succeeded by a sudden and precocious experiment with Orientalizing and other motives named, with justified misgiving, Protogeometric B. Favourite ornaments are loop patterns, either single [PLATE 7B on the neck] or opposed and with hatching between, cables, double arcs, the mill-sail pattern, hatched zigzags, cross-hatched lozenges and triangles. Concentric circles and semicircles survive on more traditional pots. The meander is rare and clumsily used. Occasionally figures, animal and human, make an appearance; they are loosely drawn and even in part outlined. The decoration is in general planned and executed with neat facility, and sometimes it covers most of the surface of the pot. The hydria of PLATE 7B is typical.

There are innovations in the shapes too. Of these the most distinctive are the pithos with straight sides and angular shoulder, and the low-bellied hydria. The stirrup vase is at last abandoned. Small pots, especially a squat jug, develop. The technique as in the preceding Protogeometric is poor, with coarsish light brown clay and often a thin whitish slip.

This Protogeometric B style contains some traditional elements, notably the triangles, and some derived from standard Geometric elsewhere, such as the chain of lozenges. Others – particularly the cables and the loop (or spiral) bands – look like borrowings from Oriental art and are paralleled in metalwork which seems to have been made about that time in Cnossus by immigrant Eastern craftsmen. The mill-sail motive and the new shapes may be credited to local inventiveness. For the home of this curious style the evidence points fairly clearly to Cnossus, artistically the principal city of Central Crete, but it spread widely, even into East Crete, though there the painters preferred to hatch the background and not the body of curvilinear ornaments. Outside the island no effect is apparent. A few imports and still fewer imitations of Attic or Atticizing Cycladic wares suggest that the period of Protogeometric B was short, roughly from 840 to 810 B.C. according to the current chronology.

Geometric

Around the end of the ninth century the Attic style at last imposed itself on Cretan vase-painters and there arose a fairly orthodox Middle Geometric school, which quickly rejected most of the innovations of Protogeometric B. After a brief and turbulent initial phase a compact and even ornate style sets in, particularly on the large pithoi which are its most careful products: here the influence of Athens is especially strong. The Late phase, which begins in the 740s, soon dispenses with Attic models and, while borrowing casually from Corinthian and Cypriot, can claim independence, if not creative power. Though an Orientalizing style emerged in Central Crete around the end of the eighth century, for most of the seventh the stock product was aridly Subgeometric.

The decoration is modest in extent. The pithos, for instance, usually has a main field on the shoulder, later supported by a band of ornament below, and the rest of the body has groups of reserved stripes to relieve its dark ground. Of larger motives the meander is the most common, of lesser cross-hatched lozenges and grouped zigzags. More progressive are the freehand curving ornaments, especially the simple cable and the newly invented tongues. In the Late phase a closer system of panelling is introduced, concentric circles are often set in long bands or used as borders, and birds – sometimes with heads turned back or multiplied – show a wayward originality. Towards the end some use is made of white paint on a dark ground, especially for the rows of concentric circles. In general the smaller vases are decorated more simply and carelessly and for that reason are harder to date.

In the shapes there was some Attic and later a little Corinthian and Cypriot influence, but local tradition and initiative were not swamped. The large pithos some twenty inches high remained the standard ossuary of Central Crete and was probably copied in Thera: its Geometric form has no neck and tends to become narrower, and the lid (which it regularly possessed) is usually conical with a central knob. Several varieties of oinochoe are found, mostly small; among them is the round-mouthed jug that approaches the aryballos. There are also kraters, at first pedestalled, cups and – later – the kotyle. Cretan technique shows an improvement in Geometric. The clay fires light brown to pink. Usually there is no slip. The paint is dark brown to coarse red. White is used as already described. Clay and paint have a fair sheen.

There was some export of Cretan to Thera, but very little has been found elsewhere. Imports are rather more numerous – of Attic, Cycladic, Cypriot and finally Corinthian.

13. Italy

The Mycenaean Greeks had left their pottery in Italy and Sicily, and it would be odd if in the early Iron Age sailors from the Ionian islands did not sometimes cross the straits. But Greek contacts with the West, to judge as usual by imported pottery, did not become regular and close till the eighth century. The first traces, some probably Euboean cups at Veii in Etruria, seem to precede the earliest Greek settlement – that of the Euboeans at Ischia (or Pithecusae), which can hardly be later than the 760s, and a generation later the massive colonization of the coasts of Sicily and South Italy was beginning. The circumstances were fortunate. In the south the native tribes had a weaker organization and a lower culture, and in Central Italy another new people – the Etruscans – though able to prevent Greek encroachment on their territory, welcomed Greek trade. One result of these contacts was Italian Geometric pottery.

The term Italian Geometric is elastic. It is properly used only of those wares which were made in Italy and Sicily outside the Greek colonies and are in the Greek sense Geometric. But it is often extended with confusing and absurd results to any subsequent Italian pottery on which the decoration consists of simple lines or nondescript patterns. Although plentiful enough, both Italian Geometric and still more the later linear wares have been neglected. This is not surprising, since artistically they are negligible.

In the *Greek colonies*, anyhow in their early years, there was more local production than used·to be credited. At Ischia and Cumae close imitations of Corinthian Geometric have been found and, though in lesser quantity, of Euboean: these imitations, of which the Euboean group ventures on figures, are often distinguishable only by the clay. In Sicily and South Italy, where settlement was later, colonial imitation was only or predominantly of Corinthian and its style generally tame and weak. So far these colonial wares have rarely been studied or even closely defined, but their importance is more for the history of Greek colonization than art.

Outside the new Greek territories *Etruria* produced a robust and confident Geometric, capable of sizeable pots and elaborate decoration. Favourite motives are hatched or solid birds, quatrefoil, hatched meanders, lozenges, the row of concentric circles, and the usual zigzags and wavy lines. The commonest shapes are the ordinary Geometric cup, kraters with high foot and oinochoai. The clay is often yellowish. Some examples would pass as respectable Greek – and indeed experts do not always agree whether a particular piece is Greek or Italian – but others are more boorish. A large and probably rather later group is best known for its flat-rimmed, high-footed bowls, tamely but neatly decorated with stripes and below the rim with panels which contain a cross-hatched lozenge or horizontal zigzags. With these go some oino-choai and a sort of squat kantharos. Outliers of the group merge with early Italocorinthian, which began about 700 B.C. and may sometimes have been made in the same workshops. This Etruscan version of Geometric, which shows some freedom in its choice of shapes, appears to be based – whether directly or by way of Ischia – on Euboean models of Atticizing character. It was established not later than 730 B.C. and lasted for a century or so.

One stage remoter from Greek are other Etruscan pots of coarser ware, strange proportions and helpless decoration. Typical are a nearly globular krater with low flaring neck and narrow but highish foot, an amphora of Villanovan shape, and bulbous stands. Large zig-zags, sets of triangles, lozenges, meanders and concentric circles, all sketched with a thick brush, are spread over the surface. The effect is barbarous. Such depravities last in Central Italy till the end of the seventh century, in backward parts even later.

In the extremity of *South-West Italy* a few native cemeteries con-tained Villanovan amphorae and other pots of impasto together with painted amphorae, oinochoai and cups of simple Geometric style. The important motives are hatched birds, vertical zigzags, lozenge, quatre-foil and hatched units of meander. Shape, style, clay and paint might often be taken for inferior Greek. Again the Greek models may be Atticizing Euboean. The date looks to be the generation around 700 B.C. In *Apulia* and *Lucania* native schools absorbed some Greek motives, but remained independent.

In *Sicily* the Geometric style is looser and less Greek than in Italy. Birds, zigzags, straight and wavy lines, and concentric circles are the staple ornaments. The main shapes are an amphora with broad out-curving neck and handles set vertically on the belly, oinochoe and a one-handled drinking bowl. Clay and paint are fairly good. This Sicilian school, which is Subgeometric rather than Geometric in character, belongs to the south-east of the island, and elsewhere in other native sites the Greek element is more dilute. This phase, which corresponds to what is called Siculan III, begins in the late eighth century and lasts till the late seventh. Its successor, Siculan IV, which is slighter and more sophisticated and has lost almost all trace of Geometric, continues into the fifth. In the main Siculan Geometric is derived from Corinthian, probably by way of colonial imitations of that style. Not surprisingly, some Euboean traits too have been detected.

4 The Orientalizing and Black-figure Styles

1. Introduction

From the beginning of the Iron Age Greece had been self-sufficient in its economy as well as in its art. During the eighth century this changed. Around 800 B.C. Greeks, apparently from Euboea, were settling in Syria, most notably at Al Mina near the mouth of the Orontes. Not much later other Euboeans established themselves in Ischia (Pithecusae) on the north of the Gulf of Naples and seem to have been active in Etruria. Towards the end of the century vigorous colonization set in of coastal sites in Sicily and South Italy. This expansion had different objects. In Syria the Greeks were traders, shipping home luxuries, which included small objects of art; in Etruria they were again traders, but offering luxuries for raw metal; in Sicily and South Italy they came to make a living from the land and, as they prospered, could buy manufactures with their surplus corn. For the development of Greek art the Western markets stimulated production, but the imports from the East had more obvious results. This was not simply because the Greeks now first became aware of Oriental art; some imports had filtered in throughout the Early Iron Age, though admittedly in much less quantity, and the Protogeometric B style of Crete shows a premature attraction to it. Nor was the effect of closer contact immediate; the Dipylon painter must have known but ignored Oriental metalwork when he was thinking out his abstract formulas for figures. More important was the growing exhaustion of the Geometric style, which opened the way to new influences, and Oriental models were handy. In vase-painting these influences were indirect, since painted pottery was a minor craft in the Oriental world and the models used by the Greeks were works in metal and ivory, of which we have a fair number of specimens from Greek sites, and perhaps also textiles, which had no chance of survival. The technique of these works is generally competent, their style often a stale and varying medley of the traditional Hittite, Assyrian and Egyptian elements that were currently available in North Syria. Fortunately the Greeks were not overwhelmed by the example of this more finished art, but selected and adapted to suit their needs, after the first experiments only casually. So even the beginner can usually distinguish between what is Greek and what Oriental in manufacture.

The pots reproduced on PLATES 8c and 9A illustrate the first stage of the new style. Geometric painting had been abstract in its conception and analytic in its expression. Now there appeared a freer use of curve and a more organic sense of form. New ornaments and a richer fauna were introduced, and there was some stirring of vegetable life. The composition in its turn loosened: here Late Geometric had prepared the way, but the oblique asymmetry of the volutes of PLATE 8c shows a new advance. There were experiments in drawing also; reservation and incision enliven the Geometric silhouette. The results are often crude, but they are vigorous and confident.

The phase of Greek art that now began lasted for some two centuries. Its two main branches are concerned one with displays of animals, the other with scenes of human action; and though men and animals often appear on the same pot, they rarely mix in the same field. The *animal style*, decorative in its intention, did not progress far. Its common fauna was lion, bull, boar, sphinx, griffin, goat, deer, dog, hare, eagle, cock, goose. Of these goat and deer were already familiar in Geometric, and some of the others (borrowed from the East) intrude occasionally at the end of that style. In the second half of the seventh century further species became popular – Corinth at least seems to have admitted some new Oriental influence – and there starts a plague of 'panthers', that is lions or other felines with head drawn in full face, and various hybrids such as the siren (or bird with a woman's head). The arrangement of animals in file, which had been normal in Geometric, was continued in Old Greece for dogs chasing and in the Wild Goat style of the East Greeks for the regular procession of goats or deer. Otherwise the animals are more usually assorted and disposed in confronting pairs or less formally in threes. The poses are conventional, as a glance through the PLATES will show, and the general absence of aggression or even activity would have satisfied Isaiah: in the sixth century lions or panthers mauling other beasts become commoner but never the rule. Once suitable formulas had been discovered there was little development except towards delicacy and slickness of drawing. It is true that vase-painters had no chance of studying some of their favourites, but the Greeks were not much interested in animals except for the noble horse (which is very rare in the animal style) and less so man's humbler friend the dog.

Progressive artists turned increasingly to depicting the *human figure* in action. Here the debt to Oriental art was small: in Attica indeed one can trace step by step the evolution from Geometric to the new type of man. The layer-wigs of the early figures of PLATE 9B come second-hand from Egypt, but this fashion appealed less to vase-painters than to sculptors. The conventional pose of flying figures, such as the Gorgon of PLATE 17, is probably Oriental too. But even in early Greek sculpture the foreign contribution to human studies was superficial, and in painting it was smaller still. Battles, races and processions were favourite subjects. To these, as competence increased, were added more particular incidents from mythology, drunken revels, and quieter scenes of domestic life. Horses are common, other animals rare apart from dogs and those monsters which complicated human life in the Heroic Age. Scenes of action made for the overlapping of figures and a considerable freedom of pose; in the orthodox animal style neither was necessary. The view of the figure was similar to that of the Geometric artist – a profile head in which the eye is frontal and profile limbs, but painters soon learnt to draw the human chest in profile as well as frontally and to add and improve anatomical details. There is no background to the scenes and a deliberate avoidance of spatial depth. It is unreasonable to complain of these conventions, which have an artistic justification in the medium; a vase is not a canvas.

The new range of *ornament* includes such abstract motives as hooks, spirals, cables, rays, crosses; some of these came from the East, others were native inventions. Volutes, palmettes, lotus flowers and buds, and often rosettes still show their vegetable origin: the Oriental models were already stylized, the Greek versions though more stylized in detail have a greater vitality. But generally ornament had a subordinate function in Greek vase-painting.

Roughly the animal style, which constitutes the Orientalizing style (properly defined), was the standard style of the seventh century, went out of favour in the sixth, and lingered on through the Classical period. But it was an interlude rather than a necessary stage in Greek art, and if there had been no Oriental contact in the eighth century Attic vase-painting of the mature black-figure and the red-figure styles might not have been much different. For the characteristic subject of Hellenic art was the human figure, and this developed out of Geometric in slow but almost complete independence.

Corinth about 720 B.C. was the first Greek city to develop the Orientalizing style. In Athens, some of the Cyclades and Crete the change began around 700 B.C. The East Greek cities were later still, perhaps by a full generation. How the Orientalizing impulse reached each area is not known. Corinth presumably had it direct from the Syrian coast, her neighbours perhaps from her. But the influences that formed the Wild Goat style of the East Greeks [PLATES 30–31] certainly came separately and perhaps in another medium or from another source. The Mycenaean vestiges that have been detected in Orientalizing art were not local survivals: either they are casual resemblances, or they were repatriated from the Levant where Mycenaean art had in its prime transplanted itself.

The two centuries that followed saw the growth and decay of a rich assortment of local schools. In Greek art as in much of Greek life there were two opposite tendencies, a striving for local independence and the assimilating attraction of some major power. Since Mycenaean times local schools of vase-painting, though based on a common tradition, had on the whole been diverging, and the new movement with its new repertory encouraged further divergence. But the new style required a more accomplished draughtsmanship than had Geometric, and soon lesser schools began to imitate more closely their greater neighbours and gradually to give up the unequal competition. By the end of the sixth century Athens was left in undisputed supremacy.

The history of this period is largely the history of Corinth and then of Athens. Corinth, the pioneer, kept her lead into the sixth century and set a standard for much of the Greek world. The early or Protocorinthian stage established a precise and elegant animal style [PLATE 11A], based on the black-figure technique – that is the use of silhouette with incised detail and occasional patches of added colour – and there are a few admirable examples of human scenes [PLATE 9C]; but pots with Subgeometric, linear or other simple decoration still greatly outnumbered the figured pieces. Then in the third quarter of the seventh century the Corinthians turned over to a popularized version of the animal style [PLATE 11B and FIG. 6G–I] with which they flooded Greek markets and Greek taste; this Ripe style lasted till the second quarter of the sixth century. Meanwhile some enterprising painters concentrated on human scenes and in the early sixth century formed a gaily handsome school [PLATES 12C–13]; but Attic competition was growing, and in spite of concessions to the new fashions the Corinthians had by 550 B.C. succumbed. After this Corinthian vase-painting was reduced to very simple patterns. In Athens the new style pursued grandeur without having learnt discipline or consistency [PLATES 14 and 16], till finally in the last third of the seventh century Corinthian example established the black-figure technique and a steadier tradition [PLATE 17]. But Corinthian influence did not stop at that, and the grand style of late Protoattic declined towards pettiness: some of the Corinthianizing painting of the early sixth century is humiliating [PLATE 20A]. Other Athenian painters, though they borrowed much from Corinth, kept and refined their standard [PLATE 18] and by the 570s the character of the mature Attic black-figure style is becoming clear [PLATE 19]. It is a style that inherits the old Protoattic interest in human subjects, is tenser and more austere than contemporary Corinthian, and has a more sober balance of colour. Round the middle of the sixth century a generation of able painters, culminating in Exekias, brought the black-figure style to its perfection [PLATES 22–23]. It was the need for a medium more subtly expressive that about 530 B.C. created the red-figure technique and style. Though the black-figure style survived into the fifth century, its artistic work was done.

In Boeotia there were some simple original experiments [PLATE 28A], but imitation of Athens proved stronger; though there is little artistic merit in the products of Boeotian workshops, at least they continued in production. Eretria till the early sixth century was clumsily dependent on Corinth and Athens. In the Argolid the local Geometric style had been impressive, but no new style followed it. Laconia made timid and sluggish use of the new repertory till about 620 B.C. [FIGS. 11–12], when it began to admit from Corinth the black-figure technique and modern ideas; the early sixth century saw the emergence of a vigorous local school [PLATE 27], provincial but self-confident, which flourished for fifty years and then rapidly decayed. One or two workshops in Messenia may have attempted an Orientalizing style, there is rather more from Elis but of no better quality, and Ithaca had an undisciplined local version of Protocorinthian; but generally the potters of Western Greece found the new standards beyond their powers. In Crete, where the Geometric tradition remained firm and the Orientalizing spirit fluid, there was a century of futile experiment. In Thera its peculiar adaptation of Geometric survived for a time, accepting little innovation. The Cyclades in the early seventh century possessed some short-lived small workshops [FIGS. 14–16], skilful but mannered in their individual ways, and providing exemplary definitions of the terms Subgeometric and Early Orientalizing: from one group developed the so-called 'Melian' school which for a generation on either side of 600 B.C. produced a showy but conventional pottery, heavily indebted to its neighbours to west and east of the Aegean. To the East Greek cities, where Geometric may have lasted through the first quarter of the seventh century, the new movement brought the Wild Goat style [PLATES 30 and 31A], an animal style executed in a slack reserving technique, in Ionia and

Rhodes decorative but costive and in Aeolis (where Grey ware or Bucchero also persisted) sliding into barbarism. Rather before 600 B.C. Corinthian ideas intruded and for some twenty or thirty years the black-figure technique is found alongside that of reservation [FIG. 18 and PLATE 31B]; but by the 570s the Wild Goat style had disappeared, at least in the southern cities, though it re-emerged some fifty years later on Clazomenian sarcophagi. Chios in the early sixth century developed two new schools, one notable for its human subjects, ably drawn in outline and sometimes brightly coloured, the other a miserable perversion of black-figure. Elsewhere the successors of the Wild Goat painters recognized the supremacy of the black-figure style; it was accepted in northern Ionia, which broadly followed Attic models [PLATE 32B], and imitated in the more traditional south by the reservation of details within a full silhouette [PLATES 32A and 33]. But in spite of some excellent and original pieces these later East Greek schools soon declined and did not outlast the sixth century. On the other side of the Greek world Ithaca and Sicily have provided evidence of provincial schools producing Protocorinthian to a local recipe, and rather earlier a more orthodox Protocorinthian was made at Ischia and Cumae in Italy. In Etruria – which had also its own Bucchero – local craftsmen imitated with varying degrees of fidelity Protocorinthian, Ripe Corinthian, and from about 550 B.C. Attic black-figure. Most of these imitations were begun presumably by immigrant Greek craftsmen, and in the middle and later years of the sixth century there are also some wares of first-rate and more original quality – notably what is called 'Chalcidian' pottery [PLATE 36] and the more eccentric Caeretan hydriai [PLATE 35]. Further research will no doubt discover still other local schools and perhaps make the history of this period more bewildering. But its end shows Athens triumphant; in Boeotia and Etruria and Campania local workshops turn out indifferent or distorted renderings of Attic; elsewhere there may occur some trivial Atticizing (as in Rhodes and even at Corinth), but vase-painting as a serious art is not even attempted.

2. Corinth

Corinth, on whose happy commercial situation Thucydides remarks, was the first Greek city to adopt the Orientalizing style and so established a dominance in vase-painting which she kept till the early sixth century. Most of her rivals at one time or another imitated her, and Corinthian pottery is found on almost every contemporary Greek site both at home and overseas. Fortunately the style of Corinth is easy to classify, since its evolution is generally even and steady.

Early Protocorinthian (c. 720–c. 690 B.C.)

The Late Geometric style of Corinth, as was mentioned before (pp. 24–5), had begun to discard the strict Geometric principles. Within a generation Orientalizing elements were welcomed in, and by about 720 B.C. the so-called Protocorinthian style is apparent. The first phase, the Early Protocorinthian, covers the process of digestion, which was remarkably quick and sure. There is nothing hesitant about the swing of the volutes on the oinochoe of PLATE 8C, and nothing Oriental although they are inspired by Oriental flora. The carefree balance of the composition and its invasion of three-quarters of the body of the pot are a manifesto of the new movement which rejected the rigid symmetry and the restrained emphasis of Geometric art. The decoration is conceived as an object of beauty in itself. Equally assured is the ring of rays or solid triangles from which the vase seems to spring. This favourite Protocorinthian use has a subtlety that would have repelled the true Geometric artist who cross-hatched his triangles and disposed of them only as ornament. But when he came to the neck the painter of this pot reverted to his Geometric training [cf. PLATE 8B].

The commonest and characteristic Protocorinthian shape is the aryballos, a small flask two to three inches high, intended for oil or scent and so narrow in the neck. The Early type [PLATE 9A] has a roundish body with a low ring foot, short neck, simple lip and narrow handle. This is called the 'round' aryballos or the aryballos 'pansu'. It was derived, probably at Corinth, from a simple type of small jug that was common throughout the Geometric period. The shape gradually narrows in body and widens in lip and handle, and the 'ovoid' aryballos is regular for Middle Protocorinthian [PLATE 9D]. Continued evolution leads to the rather taller 'pointed' or 'piriform' aryballos of the Late Protocorinthian and Transitional periods [FIG. 5B]. This top-heavy form is then replaced by a new round shape [PLATE 10B]. Because of their frequency and regular development the aryballoi have become type-fossils for excavators of late eighth- and seventh-century Greek sites.

An aryballos in Naples [PLATE 9A] shows again a mixture of Orientalizing novelties and Geometric survivals. Geometric are the row of triangles, cross-hatched and on the shoulder, and the fine banding that contains the lower part of the body. But the strokes round the base of the neck are already turning into tongues, and the main field is wholly

Orientalizing. The cock, which had only recently made his entry into Greek art and perhaps backyards, struts with an assurance justified by his substantial build and gay detail; a demure hen awaits him further round the vase. Geometric figures are patterns, abstract and stiff, but here is a creature of flesh and blood, drawn with the same organic curves as the volutes of the oinochoe already discussed [PLATE 8C]. Behind the cock two of the new ornaments, a cable and a rosette, have been casually added. The inner details are reserved. Incision was still exceptional and, as on the volutes of PLATE 8C, tentative.

This phase, which lasts about thirty years, was experimental. The animals and birds, which are rare, vary greatly, partly perhaps because Corinth had had little concern with the regular Geometric fauna. There is more unity in a larger group of aryballoi with spiral hooks or tongues round the shoulder and banding on the body. But the great majority of pots made in the Early Protocorinthian period stayed close to the older Geometric tradition (see below, p. 62). The commonest shapes were the aryballos and the kotyle, and after them the ordinary oinochoe, the conical oinochoe, and the straight-sided pyxis with flattish knobbed lid. In general only the aryballos and the oinochoe, and they not regularly, carried the new decoration. Even so, Corinth was now the dominant supplier of the growing export trade in Greek pottery.

Middle Protocorinthian (c. 690–c. 650 B.C.)

In the early seventh century Corinthian painters settled down into a style of sober correctness. The most important single factor was the invention of the black-figure technique, which became for nearly two hundred years the medium of the progressive schools of vase-painting. The technique consisted in making first a silhouette of the chosen subject, and then engraving the details with a sharp point; this was done, of course, before the pot was fired and while its surface was still only leather-hard. It soon became regular to supplement incision with colour, first purple and later white also. Geometric artists had occasionally incised a zigzag line to relieve a dark band, but the systematic use of incision probably came from the engraving of metalwork, a process introduced into Greece from the East; this would account for the unnecessary incising of outlines in earlier black-figure work. Still, whatever the causes, the effects of the new technique were immediate. Incising lends itself to fine sharp lines, which the miniature scale of normal Protocorinthian figures required. Brush strokes can be sketched with fluent ease, but an incised line if it is to be clean must be traced more slowly and carefully. Lastly the dark silhouette to which the details are added discourages an illusionist treatment of the subject, and emphasizes the enclosing contour. So a new conventional style was created, dependent on delicacy of line and balanced masses. The dog on PLATE 10A will serve as an example. The animals of the rather later East Greek oinochoe, PLATE 30A, which are drawn in a more freehand technique, are by contrast flabby.

FIG. 4. A. *Protocorinthian kotyle*

Ht 7·5 cm. Subgeometric style: first half of 7th cent. B.C.

B. *Protocorinthian cup*

Ht *c.* 5 cm. Subgeometric style: mid 7th cent. B.C.

On PLATE 9D is shown an aryballos in Boston of about 675 B.C. It is a small vase, little more than two inches high, of the new ovoid shape. Round the lip there are spiral hooks. The shoulder carries a chain of lotus flowers and volutes, a severely stylized version of a favourite Oriental design; the outline technique, abandoned in the drawing of figures, is still used for subsidiary ornament. In the main field, which is less than a thumbnail deep, two black-figure sphinxes confront each other in a now standard grouping. The species sphinx, the wig-like coiffure and the filling rosettes are all of Oriental origin, but the style is entirely Greek. Below there is a file of dogs hunting: such hunts, black-figure or on less elaborate pots in silhouette [as on FIG. 5A], are now a stock item of decoration. The inevitable rays surround the base. The exuberance of Early Protocorinthian has been tempered by discipline.

Another ovoid aryballos in Boston has round the mouth tongues, spiral hooks, and short rays pointing outward, and down the handle a complicated triple cable. On its shoulder in black-figure style a lion [FIG. 6B] faces a ram and a goat stalks away; the necks of these animals

FIG. 5. *Protocorinthian aryballoi*
A, ht 6·2 cm. B, ht *c.* 8 cm. Linear style: third quarter of 7th cent. B.C.

are overpainted in purple. The main scene round the body is drawn out on PLATE 9B a little under natural size. On the right a bearded figure wearing a sword and grasping sceptre and thunderbolt, and therefore to be identified as Zeus, is attacking a monster compounded of man and horse. To judge by mythology and later monuments this must be one of the Giants; the man–horse hybrid, already known in Attic Late Geometric art, had not yet been fixed particularly as a centaur. Between the Giant and the armed male who is rushing up there stands a curious object, which is most probably a krater with pedestal. If so, the krater is viewed from above according to a perspective that would be more intelligible in Geometric painting. The figures are drawn boldly with full rounded forms and in postures of extravagant vigour, as if in deliberate defiance of the old Geometric rules. Details are sparingly but effectively marked by incision, and purple is freely added for its decorative value. Four eagles and a variety of the new ornaments are spread generously in the field. Round the base we have again the narrower rays that are well suited to the narrower shape of aryballos. This pot also is of about 675 B.C. It is one of the first scenes in Greek art certainly taken from mythology.

On these foundations Corinthian vase-painting in the second quarter of the seventh century reached remarkable heights. The animal style is refined to a delicate vigour [cf. FIG. 6A–C]. The filling ornament lightens; stalked dot-rosettes become the commonest form, but often even they are omitted. Chains of lotus flowers and palmettes are drawn, still in outline technique, with an elaborate grace that later vase-painters never equalled. The Macmillan aryballos of the British Museum [PLATE 9C] shows the achievement in human figures. This frieze, reproduced a little under natural size, comes from an ovoid aryballos with a plastic lion's head for its neck, a lotus and palmette chain round the shoulder, and on the body below the main battle frieze three narrower bands containing a horse race, a hare hunt and double rays. Eighteen soldiers in hoplite armour are engaged: their long trim limbs and easy agility show what full use Corinthian artists had made of the twenty or thirty years since the Boston aryballos of PLATE 9B. The admirable composition contrives to keep the figures, if not quite in a single plane, yet in a shallow register, as though on the stage they were acting in front of the curtain. This principle, which obviates the need for perspective, was maintained by vase-painters until towards the middle of the fifth century some of the bolder Athenians – with unhappy results – tried to emulate the novelties of contemporary murals. Greek relief sculptors resisted the temptation longer.

The Macmillan aryballos is one of a small number of Corinthian pots of about the middle of the seventh century which experiment with a more natural coloration, notably by the use of a warmish brown painted directly on the clay to represent human flesh. But the colour is laid on in a flat wash and details are incised, and the treatment as well as the technique is essentially that of black-figure. Here the rather laboured arrangement of shields and the helmets and greaves leave little flesh exposed. But on other pots, of which the most famous is the slightly later Chigi vase of the Villa Giulia in Rome, the areas of flesh are much larger and give a brilliant air of gaiety. This venture in polychromy, so contrary to the general current, was short-lived. It was probably inspired by free painting, of which we have examples of Corinthian style some fifteen or twenty years later in the painted terracotta metopes from Thermon and Calydon in Aetolia. These metopes, which incidentally are our earliest relics of Doric architecture, have fields up to two feet square containing single figures or small groups. The figures are drawn in dark outline on the yellowish clay and then filled in with a variety of flat colours, on which anatomical details are marked in dark paint with the same economy as in vase-painting. Till about 500 B.C. the principles of composition and anatomical drawing were similar for the two arts, which were very closely related. Yet though the Protocorinthian *Polychrome style* (as it is called) is probably indebted to free painting, some large plaques of the sixth century were decorated in the full black-figure technique. But too little of free painting has survived.

The vase-paintings so far discussed have all been of small scale. Protocorinthian was essentially a miniaturist style. There are a few examples of drawing on a larger scale, of which the kotyle in the British Museum [PLATE 10A] is one of the best preserved. The height of the main frieze is about four inches. The formalized anatomy of the dog has the torsion of a steel spring, and the effect is enhanced by the precise beauty of the incised lines. Yet there are signs that this is not an independent grand style, but an enlargement of something smaller; the double and treble incisions of the head and the large blank area of body and rump suggest perhaps that the artist was not familiar with the decoration of surfaces of this size. The throat of the dog has been picked out in purple and the scruff of its neck in yellow, a colour which now began a short vogue. The filling ornament is restrained. The date of this kotyle should be about 660 B.C.

The style now about its zenith depends on the clarity and elegance of its line. Though purple is often used, especially on the necks of animals, it is not indispensable. The animal style, in which action was neglected, was reaching its decorative limits. There was more scope in the human figures, although the engaging polychrome style proved a blind alley. A similar neatness and delicacy refined the floral motives and reduced and simplified the filling ornament. The aryballos remained the favourite shape. Next come the kotyle, the flat-bottomed oinochoe (with stumpy body and short broad neck), the pyxis with slightly concave sides, and the ordinary oinochoe. But pottery painted with Subgeometric or Linear decoration (see pp. 62–3) is still much more frequent; besides the shapes just listed, cups and conical oinochoai are common in these styles.

Late Protocorinthian (c. 650–c. 640 B.C.) and
Transitional (c. 640–c. 625 B.C.)

The twenty-five years that followed the middle of the seventh century saw a transformation of the black-figure animal pottery, which now became the staple line of the Corinthian industry. The style was cheapened too. The series of lions on FIG. 6 illustrates the descent from fine and sensitive quality to pretentious mass production. The total effect is still more striking, if one compares for example the two pots on PLATE 11.

There is first a tendency to bigger, and then to longer animals. This was partly reaction against the miniaturists, partly a deliberate device to cover larger areas more quickly. Inner detail, both incised lines and purple patches, correspondingly increased and coarsened; forms grew lumpy, and postures wooden. New species, flashier or easier to draw, were introduced; so the panther now begins to replace the lion. In long friezes the group of three animals – as for example a bull between a lion and a panther – becomes stereotyped. There is a greater change in the general composition, in the relation of the animals to the field they are set in; the filling ornament is by its density becoming as important as the figures. Protocorinthian paintings are worth detailed study, but the new Ripe style can be appreciated at a glance.

The first stage of this progress improved the Protocorinthian style towards a slightly mannered charm. The well-bred animals have not lost their vigour, and the filling ornament, standardized as dot-rosettes which are usually stalked, is scattered lightly in the field. Hitherto the divisions between friezes had, following the Geometric practice, been composed of two or three narrow lines; now painters prefer a broad band of the dark paint, on which there may be a few narrow stripes of purple and of yellow or white – generally yellow is earlier than white. The subsidiary ornament too is adapted to the black-figure style. The outline floral designs that had been common on the shoulder of aryballoi give way [as on FIG. 5B] to tongues, some of which are painted over in purple. More logical still is the *black polychrome* system of decoration, well exhibited in the scale pattern on the olpe of PLATE 11A. Here the pattern is incised by compasses and in alternation left dark and filled with purple and yellow or white. The regular motives are scales and, round the shoulder, tongues. On the necks of olpai and oinochoai, which are painted dark, white dot-rosettes are evenly spaced. Some pots are wholly in black polychrome style. This kind of decoration to be effective must be carefully and accurately done, as is painfully evident a

FIG. 6. *Protocorinthian and Ripe Corinthian lions*

A, beginning of 7th cent. B.C.   B, *c.* 675 B.C.   C, *c.* 660–650 B.C.   D, *c.* 650–640 B.C.   E, *c.* 650–640 B.C.   F, *c.* 640–625 B.C.   G, *c.* 625–600. B.C   H, *c.* 615–600 B.C.   I, *c.* 600–580 B.C.

generation later. The new fashion for a dark ground also encouraged painters to paint figures in white on dark, and there are one or two examples of what one may call black-figure on a black ground.

In the so-called Transitional phase the new tendencies in the animal style harden. Compare the lions of FIG. 6C, E and F, and it is plain that spontaneity is being replaced by a standardized repetition of types. The olpe PLATE 11A is a handsome and careful piece, but its line-drawing has not the sensitive precision of the best Protocorinthian. On other pots the Ripe style is more obviously foreshadowed.

The change in style was accompanied by changes in the shapes of pots and by the adoption or invention of new decorative types. The types, which show a renewed artistic contact with the East, will be mentioned in the section on the Ripe style. The commonest shape was still the aryballos, now lengthened and narrowed to the 'pointed' or 'piriform' variety [as FIG. 5B]. The alabastron [a later example is shown on PLATE 10C] appeared just before the middle of the century. The Protocorinthian form is squat with a small bevelled mouth. By the Transitional period the wide flat lip is canonical, the body is slimming, and manufacture increases rapidly. The new round aryballos [see PLATE 10B] also begins its career. Among larger vases the olpe is new; as can be seen from PLATE 11A its sagging belly shows a kinship with the alabastron, and it too grows narrower. The ordinary oinochoe becomes more popular – a willingness to paint larger pots was another result of the impulse that led to larger figures – and the shape was revised. Till the middle of the seventh century Corinthian painters had been content with the old Geometric shape [see PLATE 8C], and though the belly of the pot had shifted slightly upwards a Subgeometric decoration of the neck often emphasized its ancestry. The new shape with broad high-bellied body and squat neck has a certain heaviness of form that suits the new animal style: the example of PLATE 11B belongs to the Ripe style, when necks were becoming narrower. Flat-bottomed oinochoai, conical oinochoai, kotylai and concave-sided pyxides continued.

The Ripe Animal style (c. 625–c. 550 B.C.)

The general character of the Ripe Animal style has been described in the last section and is more clearly illustrated by FIG. 6G–I and PLATES 10B–C and 11B. The *Early Ripe* period, which covers the last quarter of the seventh century, was its heyday. The painter's aim was to obtain quickly and easily a rich and immediate decorative effect. So he preferred broad friezes, long careless animals, and thick gaudy detail and filling ornament. His success may be judged by the comparison of FIG. 6H and PLATE 11B; in its proper environment the lion is inconspicuous. The solid incised rosette had made a modest entry in the Transitional period, but it is now enlarged and fragmented to fill every corner in the background of the frieze. This practice has sometimes been attributed to the imitation of textile models, but weaving has no monopoly of close decoration. Imagination found its outlet more in the introduction of novel creatures, some for variety and others for convenience. The new Assyrian breed of lion had arrived soon after the middle of the century and by the beginning of the Ripe period had driven out the older 'Hittite' (that is Syrian) type – on FIG. 6 C–E are 'Hittite', F–I Assyrian: the mane is often cross-hatched in summary rendering of the more laborious flame-like tufts of hair. Common though the lion is, the panther has become commoner. Other traditional animals – boar, bull, goat, deer – remain popular. Eagles, geese, hares and snakes are from the Transitional period regular central motives on alabastra. Owls grow more numerous. Cocks reappear. The sphinx and the griffin survive, but no longer walk. The siren (or human-headed bird) becomes a favourite, as do many other hybrids – the griffin-bird, the panther-bird, the snake-tailed man ('Typhon'), the fish-tailed man ('Triton'), the winged man ('Boread'), the winged woman gripping a pair of birds (the 'Mistress of the Beasts'). The siren and the Boread appear already in Protocorinthian, but are more congenial to the Ripe style, where figures with wings, worn outstretched in the new fashion, one to the front and one to the back, have the merit of filling more space. Whatever the origin or ultimate significance of the half-human creatures, their use was almost always decorative. It is futile to ransack catalogues of Corinthian vases for evidence of obscure cults. The Gorgon, though, may truly be a Gorgon. Its disembodied head, the Gorgoneion, is an ornamental – perhaps also an apotropaic – device from early in the seventh century, but the full-length type in the familiar story of Medusa appears at Athens before and in Corinthian not long after the middle of that century.

PLATE 11B is an average specimen of the Early Ripe style. On the alabastron PLATE 10C the effect is much lighter. The explanation is probably in the shape. The earliest Corinthian alabastra, which are of about the middle of the seventh century, are naturally decorated in friezes, but the growth in the size of friezes and of animals led to the treatment of the whole body as a single field, carrying either a solitary figure or a small group. These groups are as a rule arranged heraldically, two lions or cocks for instance facing each other over a hare or snake or other suitable marker. The standard was fixed by the Transitional painters, and their light use of filling ornament was continued on the small alabastra, some three or four inches high, as well as in the group of round aryballoi which adopted their scheme of the single field. It spread too to the large alabastra of ten inches or more in height, which were common by the end of the sixth century: earlier examples are usually decorated in friezes.

One embellishment of the black-figure style is not illustrated here – the emphasizing of incised lines by rows of white dots. The practice, said to be borrowed from metalwork, flourished in the early sixth century. This decorative trick takes the animal style even further from nature.

Floral ornaments, now regularly in the black-figure technique, are composed mostly of the lotus and the palmette. In spite of stylization and haste their structure has still an organic clarity. Besides continuous chains there are independent forms, of which the commonest are the doubled lotus (used especially as a central motive on the heraldic alabastra), the quadruple lotus, and the lotus-palmette cross. At the same time a new outline ornament was developed, of four lotus flowers and four buds arranged radially and much cross-hatched; this quatrefoil, which originated in Assyria, became popular on aryballoi in the Middle Ripe period, and simplified and debased lasted out the sixth century.

Mention has been made of Assyrian art as influencing Corinthian. For the quatrefoil and the new lion this is certain, and it is possible for some traits of the horse, the scale pattern and the solid rosette. The influence came during the third quarter of the seventh century, probably by way of Syria. In themselves these borrowings are not important, but if the thick filling of the background also is Assyrian, then this phase of the Corinthian and other Greek schools owes more to the East than is usually thought.

To the taste for new types there was joined a taste for new shapes, particularly in the middle and larger ranges. The commonest Early Ripe vases are however the round aryballos and the alabastron. The kotyle and the olpe continue, and the ordinary, broad-bottomed and conical oinochoai. The concave-sided pyxis becomes more concave, and new types of pyxis are invented. More significant is the appearance of the neck-amphora and the new column-krater [PLATE 12C].

The popularity of the Ripe style is striking. Not only was output and export immense – the number of aryballoi and alabastra surviving whole or in fragments must be in the tens of thousands – but imitation by other Greek schools was widespread. The conclusions for Greek taste are of interest.

In the *Middle Ripe* period (*c.* 600–*c.* 575 B.C.) the Animal style is disintegrating. Generally the figures become clumsier and dispirited and the repertory smaller, while the filling ornament melts into rosettes and little dots. FIG. 61 shows the characteristic trend of this period. There was, though, a more delicate style, especially among a group of painters who were interested also in the drawing of the human figure. Here the animals are slender and filling ornament is often omitted. The Gorgoneion group, which will be discussed later (p. 60), specialized in a now important shape, the cup. The Chimera group, which dates to the end of the Middle period, consists mainly of plates handsomely decorated with a large, often heraldic design; their painter, it is plain, owed something to the alabastra. By now the commonest shapes are alabastra, usually large, kotylai, and round aryballoi (some with a very low foot). In the second rank are various types of pyxis with convex sides, the cup [with broader foot and so rounder bowl than the Subgeometric type of FIG. 4B], the plate, the phiale, various bowls, ring-vases (shaped like an invalid's rubber cushion), the ordinary and also the broad-bottomed oinochoe, the olpe, the neck-amphora, the amphoriskos and the column-krater (which is now the pre-eminent large vase).

The *Late Ripe* period (*c.* 575–*c.* 550 B.C.) sees the extinction of the Animal style. The stock has shrunk to sphinx, siren, panther, goat, goose, griffin-bird and cock – emaciated creatures perfunctorily drawn. White is now freely used for broader areas, as in bands along wings. The quatrefoil aryballoi flourish. But artistic interest has passed altogether to human figures and the Red-ground style, and for cheaper ware a development of the Linear style predominates. The Animal style is chiefly found on aryballoi and alabastra, on kotylai, cups, lekythoi and oinochoai; and in subsidiary friezes on column-kraters. Floral chains are common on the convex pyxides. For hydriai, amphorae and the main fields of kraters the Red-ground style is normal. This interest in larger vases, general by the middle years of the sixth century, perhaps reflects the influence of Attic, which was now capturing the Corinthian markets. The old Animal style was obsolete.

The Ripe style – Human figures (c. 625–c. 550 B.C.)

Protocorinthian pots with human figures are rare, and Ripe Corinthian not common. There are two influences discernible. The first is that of the black-figure technique of the Animal style, which was practised by the same painters, though generally they put more originality into their human scenes. The second influence, which is intermittent, comes from free painting. Of this the painted metopes from Thermon and Calydon, works of the Transitional period, are our only direct evidence and there, since the fields are square, the compositions are necessarily simple. The numerous small clay plaques from Penteskouphia, which range in date from the middle of the seventh to the end of the sixth century, belong rather to vase-painting than to free painting. So the influence of free painting must in the main be inferred from tricks and trends in vase-painting that cannot be explained otherwise, as for instance the short-lived polychrome style of the middle of the seventh century, which shows not only a new and more natural range of colour, but also a sudden and assured elaborateness of composition.

During the Early Ripe period there are a good many examples of a humdrum, and sometimes slovenly, style. It is closely related to and often infected by the Animal style, and the protective background of rosettes is equally necessary. But in general proportions are better than in Protocorinthian, particular features less exaggerated, and inner details more extensive. The common subjects are riders, soldiers and the 'padded dancers' whose identity has teased many scholars [for the type see PLATE 12B]. Most of these human subjects appear on simple aryballoi and the composition too is simple, with figures placed clear of each other, though in battles shields may overlap. PLATE 10B is a fair sample.

A few large vases of the end of the Early Ripe period offer more ambitious scenes in a more independent style. The best is a column-krater in the Louvre [PLATE 12C] with conventional animals round the flat of the rim and two zones with human figures on the body. The lower and subsidiary frieze has a rather perfunctory horse-race. The main field contains on one side a battle, on the other the entertainment of Heracles by Eurytos. On this unhackneyed subject the vase-painter exerted himself. Four couches stand in a row, and on them recline Heracles, Eurytos, and his four sons, while his daughter Iole stands coquettishly between a brother and the hero. The composition has a spaciousness due not to the absence of filling ornament (which is indeed partly compensated by the sprawling names painted against each figure) but to the relation of the figures to each other and to the frame. Their anatomy is conventional, but the varied posing – with all the unnatural mobility of early Greek art – has a new and pictorial dignity. Except for the small exposed parts of Iole's person the figures are done in the black-figure technique with plenty of added purple. Their dark masses are balanced by the low tables with food and drink and by the dogs tied

under the couches, cheerful accessories which are mostly drawn in outline with painted inner detail. The outline technique is used also for
Iole's face and throat, finger and feet, and contrasts strongly with the
purple heads and dark bodies of the men. This secondary distinction of
sex was now becoming regular in the black-figure styles of the Greek
world; it is not certain where it was first established, though Corinth is
likely. A certain unevenness in style resulted from the compromise between the techniques of incision and outline in a single scene, but it was
an unevenness that vase-painters turned to good account.

The larger scale of drawing – the main panel on the Eurytos krater
is over four inches high – offered more scope than the aryballoi and
other small vases. But during the early sixth century some competent
Corinthian vase-painters were content with small figures. The cups and
kotylai of the Gorgoneion and Samos groups, though their subjects are
often conventional, show a neat and delicate vigour. On PLATE 12A–B
are details from two of them, reproduced at about two-thirds of their
natural size. These groups, which belong to the end of the Middle Ripe
period, had a strong influence on Attic, particularly on the Comast cups.
But in Corinthian vase-painting the small black-figure tradition wilted,
though something of it survived in the Penteskouphia plaques. A bottle
by Timonidas, the only Corinthian vase-painter whose name we know,
is contemporary with the Gorgoneion and Samos groups, but the composition and contrast of colour in its ambushing of Troilus is more akin
to the Grand style.

The broader style of the Eurytos krater was continued in the first
quarter of the sixth century in a group of large vases. The compositions
are now bolder and more involved, the contrast of incision and outline
drawing is more fully employed, and the profiles of figures become
milder and more fluent. The favourite subjects are battles, riders and
banquets, of which some are not heroic.

About the end of the Middle period a new technique was introduced
of using an orange-red slip. This slipping became regular in the second
quarter of the century for the larger shapes preferred by the few progressive artists, but it is used only for the principal fields, which gain
in emphasis by the contrast with the pale yellow surface of other parts
of the vase. The cause of this change was presumably the growing competition of Athens and the desire to emulate the redder Attic clay, but
its stylistic consequences show an original Corinthian spirit. Attic vase-
painting continued to be strongly black-figure in style, and the purple
and white embellishments are normally subsidiary. In Corinth the white
and purple are used more freely and the picture is conceived in terms of

colour, so much so that white (now regular for women) is sometimes used also for the flesh of men, if it is felt that too much black-figure would give a sombre effect. The drawing progresses in accomplishment. Profiles soften, the side view of the chest is better understood, limited facial expression is attempted, but drapery is still painted as flat surfaces without folds. Compositions are often elaborately crowded, sometimes with an architectural setting. The krater of PLATE 13 is to be

FIG. 7. *Ripe Corinthian column-krater*
Fragment: scale 1 : 1. *c.* 565 B.C. White for flesh and plume of helmet

dated about 570 B.C., the sherd of FIG. 7 a little later. There are also less elaborate pieces, some with sirens or cocks, which are painted with the same enjoyment of colour. This brilliant style came to an end about 550 B.C.

The subjects of this *Red-ground style* are more varied than those of preceding periods. From human life come wedding scenes, banquets, drunken dances, races, the soldier's farewell, and battles, sometimes anonymous, sometimes labelled as heroic. Of the heroes Heracles is most popular, and there are scenes from martial legend or epic – the theme of the *Odyssey* was little used by early Greek artists. The moment represented is, as in all Archaic art, one of dramatic emphasis, which summarizes the story or incident. It is probable that many of the subjects popular in the sixth century were first invented or adapted for vase-painting in Corinth. But for all its brilliance the Corinthian Red-ground style succumbed about 550 B.C. Though a local style persists for a generation or more on the clay plaques from Penteskouphia and the wooden ones from Pitsa, the rare contemporary pots with human figures are straightforward imitations of Attic black-figure.

Subgeometric and Linear styles (c. 720–5th century B.C.)

The invention of the Protocorinthian style did not kill the Geometric tradition. There was instead an immediate enrichment of the repertory of ornament by borrowing such Oriental novelties as the spiral hook and the four-leaved rosette for contexts that were traditional. Less ambiguous are the net of dotted lozenges, files of puny silhouette birds [as on PLATE 14A and FIG. 8], and the sinuous snakes or wavy lines with stars and swastikas in their curves. But the most important innovation was the adoption of the new rays of solid triangles, at first still hung round the shoulder [as on PLATE 9A], but about 700 B.C. transferred to the base, where they soon became indispensable. Till the end of the eighth century the new and the old styles run close together, and are often mixed. In the seventh *Subgeometric* drops behind and is content with a poorer repertory of ornament: the kotyle FIG. 4A is typical in its neat and simple linear decoration, and a comparison with the Late Geometric example of PLATE 8B shows the nature of the change. After 650 B.C. Subgeometric hardly continued except on the long narrow necks of conical oinochoai. A meagre tradition can be traced in the kotylai and the cups with offset rims, some still close to the Geometric shape and others more developed [FIG. 4B], but the fine narrow banding has generally been replaced by solid areas of dark paint often enlivened with thin stripes of purple. These survivals did not outlast the seventh century.

There are many other Corinthian pots which are also called Subgeometric, though there is nothing particularly Geometric about them. A better description is *Linear*. Examples of two common types are shown on FIG. 5. The Protocorinthian black-figure style was a luxury style, and the great mass of pottery produced at Corinth in that period was decorated more simply. Plain bands of paint played a big part, but the easier of the black-figure fashions were copied. Rays for instance soon became regular, and about the middle of the century broad bands (often enlivened with purple) replace the older narrow striping. A common motive throughout the seventh century is the simplified hare-hunt, reduced to a row of dogs clumsily drawn in silhouette [FIG. 5A]. In the sixth-century version we have goats or soldiers, sometimes with closely packed dots as filling ornament. Bands of small chequers are also very common [FIG. 5B]; these begin early in the seventh century and in the second quarter of the sixth merge into the White style. Broad areas filled with dots were popular in the Early Ripe period. All these forms of decoration, which are most frequent on aryballoi, kotylai and alabastra, were sedulously and closely imitated in Etruria.

Later styles (mid 6th–4th centuries B.C.)

The *White style* appears in the second quarter of the sixth century. Its characteristic is that broad areas, often decoratively the most important, are left blank, and for the rest there are simple bands of dark and purple paint or meagre linear ornament. Such unambitious but pleasant decoration is found on a wide variety of shapes as the exhausted Animal style recedes. A similar phenomenon is found rather later in Fikellura, the result not of imitation but of a similar weariness with tradition. The *Black Pattern style*, as it has been named, pursues an opposite effect. Its main decoration consists of floral or linear patterns such as palmettes and meanders, purple bands are common, and no large area is left reserved. It begins in the Late Ripe period, in its way develops, and lasts into the fourth century. Towards the middle of the fifth century interest revived a little in animals, but not of any evident Ripe Corinthian ancestry. They are done in dark paint, either in full silhouette or with reserved or unintelligently incised details: the style, though hasty, can be lively. Sometimes too animals and ornaments are painted in white on a dark ground. None of these late wares (which used to be called *Conventionalizing*) achieves or regularly attempts more than a respectable mediocrity. Besides such products of local character we find at one time or another a little straightforward imitation of contemporary Attic (see also p. 187).

Technique

Corinth has deposits of a fine whitish clay which contains very little iron oxide and so fires a pale yellowish colour. It can easily be distinguished from the redder clays used in most schools of Greek pottery, though some Etruscan and Campanian clays have a similar, but generally muddier, appearance. The pale clay was regularly used at Corinth from the second half of the eighth century. At first it often has a pinkish tinge, but by the late seventh century a greenish tinge is common. It does not seem when fired to be as hard as good Attic, and the paint does not adhere to it as firmly. The paint is at first often red or a medium brown, but during the seventh century it becomes darker and red tones are avoided. Both clay and paint have a good sheen. The Red-ground ware of the second quarter of the sixth century and later some of the imitations of Attic employ an orange-red slip for the principal fields. Purple additions are frequent from early in the seventh century. White for ornament on a dark ground is not uncommon from the last quarter of the eighth century. White details on figures appear at the beginning of the sixth century, and in the Red-ground style white is a principal colour. The shaping and the firing of pots are generally competent.

Export and influences

From the last quarter of the eighth century to the last quarter of the seventh Corinthian pottery – figured, Subgeometric and Linear – was exported to all parts of the Greek world and was, except in the East, the only pottery that was at all widely exported. It is especially frequent in the western colonies, since they imported a great part of their painted pottery. The trade reached its peak in the Early Ripe period, although some competition was just appearing. During the sixth century Corinthian exports declined rapidly, but did not entirely disappear.

The popularity of Corinthian naturally provoked imitations. Around the end of the eighth century there was widespread, though mostly trivial copying of the Subgeometric style, particularly on kotylai. But the Protocorinthian style proper, while influential in Greece, the Cyclades and Crete, was only casually imitated except in the West. In Ithaca (cf. p. 27) a wild version of Protocorinthian was current in the first half of the seventh century; it is most interesting for its oinochoai with high shoulder and narrow conical neck, which are decorated with great loops in a bold early Orientalizing style. In Corcyra the Animal style was copied. At Ischia and Cumae in Italy the local Protocorinthian of around 700 B.C. cannot always be clearly distinguished from genuine Corinthian (see p. 145). In Sicily there are kraters of the early seventh century which develop the Protocorinthian style in their provincial way and both there and in South Italy smaller, less ambitious pots were made longer and in some quantity (see p. 146). In Etruria from the end of the eighth century to the middle of the sixth the prolific Italocorinthian school copied and adapted with varying fidelity (see pp. 148–15).

The Ripe style was still more effective. It was accepted and modified not only in Etruria, but also in all the surviving Greek schools of the end of the seventh century. During the early sixth century the progressive group of Corinthian, that interested in human figures, was influential so long as it lasted.

There appears to be no influence of other Greek schools on Corinthian till about the second quarter of the sixth century. Then in the red ground of the Red-ground style and perhaps in its preference for larger shapes Attic competition is recognized. Finally, in the later sixth and earlier fifth centuries, a few red-ground and white-ground Corinthian pots are creditable imitations of current Attic black-figure.

3. Athens

The Geometric style of Athens had been distinguished by a strong sense of order, and both collapsed together. During the next two or three generations Attic vase-painters showed a readiness to experiment and a grandiose imagination that was not troubled about scale or balance. But at the end of this period, which is known as Protoattic, discipline and a black-figure system were adopted and a new monumental style emerged. It is all very different from the steady refinement of contemporary Corinth; in the seventh century Corinthian vase-paintings can generally be visualized from a short verbal description, but only illustrations do justice to the unexpectedness of much Protoattic. Students do not agree whether to class the monumental style as Protoattic or Attic black-figure. It has the grandeur of the one and the technical manner of the other. But perhaps it is better to put the division (which is anyhow conventional) after the monumental style, when for a generation closer imitation of Corinthian and a preference for correctness rather than originality shows a more modest and even timid spirit. Then, in the second quarter of the sixth century, the Attic black-figure style found itself and became the standard of the Greek world.

Both Protoattic and Attic black-figure pottery is plentiful, since excavators, mercenary and scientific, have been busy in Attica and Italy. This and the strongly individual quality of the style enable us to see in fair detail the personalities of the artists and their relations to one another. That they were artistically wilful cannot be excused by isolation; a tenth of the contemporary pottery found in the Agora at Athens was imported from Corinth.

Early Protoattic (c. 700–c. 675 B.C.)

The hydria from Analatos [PLATE 14A and FIG. 8] is one of the earliest of Protoattic vases. The lower half of the body is still Geometric, though the deer are a little more supple and the bands of birds and oblique zigzags are borrowed from Corinth. Above we are in the new world. The lions, crick-necked bird and vegetable medley show a delight in curve and vitality that is the antithesis of the Geometric below, and

A

B

FIG. 8. *Details to supplement* PLATE 14A

A, neck; B, belly

the filling ornament repeats the contrast. Round the shoulder are the solid rays, which as in Protocorinthian replaced the cross-hatched triangles. In the main field of the body we have witnessed a revolution; the neck offers evolution. Between a row of double spirals and a band of lozenge ornament modernized by spiral hooks six men led by a lyre-player are confronting four women; each party has joined hands and carries branches. Compare the men with their ancestors on the Dipylon amphora [PLATE 5] – their calves, thighs, buttocks, waists, shoulders, arms, necks, heads, their stance and poise. This is a native development from Geometric, not the adaptation of Oriental models. In shape too this pot belongs to the new era, with its lankiness and more fluid articulation, the panelling-in of the vertical handle, and the plastic snakes that wriggle round lip and handle and mask the junction of shoulder and neck. The date must be near that of the later of the Early Protocorinthian aryballoi, say about 700 B.C.

The Analatos painter was brought up in a Geometric school, the progressive Late Geometric school already mentioned (p. 21), and this hydria owes much to his teachers. The proportions and contours of the shape, the decorative scheme, the spiral hooks, even the litheness of his men originate in their work. But his robust individuality went much further. We can trace for a good thirty years the career of this untiring artist, who as much as anyone determined the course that Protoattic took. The bell-krater in Munich [PLATE 14B] shows him at a later stage, about 690 B.C. One link between krater and hydria is a fragmentary plaque from Cape Sunion, painted with a warship; the marines by their faces are brothers of the women of the hydria, the steersman of the krater's charioteers. The comparison of the lions as well as the men shows the distance and the direction that the Analatos painter has travelled. There is little that is directly Geometric here. Instead we see a new massive style, that is willing to be crude provided it can be powerful. The Analatos hydria is not so different from contemporary Protocorinthian, the Munich krater is.

Besides the men and lions and horses which are illustrated here the sphinx was popular, often with scaly wings. Winged horses had been introduced at the end of Geometric as well as 'centaurs' (their identity is discussed on p. 50). Dogs, cocks, eagles [as on FIG. 9] usually decorate smaller pots. The figures are bulkier and more active than before, their structure organic, the details bold. In composition there is less constraint – the Analatos painter did not feel obliged to show how many horses are pulling each chariot on the Munich krater [PLATE 14B] – and the balancing of groups is not always symmetrical. Of the new ornaments the most characteristic are the spotted leaves and palmettes and the heart-shaped pair of spirals; the hooks, known in Late Geometric, grow in size and often (as on the Munich krater) perversely substitute for the rays of Corinthian; and the horizontal rows of zigzag filling acquire a new and sometimes overwhelming character. The favourite subjects are processions, gay or sad, parading chariots and horsemen, 'centaurs' hunting, and monsters and animals in file or less often heraldically confronted. The technique is outline drawing and partial silhouette, occasionally and unintelligently broken by incision.

Of the other Early Protoattic painters some followed the Analatos painter and some played with a mannered archaism. Others were more

FIG. 9. *Protoattic oinochoe*
Ht 17·3 cm. *c.* 700–675 B.C.

frankly Geometric and continued for a time the tradition of abstract ornament. The new shapes had already begun to evolve at the end of the Geometric period, but there is still variation. The progressives preferred slimness and the slurring of angles, the old-fashioned clung to rotunder forms. The hydria, a new invention, is illustrated on PLATE 14A; from it can be imagined the change in the amphora and the small globular oinochoe [for the new form see FIG. 9], and also in the

stemmed bowl and the mug. The old stemmed krater (distinct from
the low open krater or bowl which also is common) loses its vertical
lip and contracts to an oval body. The wide-necked oinochoe disappears. The kotyle replaces the Geometric cup, and round aryballoi also
show the influence of Corinth. But the chosen vessels of the new style
are hydria, amphora and krater. Outside Attica, Early Protoattic has
been found in Boeotia and Aegina. At home it had to contend with
Corinthian, which it sometimes imitated, especially on small pots.

The Black and White style (c. 675–c. 650 B.C.)

The works of the Analatos group still show their Geometric breeding,
but the second generation of Protoattic artists was born free. In the
drawing of figures the silhouette had been the basic form, broken by
the reservation of heads and sometimes other areas. But to the new
school outline drawing came naturally, and light and dark had equal
value. The result was a style of broad contrasts, turbulent and im-
patient. The first stage from its generous use of white paint has been
called the Black and White style and lasted till about the middle of the
seventh century. It was apparently initiated by the Analatos painter.

The New York Nessos amphora (to be distinguished from the later
and more celebrated 'Nessos amphora' in Athens) is a fair work of about
660 B.C., though not one of the best. PLATE 16 shows a side view. In the
main field the centaur Nessos collapses in front of Heracles, while
Deianira is slumped in her husband's chariot, faint but self-possessed
enough to hold the reins; beyond the horses a rubber-legged Iolaos
comes running up. The scale of the figures is unequal – Deianira must
be a head taller than Heracles. Unequal too are the style and the planning of the figures. To the powerful forms and action of Nessos and
his executioner correspond four old-fashioned horses with their heads
in a finicky fan and the caricatured manikin Iolaos. Such lopsidedness
is common in this period, as if the artist began his picture before he
had fully conceived it. Both outline drawing and incision are used, and
the flesh of the human figures and other details are painted in a yellowish white, which contrasts more strongly than appears in the photo-
graph with the brown of the clay. The subsidiary frieze of the shoulder
contains a couple of grazing horses, old-fashioned hackwork; and on
the neck a moon-faced panther mauls a deer. The filling ornament is
less obtrusive and less Geometric; it is only natural that the belated bird
between the centaur's hindlegs should be wilting. The other ornaments
show the new preference for solid forms, and the cable on the shoulder
is characteristically painted in alternate strands of dark and white. The

back, as of most large Protoattic vases, is very much the back, though the neck has an unusually charming floral pattern.

The fragments of another contemporary amphora shown on PLATE 15A reveal a greater artist, the Ram Jug painter, who was busy in the 660s and 650s. His earlier work has a gauche heaviness, particularly in the ill-proportioned human figures; and even in this more elegant scene, where Peleus is carrying Achilles to be tutored by the good centaur Chiron, Achilles has a puny arm (visible on the smallest of the fragments). The big almond eye and heavy brow are normal in the developed Black and White style, but the fleshy nose is more of an idiosyncrasy, as is the palmette sprouting from the forehead of Peleus. Compare this amphora with the contemporary Protocorinthian kotyle of PLATE 10A: both have a feeling for line, but the Corinthian painter has refined it with studied precision, the Athenian is more of a dilettante and a humorist.

In composition vase-painters are much bolder. There are comparatively few stock attitudes, and the use of outline or white as well as black-figure silhouette invited the overlapping of figures, the more so since (as in the later Red-ground style of Corinth) dark and light were not distinctive of sex. Though staid processions continue, there is also much varied and violent action – battles for instance, chariot races and even jugglers. Mythological scenes, such as the fate of Nessos, occur from the beginning of the period. In the drawing of figures anatomy progresses and there is an increase in inner detail, sometimes merely decorative as, for example, cables on the naked thigh or circles on a buttock – on PLATE 16 Heracles wears a similar device on the tail of his chiton. The black-figure technique is known – it had indeed been known to the Analatos painter – but it remains subordinate to the gayer variety of outline drawing and colour; sometimes, especially about the middle of the century, white lines accompany incision on dark surfaces. The filling of the main fields is sparser, a prudent reform now that the subsidiary areas of the vase carry stronger decoration of their own. In general the ornaments are Orientalizing, but Attic originality adapted and invented. So the spiral hooks are often adorned with birds' beaks, and palmettes may reproduce themselves till they look like bunches of grapes. Many of the more solid ornaments, such as cables, rosettes, rays, rows of leaves, are variegated by painting alternate members in dark and white paint. Altogether it was an era of exuberant and spontaneous creation. Among the shapes the hydria disappears and kraters become more popular. The oval krater grows taller, then about the middle of the century gives way to the kotyle-krater, which evolves from the open bowl. Pottery of the Black and White style has been found in Aegina and Boeotia, a little too at Megara, Perachora near Corinth and the Argive Heraeum. In this period the effects of Corinthian on Attic were vague or casual.

Later Protoattic (c. 650–c. 610 B.C.)

During the next twenty or thirty years Attic vase-painting settled into a disciplined black-figure style. The planning of the decoration becomes more thoughtful, the execution more precise, the colouring more sober and outline drawing disappears. Vase-painters were learning the virtues of concentration on definite and limited objectives. In all this the influence of Corinth is visible, as also in many details. But there is a scale, physical and imaginative, that is peculiarly Attic.

The Black and White style fell into a decline about 650 B.C., when the use of purple first became regular. There was for a time a three-colour school, which produced some admirable effects, as when a near-black wing is feathered alternately purple and white, but gradually white lost ground. For animals the black-figure technique was already in partial use; the new movement met no obstacle here, and purple necks and belly stripes and feathering were soon the rule. Human figures resisted longer, for it was with them that the outline technique was chiefly concerned. The Cynosarges amphora, for example, has on its shoulder dull black-figure animals, but the wrestlers on the neck and the farewell group on the body are painted with white flesh and much purple on their drapery. On some pots there is a more elaborate polychromy – reds, yellow, browns and bluish green have been observed. This short-lived venture was roughly contemporary with the polychrome figure style at Corinth, but the Attic colours are not fast and the pots on which they appear were apparently specialities for graves. By the last quarter of the century a black-figure style was established.

The Nessos vase in Athens [PLATE 17] marks the consummation of the process. It is an amphora about four feet high, intended like the big Geometric pots as a marker for a grave. On the neck once more Heracles is killing Nessos. Below two Gorgons take off in pursuit of Perseus (wisely out of sight), while their sister Medusa collapses behind them. This is a monumental style, carefully planned and admirably executed. Comparison with the New York vase [PLATE 16] shows what Attic art has gained in compactness and unity, and in subtlety too. The Gorgons vanish round the curve of the pot, their speed underlined by the opposite movement of the dolphins below. Purple is used freely, for the faces of Heracles and Nessos, for the drapery, and on other details.

The white paint that was added sparingly, as on the teeth of the Gorgons, has peeled off, but cannot have much relieved the dark masses of the figures. The filling ornament is now light and subdued. The back, neglected as usual, is scumbled over with streaky paint. The Nessos

FIG. 10. *Attic Bf bowl*
Details of panels: scale *c.* 1 : 2. By the Nessos painter: *c.* 605 B.C.

vase is much indebted to Corinthian, in its fully black-figure technique, the choice of inner detail, the type of the Gorgon, the purple faces (a trick that became common in Corinth in the thirties and lasted for some sixty years), the filling ornament, the floral chain, the birds on the facings of the handles. Such borrowings are general on Attic pots of this time, which draw freely on the Corinthian repertory. But there is no slavish dependence on Corinth. Athenian vase-painters kept their sense of scale – large pots with large decoration were still favourites – and there is spontaneity, even in the Animal style current on minor works. The same is true of the subsidiary ornaments, the most striking of which are mill-sail patterns and the strip of oblique meanders [as on FIG. 10] which is first found on the large Corinthian kotylai that were made just before the middle of the century. The filling ornament of the Nessos vase is typically eclectic, on the body neat dot-rosettes, in the panel on the neck the same rosettes mixed with older Attic motives, and in the vertical strips that frame the neck and on the handle-plates incised rosettes. Attic vase-painters were critically choosing Corinthian elements and making them their own. So it is not surprising that resemblances to different periods of Corinthian vase-painting can be detected on a single pot. The Nessos amphora may perhaps be dated about 615 B.C.

The favourite shapes were the big amphora; the kotyle-krater, often united with its stand and furnished with a lid; and towards the end of the period the new one-piece amphora, where neck and body make a single unbroken curve and the proper decoration is a panel let into the dark surface [as on PLATE 21A]. The popularity of Attic pottery is about to begin. A fragment by the Nessos painter has been found at Caere in Etruria, and about the same time there may be some Attic influence in Eretrian and 'Melian'.

Attic Black-figure: the period of Corinthian Influence (c. 610–c. 550 B.C.)

Like other leading painters of his day the Nessos painter straddles the uncertain boundary between Protoattic and the Attic black-figure style proper. On one side is the big amphora in Athens [PLATE 17], on the other the fragmentary spouted bowl in Berlin [FIG. 10]. Here the earlier grandeur and freedom are being replaced by correctness and convention. The wide shallow shape is tauter and finer, as it stretches from narrow foot to high belly and then returns quickly to the mouth. Compared with the simple sturdy contours of Protoattic it shows an advance in the potter's skill and delicacy, but to the painter it no longer offers a large unbroken field. This change in aesthetic principles is most obvious in the substitution of the dinos for the kotyle-krater; PLATES 18 and 10A will serve to illustrate the relation between shape and decorative system. The Berlin bowl is then decorated in narrow bands. Round its shoulder were four panels, in one Perseus and Athena, in a second the Harpies, while the other two which are lost presumably completed the stories with the Gorgons and the Boreads. Poses, details of the figures, and both the filling and the independent ornament are very much as on the Nessos amphora, but the effect is tamer and more constricted. On the lower part of the bowl came first a band of animals and monsters in confronting pairs, next – below a strip of small chequers – a row of lotus flowers and palmettes, and round the base rays. Attic now is borrowing not only Corinthian motives, but something too of the Corinthian spirit. If the Nessos vase is of about 615 B.C., the Berlin Harpy bowl is perhaps ten years later.

The Nessos painter was followed by the *Gorgon painter*, who has his name from his most elaborate work, a dinos in the Louvre [PLATE 18]. The main frieze runs round the shoulder – Perseus in flight from the Gorgons with Medusa collapsing behind them and Athena and Hermes looking on, and a duel of two hoplites flanked by their chariots. The two scenes have no connection of subject, but early artists were not pedantic when filling a long frieze. The duel is the better side with its intent men and horses, as neat and well-bred as the band of lotus and palmette below. The Gorgons of the other side have lost the gusto of the Nessos painter; art has found a human level and there is less sympathy for the old monsters. On the lower part of the bowl and on its elaborately turned pedestal tier on tier of animals go through their paces: a couple of uneasy lads have intruded and the drawing is not yet jaded, but it is clear where Attic art has been busy. Yet the Gorgon painter still takes pride in his lions, whose fine square heads and well-combed manes make them the worthy last representatives of the old square-headed Attic breed, and he knew how to pair them heraldically as the principal decoration of a one-piece amphora or an olpe. After him no Attic vase-painter was interested in the Animal style.

Corinth had now for a generation or more been steadily influencing Attica, and the Gorgon painter kept abreast of current Corinthian improvements. The airy spaciousness of the main frieze of his dinos recalls the Eurytos krater [PLATE 12C]; so too does the achievement of expression without action, as in the charioteers and the soldiers waiting with spears poised. It is in increasing subtlety rather than in violent movement, though there will be plenty of that, that the future of Attic vase-painting lies. Among minor details the artist has at last after a century of experiment ventured to draw the chariot rail in strict profile. The Louvre dinos, a mature work of the Gorgon painter, is about 590 B.C.

Sophilos, the first Attic vase-painter whose name we know, was a contemporary of Timonidas of Corinth. His style comes from the same school as the Gorgon painter's, but is clumsier and more laboured.

Sophilos was an ambitious but lesser artist. He too followed Corinthian fashions – in shapes as well as in massed compositions and the lavish use of white paint for the near horse of a team, for drapery, and for the flesh of his women [PLATE 15B]. For horses and drapery the innovation soon failed; but from the 570s Attic women are regularly white and their menfolk are black, even if often at first still purple in the face. Attic vase-painters, though not Sophilos, are now beginning to paint their white over a coat of the blackish paint and much of the detail on it is incised; the black-figure tradition had taken deep roots. On a fragment of a dinos by Sophilos [PLATE 15B], found at Lindos and made in the 570s, is one of the earliest appearances of the tribe of good-for-nothing satyrs. If there is doubt about the satyr's origin, there can be none of his intention. The art of the eighth and seventh centuries had been indifferent to sex, the early sixth displayed its urgency, and the middle added its tendernesses. The progress may be inferred by comparing the New York Nessos amphora [PLATE 16] with the fragment by Sophilos, and this again with one of the amphorae by Exekias in the Vatican [PLATE 22]. Other new types that are making their debut are the old man with a fringe of white hair, the athlete, the drunk, and soon the lover and the adolescent. Artistic interest was changing, but at least as important was the increasing ability of the artists.

Three other dinoi of Sophilos, two fragmentary but all signed, show more fully the complex scenes in which his imagination surpassed his execution. One, found at Pharsalus in Thessaly and now in Athens, has perfunctory animals on the rim and the lower part of the body, and round the shoulder, as an ill-spelled title informs us, the games at Patroclus's funeral are being run – what we have are the horses of the winning chariot and a terraced bank on which grotesque little spectators sit cheering. The other two, which are more or less duplicates, have in the principal field the procession of gods and goddesses to the marriage of Peleus and Thetis, an occasion better known from the slightly later François vase. One of the nymphs here has turned her face to the spectator; but frontal heads, though they appear occasionally from about this time, never became normal in black-figure. To his human figures Sophilos gave all he had; witness the painstaking detail of the chitons [as PLATE 15B] and his careful labelling of persons. Such inscriptions, painted on the pot before firing, had occurred at Athens and Corinth from rather before the middle of the seventh century, but suddenly become the fashion in the 570s. Their purpose is less explanatory than ostentatious as on the Tyrrhenian amphorae, or decorative as on lip cups, and often enough they are meaningless jumbles of letters.

The *François vase* [PLATE 19], found near Chiusi in Etruria and now in Florence, is a volute-krater some twenty-two inches high. It was, so the signatures say, made by Ergotimos and painted by Clitias. No other black-figure vase so elaborately decorated has survived so complete, and its rich repertory of subjects makes it in itself a compendium of Attic vase-painting around 570 B.C., when it was made. Here we see the gay mastery of drawing and composition that Sophilos could not achieve. On the lip Theseus returns from Crete, on the neck Lapiths fight Centaurs: the other side, which is the front if either side can claim precedence, has the Calydonian boar-hunt and the funeral games for Patroclus. In the main frieze the divine guests are arriving at the marriage of Peleus and Thetis; the procession encircles the vase, passing under the handles as if behind arches. Then the return of Hephaestus, and on the opposite side the ambushing of Troilus. Further below are animals, and at the base rays. The cranes and Pygmies fight it out round the foot. From the handles proper which are painted black spring broad volutes, their outer surfaces decorated too – Ajax carrying the dead Achilles, and above him the 'Mistress of the Beasts' ('Potnia theron'), a winged female gripping on one volute a lion in either hand, and on the other a panther and a deer, to the Orientals a deity but to the Greeks (at least of Europe) no more than a decorative type. The inner face of the volutes carries the now decrepit Gorgon. In all there are over two hundred figures, many of them named, and the detail is equally meticulous. White, in larger areas still put directly on the clay and with details usually painted on it, is in the main restricted to the flesh of the women and to the microscopic patterns and animals of dresses. Much of it has perished, but it matters less since Clitias relies for his colouring on the shiny black paint and plenty of purple.

The drawing of the figures is sure and elegant, their poses varied and convincing in spite or perhaps because of the archaic conventions of anatomy. The composition, clear and well-knit, knows how to mass figures in the shallow focus of the pictorial field – eight deep at times in the wedding procession. Men's faces are still purple on occasion – the François krater is one of the last important pots on which they are – and there are several curiosities, typical of the time. Polyxena's hydria, Priam's stool, the fountain are all labelled with their names; Zeus and Hera, welcoming back Hephaestus, sit tandem – the old-fashioned alternative to the overlapping of figures; and two charming little buildings, the house of Thetis and the fountain outside Troy, tease the Classical architect. A rarer detail is the young Athenian swimming ashore from Theseus's ship. Generally the spirit of this vase is lively and cheerful, yet polite. But the pygmies of the foot are comic, if not burlesque; and in the little panels where Ajax staggers under the body of Achilles there is a new and tragic solemnity.

Much on the François vase is derived from Corinthian; but it comes at second hand, incorporated in the Attic tradition that Clitias inherited. Even the Animal style of the lowest figured zone of the body has a new if artificial animation; the sphinxes and griffins pose, the lions and panthers pull down their prey, all with a mechanical elegance that contrasts with the spontaneous life of the other scenes. Compare this krater with any of the more elaborate Red-ground vases of Corinth [as PLATE 13]; the styles are parallel, but distinct. Attic art has declared its independence, and indeed is threatening Corinth. Not only did Corinthians from the 570s imitate the colour of Attic clay, but about this time Attic painted pottery began to be imported into Corinth itself.

The François vase has long fields, and Clitias chose subjects that could be extended almost indefinitely. His style is therefore often called 'narrative', but the term can be applied to most black-figure pottery that is not merely decorative. Not till Exekias does mood become important. Several of the scenes of the François vase are found elsewhere, on Corinthian Red-ground, the remnants of Sophilos, Siana cups and Tyrrhenian amphorae; and in literature we have the Chest of Cypselus seen by Pausanias at Olympia and the Hesiodic *Shield*, both of them contemporary with the vase-paintings. The resemblances between the different representations are sometimes striking; for instance in the episode of Troilus Polyxena's hydria is regularly there, lying on the ground or falling in mid air. Details like this perhaps suggest that the source was often the memory of some famous wall-painting rather than direct illustration of one of the epic or heroic poems then popular. But of course vase-painters regularly borrowed from each other.

The cup appears in Attica in the 580s and from then on remains one of the most popular shapes. The first stage, that of the *Comast cups* [PLATE 24A], has a low flaring foot and short offset lip. Both shape and decoration are taken from Corinth, where similar cups become common in the early sixth century (see p. 60). The Attic cups usually have three dancers a side, at first in padded chitons, later naked and undeformed; sometimes a short-skirted wench joins them. Purple faces and chests are common. Under the handle is set a lotus flower with sprawling tendrils – floral ornament is now more cursorily drawn – and the lip carries incised rosettes or a rough net pattern. The inside is painted black. The Comast Group includes other Corinthian shapes, kotyle, column-krater and lekane. The clay tends to be more orange, and the technical standard is improved. The date of this group is from about 585 to rather after 570 B.C.

The Comast cups are succeeded by the *Siana cups* [PLATE 24B], named after the village of Siana in Rhodes near which two were found. The rim has grown higher, the bowl wider, the foot taller, the contours more precise: the average diameter is now about eight inches. The new elegance reforms the decoration too. The Comast cup has a casual top-heavy look, the Siana is planned for a balance of light and dark. Some-times the lower part of the bowl is elaborately patterned, usually it is painted black (as is the stemmed foot) except for a narrow striped band two-thirds of the way up. The edge of the foot too is reserved. The distinction of handle frieze and the lip is emphasized by a narrow black line, but more often the figured decoration which has now shifted up the cup ignores the division and awkwardly straddles the two fields. Or else the lip is patterned – an ivy branch for instance or dogs cours-ing a hare – and half-size figures keep within the narrow handle frieze. The overlapping system of decoration is unhappy, the two-zone cum-bersome. The Attic lip cup (see pp. 81–2), that triumph of archaic trimness, was the logical consequence. For the friezes the familiar themes are riders, battles split into duelling pairs and dinner parties. Inside, an elaborate frame – usually of tongues and bands of dots – sets off the large tondo filled with a flying or running figure or some other convenient subject; the surround is black, except for a narrow reserved stripe near the edge of the lip. The greater number of the Siana cups are by the C painter and his followers. He owes much to Corinth – his favourite subjects and his lavish use of white as well as purple – but he is an Attic painter and makes full use of the orange-brown Attic clay and shiny black paint. The Siana cups belong to the second quarter of the sixth century, overlapping with the later Comast and the earliest Little Master cups. They have been found even in Corinth.

There are other groups of vases, where the standard of drawing is lower. The best known are the *Tyrrhenian amphorae* [PLATE 20B], so-called because most of them have been found in Etruria and they were once thought to have been made there. The long egg-shaped body balances on a spreading foot and ends at a squat neck, and the average height is about sixteen inches. The shape comes from the larger *S.O.S. amphorae*, a line of utilitarian pottery named from the form of the pat-terns of the neck, which is the only part of the pot not painted black;

this simple ware was made through much of the seventh and sixth centuries and widely exported, presumably for its contents. But the Tyrrhenians have more decoration. On the neck a chain of lotus and palmette or animals, on the shoulder human figures, round the belly two or three bands of animals, at the base rays – such is the usual formula. Their interest is in the human subjects – the sacrifice of Polyxena, the departure of Amphiaraus, the battle with the Amazons, to mention a few – and in the representation, sometimes in an architectural setting. The draughtsmanship is careless and rough. It is a pretentious and inferior style, which offers cheaply all the latest improvements of the leading masters of Athens and Corinth. There is of course plenty of purple and of white, though this is put on in the Attic method; and the inscriptions that litter the field, usually nonsensical and sometimes mere blobs that imitate letters, show painters often too hurried to clean their brushes. The Tyrrhenian amphorae are only part of a wider class, of which the most striking are some amphorae which under the influence of the panel style (see p. 80) replace the subsidiary decoration of the belly by a solid area of black paint topped with narrow purple stripes. The period of the whole group is the second quarter of the sixth century.

So far the discussion of Attic black-figure in the early sixth century has kept mainly to the human figures. But the tradition of the Animal style died hard. We can see the creatures, still lively, on the Nessos painter's bowl in Berlin; newly broken in on the Louvre dinos of the Gorgon painter [PLATE 18]; cowed and weary in the works of Sophilos and his successors [so on the lower friezes of PLATE 20B]. The main tradition of the Animal style shows a temperate admiration of Corinth. The listless groups recall the Early and Middle Ripe periods, though details and the popularity of species differ. This is a numerous class, more so indeed than the groups of vases with human figures, but the animals have little artistic merit or religious interest, so that few of them are published or exhibited in museums. The Animal style faded out about 550 B.C. together with the old system of decoration in several zones.

Two other developments of the Animal style are conspicuous. On one side are the wholehoggers, such as the *Polos painter* and his friends [PLATE 20A]. If any particular phase of Attic vase-painting should be credited directly to Solon, it is perhaps this uncritical adulation of the Animal style of Corinth, which so abjectly renounces the native tradition. Corinthian too are the shapes of its dumpy amphora and hydria, lekane, kotyle and plate. This Polos style, if style it may be called, lasted perhaps from the 580s to the 560s and somehow found a ready market overseas. The other variation tries to inject elegance if not life into its animals. So Clitias on the François vase [PLATE 19]; so too the miniaturists of the Little Master cups; and till the end of the sixth century there can be found small friezes of animals supporting the main picture, especially on hydriai, while shield signs carry them still longer.

There is one other strand in the early black-figure of Athens, ultimately as important as any. At the end of Protoattic there had suddenly appeared the one-piece amphora. The prototype is a heavy sagging pot, not unlike the later pelike. Gradually its belly lifts, and by 600 B.C. is about the middle of the body [PLATE 21A]. Later changes are to slimness and greater delicacy of contour, and finally to a still higher belly [PLATE 22]. The shape of the body is in one piece, so too is the decoration; indeed it is plain, if one looks at the illustrations, that it can hardly be otherwise. The same is true of the new olpe that appears at Athens just before 600 B.C. and is borrowed by the Red-ground school of Corinth. Some of the earlier of these amphorae try to follow the ordinary decorative convention. One of the most determined is a fine piece in the Louvre by the Gorgon painter. On the front two of his magnificent lions with heads turned back sit up on either side of a floral ornament, on the back a pair of sphinxes respond, above is a chain of lotus and palmette and below a band of animals. Yet even here the main picture by its size and position dominates the pot. But from the beginning there was also a new system of a reserved panel let into a dark ground. On this, as if seen through a window, there is generally the head of a horse, or of a man or a woman [PLATE 21A]. This panel amphora, simple and conservative, was untroubled by the major changes and fashions of the early sixth century; it was not till the 560s that it was caught up in the current of progress.

The shapes preferred during the half century down to the 560s show a general replacement of the older Attic favourites by Corinthian types. The neck-amphora, now that the huge size of Protoattic has been abandoned, loses in interest for artists, but still remains one of the commonest shapes. The one-piece amphora has also established itself. But of the large pots those that most exerted vase-painters were kraters and dinoi. The kotyle-krater survived into the first quarter of the sixth century, when the dinos became popular, a footless bowl which was rare at Corinth, but appeared frequently in East Greek too about 600 B.C., though there less ornately decorated and provided with handles. The kantharos and kotyle continued. The olpe was invented at the end of the seventh century. From Corinth came lekane, column-krater, hydria, lekythos, plate, the new cup, and perhaps the tripod cothon, as well as the alabastron, aryballos and pyxis: the greatest borrowing, as in the decoration, was at the beginning of the sixth century.

For the last years of the seventh century Attic pottery is found outside Attica in Aegina and Boeotia, and there are rare fragments from Troy, Naucratis in Egypt and Caere in Etruria. During the first quarter of the sixth century export was increasing rapidly, to the Aegean islands, the Black Sea colonies, Naucratis, Delphi, Ithaca, Etruria and Marseilles; very little has been reported from Greek Italy and Sicily. During the second quarter the advance continued, and Attic black-figure pottery became the favourite painted ware of the whole Greek world.

Attic Black-figure: the Mature style (c. 570–c. 525 B.C.)

The François vase [PLATE 19 and pp. 76–7] stands at the beginning of the maturity of Attic black-figure, although – as is not surprising on so elaborate a vase – it has some old-fashioned traits. Purple faces and the use of white directly on the clay are details; more significant is the diffusion of the decoration in many shallow zones. The new generation prefers instead a single large design, and if this is framed by bands of minor decoration, they are both in size and emphasis subordinate. So the principal field recovers the importance it had in Protoattic. Its new proportions, higher and relatively narrower, reacted on the drawing and composition. Larger figures gave the artist more scope, and groups became smaller and compacter – the picture replaces the strip.

Something of the old tradition survives in the *Little Master cups*, but remodelled and refined to a new if sterile delicacy. At a time when the scale of figure drawing had enlarged they create a new miniature style. The Little Masters, that is miniaturists, were often also the painters of larger pots; but the style of the cups is distinct and they are best treated separately. There are three chief varieties, all evolved from the Siana cup [PLATE 24B and p. 78] – lip cup [PLATE 25A], band cup [PLATE 25B], and Droop cup – as well as some intermediate forms. Their common features are the tall stemmed foot, the spreading bowl, a clearly marked lip; the sensitive balance of dark and light; the decorative emphasis on the outside, with which goes the careful finish of the bottom of the foot and even of the hollow within the stem – evidently these cups were meant to be seen when hung against a wall. The canonical proportion of height to breadth is about two to three, and there are two common sizes, a larger some eight inches across and a smaller about five. The exquisite precision of the shapes has provoked the unnecessary suggestion that they were modelled to a mathematical formula.

The typical *Lip cup* [PLATE 25A] has a slightly outcurved lip, set off sharply from the bowl, and bowl and stem meet at an angle. Outside both lip and handle frieze are reserved, and so are a narrow stripe on the lower part of the bowl, the sharp edge and the underside of the foot, the hollow of the stem, and the inner face of the handles: the rest is black. So two fields are vacant for the painter, and the angle that separates them is underlined by a narrow black stripe. The upper field, the lip, concentrates its decoration in a single figure, or less often a small group or even an outlined female head; or else it is left entirely blank. The inscriptions that frame the figure on PLATE 25A are abnormal. The lower frieze stresses the handles: from their dark bulk usually spring small palmettes, and the space between carries a neatly lettered inscription or is empty. The inside is most often black, except for a narrow stripe near the rim and small reserved circles in the middle. A few lip-cups have a tondo, but narrower and less elaborately framed than in the Siana group. The commonest subjects on the lip are animals and cocks, drawn with a brittle elegance. There are human figures too – Heracles introduced to Olympus and the Birth of Athena on one of the most famous of these cups. The lip cups begin about 565 B.C. and were popular for some thirty years. They were imitated in Ionia (see pp. 129–30).

A few early lip cups form a loose group known as *Gordion cups* from the city in Phrygia where one was found. The foot of some is still lowish, the tondo has the Siana's elaboration, and the offset lip is painted black. They belong to the years when the canon was not yet fixed, and may be the stage of transition to the band cup.

The *Band cup* [PLATE 25B] differs from the lip cup in its effect even more than in its details. The black concave lip passes into the bowl in a smooth curve, and in correspondence the transition from bowl to stem is often masked by a purple fillet. The decorative accent is on the handle frieze. Usually there are neat palmettes at the sides: between them there may be a figure or small group in the centre as on the lip of lip cups, or an inscription as on the handle frieze of lip cups, or less often the whole space is filled with figures loosely or closely set, or again the field is left empty. Inside, tondos are rare. The band cup runs later than the lip cup, by which its type is influenced. Its popularity is from the 550s to the 520s. The Floral band cups, small tedious pieces with chains of palmettes along the handle frieze, are a late variety which probably lasted longer. Another byform is the *Cassel cup*: the shape is normal, the size small, the outside of the bowl usually entirely covered with bands of simple ornament. The band cup was the model also for a group of low cups (cup-kotylai); the shape is that of the bowl of the cup, but deeper and set on a ring foot, and the decoration is orthodox.

The *Droop cup*, named after its first classifier, is related to the band cup. Its characteristics are generally the broad unpainted channelling of the top of the stem, the convex black edge of the foot, a black border to the inside of the stem, and except in some early specimens the decoration of all the lower part of the bowl. The handle frieze has most often a chain of buds; then comes a band of silhouette animals upside down (perhaps because they were easier to paint that way) or some not too meticulous ornament; and round the base are rays. These main zones are separated by stripes. There are some good early examples with careful figures in the handle frieze, but much is mediocre and more is shoddy. The Droop cup begins to acquire its separate identity about 560, and is frequent from about 540 to about 510 B.C., but trivial pieces were made even later. Its prodigal decoration probably was inspired by some of the Siana cups, and its influence can be seen in Laconian (see pp. 96–8). There are also the so-called Black Droop cups, with bowl painted wholly black.

Thanks to the decorative use of inscriptions we know the names of the painters and makers of unusually many lip cups. Fewer band cups are signed, and very few Droop cups. Clitias and Ergotimos of the François vase signed Gordion cups, and a son and perhaps a grandson of Ergotimos were makers of lip cups. Nearchos, another painter of large pots, painted a lip cup; and his son Tleson has left us more than fifty signatures as maker. Even the great Exekias made lip cups, and two band cups are painted by the Amasis painter. Sakonides painted and Hermogenes made lip cups with outline heads. But the first places belong to Tleson, son of Nearchos, and to Phrynos or whoever painted for them.

There is so much on the François krater that discussion of Attic vase-painting of its generation keeps returning to it. This time it is the groups on the handle-plates of Ajax and the dead Achilles. In *the Painter of Acropolis 606* the new seriousness is dominant. His name-piece, a fragmentary dinos in Athens, has, to be sure, animals on the rim and in the third (and lowest) zone of the body, dull creatures akin to though neater than those of Tyrrhenian amphorae. Beneath, in the centre of the base, the whirligig has been metamorphosed into the foreparts of six leaping lions and horses, and in the middle zone cavalry with javelins attack mounted archers. But what interested the artist was the top zone, a battle scene six inches high, which occupies the whole upper part of the body and is conceived too on a larger scale. From left and right chariots are driving up, and beyond the horses hoplites are engaged. There is in these figures a severity and even grimness that comes partly from the solid forms, partly from their workmanlike action; the detail too is plainer. Spruce elegance has given way to a robuster appreciation of anatomy, and the strong full features make the figures look larger than life. For all its purple and white – and there is plenty of both – this is a sombre masterpiece. Another of the painter's works, a one-piece amphora in Berlin, is still more austere. On back and front two mounted hoplites ride abreast, behind them an eagle in flight, below on one side a hare and on the other a dog. These pieces are of about 565 B.C. Their style with its deliberate severity and under-emphasis leads to the grandeur of Exekias; in lesser hands it can become rough and meaningless. The Burgon amphora in the British Museum (PLATE 21B), one of the very early Panathenaic amphorae, is a second-rate work of this trend and time.

Attic vase-painting in the sixties and fifties was in transition. The Painter of Acropolis 606 pursues the monumental, the Little Masters elegance, the Tyrrhenian group quick returns. Between these extremes were other less single-minded painters. Nearchos, from whose hand we have also an early lip cup, combined on larger pots the delicacy of Clitias with the new enlarged concept of humanity, a fragmentary kantharos in Athens with Achilles standing by his horses' heads has a delicate melancholy that recalls the *Iliad*. Tleson had good reason to advertise himself as 'son of Nearchos' on many of the lip cups he made and to judge by the kindred nicety of style painted too. *Lydos*, whose career lasted from the 550s to the 530s, has a robuster quality with more of gusto and less of grace: his firm, solid figures suggest more plainly their third dimension. His best work is in scenes of lively action, as on the krater in New York; here his satyrs and maenads show a remarkable and convincing variety of pose, which compensates for the uniformity of their pouting faces. On another vase, a fragmentary dinos in Athens, he experiments with landscape and a crowded procession. Towards the end, on an oinochoe in Berlin, he was tempted into delicacy, but though his workmanship was equal to it the effect is mannered. His name means 'the Lydian', but his art is consistently Attic.

About 550 B.C. two other masters begin their careers, Exekias and the Amasis painter. The *Amasis painter* was an admirable draughtsman with a strong decorative sense. His early work is conventional and tame, but as he matures he displays a more individual assurance. For the dignified and the sublime he lacked talent, and his best work has a touch of the comic. So he is happiest when portraying the tipsy gaiety of Dionysus and his satyrs and maenads [PLATE 23]. His heroic scenes have sometimes a cheerful irreverence, but often they are empty of meaning. Throughout his working life he kept abreast of changes in general design and in the details of figure-drawing, but was himself no innovator, though he had a fondness – unusual in his time – for the technique of outlining female flesh instead of overpainting it in white. We have over a hundred pieces that he painted, representing an unusual range of shapes. Besides the one-piece amphora, neck-amphora, oinochoe and olpe he tried his hand on lekythos, band cup, eye cup, cup-kotyle, alabastron, 'Sosian' stand, little bowl and plaque. His potter, if it was not the Amasis painter himself, showed an equal technical dexterity. He introduced for larger shapes the elaboration and refinement of profile that had before been applied to the Little Master cups [compare for instance PLATES 20B and 21B with 22 and 23], but his passion for novelty at the expense of harmony lost him his lead. The activity of the Amasis painter is from about 550 to about 525 B.C.

The Amasis painter stands apart from the run of Attic vase-painting of his time, which followed Exekias. For that reason he has sometimes been claimed as an immigrant to Athens from Ionia, and his personal peculiarities have been dubbed Ionian. In fact his decorative elegance has its origins in the style of Nearchos and Clitias, and its counterpart in the Little Master cups. From Ionia we have nothing comparable. For all his excellence the Amasis painter founded no lasting school, though a few of his lesser contemporaries admired his obstinacy against the new Exekian spirit. 'Elbows Out', whose neat manikins earn him his name, and the Affecter with his larger gawky figures are both excellent technicians; their styles (and even their shapes) are self-consciously old-fashioned, more concerned with obsolete types, including even starveling animals, than with coherent subjects. The black-figure style has reached the stage where archaism can be engaging.

Exekias is as a draughtsman the equal of the Amasis painter, but in spirit his opposite. His style has a grave inwardness inherited from the Painter of Acropolis 606, to whom he comes nearest in his set battle scenes; but his best work is in quieter figures and groups. It is natural that he preferred to paint amphorae. There are few artists in whose work shape and style progress so harmoniously. Of his earliest amphorae, squat and pot-bellied, the majority are necked and some have subsidiary zones of little animals; later the shape tapers and the one-piece amphora predominates. At first his style is conventional and close to the so-called Group E. But already in the 540s a neck-amphora in Berlin, one of the earliest of his slimmer vases, gives a foretaste of his individual quality. On the front Heracles grappling with a lion is fine drawing though not particularly sensitive, but Iolaos, hands locked in sympathy, is something new. The Athena who completes this scene and the dismounted riders of the back are undistinguished. In the 530s comes the maturity of his style. The one-piece amphora in the Vatican shows on one side [PLATE 22] a domestic idyll, full of sober charm; even the horse is thoroughbred. On the other side the incident is trivial, Ajax and Achilles armed and playing backgammon, but their intentness on the game, as they while away their watch, invests the picture with a universal quality. Another one-piece amphora in Boulogne gives a new tragic grandeur to the suicide of Ajax: earlier artists had shown him spitted; here with furrowed brow, quietly and methodically, the hero fixes his sword in the ground. The same reflective dignity reforms even Dionysus on a rather earlier neck-amphora in the British Museum; there is a sacramental feeling as the wine-god takes the cup from his server Oinopion. Dionysus appears again on one of Exekias's latest works, the eye-cup in Munich, reclining in his ship while beside him sprouts a giant vine and dolphins tumble around: this scene fills the whole inside of the bowl – a rare variety of the tondo throughout Attic cup-painting – and on the outside beyond the eyes hoplites fight grimly across the handles [FIG. 30A]. Exekias was the greatest of black-figure artists, and he brought the style to its limits. It is hardly credible that so much human dignity and pathos can be expressed in so artificial a convention. Besides the amphorae and his one eye cup we have by Exekias a calyx-krater, a dinos and two sets of fine plaques some fifteen inches high designed with funeral scenes to adorn a tomb. There are pots of other shapes signed by him as 'maker', but with trifling imper-sonal decoration. If it is fair to judge by what is known, he painted com-paratively little. But his influence on his contemporaries – not only in style of painting and in types, but also for the shape of the amphora – was profound and enduring; and it is from Exekias that the Andocides painter and the main stream of red-figure painting derived. His activity as a painter lasted from about 550 B.C. into the 520s, but he did not so far as we know himself attempt the red-figure style.

Exekias, the Amasis painter and Lydos are the most considerable black-figure artists of the third quarter of the sixth century, and they had their followers and friends. There are other painters who stand apart, some laggards from an earlier phase, others of slight but original talents. The Swinger, one of the most prolific, will serve as an example, pleasant and uninspired; his composition is careless, his figures simple and without expression, but his drawing is clean and his range of subjects untiring. There were also in the 530s the devotees of the *Eye cup*, which was now replacing the Little Master cup; to a generation that approved the rhythm of the one-piece amphora the lip cup was a *tour de force* and band and droop cup trivial. As early as the 560s there had appeared a cup with bowl shaped like the segment of a sphere and a knob standing on each handle (the 'merrythought' cup), but this had not become popular. The new eye cup retains the single curve of the bowl but is generally shallower, and the stemmed foot which is surmounted by a broad purple fillet is stumpier. Progress is towards shorter stem and deeper and more strongly modelled foot, to which Exekias gave a fine concave profile [FIG. 30A]. The inside of these cups is generally simple – a small reserved circle or a shabby Gorgoneion. The outside is distinguished by a pair of great eyes on each side in black and white and purple, with strong brows above; between them may be a rough nose or a figure, at the sides more figures; and round the base run bands and often rays. The eye cup and its decoration are an Attic invention. At the beginning of the sixth century a group of rough East Greek cups had been decorated with eyes (p. 117), but these probably ceased a generation earlier; and Greek ships were often painted with great eyes, as were other things that had to find their way home. The eye cup was imitated in Italy (see p. 157). There are also other Attic cups of eye-cup shape, but decorated more conventionally with a frieze of human figures.

The character of the Mature style is evident in composition, the drawing of human figures, the subjects and subsidiary ornament, as well as in its choice and remodelling of shapes. The standard amphora offers a field, whether framed in a black ground as on the panel-amphora or supported by minor decoration as usually on the neck-amphora, that is not much broader than high. So the typical scene contains not more than five or six figures and only a single incident; the importance of the action is concentrated. There is no longer room for old favourites like the chariot race, the fight between Lapiths and Centaurs, or the thronged return of Hephaestus; instead we have the soldier waiting to drive off, Heracles strangling the lion, Dionysus with a few intimates. The figures, fewer and larger, have to stand a closer scrutiny. Greek artists, as is often said, did not till much later model from life; but they observed it. Anatomy now becomes more coherent, particularly in the region of the waist and belly, and poses are easier and more natural, though oblique views are still avoided. Drapery too is studied. Earlier artists had been satisfied with a flat surface, varied sometimes by a border or a vertical panel. By the time of the François vase there are three techniques, one for each of the three common garments. The peplos, a thick long dress, is still flat though often elaborately patterned; the chiton, a light-weight shift, has wavy lines running down it; the himation, worn short as a cape, ends often in formally stepped folds. To these fashions a fourth is soon added – diagonal striping of black and purple that follows the lie of the long himation or cloak. Figures so enveloped, 'mantle figures', are often brought in as supers when the central group does not of itself fill the field. The tendency during the Mature period is towards simpler patterning and more natural folds [note the right-hand and central figures of PLATE 22]. The change in subjects is the result partly of the shape of the normal field – much as in sculpture friezes and metopes are differently designed – partly of greater technical competence and the desire to express mood. Greek artists had never set up a separate hieratic style for the representation of gods and heroes, and they as much as ordinary mortals begin to respond to the natural pleasures and sorrows of life.

The subsidiary ornament has lost in importance. On the one-piece amphora the panel is usually framed above by a narrow band of lotus and palmette, and there are narrow rays round the base. The neck-amphora has most often lotus and palmette on the neck, round the shoulder a chain of buds, or sometimes a small figured scene, bands of simple meander and buds below the main scene, and rays at the base; and after the middle of the century there are often fine volutes springing from the handles [as on PLATE 23]. The hydria, remodelled in the fifties, has commonly a figured scene on its flat shoulder, on the belly a broad panel bordered at the sides with ivy leaf, and rays round the base. These and other ornaments are generally careless, and sometimes slatternly. It is clearly the day of panel decoration.

The chief shapes are one-piece amphora, neck-amphora and cup. Hydria, olpe, oinochoe, lekythos and column-krater come well behind. The modelling is becoming precise and delicate. Export was vigorous and universal throughout the Greek world, and competition was negligible. Vase-painters in Boeotia, Eretria, Thasos and the East Greek area tried to imitate Attic, and so did a few Greek and Etruscan artists in Italy. If foreign vase-painters emigrated to Athens, they must have been very quickly assimilated into the Attic tradition.

Late Attic Black-figure (c. 530–c. 450 B.C.)

The production of black-figure pottery, so far from ceasing at the introduction of the red-figure technique, continued to increase in quantity and for a generation red-figure decoration is comparatively rare. This is still evident in the offerings found at Marathon in the grave-mound of the Athenians who died there fighting the Persians in 490 B.C. But it was the red-figure technique that attracted the greater vase-painters, even though for forty years some of them worked in black-figure too; and the red-figure style they created and developed became increasingly the model for the lesser painters who held to the black-figure technique. For a time tradition and even rivalry maintained a competent standard, but by the end of the first quarter of the fifth century competence was lost, and during the second quarter production (now mainly of the small lekythoi) petered out. Only the official Panathenaic amphorae preserved a senile reminiscence of the black-figure achievement.

For a generation the black-figure style continued to develop. Compositions are often fuller, with closer grouping and much foliage (perhaps because leaves and branches are more easily done in the black-figure technique). The relations of the figures are carefully worked out, and supers no longer stand by but have been taught to act – and overact – their byplay; there is plenty of expression in faces, hands and attitudes. This histrionic business is in strong opposition to the simpler movements of contemporary red-figure. The black-figure champions are responding to the challenge. The Andocides painter, the pioneer of the red-figure technique and style, was more prolific of black-figure. Some of his vases conveniently show the same scene on front and back but in different techniques, an illuminating contrast. His red-figure, fittingly for a pupil of Exekias, becomes bold and clear; but his black-figure, though the drawing is neat and expressive, tends to fussiness both in composition and in detail – he does not instinctively know when to leave well alone. But Psiax, another very early red-figure painter, is at his best in black-figure. His is a slighter finicky style, with a gift for the drawing of character; a three-quarter torso, done with conviction, is a sample of his interest in anatomy. Close to Psiax is the Antimenes painter, who seems to have worked only in black-figure. Both pursue charm and humour rather than grandeur, and it is not surprising that the Antimenes painter occasionally puts his figures in a setting that is artistically of equal importance, as on his well-known amphora in the British Museum with a scene of olive picking.

The stronger style has its last flowering in the *Leagros group* in the years around 510–500 B.C. The subjects are predominantly heroic, but the harnessing of a racing chariot is popular too, and there are several hydriai with women at the fountain house – an appropriate subject for a water-jar. In the 480s the Cleophrades painter could still paint a worthy Panathenaic amphora. But after him the special character of the black-figure style faded away. For the black-figure style does not stand to the red-figure style in the relation of simple reversal of colour. One is an engraver's, the other a draughtsman's style; and – more important – the optical balance of light and dark is totally different. The last painters of black-figure lekythoi were purblind hacks.

The better of the black-figure recusants asserted their independence in their favourite compositions and subjects, and to some extent in their choice of shapes. But even they could not ignore the inventions of their red-figure rivals. In dress, for instance, the soft chiton is from the beginning normal in red-figure, and the black-figure painters, used to the heavy peplos, followed reluctantly. The drawing of folds is also imitated from red-figure, but when translated into the black-figure technique becomes tiresome or cursory. Anatomical structure and occasionally foreshortenings are also copied. The use of purple decreases. It is easy enough to distinguish black-figure vases painted before and after the establishment of the red-figure style.

Early in the red-figure period specialization increases. One painter generally decorates large pots, another cups and small pieces. In late black-figure the painters of large pots are vastly superior; the cups are mostly trivial and miserable pieces. Eye cups are very numerous till the end of the sixth century, and some amphorae and hydriai borrow the notion of eyes with unhappy effect. Many of these cups combine both styles, black-figure for the tondo and red for the outside. An innovation that was later fruitful (see p. 176) was the introduction near the end of the sixth century of a white ground, principally on lekythoi. The commonest shapes till the early fifth century are neck-amphora and hydria (both these deliberately conservative, and the hydria often provided with a subsidiary animal frieze), one-piece amphora, cup, lekythos, and the small Nikosthenic amphora (a vulgar translation of a metal shape related to the small amphora or amphoriskos of Etruscan bucchero that is mentioned on p. 152). Next come of the old shapes column-krater, plate, alabastron, oinochoe; and there are also new shapes invented for the red-figure style, such as stamnos and pelike. Export, even of the poorest black-figure of the decadence, was as wide as ever.

Panathenaic amphorae

In the athletic section of the Panathenaic Games, which (it is said) was inaugurated in 566 B.C., the prizes were amphorae filled with oil. These amphorae are of a special type, though not all the amphorae of this type were prizes: some have no official inscription and others, to judge by the places where they have been found, were or became ordinary articles of trade.

The Burgon amphora [PLATE 21B] is one of the earliest Panathenaic amphorae and should be of the 560s. With its fat body and small neck and foot it is a neater version of the old S.O.S. amphora, naturally enough since that too was a container and not table crockery. The shape persisted, though of course revised to suit changing taste. The principal decoration is in the panels of the body, on the front an armed Athena with the legend 'a prize from Athens' and on the back a picture of the event. Early modifications were that a column was placed on each side of Athena, and that a chain of lotus flowers and palmettes became regular on the neck and below them tongues. With minor alterations this scheme continued to the end. So too did the convention that Panathenaic amphorae should be black-figured.

Orders for these amphorae were placed with leading artists. So in the early fifth century the Cleophrades painter and the Berlin painter, two of the great red-figure artists, turned their hand to black-figure Panathenaics. In the next generation understanding of the black-figure style had been lost and the technique becomes little more than red-figure with incision and reversed colouring, at least for the athletic scene. The Athena suffered a more curious fate, since conservatism decided that (as on coins) she should remain archaic or rather archaistic. A fortunate innovation in the early fourth century was the addition of the name of the archon of the year when the amphora was made. Since the archons' dates are known, the pots too can be dated. But towards the end of the century there were substituted the names of lesser magistrates whose dates are mostly unknown. About the same time red-figure came to its end in Athens and there were no more vase-painters worth the name. Though Panathenaic amphorae were made much longer – until the second century B.C. and perhaps till the fourth century A.D. – and though in the Hellenistic period some of them were painted in a white-ground style, these later products have little interest of any sort.

Technique

In general early Protoattic, from negligence rather than incompetence, is technically inferior to the preceding Geometric. The clay is paler and coarser, the paint less evenly dark, the sheen duller. There is some improvement in later Protoattic and early black-figure. Then about 580 B.C. a new standard is set with finer clay of a deeper orange-red colour, paint that may be described as black, and a high sheen. This is first regular in the Comast group, where for the first time since the late eighth century the potters of Athens interested themselves in small fine shapes, and soon becomes characteristic of Attic black-figure. A yellowish slip is correspondingly common in Protoattic, as it had been in Protogeometric and Early Geometric, but very exceptional during most of the sixth century, though at its end a whiter slip becomes popular for lekythoi and some other small pots. White as an accessory colour is used erratically on some Late Geometric pots, becomes important in the Black and White style of the second quarter of the seventh century, and then declines to a minor aid. In the earlier part of the sixth century some Corinthianizing painters are more lavish with their white, but in the mature phase its main purpose is to distinguish female flesh, and in the late phase it becomes rare. Protoattic white is often yellowish. Till the beginning of the second quarter of the sixth century Attic painters put white directly on the clay or over dark paint as was more convenient, and details on white were usually painted. Afterwards the dark undercoat and incision of detail are normal. Purple, regularly over dark paint, is frequent from the middle of the seventh century. Outline drawing is common and reputable in Protoattic, though less so towards its end, and it recurs occasionally in the black-figure of the sixth and fifth centuries.

4. The Argolid

The Argolid had like Athens a rich and heavy Late Geometric school, but there is no sign of a similar progressive group which by simplifying the current Geometric style cleared the way for new developments. It is likely that this entrenched conservatism of the Argives resisted the Oriental impulses till Protocorinthian, rapidly advancing some thirty easy miles away, had taken too big a lead to be caught up. In the first half of the seventh century some simple Orientalizing ornaments were admitted into the Subgeometric workshops, and later there was a humble use of floral and linear designs. One ambitious but fragmentary krater from Argos recalls Middle Protoattic and another from Mycenae Attic black-figure of about 600 B.C., but these are exceptional.

It is, no doubt, surprising, till accepted, that in the Argolid no advanced style succeeded Geometric. The lack used to be made good by

attributing awkward pieces from other schools. The odd Fusco kraters
from Syracuse are still sometimes classed as Argive, but the resemblances may well be collateral. More remote is a krater from Etruria
which from the painted name of the maker is called the Aristonothos
krater; this much illustrated vase has on the front (like the krater from
Argos) the blinding of Polyphemus and on the back a naval battle that
recalls the Attic Black and White style. Here without much doubt we
have provincial Greek products made respectively in Sicily and Italy.

5. Laconia

The reserving period: Transitional and Laconian I (c. 690–c. 620 B.C.)

Laconian vase-painters after the Geometric period did not show much
enthusiasm for the Orientalizing style and it was not till about 620 B.C.
that the black-figure technique was accepted. In the later eighth century
the new trends of Corinthian Geometric had had their effect in Laconia

FIG. 11. *Laconian lakaina*
Ht *c.* 7·5 cm. Third quarter of 7th cent. B.C. Restored

and from Corinth too came specimens of the new art, but though there
are some faithful Laconian copies of Early Protocorinthian the impulse
soon weakened and the native style proceeded on its leisurely way.
Third-rate and unpretentious, but still independent, it escaped the fate
of Argive pottery.

The so-called Transitional style is an assortment of Subgeometric
and Early Orientalizing, not yet understood. From this around 650 B.C.
emerged a more consistent school, Laconian I. Here the traditional

chequers and other solid ornaments presumably continued for some time, and new motives – broken and unbroken cables, rosettes (sometimes reserved on a dark ground), tongues, rays, rows of pomegranates, spirals, hollow squares with a dot in the centre, and even clumsy palmettes – make modest appearances. A common and characteristic ornament of the finer vases is the row of squares set between two rows of dots that runs round the rim of a pot [see FIG. 11: as time goes on these squares are more widely spaced]. Broad painted areas and bands of purple have a large part in the decoration [see FIG. 11]. Animals are not common, and human figures and heads set in panels are rare. They are drawn in the reserving technique with large outlined heads and little body detail [as in FIG. 12] and sometimes patches of purple or

FIG. 12. *Laconian animals*
Fine style: third quarter of 7th cent. B.C.

white are added. There is not much filling ornament. The negligent and extremely simple style often has a liveliness that suggests caricature. Laconian I is divided into a finer and a rougher school, both contemporary. The rougher vases, especially the larger of them, show a clumsy and intermittent taste for experiment. The finer school, which limits itself to small vases, is excellent in technique but conservative and restrained in decoration; it is for long content with linear and abstract patterns, and seems to have admitted the animal frieze only about the end of the period. The lakaina of FIG. 11 is a fair example of its unpretentious merit. Slip is now regular, and at least on the finer pots thicker and better. In shapes, which have a strong local individuality, there is a liking for ridges and angles that interrupt the smooth curve of the contour. The commonest are the low cup with shallow ring foot and large offset lip, the cup with high straight lip, small bowls, the chalice or low handleless cup on a high stem, the mug with boldly outcurved wall, the kalathos, the dish, the lakaina [FIG. 11: the Geometric type has often a convex, Laconian II a concave lip], a squat jug of olpe, oinochoai, large bowls and pierced stands. Plastic heads are sometimes attached to bowls and oinochoai. There was during this period almost as little export as before, though a fragment has been found in Samos. Some Corinthian was imported.

The early Black-figure period: Laconian II (c. 620–c. 580 B.C.)

About 620 B.C., to judge by parallels with Corinthian, Laconian pottery took a firm step forward. The black-figure technique was adopted, ornament becomes more assured and varied though still abstract in form, and a more unified and vigorous style developed. These changes coincide with the establishment of the black-figure style in Athens and are in part the result of a similar relation to Corinth, where the new Ripe style with its increased productivity was starting on its commercial triumph. But Laconian vase-painters, content to remain provincial, kept their own character.

Around the end of the eighth century Laconian painters had occasionally imitated the simple incision of Early Protocorinthian, but the experiment was soon abandoned. The black-figure technique was therefore strange to the painters of Laconian II and it took them a generation to master it. At first the incision often does little more than follow the outlines of the figure and border the internal patches of colour, and there are later sherds that show the opposite fault of meaningless detail. But by the beginning of the sixth century a workmanlike black-figure style had been created. From the scanty remains it seems that the Laconian animals and monsters were selected from the simpler of the Corinthian types, but the composition favours files of creatures of the same species and there is little filling ornament. The most original design is that on an early sixth-century cup found at Tarentum, inside which fishes swarm about a central rosette, reserved in a dark circle, and dolphins circle them [cf. PLATE 26A]. Commoner than any incised animals are silhouette birds with drooping purple tails [PLATE 26B]. Human figures are rare, though there are from the centre of cups a few large Gorgoneia drawn mainly in outline.

The majority of Laconian II pots were more simply decorated with a little ornament to relieve the plain banding. The row of squares between two rows of dots remains common for rims, though the squares are more widely spaced [cf. PLATE 26B], and rays are sometimes doubled. Of the new ornaments many are variations on the step and hook meanders, often built up of rectangular units like the patterns on old-fashioned linoleums, and there are also chevrons, tongues, cables, pomegranates and rosettes. Purple is freely used, and there is strong contrast of colour in the ornament and in the plain bands. The shapes include the lakaina, the mug – both these with pronounced ring foot and outcurving wall, the cup which is closely modelled on Corinthian, the chalice, the plate, the stemmed dish, bowls, a primitive bell-krater, the convex pyxis, the squat olpe and various small closed pots with spouts. Ridges, grooves, knobs and plastic heads, strong angles and bold curves are popular. In this period export begins. Examples – mainly cups – come from Olympia (where Laconian artists were active), from Samos which during the sixth century had seemingly intimate relations with Sparta, from Delos, Rhodes, Ephesus, Naucratis, Tocra in Cyrenaica, Tarentum (a Laconian colony) and Caere in Etruria. Corinthian import continued, and there are some Laconian imitations of East Greek Bird bowls and helmet aryballoi of the Gorgoneion group.

The developed Black-figure style: Laconian III (c. 580–c. 550 B.C.) and IV (c. 550–c. 525 B.C.)

About 580 B.C. – the date is fixed by grave groups that include Corinthian – there begins the phase of Laconian pottery that is best known and was once called Cyrenaean. Human figures and vegetable ornament now become common, and since also much has been preserved the work of individual painters can be recognized. The cup which grows a stem appears as the principal shape, partly because of its popularity in overseas markets. This blossoming of Laconian art, which is visible also in the painted architectural revetments, could not have happened without the fertile contact of Corinth, but the new style has a native character that is to be explained not by incompetence (though there is some of that) but by a restrained and independent judgement which does not strain its limited capacity and perception. From this come the honest, simple charm and liveliness of much Laconian vase-painting at a time when imitation of Corinth was having disastrous effects elsewhere.

The outside of a typical cup of the mid-sixth century is illustrated on PLATE 27B. The shape, compared to PLATE 26B, shows a development similar to that of Attic and East Greek cups. The lip has grown more important, the bowl shallower and its curve flatter, the stem is taller and often ends in a rounded moulding. The decoration has a richness that is comparable to some of the Siana cups of Athens and to their successors the Droop cups. On other cups the lip is covered with a double network of pomegranates, which has ousted the bands and squares normal there in Laconian II, and in the handle frieze between clumsy palmettes a row of elongated flowers and buds shows a stylization of the lotus that is characteristically Laconian. Purple is freely used on ornaments and for bands, in cheerful contrast with the dark paint and creamy slip. Stem and foot are dark, except that the moulding above and the edge of the foot, if sharply profiled, are not only reserved but unslipped. Shuffle the motives, put animals or birds in the handle frieze – the formula covers most of the more elaborate cups.

On the inside [PLATE 27A] the lip is modestly painted over except for a reserved and unslipped stripe at top and bottom, with sometimes a third between; or occasionally it is patterned. The bowl reveals more fully the Laconian artist. Here, as already in the Tarentum cup (p. 95), the full space is used, and it was not till the middle of the century, when Attic influence was growing, that small tondos became common. At Corinth too the whole field of the bowl was sometimes decorated, but in concentric zones. Yet though Laconian vase-painters also used this scheme, they preferred to take advantage of the opportunity for drawing and composing on a larger scale. Composition is perhaps too definite a description of Laconian methods, since the deliberate planning of the picture to fit a round field was to them unnatural and unless they had to hand a ready-made design (such as the Gorgoneion) they tried to square the circle. In this the contrast with Athens is instructive. Attic vase-painters were more interested in the outside of the cup and the tondo – if there was one – was small and usually contained a single figure; but they took pains to choose poses which fitted that figure to the circular space. At Sparta, on the other hand, the painters of cups – at least till the introduction of the smaller tondo in the mid century – were not content with one figure and no more, and in their composition preferred the less exacting method of drawing a horizontal base-line for the main scene, as did the uninspired painters of the plates of the Wild Goat style in the early sixth century. There are some curious experiments – the division of the field into two equal halves with the figures of each group set foot to foot, the breaking of the exergue by another base-line so that it is divided into a narrow frieze above and a smaller segment below, and even the use of two opposite exergues with a narrow frieze between them. But the normal scheme is that of the cup illustrated, with a single exergue containing a lotus member or less often figures.

Besides the elaborate cups there is a smaller and simpler version, in which lip and bowl are hardly distinct and the stem has no moulding, and about 550 B.C. there appear copies of the Attic Droop cup with lightly concave lip and channelled stem. Some cheaper cups have no decoration inside or a small medallion. In the later stage simpler decoration becomes more common.

The pioneer of the new style of Laconian III was the Hephaestus painter, whose figures, based on Corinthian models but less well-knit, have a direct vigour that owes much to a firm and careful economy of incised detail. Besides the style of drawing early signs are the fringing of the tondo with a valance of pomegranates and the volutes and triangular bases of the handle palmettes. Like his successors he is lavish with purple but makes little or no use of white, even for female flesh; for this Laconian vase-painters, who already had a light ground, were satisfied with outline drawing, or else did not distinguish men from women by their colours. The Arcesilas painter, who was working in the years before 550 B.C., is so called from the cup in the Bibliothèque Nationale in Paris with – presumably – the second Cyrenaean king of that name superintending the packing of wool. It is a lively scene, full of gesticulation and jabbering and numerous properties, and notable also for being a topical sketch, but the detail is inferior and rather fussy. The Hunt painter, younger than the Arcesilas painter and at first influenced by him, is a draughtsman of greater technical competence whose solid well-built figures and firm detail give a new realism to Laconian art. His cups have the curious trick of showing a scene as viewed through a porthole, the outer figures being cut through by the frame. Clearly he learnt his composition on friezes, as of that of his hydria in Rhodes, and made no concession to the circular field of the cup. About 550 B.C. Corinthian vase-painters abandoned the figure style, and Attic standards proved too much for the Laconians. In Laconian IV there is a rapid decline, visible in the later works of the Hunt painter and his followers, and by the 520s the native tradition of figure painting was dead.

Laconian artists of this period gave their best to their human figures. The debt to Corinth is evident, but they took only so much as they were capable of digesting and so their art has for all its awkwardness a homogeneity that raised it to the third place among contemporary Greek schools. The subjects, drawn from myth and daily life, make a strange collection. Besides such widespread favourites as Heracles with the hydra and men drinking or dancing or wenching there are others that are unique – as Atlas with Prometheus, the building of a temple,

Arcesilas at his wool business, soldiers carrying home their dead. But the strangeness of the subjects must not be exaggerated, as it has been by some interpreters; much is due to the Laconian practice of excerpting incidents for their cups from larger scenes – so the ambushing of Troilus is reduced to Achilles lurking behind the well-house. Filling ornament is rare, but winged lads and birds and other creatures are fairly common, and Laconian artists have a weakness for settings – buildings, bushes and once even a creditable pond.

The animals and monsters are of Corinthian stock, but mostly show clumsy drawing and awkward grouping. The most successful are the grubbing cocks, less showy than the Corinthian breed but nearer to life. The chief vegetable ornaments have already been mentioned in the description of PLATE 27B. The pomegranate, in the seventh century shaped regularly like a ball with a spike through it, puts out two stamens for the Hephaestus painter, and after him these multiply and often add a cross-bar. Buds and flowers with austerely stylized petals grow spindlier still. Tapering 'myrtle' leaves which sprout from each side of a stem are common too – at first they have no stalks, and at the end neither stalks nor stem – and in Laconian IV ivy creeps in. These are all continuous ornaments. Other floral ornaments are the handle palmettes, the lotus and palmette unit which is used in exergues and sometimes in animal friezes, and small varieties that sphinxes and other figures sometimes wear. The Laconians soon tired of vegetable ornament, and made it even less lifelike than did other archaic Greeks. Of the abstract ornaments the most notable are the bands of squares and dots, of a sort of bracket ($\mathsf{\Gamma}$), and of hook meanders.

The cup is a shape much honoured by Laconian painters. The hydria, a tall handsome pot with high belly and flaring foot, the dinos and the volute-krater also received decoration with human figures. The lakaina, oinochoe, stemmed dish, plate, bell-krater, chalice and flat-bottomed aryballos rarely rise above animal friezes. In his shapes the Laconian potter carries still further his remarkable fondness for technical dexterity; the hydria in particular may repeat a bronze form, and bronze details are imitated by the plastic palmettes and heads on oinochoai at the attachments of the handle as well as by bosses where in metalwork there would be the heads of rivets. These are the more important of the elaborate vases, which are mostly decorated in narrowish bands from rim to foot and even on the underside of the foot, if that is flat. There are also plainer pots, mentioned in the next section. The clay, which is less fine than Corinthian or Attic, is fired to colours ranging from pink to light brown, pink if the vase is wholly slipped, brown if the clay surface is to show. The slip, at first thick and a pale cream, deteriorates or disappears in Laconian IV. The paint has usually a deep sepia tone, but after about 550 B.C. is sometimes as good a black as Attic. The contrast of cream ground with dark paint and rich purple makes an effect unusually gay for a black-figure style, and the practice of leaving parts of pots (especially cups) unslipped adds to the polychromy.

Export was considerable and wide, declining after the middle of the century. Olympia was perhaps the most important customer; there is much from Samos, Naucratis and Cyrenaica; and some pieces are known from Delphi, Kavalla, Rhodes, Smyrna, Pitane, Pergamum, Sardis, Gordion, Crete, Corcyra, Sicily, Greek and Etruscan Italy, Marseilles, and even Carthage. The catholic taste of Etruria drew on Laconian also for its hybrid art, and there was some borrowing by East Greek workshops – Fikellura took the pomegranate, Samian potters reproduced the handleless chalice, and there are one or two forthright copies. In return Laconian vase-painters occasionally show knowledge of East Greek, as in the concentric rings on some of the cups of the Hephaestus group (cf. p. 140) and in the use in the third quarter of the century of the crescents familiar from Fikellura. Corinthian influence has been mentioned already, and the developed Laconian cup borrows from the Attic Droop cup. After Laconian IV pottery was still made at Sparta, for the home market only, but the native style has been replaced by inept imitations of Attic and the simplicity of incompetence. It is unnecessary to put up a political reason for this decline, which resulted from Attic competition, not the hauntings of the ghost of Lycurgus. Those who do not like the idea that a commercial industry could flourish in Sparta itself may prefer to find the workshops in Gytheion, the port of Laconia and a town not of Spartiates but Perioeci: Gytheion has not been excavated.

Plain ware

During the sixth century Laconia did a brisker trade overseas in plainer wares, which are not always recognized as Laconian. The numerous column-kraters, usually painted all over or with a simple linear pattern on the reserved and slipped outer face of the lip, deserved their popularity for the excellence of their shape. Aryballoi of Ripe Corinthian shapes are very common. During the first half of the sixth century there are three main groups. Some are flat-bottomed and have all or most of their surface painted dark; but most are of the simpler round type with a little decoration – the upper part dark and the lower left slipped (much like a darning egg), or the whole pot covered with paint and the belly girt with a purple band which is bordered above and below by a pair of white lines enclosing dots. This last group alone survives through Laconian IV, somewhat flattened and with a plain reserved border to the purple. About the middle of the sixth century ring-footed cups, generally unslipped, come into favour: here the inside is painted over, the outside carries a single or double row of leaves and for the rest is plainly painted or carelessly striped. A few stemmed cups are similarly decorated. Other shapes include amphorae, oinochoai, mugs, kantharos, flat-based cup, bell-mouthed two-handled aryballos and miniature pots, painted dark all over and sometimes enlivened with a stripe or two of purple or white. Miniature pots, which were regularly offered at sanctuaries, seem to have continued till the third century.

6. Boeotia

For Boeotian pottery of the seventh century we rely, as before, on style. A basically Geometric school continued for a while to work in a tradition derived from Attic and Corinthian, but at the same time Orientalizing motives were becoming acceptable. This is most evident in a class of big amphorae with a high conical foot, which may be fenestrated, and a broad neck passing into a flaring lip. The principal decoration, of Subgeometric or early Orientalizing figures or ornaments, is set – sometimes in wild confusion – in a panel on the shoulder; neck and often the foot and the band round the belly are crudely filled with a row of thick vertical zigzags. The shape, the system of decoration and the zigzags were current too in Euboea and the Cyclades where they belong particularly to the Linear Island group [PLATE 29A–B]; but the Cycladic decoration is quieter and finer, and Euboea – which is also nearer – was probably the immediate source for Boeotia. Later examples, which are more Orientalizing than Subgeometric in effect, show peculiar forms of plant ornament, have tidier zigzags and add a plastic rim below the lip. There are besides pots of other shapes and more humbly decorated which have similar zigzags and banding. Dating is difficult. Some of the figures and ornaments can be paralleled elsewhere in the first and also the second quarter of the seventh century; but unless there is a gap in the present sequence of Boeotian, this zigzag manner may have lasted through the seventh century and even into the early years of the sixth. The coarsish clay is buff to pink, with a cream slip or wash, and the paint is dull and uneven.

There follows, so it seems, an original product of Boeotian taste, the *Bird cup group*, which takes its name from such pieces as that of

PLATE 28A, a clumsy sort of dish with or without a high foot and decorated in the manner of modern folk art. On the outside birds or palmettes, zigzags and cross-hatched triangles are the commonest components. The birds and other ornaments are regularly upside down,
whether because the cup was meant to be hung high up or that the
painter found it easier to work that way. The inside is simply banded.
Of other shapes the kantharos is most important. The clay, buff or pink,
has a pale slip. At first this slip is cream, and the decoration in the
standard dark paint and red or purple; but from about 520 B.C. the
slip becomes whiter, purple and yellow are used liberally, and the
surface is powdery. The effect is remarkably colourful. At Rhitsona,
the ancient Mycalessus, the only Boeotian site where a cemetery has
been carefully excavated and reported, the series of Bird cups begins
about 560 B.C. and lasts till about 480 B.C. Examples occur throughout
Boeotia and are very numerous.

During the seventh and for much of the sixth century Corinthian
pottery was imported in great quantity. Some simple Boeotian imitations have been recognized; since recognition depends on the clay, inferior workmanship and place of finding, but not on a coherent local
style, they are often disputed. A *black-figure style* was not established
till the early sixth century, and then naturally under Attic influence, if
not by graduates from Attic workshops. The first models are in the
Comast group and the Animal style of the time. Animals, now as in
Attic tamer and thinner, remain popular during the middle and third
quarter of the century, but the Boeotians surround them with thick
filling ornament. Human figures are rarer and lag further behind Attic
standards. A large class regularly does without incision and added
colour, though the forms and disposition of figures and of ornaments
are those of contemporary black-figure. This use of full silhouette is
sometimes described as Geometricizing, but there is no need to derive
from the Geometric style of a century and more earlier a practice that is
readily explained by indolence or the example of Droop cups then
being made in Athens. Both silhouette and incising black-figure continued throughout the fifth century, first following the minor tradition
in Attic black-figure and when that ended with a new vigour. Even
at the end of the fifth century output was large, especially of cups decorated with floral ornament or with a figure or small group, usually in
silhouette, between heavy palmettes. Early in the fourth century even
the floral style withered away. The notable shapes are at first kantharos
and tripod-pyxis, lekane and kotyle; later cups of various types become
increasingly common.

This late black-figure is redeemed by the *Cabiran style*, so-called because of its popularity at the Cabiran sanctuary near Thebes. The school begins soon after the middle of the fifth century and lasts till near its end. The drawing, which uses incision and added white, sometimes shows a skilful translation of the manner of Attic red-figure, but much more often it is perfunctory or negligent. Besides Cabirus reclining at the banquet there are less elevated scenes from mythical, human and pygmy life, grotesque in poses and proportions but vivacious and convincing [FIG. 13]. This is the only truly comic school of Classical Greek art. Some instances of what appears to be actor's costume suggest a connection with farce. These pots with human figures are, especially

FIG. 13. *Boeotian kantharos*
Detail: scale *c.* 2 : 5. Cabiran style, workshop of Mystae painter:
later 5th cent. B.C.

in the later phase, less common than those decorated with a band of ivy or other floral ornament; and sometimes a floral ornament surmounts a figure scene. The characteristic shape is a kantharos like a deep mug, narrowing towards the rim: it has a low foot and a pair of vertical ring-handles, to which one or two spurs are attached. The lower part of the pot is often left unpainted. A few vestiges of the Cabiran style appear in the early fourth century.

The clay of Boeotian black-figure is normally a pale brown. Sometimes the surface or part of it is given a reddish wash to imitate Attic or to contrast with the main field. The paint is often rather dull and streaky. A few pieces resemble Attic very closely. Thebes was perhaps the chief place of manufacture; it was accessible to Athens, the largest Boeotian city and probably the home of the Cabiran workshops. Inferior contemporary groups seem to come from northern Boeotia and

perhaps Euboea. A few Boeotian pots have been found in Attica and
other parts of Greece, but there was no regular export, unless to more
backward neighbours.

7. Euboea

The two big cities of Euboea, Chalcis and Eretria, were only a dozen
miles apart. From Eretria we have enough pottery to judge the school
current there, from Chalcis nothing of importance. But it is not likely
that if pottery was painted in Chalcis it differed much from what may be
called Eretrian. The admirable ware known as 'Chalcidian', which many
think was made at Chalcis, is here assigned to Italy for the reasons set
out on p. 158.

A largish amphora with broad neck and high conical foot appears
at Eretria (as in Boeotia and the Cyclades) about the beginning of the
seventh century, soon becomes the principal shape – at least for infant
burial – and with modifications lasts well down the sixth century. Dating, though by stylistic analogies, is fairly secure. The earliest of these
amphorae, of the groups A and B, make much of vertical zigzags, big
and little, in a close row or more often spaced in groups: the main
panel, between the handles, has sometimes Subgeometric animals and
sometimes simple Orientalizing ornament. Corinthian influence is evident, though the effect is nearer Boeotian. Later the decorative bands
grow fewer and much of the pot is covered with dark paint, relieved by
stripes of purple and white: a peculiar ornament is an upright bar,
shaped like a sausage, which repeated in the centre and singly at the
sides gives weight to the main panel. In group C [PLATE 28B] a new kind
of decoration is introduced. Usually the front of the amphora has
women on the neck and a lone animal or monster on the upper part
of the body, while the back is filled in with heavy loops. The figures are
drawn in partial outline, white and not incision is normally used for details on dark areas, and purple is added freely. The helpless style and the
repertory of filling ornament most resemble 'Melian', but may rather
be debased from Attic. In spite of old fashioned traits this group is
probably of the last quarter of the seventh century. In contrast group D
attempts a regular black-figure technique with incision, though still
allowing itself outlined heads. The model, as elsewhere in the early
sixth century, is the Corinthian Animal style, but mixed with other
elements, some local and others paralleled in Attic or 'Melian'. Probably the Corinthianizing style came through one or other of these
schools. The result anyhow is singularly uncouth. Here the strictly

Eretrian school ends. Its style had been costively provincial, moving –
when it moved – by sudden jerks. Groups A and B (and for that matter
D) show some resemblances to contemporary Etruscan: either Eretrian
was imported to Italy – and for this there is no evidence – or, more
credibly, both Eretrian and Etruscan sometimes made similar use of
their Corinthian models.

A few amphorae found at Eretria, of the same type but more finely
modelled, are elaborately and competently painted in a black-figure
style that in large part is pure Attic of the middle of the sixth century.
The painters must have trained in Attic workshops; but some of the
details of the decoration are foreign to Attic, and shape, use and place
of finding are Eretrian. Some smaller pots with similar un-Attic details
may also have been made in Eretria, but attributions of this kind are
dangerous. Finally, in the late fifth century a sort of black-figure akin
to Boeotian may belong to Euboea.

Clay and paint cannot regularly be distinguished from Attic. There
was hardly more export of Eretrian than of Boeotian pottery, though
odd Atticizing pieces of the late sixth century have been noticed at
Megara Hyblaea in Sicily and Olbia in South Russia.

8. The Cyclades

The Orientalizing movement reached the Cyclades early and more or
less independent workshops concocted different mixtures of Subgeometric and Orientalizing. Some clung to a looser version of the old
style, admitting a few new motives. Others innovated more frankly, but
with a tendency to mannerism which was refined and exaggerated by
their successors in the middle of the seventh century. The black-figure
style with its regular use of incision was not accepted. The general
impression is that there were scattered round the islands a few progressive painters, gifted but isolated, who could not establish a living
tradition of their own and though casually imitating would not adopt
the tradition of others. The one exception is the showy 'Melian' school,
which through the later part of the seventh century and the early part
of the sixth drew what can hardly be called inspiration from the major
schools of its time.

The study of Cycladic Orientalizing is confused. Many more or less
complete pots, among which amphorae have a probably unrepresenta-
tive importance, have been found in the Purification enclosure on
Rheneia (to which were transferred the contents of graves on Delos)
and in the cemeteries of Thera. There are also sherds from Siphnos,

some pots from Melos and Kimolos, and a few oddments from else-where. These finds give some idea where particular groups were or were not current, and in Thera a few early pots were noted in useful contexts. A better knowledge of the Late Geometric of the Cyclades has helped to locate some of the schools that developed from it, but there remains much for which specialists rely mainly on intuition. The opinions that follow are possibly too sceptical, but a short concordance of other opinions is added on p. 343. The dating of Cycladic has often been too early, and perhaps the dates proposed here have not all been lowered enough; for if (as is likely) the deposit on Rheneia conceals a steady series of Cycladic pottery, some of the earlier Orientalizing groups must continue beyond the middle of the seventh century to link with 'Melian'.

Several groups had some general currency within the Cyclades, but only 'Melian' was at all regularly exported beyond them. In the seventh century there was much import and some imitation of Corinthian, less import but perhaps more imitation of East Greek. In the early sixth century Attic became dominant, and its simpler forms were occasionally copied.

The Linear Island group

Linear Island is the least prejudiced name that has been proposed for this group of pots, mainly neck-amphorae around twenty inches high; PLATE 29 offers an example typical in shape and system of decoration. The vertical zigzags on the neck are standard. In the three panels of the shoulder, the principal field of decoration, various motives occur. Some, not necessarily confined to the earliest stage of the group, are of Geometric origin, such as the heavy concentric circles (often flanked by four dots), the quatrefoil, the big lozenge that sprouts extra corners from its sides, and opposed or boxed triangles. Others are Orientalizing – rudimentary florals or simple curvilinear patterns, birds of various forms and structure, and the lion. The style has a simple but studied elegance which relies on line. This is obvious in the narrow stripes surrounding neck, shoulder and foot, and in the groups of thin up-rights, stopped by thicker, which separate the panels. It appears more subtly in the fauna, wiry and boneless, and unencumbered by filling ornament: the lion of the illustration is treated as a linear pattern, its body lightly sprinkled with dots except on the shoulder (which, as often in Cycladic, is defined with inorganic emphasis) and its pose adapted to the panel rather than for action. With these amphorae go a few kraters of the low Geometric shape. Many cups and other simply decorated pots have also been connected, without much more reason than general similarity of clay. This in Linear Island is fine, varies in colour from reddish to yellowy brown and contains some mica. There is usually a yellowish slip or wash. The paint is normally dark brown.

The origin of this group is disputed. There is nothing distinctive about its Geometric components, its Orientalizing forms seem to be independently received or adapted (though some of the birds have relatives in Cretan), and the shape of the amphora was evolved in Cycladic Late Geometric. Nor is its distribution decisive. The humbler candidates for the group appear in Thera, Delos (including Rheneia) and Paros, which is often accepted as its home. But almost all the important amphorae and kraters have been found in Thera, though their style is very different from the contemporary Theran Subgeometric.

The end of Linear Island is also obscure. Its only recognizable descendant is a close group of three amphorae in Leyden, Stockholm and Paris. Their shape is tauter and more subtly proportioned, their decoration simpler and bolder with the central panel extended to take a crouching lion or grazing deer. In some details they resemble the Protome group, but not more closely than might be expected from two workshops of much the same time and region.

On style and the contexts of Theran graves the date of the Linear Island group should be the early part of the seventh century, though what looks like a fragment of this ware has turned up at Aziris in Cyrenaica in a context not earlier than the 630s. The shape of the amphora and some elements of the style were probably borrowed and debased in Eretria and Boeotia. The Leyden group appears to be of the middle of the seventh century.

The Ad group

The Linear Island group is calligraphic and primly modern. The contemporary Ad group prefers crude contrast of dark and light and an antique manner. Here the whole surface of the pot is decorated with coarse but effective brushwork. On the broad neck-amphora, a standard shape, the full width of neck and shoulder is taken for the field; the neck usually has an elongated horse and the shoulder two or more animals, grouped or in file. Below come two, three or four bands of ornament, and at the base heavy rays. A few close stripes bound each field and band. The favourite animals (sometimes reduced to protomes) are horse, with or without wings, deer, griffin and lion. Of these the lion is Orientalizing in build and in its technique of reserved head and dotted – and even chequered – body. The other creatures are typically Subgeometric in their exaggeration of Geometric traits: note on FIG. 14 the overgrown hindquarters and the extensible body, which is sometimes broken by sections reserved and filled with dots. Columns of horizontal zigzags and compositions of lozenges fill the vacant spaces.

FIG. 14. *Cycladic oinochoe*
Detail of shoulder: ht of field 7 cm. Ad group: first quarter of 7th cent. B.C.

These ornaments also appear together in the bands on the lower part of the body, as do flattened chequers, the open cable, tall blobs and short vertical zigzags. Other shapes are hydria, krater, oinochoe and skyphos; and from Siphnos came a terracotta figure, originally about a foot high. The clay is fine and brown. There may be a creamy slip. The paint is dark and dull.

Pots or sherds of the Ad group have been found on Rheneia (in the

Purification deposit), Siphnos, Kimolos and Paros, and at Al Mina, but not on Thera. In decorative details the closest parallels are in 'Parian' Geometric and, since the clays are similar, 'Paros' may be considered the home of the Ad group too. It is, though, a compact group of very personal character – many of our pieces are evidently by one painter – so that purely stylistic argument is less secure. The date, by the look of the animals, is in the first quarter of the seventh century.

The Heraldic group

The Heraldic group, of much the same date, uses a similar repertory in yet another mode [FIG. 15]. The principal shape is a slim neck-amphora with handles on the shoulder, some eighteen inches high, an

FIG. 15. *Cycladic amphora*
Detail of neck: scale *c.* 3 : 7. Heraldic group:
first or perhaps second quarter of 7th cent. B.C.

exaggeration of a standard Late Geometric type. The lower half of the pot is striped. The back of the upper part has sprawling lozenges, loops, cables or grotesques. The front of neck and shoulder receives elaborate decoration. On each there is a main field, bordered above and below by one or two bands of simple ornament, and divided into a narrowish central panel and flanking strips or subsidiary panels. The panels contain a couple of dancing lions, a solitary lion or horse (winged or wingless), a sphinx, or the head and neck of a horse – all these in a rubbery Orientalizing style and with reserved heads – or else simple curvilinear or even floral designs, or step-pattern. In narrower strips a simple cable and latticing are frequent. For the horizontal bands the favourite ornaments are lozenges, void or cross-hatched, and S-shaped blobs: sometimes there are simple tongues or floral chains at the top of the shoulder. The sphinxes are notable for the three-leaved drape over their forelegs, a misunderstanding of the ultimately Egyptian skirt. The drawing is cursory, with more attention to a general effect of vertical elaboration than to detailed accuracy of line or anatomy or to grand composition. Of shapes other than the amphora the most remarkable is a large figure from Siphnos. The clay is reddish brown, with a creamy slip, and the paint is dark and shiny.

Most of these amphorae are by one painter, a decorative mannerist who had some knowledge of Geometric but was familiar with the early Orientalizing style. Similarities in shape and the use of striping suggest a connection with Naxian Late Geometric, and the clay and slip agree; but stylistically the Heraldic group looks invented rather than evolved. One example has been found on Thera, one on Siphnos and more on Naxos; the rest are from the Purification deposit of Rheneia and from Delos itself. Style suggests a date early in the seventh century, though the context of the amphora from Thera is later.

The Protome group

The consummation of Cycladic mannerism is reached in a small group of neck-amphorae, hydriai and one cup, which has been named the Protome group. The decoration is disposed and designed in harmony with the fullbut simple shapes. The amphora is especially successful. Here the lip has a band of simple ornament – trios of S-blobs separated by grouped strokes. On the neck a central panel displays usually the head and neck of a horse or the forepart of a lion, and the narrow flanking panels some simple linear or floral motive. The shoulder is decorated like the neck, but on a larger scale, and below comes a border of ornament as on the lip. The lower half of the pot makes a good setting with its deep band of dark paint, relieved by two thin purple stripes, and the thick rays round the base. The sophisticated simplicity of the style may be inspected in FIG. 16. The balance of light and dark is carefully studied, most obviously in the structure of the lion; and, as the horse's jaw shows, line is developed for its own sake in defiance of anatomy, something very different from Corinthian calligraphy [of which FIG. 6c and E gives mature examples]. This is a style complete in itself; it can advance no further. Some students assign the Protome group to Paros, others to Naxos. But the painter of the amphorae was an individualist rather than an adherent of a school. The clay is brown and micaceous, the slip cream, the paint dark and usually dullish. The

FIG. 16. *Cycladic amphora*

Details of shoulder (front and back): scale 2 : 3. Protome group:
mid 7th cent. B.C.

date should be about the middle of the seventh century, if only because
of the teeth of the lion: till the second quarter of that century Greek
lions are fitted only with incisors. So far this group is recorded only
from the Purification deposit on Rheneia.

Other Orientalizing groups

Many Orientalizing pots and fragments, especially from the Rheneia
deposit, do not fit into any of the groups already described, though
place of finding and various stylistic connections argue that they are
Cycladic. A group consisting in the main of miserable one-piece amphorae and hydriai and of big cups – *group D* – is decorated in an

execrable style, probably of the first half of the seventh century. The upper part of the body has a row of birds or lions' heads or a whole animal, supported by such ornaments as simple florals, lozenges, thick vertical zigzags and open cable. On the lower part are stripes and rays. This group has not been observed outside Rheneia and Delos. The clay is fine and brown, with a dirty slip, the paint dark and shiny.

Theran Subgeometric, as has been said (p. 32), flourished well into the seventh century and some pots show Orientalizing motives, though it would be supererogatory to separate them into a Theran Orientalizing style.

Imitations of Corinthian, not always close, occur sporadically in the first half and middle of the seventh century. *Imitations of the Wild Goat style*, rather more frequent, are mostly of the second half of the century. Where the style does not betray them, these imitations are recognized by their rougher clay and yellowish slip. Other pots show a style *related to 'Melian'*, if not an early stage of that school. The most remarkable are some pieces from Naxos, of the mid seventh century, which use a light brown for male flesh and other parts of the decoration. A number of *ring-vases* (shaped like a bloated lifebelt with a vertical spout) are on their distribution probably Cycladic; they are palely slipped and are decorated simply with cross-hatched triangles, tongues or flora forms. Finally, there is an assortment of pieces, a few reputable but more inept, which display Orientalizing patterns, vegetation or figures.

'Melian'

The 'Melian' school takes its name from a series of big amphorae found on Melos and published as long ago as 1862. At that time they were the largest and gaudiest of known Greek pots, and their importance and age were and still sometimes are exaggerated. But the school is sluggishly imitative, not pioneering.

The decoration is by monotonous formula. The big amphora (or krater), which runs about a metre high, is a modernization of the Linear Island type. The neck is broader and taller, the body more elegantly ovoid, the foot higher and slit by vents. The decoration, as always in 'Melian', covers the whole pot. On the neck there are usually a human or divine pair in the central panel and double volutes at the sides and back. On the body a grand scene is exhibited in front, confronting horses or other unimportant figures at the back, and below them come a band of double spirals or other large ornament and a deeper band of volutes. On the foot female heads or more volutes occupy the panels between the vents, with a band of ornament above and below. Round the moulding at the bottom reversed rays are normal. The subjects of the main field are sometimes mythological. A smaller and more simply decorated version of this type of amphora is illustrated on FIG 17. The ordinary neck-amphorae and hydriai, which are very frequent, are of course less ambitious, but again the whole surface is decorated. The

FIG. 17. *'Melian'* amphora
Ht (without lid) 45·5 cm. Early 6th cent. B.C.

shapes are not well defined: some are tallish with ovoid body, others (perhaps later) more squat. The familiar motives are: on the neck a female head, double volutes, or occasionally a complete figure; on the shoulder, volutes or animals; on the body, in the main field animals, and below it meander or chevrons and then rays or even tongues. The shallow dishes (or deep plates with two handles) are usually surrounded with volutes on the outside and banded or plain inside. Other shapes include the one-piece amphora, the plate and the phiale mesomphalos.

The drawing is unequal and rather coarse. The human figures and still more the female heads are often gawky and angular, and the detail is stupidly excessive: there is much resemblance, and presumably indebtedness, to Corinthian (as on the neck of FIG. 17). The animals are more varied: on some earlier pots the horses have a Cycladic look, but soon the fauna of the Wild Goat style is copied, and that is succeeded by Corinthianizing birds and beasts. The filling ornament changes in harmony, though it too keeps its own flavour. Of the larger ornaments volutes in one form or another occur on almost every 'Melian' pot and with their latticed appendages make identification easy. Also common are double spirals and lotus chains with flowers of an undeveloped type known earlier in Cycladic. Samples of volutes and flowers are shown on FIGS 17 and 24. For minor bands there are tongues, meanders, chevrons and other angular patterns, big round dots, and spiked dots that are perhaps derived from the Laconian pomegranate. Latticing is frequent for the side frames of panels. Under handles set horizontally eyes often peep out, as in some earlier Cycladic groups. The technique of figures is at first reserving, that is heads and other appropriate parts are outlined, but in time a little unsystematic incision is attempted, and for Corinthianizing animals there is especially in the late stage a sort of black-figure method which substitutes white lines for incision. Purple is used freely throughout, and on the big amphorae a light brown denotes male flesh. The coarse clay is a greyish brown ranging to pink and contains a little mica. The slip is yellowish. The paint varies from brown to blackish and is rather dull. The general effect is loud.

The 'Melian' school, as at present defined, is compact and not of long duration. Imitation of Corinthian, which appears early, is of the last quarter of the seventh century and the first of the sixth. Even if some disputed pieces are included, it is hard to date the beginning before 650 B.C. The main finds are from Rheneia (where over three hundred pots, still unpublished, were recovered in the Purification deposit), from Delos itself, and from Melos; there is a fair amount from Thasos and Tocra in Cyrenaica; other examples are recorded from Siphnos, Paros, Naxos and Kavalla (the Thracian Neapolis), and isolated fragments from Icaria, Samos and Lindos.

Where 'Melian' was made is a puzzle. It does not obviously evolve from any earlier group of Cycladic, although some father it on the Heraldic group. Since a 'Melian' amphora or hydria was for some thirty or forty years the standard show-piece in graves on Delos, it is convenient to put the workshops in one of the nearer islands, perhaps Paros, which also was the mother city of Thasos.

Polychrome plates

A few plates of the early sixth century pose in a field of blue human figures or animals done in white, red and the usual dark brown. The style is not specifically Cycladic, but finding places point strongly to the Cyclades: there is one each from Thera and Tocra, the others come from Delos (including Rheneia) and from Paros.

9. The East Greek Cities

Ionia and Aeolis were pioneers of Greek literature, but in their barren vase-painting rare spurts of energy were followed by long spells of stagnation. East Greek Geometric was irresolute, the Orientalizing style tame, the black-figure without roots. A little isolated imitation comprised East Greek influence in European Greece, though there was naturally more in the Cyclades, but Corinthian and then Attic models dominated East Greek in the sixth century. Exports tell the same story: from the later seventh century the pottery of Corinth and then of Attica becomes common on East Greek sites and even Laconian not unknown, while East Greek pottery was rarely carried across the Aegean except perhaps to such East Greek foundations as Gela in Sicily. It is often said that there is much that is East Greek in the art of Etruria. The claim is exaggerated, for part of their similarity is that neither is Attic.

It was probably not till the second quarter of the seventh century that East Greek vase-painters turned their backs on the Geometric tradition. From Smyrna some tantalizing fragments suggest a mood of uncoordinated experiment: but the successful Orientalizing style, wherever it first established itself, was an Animal style, which from its commonest species is best called the *Wild Goat style*. In no part of the Greek world is the contrast stronger between old and new – in decoration, shapes and technique – and the intermediate stage is less a transition than an uncompounded mixture of the two styles. Here the influence of Oriental models is more persistent, and if the source was the same as that on which the Greeks of Europe drew, the vehicle was not. Protocorinthian has a fine precision of line that suggests engraving, the Wild Goat style with its thick careless brushwork and dependence on mass and colour has a textile look, and that there was anyhow in the sixth century a textile Wild Goat style can be argued from the Clazomenian sarcophagi (see p. 137). In Greek vase-painting of the seventh century it was the human figure that more and more attracted the progressive artists; there were no progressive artists on the east of the Aegean and once established the Wild Goat style steadily declined. A little before 600 B.C. it attempted to graft on to its old reserving tradition the black-figure Animal style of Ripe Corinthian, but even so rejuvenated succumbed in another thirty years. The Wild Goat style had been universal in the East Greek region, except that in Aeolis its provincial school could not oust the older Grey ware (or Bucchero), but in the sixth century there was divergence. In the south from Samos to Rhodes the *Fikellura* style continued some of the Wild Goat tradition, at first with revived delicacy, then more carelessly till it petered out in clumsy linear and vegetable patterns: its period is from the second quarter to the end of the century. *Chios* during the first half of the century developed a polychrome style, sometimes elegant, for scenes with human figures. There were also groups inspired by or imitating Attic black-figure, notably the *Ionian Little Master cups* of the years round 550 B.C. and the slightly later *Clazomenian* ware. Yet another school produced the *Situlae*, mostly found at Tell Defenneh in Egypt and posing a curious problem. But by 500 B.C. East Greek vase-painting was deservedly dead. Only the *Clazomenian sarcophagi*, tedious monuments of painted terracotta, show that from about 530 to the 460s B.C. there were still one or two workshops which not only imitated contemporary Attic but remembered the old tradition of the Wild Goat style. Disappointing as the admission may be, the Persian conquest in the 540s had no visible effect on East Greek vase-painting.

The East Greek sites from which we have material have been mentioned on p. 33. In this period Rhodes, Samos, Smyrna and 'Larisa' are the most prolific, and there is much pottery from overseas settlements also – Naucratis and Tell Defenneh in Egypt, Al Mina in Syria, Istria in Rumania, Olbia and Berezan in the Ukraine and now Tocra in Cyrenaica. But Rhodes provides the clearest evidence, since there we have graves and after about 630 B.C. these graves regularly contain Corinthian or Attic as well as East Greek pots.

Subgeometric and Bird bowls

In the early part of the Orientalizing period there was much Subgeometric pottery, though hardly a Subgeometric style. The best-known examples are round-mouthed oinochoai decorated wildly with Geometric ornaments and birds, with which simple Orientalizing motives may be mixed. Such Subgeometric occurs on most East Greek sites which have deposits of the mid seventh century.

A peculiar East Greek byform is the *Bird bowl*, of which PLATE 29D offers a sample: the inside is covered with dark paint. The Bird bowl evolves in shape and decoration from a Late Geometric kotyle and once established shows little variation, even in the placing and forms of the filling ornament. Generally nicked rim, ring foot and the painting over of all the lower part of the bowl are signs of an early date; and smooth rim, moulded foot, rays round the lower bowl and bands of white–red–white on the painted inside are late. The clay, usually light brown and unslipped, is like much of the ornament Geometric, but the mannered style betrays its later date. The period of the Bird bowls is roughly the whole seventh century. Some examples have a pale slip, and a few display Orientalizing fauna. They were made throughout the East Greek region, but probably originated in Rhodes. Their export was rather wider than that of the Wild Goat pottery to which they are complementary. A few examples have been found as far west as Etruria and Malta, and some local imitations occur at Sparta.

In the later seventh century the Bird bowls were being succeeded by cups of similar shape but more modern decoration. The rigid compartments of the handle frieze disappear, the ornament turns to large dot-rosettes or a lotus flower or even a roughly sketched nose and pair of eyes set loosely in the field, and the use of a slip is perhaps rather less exceptional. These *Rosette bowls* and *Lotus bowls* are still common in the second half of the sixth century; the *Eye bowls*, less frequent, may not have lasted so long. They are all rare outside East Greek settlements and imitations are rarer still.

The Wild Goat style

The Wild Goat style, still sometimes described generically as Rhodian, began not long before the middle of the seventh century and for nearly three generations was the principal style of East Greek vase-painting. It is easy to recognize even in its last Corinthianizing products [for examples see PLATES 30–31 and FIG. 18]. The clay is coarser than that of the preceding Geometric, and the exposed surface (except of some Late pieces) has a pale slip or wash. The draughtsmanship has a careless facility which might be thought spontaneous if there were not so many examples of it. It is a style without ambitions.

Early Orientalizing experiments evident at Smyrna and elsewhere came to nothing. More of a transition may be divined in the Subgeometric round-mouthed oinochoai. Here there may appear on the broad shoulder a fish or tentative goats, in silhouette relieved by a little reservation, and on the neck a simple cable. Slip is not yet regular. There are, besides, sherds on which panels with animals and ornament in a developed Wild Goat style adjoin bands of purely Geometric meander.

The Wild Goat style, ornaments and animals, seems to have been introduced very nearly in the form that became canonical and not to have passed through a long evolution. A few sherds show abortive experiments in incision. The date of the transitional phase is probably in the second quarter of the seventh century.

The next stage seems to fall into two parts – *Early* and *Middle Wild Goat style* (roughly the old style 'A'). The Early phase (*c.* 660–640 B.C.) is erratic. The staider Middle phase may perhaps be subdivided into I and II about 625 B.C., when ornament and poses become stereotyped. The round-mouthed oinochoe of PLATE 30A exhibits the Middle I style. The shoulder as usual carries the principal subject, a neat but stiff composition of two griffins posing across a lotus ornament and flanked by a bull and a goat. But there is a refreshing liveliness in the two friezes round the belly, with their broken groups of dogs coursing goats and deer. The light filling ornaments are deftly scattered in the field, the independent bands of ornament nicely judged not to overweight the figure scenes. This vase, made about 630 B.C., plainly shows the strength and weakness of the Wild Goat style. It is admirably decorative in its design and in the gay contrast of cream ground and dark paint, but it aims at nothing more than being decorative and an ideal so easily satisfied does not stimulate a progressive tradition. The result can be seen in the trefoil-mouthed oinochoe of PLATE 30B, of the last quarter of the seventh century. Oinochoai like this, some neater and some more negligent, are to be seen in most sizeable collections of Greek vases, and their cumulative effect is monotonous. On the dark lip eyes and rosettes are often painted in white; the neck carries a ribbon of simple cable or meander and square; the shoulder is still emphasized by the animals and geese which beneath tongues strike various attitudes, sometimes across a floral ornament; round the belly goats follow one another grazing, each kind of filling ornament having its appointed place; and the base is encircled by a chain of lotus flowers and buds or long rays. There are variations: the goats on better pieces sometimes run, there may be more rows of figures on the belly, an occasional creature forgets its drill, or the decoration may be simplified – for the shoulder frieze a lotus chain, for the belly frieze a broad dark band enlivened by purple stripes and enclosing some simple ornament such as the hook meander. The general tendency is towards rougher draughtsmanship, a narrower repertory, heavier and coarser filling ornament, a more lavish use of purple, and the labour-saving elongation of animals already noticed in the Ripe Animal style of Corinth.

Much the commonest species in the fauna is the goat, which in the

Middle II phase has almost a monopoly of the belly of the pot. Spotted deer, lion, griffin and bull occur throughout the Middle phase; dog and hare are usually early, sphinx and goose mostly later, panther and boar rare. Occasionally around the 620s there is the pretty conceit of swallows perching on tails and rosettes. The characteristic lotus [drawn on FIG. 19A] remains closer to its Oriental model than do its relations in European Greece. At first it is small and delicate and is used in subsidiary bands, but soon it grows large and bold. This type, in a chain of alternate flowers and buds (the two ends often carelessly united), is familiar round the base of trefoil-mouthed oinochoai; but units are also made up into compact ornaments – surmounting a pair of volutes in the middle of the shoulder, or joined in a cross in the centre of dishes; and sometimes a flower or bud stands alone in a panel. Compared with the Corinthian lotus [PLATE 12C] the East Greek type is both truer to nature and less convincing: at Corinth the stylization is more abstract, but the vigorous play of the connecting tendrils suggests organic life. Towards the end of the Middle Wild Goat style a simpler and smaller variety of lotus [FIG. 19B] was invented for shoulder friezes and dishes. Other continuous ornaments are few – the cable (on fine pieces two or more courses deep) and the meander and square are needed on necks, but subsidiary bands are rare after the Early phase. The character and general progress of the filling ornament can be seen in the illustrations. Of the shapes the oinochoe is the most frequent. The broad round-mouthed type of PLATE 30A was perhaps the only shape that survived from Geometric to Orientalizing, gradually assuming a wider and lower body: it began at the end of Geometric, had its popularity, and came to its end with the Middle I phase. The canonical trefoil-mouthed oinochoe [PLATE 30B], though it occurs in the third quarter of the seventh century, is characteristically a Middle II shape: its development seems to be towards a higher and narrower body and a feebler neck. A squat variety too appears near the end of the Middle II phase: the shoulder usually has a panel with a figure or head, the belly bands of paint striped with purple. The stemmed dishes, which become common in the Middle II phase, have a conventional charm: the decoration, on the inside, is usually a central rosette or lotus cross, then bands of dark paint enlivened by narrow purple stripes and inset hook meanders, and round the edge between groups of wedge-shaped leaves or rays six or seven panels framing rosettes, heads of goose, goat or sphinx, or curious stylized sets of a nose and a pair of eyes. Contemporary with these but without figure decoration are other dishes with ring foot and heavy flat rim. Further shapes include krater, dinos and probably the plate, though its heyday was later. The accident that so many of the pots of this period come from graves in Rhodes may give a wrong idea of the frequency of various shapes; but there is no doubt of the rarity of the amphora, the place of which as in contemporary Corinthian was filled by the oinochoe, and of the cup and other drinking pots – here probably for the technical reason that the Wild Goat fabric was coarse to the lips.

FIG. 18. *Wild Goat style oinochoe*
Details of shoulder: scale 2 : 3. Late Bf style: first quarter of 6th cent. B.C.

The *Late Wild Goat style* (or *Wild Goat style 'B'*) began shortly before 600 B.C. The conservative manner of the seventh century had remained pure-bred in spite of heavy import of Corinthian pottery into the East Greek region. Now there appeared an uncritical imitation of Corinthian black-figure [see FIG. 18], especially of the dense fauna and (though less wholeheartedly) of the filling ornament of the Ripe Animal style. The black-figure style of the Wild Goat painters is coarse and blotchy, but they thought so highly of the novelty as to give it the place of honour on the shoulder and sometimes the neck of important pots. Elsewhere the reserving tradition survived, rapidly degenerating. One of the better Late goats is illustrated on PLATE 31B below a deer of the beginning of the Middle II phase [PLATE 31A]; the new laxity is perceptible. But much of Late reserving work is execrable, particularly on the plates, so common in Rhodes, which regularly display a solitary sphinx or other animal set on a broad exergue. The end came about the 570s.

Human figures remain very rare. The most famous scene is on the Euphorbos plate in the British Museum, a unique but hamfisted work, perhaps about 600 B.C. The regular fauna of the black-figure style includes lion, boar, bull, goat, deer, sphinx, griffin, goose (or swan) in the usual Corinthian groups. In the reserving style stubby goats, grazing or running, are normal for friezes; on plates the single figure is most often an angular sphinx, but dog, bull, boar, goat and griffin are not rare. The lotus takes the lumpy form of FIG. 19C–D and loses in size and importance, long bunches of leaves sprout from corners, cables exude drops at their angles, the filling ornament solidifies, new continuous ornaments develop, and dividing bands are heavier and now often variegated with stripes of white, purple and white. There are new shapes too. The oinochoe is long and narrow, with oval body and high neck: it shares its popularity with an amphora of similar build. Other common shapes are kraters (including column krater), dinos, stemmed dish and ring-footed dish (both now less carefully modelled and more simply decorated) and plate.

In the second quarter of the sixth century the reserving ware seems to be confined to simple floral decoration and can hardly still be defined as Wild Goat style. The black-figure style develops clumsily, perhaps only in the northern area, and makes more use of human figures: it is known from Smyrna and Naucratis. Clazomenian is the most familiar descendant of this indeterminate East Greek black-figure.

Wild Goat pottery was current in most of the East Greek region and it is very likely that it was made in many places. The outline of the style just given is based on the finds from Rhodes, most of which are probably of Rhodian make; and though it is pleasant to imagine that the big cities of Ionia had something better, Ephesus is still almost a blank, the examples from Miletus have – so it seems – no distinctive peculiarity, and the not very numerous finds at Samos are perhaps of rather better quality only because they were dedications in a sanctuary. Nor are the remains at Al Mina, Naucratis and the Black Sea colonies noticeably unlike Rhodian. It is therefore probable that the Wild Goat painters of the

FIG. 19. *East Greek lotus flowers and buds*

A, Middle Wild Goat style: *c.* 630–600 B.C. B, Middle Wild Goat style: *c.* 615–600 B.C. C–D, Late Wild Goat style: early 6th cent. B.C. E, Fikellura: middle and later 6th cent. B.C.

southern part of the East Greek region – that is from Samos to Rhodes – recognized a single standard, and that the difference between one city and another was not much greater than the difference between one workshop and another in the same city. There were of course provincial groups such as the Late Wild Goat pottery of Nisyros, a little island off the Cnidian peninsula; and the loutish Late plates of Rhodes may indicate that that island was then lapsing into provincialism. But it is premature, if not futile, to try to assign an individual school to every

East Greek city: to give an example, two very fine sherds were found at Ephesus and on this evidence a superior Ephesian school has been asserted, but there are unpublished pieces by the same hand from Miletus and Sardis. If the leadership in this southern school is to be given to one place, Samos has the best claim.

In Chios there are signs of a local school. The early Wild Goat phase is not yet clear, but there are enough Middle sherds, especially from Naucratis [PLATE 31C]. Here is a reputable style, in which the most noticeable peculiarities are the horseshoe shape of the roundel (while the southern school prefers a short arc), an unusually white slip and the chalice shape. In the Late phase Chiot vase-painters took another course. A fuller account of Chiot is attempted on pp. 125–9.

The provincial workshops of Aeolis diverged so far from the southern standard that they can be regarded as a separate school. Most of the evidence comes from the excavation of 'Larisa', which was not the leading Aeolian city. Here the style of drawing is angular and uncertain, and there is a lack of proportion and restraint. Lotus flowers for example may reach seven inches high and grow extra petals; roundels and triangles often make a continuous fringe to a frieze; the loop pattern [a Rhodian specimen of which appears on PLATE 31A] becomes rectilinear. The favourite shapes are oinochoe, kotyle-krater (popular elsewhere only in Attica in the second half of the seventh century), dinos, stemmed dish, ring-footed dish. But generally Aeolian seems to have followed the trends of the main Wild Goat style. In technique a characteristic is the frequent use together of two shiny paints, dark brown and red, as well as purple retouches: the two paints are sometimes found at Corinth in the later eighth century and the method of producing them may have been widely known to Greek painters, though some think that the Aeolians were indebted to inner Anatolia. Aeolian occurs at Myrina and Pitane (mixed with standard wares) and perhaps Troy. It has connections with Chiot, and some of its traits seem to have milder parallels at Clazomenae. Smyrna appears to have kept fairly close to southern orthodoxy. But besides the painted pottery Grey ware (or Bucchero) was still made; it was, coarse ware apart, the normal pottery at Antissa in Lesbos, about equal in quantity to the Wild Goat pottery at 'Larisa', and common at Troy. Aeolian pottery, unlike the pottery of the southern and Chiot Wild Goat schools, was rarely exported and the Aeolian look of some fragments from Sardis and Amisos may mean no more than that other places too were clumsily imitating the canonical Wild Goat style.

The dating of Wild Goat pottery is straightforward in Rhodes from about 630 B.C., when there begins a long series of recorded graves containing Corinthian as well as East Greek pots, but more evidence would be welcome for the last years of the style. There is no firm evidence for the 'transitional' and Early phases, but the remains are so few and the development so little that it is hard to believe that either lasted more than some twenty years. This late dating is supported by the survival of a strong Subgeometric manner in the Bird bowls till about 600 B.C. and in the kotylai at Vroulia for almost as long, and by the date of the Corinthian and Attic examples of the round-mouthed oinochoe [of the shape of PLATE 30A].

There are other reconstructions of the Wild Goat style, of which the most considerable is the division – popular in Germany – into Camirus and Euphorbos groups, the former corresponding roughly to what is here called Early and Middle, the latter to Late. But instead of one proceeding from the other, the two groups are considered to be contemporary (or at least widely overlapping) and largely independent. A refinement of this system detaches a Vlastos group from the Euphorbos group, which is left with little but plates: the three groups so constituted are again contemporary, the Euphorbos group flourishing in Rhodes and the Dodecanese, the Camirus and Vlastos groups both there and elsewhere.

The clay used for Wild Goat pottery is generally coarse and gritty; it is usually fired from sandy brown to pink, but varies as far as chocolate and salmon red. The slip of the Early and Middle phases is thick and ranges from yellow through cream to a near white. In the Late phase the slip is often only a streaky whitish wash or omitted altogether. The paint aims at dark brown, but has the usual transformations to red; it has little sheen. From the start of the Middle II phase purple retouches are common, white except on the lips of oinochoai is mostly Late, when too there was some use of the black polychrome technique. Efforts have been made to distinguish local schools by the look of clay and slip; but though admittedly Chiot slip is unusually white, I doubt if the naked eye will do much in this field.

Wild Goat pottery was not much exported except to East Greek settlements. It is plentiful at Al Mina in Syria, Mersin in Cilicia, Naucratis in Egypt, Berezan and Olbia in the Ukraine, Istria in Rumania, Apollonia Pontica in Bulgaria, perhaps at Ak Alan near Samsun in northern Turkey, and there are isolated finds from native sites in Syria and Palestine, Egypt and the interior of the Ukraine; it has been recovered from Kavalla and Thasos; some pieces have been found at Gela (traditionally a Rhodian foundation), Selinus, Megara Hyblaea and

Syracuse in Sicily; and in its Late phase it is relatively frequent at Tocra in Cyrenaica. In Crete and Cyprus and mainland Greece it is very rare indeed. More went to the Cyclades, where the influence of the Wild Goat style is plain in 'Melian' vase-painting, and there were probably imports and imitations in Lydia and Caria and perhaps even in Pamphylia and adjacent regions. One Wild Goat painter of the Middle II phase appears to have emigrated to Etruria, where he picked up some Italocorinthian habits. Except at Al Mina, where the Wild Goat style succeeds Geometric, Tarsus and perhaps Mersin, the finds are generally not before the Middle II phase; but this is evidence not so much of a change of taste in many East Greek colonies, as of the lateness of their foundation.

The Chiot styles

The island of Chios long maintained some artistic independence. Its Late Geometric pottery differs a little from that of other East Greek cities, its Wild Goat style shows individual traits, and in the sixth century it took an original course. Since the first important finds were made at Naucratis, the later Chiot style used to be called Naucratite. Now there is a fair quantity from Chios, and especially Emporio, though again from sanctuaries. As a result the so-called chalice still has an exaggerated frequency in the finds, since fashion encouraged the dedication of that shape in particular.

A Subgeometric style seems to have lasted well down the seventh century, till eventually a Wild Goat style became established. Of this, whether or not by chance, we have little or nothing that is certainly earlier than the Middle II phase. Here the decoration seems to have been fairly orthodox, though with some minor peculiarities. Roundels of horseshoe shape become common and sometimes (as in Aeolian) they form with pendent triangles a continuous border to a figure frieze; dots along the reserved belly stripe of animals and on volutes are more usual than in the southern school, the slip is rather whiter. Generally the Chiot school looks less considered and less hackneyed, but it may only be that there is less of it. The goat is not so prominent as in the south, perhaps because so few of our fragments are from pots with secondary friezes of animals. Bull, lion, boar, dog, goose and sphinx are also common. The essentially decorative character of the Wild Goat style is very evident in the unnatural but ornamental patterns and patches reserved on many of these creatures. This Chiot school probably continued for a few years into the sixth century, declining of course in quality. PLATE 31C gives a fair example.

In the early sixth century Chiot vase-painters left the Wild Goat tradition which still survived in the southern area and turned to two new ventures, a black-figure style and what may be called the Chalice style. The *Chiot Black-figure style* (like the Polos style of Athens) is a careless small-scale adaptation of Corinthian, of the Middle rather than the Early Ripe phase, but retains a little East Greek in its details: general resemblances to Laconian are probably the outcome of a similar ineptitude. The favourite subjects are rows of crouching sphinxes or lions (these usually wearing a ham frill), and alternatively drunken male dancers with protruding rumps and clothing reduced to a band across the chest and a cap on the buttocks. The thick filling ornament consists of Corinthian rosettes and half-rosettes used as roundels, and purple lavishly supplements incision. There is not much variety; sirens and bulls occur among the animals, and there is one fragment with centaurs. All this is trivial hackwork, but a few sherds with larger and more careful human figures show that there were Chiot artists who understood and were interested in the black-figure technique. The Chiot Black-figure style probably lasted into the second quarter of the sixth century, and perhaps beyond. One late group does without the white slip.

The reserving technique continued in the *Chiot Chalice style*. As in the contemporary black-figure style human figures appear as well as animals, but not of course together. The animals – sphinx seated or standing, and lion – belong to the East Greek tradition. The new manner often dispenses with filling ornament and sets a single figure or ornament on each side of the chalice, so giving an effect of elegance in spite of the summary drawing [see FIG. 20]. The same scheme of decoration occurs with human figures, some of which are very careless. But the majority of fragments with human representations come from more elaborate compositions of battles, horse-racing, drinking parties, women's dances, processions and even mythological scenes. The common facial type, at least of the men, is taken from Corinthian of the early sixth century, as perhaps are the riders and the general inspiration of this class. But there are other faces with fleshy profile and receding forehead inherited from Middle Wild Goat sphinxes; the favourite dress is the full-length sleeved chiton; the filling ornament, which is sometimes retained, is Chiot; and the mythology includes besides the popular Heracles such rarities (it seems) as the Danaids with their husbands' severed heads. The quality of the work varies from a wooden angularity to a flowing draughtsmanship that makes good use of colour. The whitish slip makes an admirable background to the brownish-black paint, which for details is often diluted to a golden brown, and there is much purple and even a purer white. The finest group adds a buff to yellow wash for male flesh, so coming closer to the polychromy of free painting. For this appreciation of colour the nearest contemporary parallel is again in Corinthian, where too the distinction of dark men and light women is not rigid. The life of the Chalice style is probably from soon after 600 B.C. till some time in the second quarter or middle of the sixth century.

The inside of Chiot chalices and other small open vases is distinctive. The surface is first slipped and then covered with dark paint, and on this

FIG. 20. *Chiot chalice*

Ht 14 cm. Chalice style: late in first quarter of 6th cent. B.C.

after the end of the seventh century bands of ornament are often boldly painted in white and purple. In the centre there is usually a cross or a rosette; round the edge lotus flowers are common [especially of the types of FIG. 19D], alternating with buds or rosettes; and there is a selection of linear ornaments. A few sherds show white human figures floundering uncertainly on a dark ground, and on a chalice in Oxford this technique is used for a pair of riders on the outside.

The shapes that are known are in the Wild Goat style dinos, open bowl (with out-turned sides), chalice, dish, jug and – a curiosity at this stage of East Greek art – the phallus-cup; in the Black-figure style pyxis with lid, ring-vase, stemmed dish, phiale, chalice, cup, and perhaps oinochoe and bowl; in the Chalice style pre-eminently the chalice and also the phiale. Plastic heads, of which several survive, were sometimes attached to handles or in other places. Pots without painted ornament include amphora, hydria and kantharos besides the inevitable chalice, of which some late examples from Chios are very clumsy. But in all the chalice is much the commonest shape among the existing material, as it was in the sixth century, to judge by the finds overseas, the most admired. The earliest complete examples are the two from Vulci in Würzburg of the end of the seventh century, and here the lip is of only moderate height, the bowl sharply distinct, the foot low. The origin is plain; the chalice arose from a cup of the general type of FIG. 4B by the exaggeration of lip and foot, a process which is paralleled in the kantharos and the Laconian lakaina. In the early sixth century the lip grew still taller, the transition to the bowl was slurred, and the foot – concave or conical in profile – became higher [so FIG. 20]. The lip carries the main decorative field. In the Wild Goat style it is heavily framed, often with a meander, the bowl is emphasized by such patterns as double cable or meander, and the low foot is painted over. In the Black-figure and Chalice styles the subsidiary decoration becomes much lighter or disappears. The usual formula is now at the edge of the lip a narrow strip of simple ornament, between the handles the characteristic saw-pattern or something as slight, and round the base of the bowl a couple of plain bands instead of the former rays. The chalice was a long-lived shape and continued, debased and decorated at most with banding, till the fourth or even the third century.

It was once widely supposed that the pottery of these styles was made in Naucratis, and so it was and sometimes still is called Naucratite pottery. That was reasonable on the evidence then available; so little had been found in Chios and so much at Naucratis, where also many inscriptions painted on kantharoi or chalices before they were fired were dedications to Naucratite deities. But more recent excavation in Chios has shown that the Chiot Wild Goat style and its successors had their origins in a local Geometric and must themselves be local. Some diehards have compromised on a dual style with workshops both in Chios and at Naucratis, but clay and slip are uniform and painted dedications have been found not only in Chios and Naucratis but in Aegina. Chiot pots were fashionable for dedications, and evidently vase-painters in Chios were willing to oblige the whim of a customer who travelled. A newer theory, that at least the polychrome style was Naucratite, is more plausible but hardly convincing.

The clay is sandy in texture and fires usually from lightish to reddish brown. The slip is rather hard and white: its use inside open pots has been mentioned. The paint is normally dark brown, often with an olive tinge. Purple additions are common. White (except for decoration on a dark ground) is limited to the more elaborate work of the Chalice style. The walls of chalices and phialai are often very thin, and the firing as well as the shaping is competent.

The later styles of Chiot pottery are easily recognized and exports have been widely reported. It is common, of course, in Chios, and not uncommon at Erythrae, Smyrna, Pitane, Phocaea and perhaps Clazomenae. In southern parts of the East Greek homeland it is rare. Overseas there is much from Naucratis, Tocra and Cyrene, Thasos and the neighbouring Greek colonies, and Berezan, and some from Olbia, Istria and Catania. At Aegina it seems relatively common in the sixth century. Isolated pieces have turned up in most parts of the Greek world. But the influence of Chiot does not correspond to the quality of its best work. There may have been close imitation in Thasos, an Attic chalice of about 580 B.C. is like an earlyish form of the Chiot shape, some later East Greek styles which used human figures were probably influenced by Chiot types, and there are reminiscences of the reserving Animal style on a few early Clazomenian sarcophagi.

Ionian Little Masters

In Ionia as elsewhere the influence of Attic black-figure succeeded Corinthian during the second quarter of the sixth century, and though it did not generally go deep it inspired a few cups of exquisite quality. Clay and paint are close to Attic and the shapes follow the Siana and the lip cup, but the arrangement of the decoration is freer and the style eclectic. The cup was already long established in East Greek pottery (see p. 140) and from that tradition the Ionian Little Masters took their usual practice of reserving both sides of the lip, often decorating the outside with a row of doubled myrtle or ivy leaves and the inside even with birds or animals. From the Wild Goat repertory came some of its fauna, but now planned in silhouette without the outline drawing of the head, and as on the plates of the early sixth century the tondo is sometimes filled by a single large figure placed on a broad exergue. Much too is original. Tradition and originality make a useful basis for a style, but here we have virtuosity. Detail is marked sometimes by reservation that equals incision in its fineness, sometimes by incision which may be so minutely elaborated that it is finicky. Individual figures are often admirable, but the composition tends to be loose and careless. The most remarkable effect is that of the Vineyard cup in the Louvre [PLATE 33B], an archaic Greek version of the arabesque to which there is an apt contrast in Exekias's rather later cup of Dionysus at sea. In the Ionian cup the ordinary rules of top and bottom are confounded and the subject has no particular content: instead we have a brilliant exercise in decoration, which even manages to enclose in its pattern a little running man – a concession to the Greek sense of artistic propriety. The shape of this cup is that of the early lip cup and the outside decoration differs only in the doubled ivy leaves of the lip; details are reserved; the date is about 550 B.C. There are not many of these Ionian cups and only two or three are complete, but their variety is bewildering. The impression they give is of artists of great ability and little direction, and so their promise came to nothing.

The places where these cups have been found are first Samos and Naucratis; isolated examples come from Apollonia Pontica, Aegina, Perochora perhaps, and Italy; and there must be fragments not yet identified from other sites. Their home was presumably Samos, since their nearest relative is the Fikellura style which flourished in Samos and Rhodes and though the examples from Samos are not many there are none from Rhodes. Comparison with Attic and Fikellura shows that the date of the group is around the middle of the sixth century.

Fikellura

The Fikellura style, named after a modern place in Rhodes, is the last genuinely East Greek style of vase-painting. Its home was in the southern part of the East Greek region, and its life from the second quarter to the end of the sixth century. Its basis was the old Wild Goat style, particularly of the Middle phase, but modernized. Some of its new types and methods are shared with the Ionian Little Masters – for instance the man on the Vineyard cup [PLATE 33B] is in pure Fikellura style – but its spirit is less volatile and so it succeeded in fixing a tradition. But though Fikellura kept its independence and had also a shrewd originality, Attic competition was always too strong for it: even in Rhodes graves of this time contain more Attic than Fikellura.

The characteristic shape is a squat amphora about a foot high of the shape of FIG. 21. In the decoration there are some constants – on the lip rough strokes, on the neck double cable (a simplification of the Middle Wild Goat form and usually early) or meander and square or meander cross, on the three-reeded handle coarse blobs, and the low foot is painted over. Variety comes in the decoration of the body. In those groups which form the core of the style it is arranged in zones, at first numerous and with the emphasis on the shoulder, then in sympathy with Attic fashion giving more size and importance to the top field of the belly. On early vases groups of animals and men are common, but gradually such figures become perfunctory and are replaced by vegetable or linear ornaments. An amphora [FIG. 21] of about 540 B.C. in the British Museum represents the turn of the style: here the main field is on the belly and contains a partridge between large and spreading volutes, but the composition is compact and the draughtsmanship for Fikellura conscientious. The last stage is slapdash, with continuous sprawling volutes between roughly drawn tongues and crescents.

FIG. 21. *Fikellura amphora*
Ht 29 cm. *c.* 540 B.C.

The other important system of Fikellura decoration is that of the free field, of which PLATE 32A is an admirable example. This anticipates an effect of Attic red-figure of the early fifth century, but here the boldness of the conception does not need delicacy in execution. To balance the central figure the artist has sketched under each handle an ornament of about the same height. Free field decoration had been tried at the beginning of the Fikellura style in a group of oinochoai which make do with neat ornament at the top of the shoulder and short rays round the base and a blank between. But there is a gap between the oinochoai and our amphora, which was painted not before the 540s, and though in Cyprus a similar idea had been current it is best to honour the Running Man painter as an original creator. His influence survived on some later amphorae on which volutes are the sole decoration of the belly; and perhaps a group with animals on the shoulder and a blank zone below profited by this demonstration of the value of empty space.

Another original but this time unsuccessful experiment was made on some oinochoai of the 550s. The front of the body is treated as a single panel, filled in the main with scales; and from this panel broad bands, generally barred, sweep back and up towards the line of the handle. The effect is so irregular that it is hard to believe that this was an exercise in pure invention, and perhaps it was prompted by a plastic bird with feathered breast and wings laid back. This group had no successors.

Animals and birds are common at the beginning of the Fikellura style. They are drawn, as on the Ionian Little Master cups, in full silhouette with reserved detail. In the earlier groups the work is delicate and the species numerous. Lion, panther, bull, boar, deer, goat, sphinx and griffin appear in the conventional groupings; dogs chase hares; ducks or partridges waddle in file. By 540 B.C. little more is left than dogs and hares and unspecified birds, larger and summarily sketched but not necessarily feeble; and by 520 B.C. even these were extinct. Human figures fared better. Neat small figures were succeeded by larger and clumsier, but throughout the third quarter of the sixth century there were painters capable of such exquisite draughtsmanship as the Dionysus of FIG. 22, which may be as late as 520 B.C. The commonest subject is the drunken revel round the winebowl, and there are pygmies fighting cranes, satyrs (once chasing maenads) and Busiris. Isolated figures begin after the middle of the century, such as the hare of PLATE 32A or a solitary reveller or the Dionysus of FIG. 22 who is matched by Ares on the other side of the vase. There are also fanciful creations – winged man, hare-headed man, even a winged dog-headed man. Fikellura had a taste for comic and whimsical subjects.

Volutes of the type of FIG. 21 are the principal decoration of later amphorae: in the 540s, when they first appeared, it was as sidepieces to a central figure. Other ornaments used to fill the wide belly field are net pattern (often of dotted lines) and sometimes scale pattern. For minor zones the commonest and most characteristic ornaments are crescent and lotus (of the type of FIG. 19E, at first sometimes with two extra petals inserted); often there are several rows of crescents, one above the other and facing in alternate direction, and the lotus band is occasionally doubled. A chain of buds is common on the shoulder, and on some earlier pieces a band of simple cable marks the transition from shoulder to belly. Besides these there are rows of ivy or doubled myrtle leaves and of enclosed palmettes, and an effective pattern made up of overlapping leaf rosettes. Filling ornament, often sprinkled in figure scenes, is light.

The commonest shape is the amphora. The oinochoe, a smaller version of the Middle Wild Goat type but with strong upright neck, is early. So too is a little simple cup about five inches across with short

FIG. 22. *Fikellura amphoriskos*
Details of body: scale *c.* 2 : 3. *c.* 525 B.C.

offset rim and ring foot. The amphoriskos, a small very slender byform of the amphora, is common later: it often has net pattern on the belly. Of the rare shapes the most remarkable is a large cup from Samos with offset rim; its elaborate decoration, with a Gorgoneion in the centre, is exceptional.

The technique is that of the Middle Wild Goat style. The clay which fires from buff to pink is gritty, the slip creamy yellow to white, the paint dark brown to red. Details are reserved. Purple is used on early pieces, white very rarely except for eyes and rosettes on the lip of oinochoai. There is no distinction of colour between men and women. The workmanship is often very careless; note the lip on PLATE 32A.

The Fikellura painters drew heavily on the Wild Goat style, particularly of its Middle phase, for fauna, ornaments, shapes and technique. They have much in common with the Ionian Little Masters; which borrowed from the other is not clear, but perhaps they were sometimes the same individuals. Attic (or Corinthian) influence is remotely visible in the abandonment of outline drawing, directly in the change of emphasis in the decorative scheme and in some details. But generally the Fikellura style kept to itself. The crescent, the development of the volutes, the use of the free field are original. In execution the Fikellura painters were economical and even on their most careful pieces the minor detail is rapid and negligent. The Birmingham amphora [PLATE 32A] shows the spontaneity that this freehand style can achieve, but in later and less imaginative pieces it degenerates into boorishness.

Much Fikellura pottery has been found in Samos and Rhodes and perhaps at Miletus. It is common at Naucratis and Tell Defenneh in Egypt; a few pieces have been found in Cyprus. A fair amount comes from Olbia, Berezan and Istria on the western coast of the Black Sea. There are several examples from Delos and a few from Aegina. In mainland Greece and further West it is very rare. This is a normal distribution for an East Greek style. The influence of Fikellura was slight; Clazomenian probably borrowed the crescent, and there are a few casual imitations. The list of finding places shows that Fikellura belongs to the southern part of the East Greek region, and it is likely that it was made in both Samos and Rhodes, and perhaps in other places too. But if Fikellura was made in more than one place Samos was probably the leader, since the finds there are of finer quality and the related Ionian Little Masters seem to have been Samian.

Clazomenian and other East Greek Black-figure

The black-figure technique was not used regularly on East Greek pottery till the early sixth century. Then there was a little imitation of Attic and in the Late Wild Goat style much more imitation of Corinthian. From this in the second quarter of the century some North Ionian workshops developed more independent if not very distinguished lines of their own. Of various small schools that called Clazomenian is the best known, since it was occasionally shipped overseas. Most of the others were exported even less, so that we depend on finds in their home cities, of which only those from Smyrna have yet been published conscientiously. Towards the end of the sixth century there was again some imitation, more or less pawky, of current Attic.

Clazomenian, to judge by places of finding, was probably domiciled in or near Clazomenae, an Ionian city some twenty miles west of Smyrna. It is a school which took more note than others of the technique and types of Attic, but was usually content to be decorative. The earliest recognizable group, the Tübingen group, is showy and in character traditionally East Greek with an admixture of Attic. The Petrie group, which is generally rather later, is both more Attic and more original. The Urla group, later still, is their drab and degenerate heir.

The arrangement of the decorative fields follows Attic. In the principal frieze or panel human figures are regular, animals usually occupy secondary fields, vegetable and abstract ornament is less important. The commonest theme is a file of women, each gripping her neighbour's wrist or modestly holding her cloak. Besides these there are satyrs, revellers, sacrificial processions, riders, chariots and occasional excerpts from mythology. There is little interest in anatomy – witness the favourite distortion of the shoulder (as on the boy of PLATE 32B) – or in composition. The fauna comes from the ordinary repertory of black-figure and is generally drawn with a scratchy carelessness, suitable to its inferior position. But more pains are taken when a bird or animal appears on the neck or strays into the main field. The large long-necked birds, feeding in line and occasionally white, are characteristically Clazomenian. Of the ornaments scales containing a large white drop, which may have a dark centre, sometimes fill the main panel; white, or alternately white and purple, crescents on a dark band are normal below the shoulder of the early amphorae; a big palmette with matted incised fringe may occupy the neck, or a lotus and palmette cross take the centre of a field. The quality of the work varies greatly, even on the same pot, and the school has little active character. Of the old Wild Goat style almost nothing remains, there are connections with the Chiot Chalice style, some of the female heads have the shelving East Greek profile, crescents and perhaps scales seem modified from Fikellura. But for the present we cannot define closely the sources of the East Greek idiom of this adaptation of Attic.

The common shapes are various neck-amphorae and a hydria with a flat shoulder that sometimes makes a sharp angle with the belly. Other shapes are a very large low pyxis (reminiscent of an Aeolian Wild Goat form, but with a large domed lid) and some kind of krater or dinos. The typical amphora of the Tübingen group has a general likeness to Fikellura, but with some moulding and handles set on the shoulder; this type is elaborately decorated and often embellished with plastic female heads at the bases of the handles. The amphora illustrated on PLATE 32B, which should be completed with vertical handles and a lowish spreading foot, is the speciality of the Petrie painter, the most robust and able of the Clazomenian vase-painters. The broader amphora of the Urla group follows Attic models of the third quarter of the sixth century.

The clay, which varies in purity, is leathery brown, generally lighter than contemporary Attic. The paint is not far from the Attic standard of blackness and sheen. Purple and white (which is often put directly on the clay) are disposed much as in Attic, except that white is permitted for male flesh [as on PLATE 32B] and is popular for small ornaments like little stars on dresses and rows of dots between a pair of incised lines. This last trick, which goes back indirectly to Corinthian of the beginning of the sixth century, is habitual in Clazomenian. Details on white are usually drawn in dark paint. Incision is careless, if not stupid, more concerned with the creases of the belly than the musculature of the chest.

A fair quantity of Clazomenian has been found at Clazomenae and at Smyrna, and very little elsewhere in the East Greek region. Much comes from Tell Defenneh and Naucratis and some from native sites in Egypt. It is reported from Istria, but seems to be rare; and only a few pieces are published from South Russia. In European Greece it is extremely rare, and there is no certain example from the West. To judge by its style and its association with Attic black-figure and Fikellura at Tell Defenneh, most of the pottery defined above as Clazomenian belongs to the third quarter of the sixth century.

Close to Clazomenian but perhaps made in another city are amphorae and askoi of the miscellaneous *Enmann class* and the more homogeneous *Knipovitch class*. Both use scales with white drops, and the Knipovitch amphorae are fond of the forepart of a winged horse to fill the panel on their sagging bodies. These classes have a rather different distribution, being rare at Clazomenae and Smyrna, but not uncommon at Delos, in South Russia, and in Egypt. A few other pieces are legitimately, if loosely, connected, but the term 'Clazomenian' is still sometimes extended to shelter miscellaneous black-figure works that look even vaguely East Greek: some are earlier East Greek experiments in black-figure, some are feeble imitations of Attic made in other East Greek workshops, and some are Etruscan or Italian Greek. Among these last are the Campana and Northampton groups (mentioned again on p. 158)

Clazomenian sarcophagi

Simple terracotta coffins were used widely in the East Greek region during the sixth century, and about 530 B.C. one or two workshops began to make a more ambitious model. The heavier box was now (like an old-fashioned panelled bath) surmounted by a flat rectangular or trapezoidal frame, the top and edges of which were slipped and decorated. The strips at head and foot were usually painted with figures, the long sidepieces with cable and palmette, and panels at each end of the sidepieces with figures or ornaments. These sarcophagi are pretentious monuments, at best inoffensive but more often vulgar, and their interest is in their retention of a style we should otherwise suppose extinct. For much of the figure decoration – such groups as a lion and a panther posed stiffly about a boar or bull or goat – is in the Wild Goat style, not the modified version of Fikellura but a further degradation of the Late Wild Goat style of the early sixth century [PLATE 31D]. Presumably the tradition, neglected by vase-painters for a generation or more, had survived in textiles. Often also, especially on headpieces, a laborious black-figure style imitates Attic of the last years of the sixth century, but with painted white lines in place of incision; an old-fashioned trait is the rich use of purple and white, without which the individual figures in the groups are hard to separate. The favourite black-figure subjects are battles and chariot races. A few sarcophagi experiment clumsily with the red-figure technique.

Since these sarcophagi are most numerous at Clazomenae and Smyrna and the earliest group has connections with Clazomenian black-figure, they are reasonably called Clazomenian sarcophagi. Most of the hundred and more extant specimens were dug up by peasants and only three have been provided with any context useful for dating, but stylistic comparisons show that they are late and probably they cover the years from about 530 to about 470 B.C. or a little later. The clay is reddish and of the texture of brick, the slip thick and creamy, the paint very dark brown; the white and purple used in the black-figure style have almost always perished. The distribution of these sarcophagi is generally limited to within a few miles of their place of manufacture, though five examples of the latest group were found in the island of Rhodes and one at Acanthus.

The Situlae

Tell Defenneh lies at the east of the Egyptian Delta on a caravan route to Asia and was probably the ancient fortress of Daphnae. There in 1886 Flinders Petrie found with about equal amounts of Attic black-figure, Fikellura and Clazomenian about thirty of what he called *Situlae*. The shape is a tall narrow tube, swelling gradually towards the base and then curving quickly in to a low foot: the lip is flat and wide, and below it, separated by a narrow ridge, are two small handles. The outside is painted dark except for an oblong panel on each side between the handles and for groups of narrow reserved bands which divide the body into three parts.

On most of these situlae the two lower zones are decorated with large pendent lotus flowers or buds and palmettes, incised and picked out in purple (as in Vroulian), and a black-figure subject is put in the panels. The composition usually fits the space – a single kneeling animal, an interlocking group, a symmetrical pair facing across a central ornament. The clay fires from light brown to greyish, and splits badly; the paint is a dark brown with little sheen; purple is used but not white; the wall of the pot is thin. The drawing has an extraordinary range from childish crudity to a vigorous assurance and there is no stylistic unity. Two poor situlae decorated in the same way and of similar fabric have been found at Ialysus in Rhodes. These come from contexts of 500–490 B.C., while those of Tell Defenneh because of the associated pottery should belong to the third quarter or perhaps the middle of the sixth century. The distribution – they hardly occur in the East Greek region and not at all at Naucratis – suggests that this group of situlae was made by Greeks of the second half of the sixth century in the neighbourhood of Tell Defenneh, perhaps at the civil settlement of Stratopeda mentioned by Herodotus. There are a few other Greek pots found in Egypt which from their eccentricity seem also to have been made in Egypt.

A few pieces belong to a stylistically earlier group of situlae, which seem to be the product of a single workshop or painter (PLATE 33A). These are heavier pots, made of a better and browner clay and painted in a neat style which frames its figure panels with affected Subgeometric ornament. Here the lower part of the pot is dark with sparse groups of reserved bands. The places of finding are Rhodes, Tell Defenneh and Memphis. Their date, by comparison with more advanced wares, should be the second quarter of the sixth century. So far Rhodes has the best claim as the home of this group.

The later of these two groups may reasonably be derived by adaptation from the earlier, but their styles cannot generally be traced further back. For the shape there are older models in East Greek pottery, though the series is not yet continuous. From Vroulia in the south of Rhodes there are from contexts of around 600 B.C. a few squat situlae, decorated only with bands and large splashes of paint. Others found on Samos are rather earlier and not much more ornate, except for one which exhibits a competent sample of the Middle II Wild Goat style in the fields between the handles. These situlae from Samos and Vroulia are probably all of local manufacture.

Vroulian

Decoration on a dark instead of a light ground is an obvious though uncommon technique that recurs throughout Greek vase-painting. In the East Greek region it had some popularity from the end of the seventh century, probably in emulation of Corinthian black polychrome. A few Late Wild Goat pots have on the shoulder a lotus chain incised on the dark paint and enlivened with purple and white additions, and Chiot vase-painters made much use of white and purple ornaments painted without incision on the dark inside of chalices and phialai. But the fullest exploitation of dark-ground effects is on a group of cups, which are known as *Vroulian* from the discovery of specimens at Vroulia in Rhodes.

FIG. 23. *Vroulian cup*
Ht 7 cm. Early or middle 6th cent. B.C.

On these cups [FIG. 23] the whole surface is painted over except sometimes for a reserved band at handle level, and the outside – and often the inside too – is covered with large ornaments boldly incised and variegated with purple. The typical ornament is the enclosed palmette, but unenclosed palmettes, lotus flowers, buds and rosettes are common; usually there is a zigzag on the lip and attenuated sets of opposed triangles in the handle frieze (if it is reserved). The shape, still near the cup of Rhodian Late Geometric, has a low offset rim and a narrow conical foot. The clay is fine, firing from yellowish to reddish brown, and the paint near black and shiny. With their thin walls and trim decoration these cups are among the most charming products of East Greek pottery.

A few clumsy amphorae and stamnoi go with the cups. The body is divided into two or three zones by reserved bands and the ornaments are limited to lotus flower and bud and palmette, as on the situlae which probably copied them.

Vroulian pottery has been found throughout Rhodes, where presumably it was made, but there was little export except to Naucratis. Grave groups show that the cups continued from the beginning till the third quarter of the sixth century and that there was no development in the style.

East Greek cups

The cup is very rare in the major East Greek styles – Chiot developed its chalice and the others stuck to large shapes – but drinking vessels were needed and were made in large numbers. Two types had evolved by the end of Geometric, the wide kotyle without a separate lip (from which the popular Bird bowl developed) and the lower cup with short out-turned rim and narrow foot. During the rest of the seventh century this cup continued with little change in shape except for a tendency to a rather higher conical foot, and the type survived till the middle of the sixth century as is shown by the Vroulian cups and by the still more old-fashioned Fikellura cups with ring foot. But in the first half of the sixth century there begins a development parallel to Attic which leads to the canonical lip cup. In the later sixth century the finer East Greek cups disappear.

The decoration consists principally of reserved bands, usually one at handle level (occasionally with hour-glass ornament) and often another below it or on the lip. A small fine group of the late seventh century uses instead white–red–white bands on a dark ground. On the progressive shapes of the early sixth century the decoration too advances until eventually the inside of the lip or even the whole of the bowl is ringed with groups of very fine bands in dilute paint alternating with broader, darker stripes; on the outside of the enlarged lip a garland of doubled myrtle leaves is common. A special class of these cups, the Ionian Little Master cups, has already been discussed (see pp. 129–30.) There are also a few cups and bowls with plastic ornament in low relief in the handle frieze – hands, knucklebones, garlands and suchlike.

The clay varies from a sandy texture and colour to a clear light brown that is close to Attic and the paint ranges similarly from dark brown to near black. Cups of this general type were made at Athens too, Corinth and in the West. The fabrics are not often distinguished and there is a misleading practice of claiming all for East Greek.

Banded wares

Many other pots besides cups were simply decorated with bands of paint. Most are of coarse clay firing from pink to pale brown and very rarely slipped, but some are of shiny orange-brown clay with good near-black paint. Their export has been greatly exaggerated, since there is an inclination to describe as East Greek almost any pot of brownish clay and banded decoration that is found on a colonial site: in fact most of these banded wares have no particular character. It is anyhow unlikely that the plainer East Greek wares were imported where the fancy wares were not.

10. Thasos

Thasos, founded by Parians early in the seventh century, was the oldest and for long the most important Greek city along the southern coast of Thrace. Excavation has been intensive only at Thasos, a sizeable deposit of painted pottery has been discovered at Kavalla (an ancient Neapolis), there is some material from Abdera, and from other sites we have little more than casual finds. Not much has been published.

The principal, though not necessarily the only place in this region where painted pottery might have been made is Thasos, but it is hard to judge how much of what has been found is local, partly because the schools said to be imitated are not themselves well enough known. First, there is a class of Subgeometric pottery, especially cups with sets of concentric circles ringed often by dots and separated by vertical strokes. These cups are of a type which evolve from 'Parian' Late Geometric, and in the south as well as in the northern Aegean seem to have persisted till the late sixth century. Still it is easy to believe that most of those found in Thasos and on the Thracian coast were made locally.

For the late seventh and early sixth centuries much pottery of the 'Melian', Wild Goat and Chiot styles has been discovered in Thasos and on the mainland opposite. Some of this is evidently imported, but there are other pieces of high and even superior quality for which local manufacture has been claimed. The claimants include students who are the most familiar with the finds from Thasos: on the other hand it seems unlikely that several distinct and competing styles were being practised without serious contamination in a single place, even if the practitioners were immigrant craftsmen who arrived with their style already formed. Here analyses of clay might be decisive.

Further, through much of the sixth and into the early fifth century we have a black-figure style based in the main on Attic but on pots not of Attic clay, and this must be local. Though there is some careful work, more is clumsily debased. The frequency among the shapes of lekane and plate is notable.

11. Crete

When towards the end of the eighth century the new Orientalizing movement was felt in Crete, the local Geometric was still strong and healthy and already possessed some of the freehand órnaments – tongues and cables – which were favourites of early Orientalizing elsewhere. So for a time the two styles ran together, combining rather than in competition, and differing not so much in the syntax as in the units of the decoration. Older traditions had delayed the establishment of Geometric in Crete, and now the persistence of Geometric hampered the growth of an original Orientalizing style.

In the first stage of Cretan Orientalizing the decoration is compact and tight. The commonest ornaments are cable patterns, often elaborate; heavy close-set tongues; both leaf and star rosettes; rudimentary volutes and palmettes; lotus flowers and buds, drawn with unusually inorganic abstraction [examples on FIG. 24] – and sometimes flowers are even transformed into bees. Birds are many and varied: the strangest, already known in Late Geometric, are freaks with two or more heads, or bodies split into a 'U' and a forked tail floating loose in the gap. Animal and human figures are few and clumsy. All these are combined readily with such old favourites as concentric circles, and since the old Geometric division into narrow zones and panels is maintained the effect is less of a new independent style than of well-mannered variation on the old theme.

The most curious product of the early Orientalizing style is a group of polychrome pithoi found so far only at Cnossus. They have a thick white slip and are painted, sometimes over the whole surface, in bright red and indigo. Slip and paints, which are matt, are very friable and may have been intended for use only in burials. There are instances where pithoi painted in the ordinary Geometric manner were then slipped and repainted in polychrome. The decoration, painted with a sure but thick brush, appears more consistently Orientalizing than on the unslipped pottery, partly because of the freer use of new ornaments and partly because solid colour often replaces Geometric hatching. In composition the most remarkable experiment is a scene of birds perching in a thicket; the detail is conventional, but there is an appreciation of nature very rare in Greek art. The idea of such polychrome decoration, where the two colours have about equal value, is new to the Greek world and possibly came from Cyprus, to which Orientalizing Crete had other debts.

During the seventh century the Geometric tradition weakened and the Orientalizing style becomes looser and its vegetable ornament more exuberant. Figures, especially sphinxes, are commoner and there are such decorative fancies as long slanting volutes that end in a panther's head. Bees are popular as ornaments; and the row of � solid or in

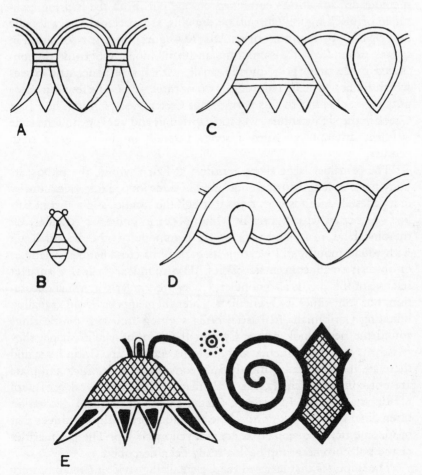

FIG. 24. *Cretan and 'Melian' lotus flowers and buds*
A–D, Cretan: early 7th cent. B.C.   E, 'Melian': late 7th to early 6th cent. B.C.

outline, is characteristic. The drawing occasionally has a delicate charm and a few pieces show something more, but though some Cretan vase-painters were versatile and receptive they lacked direction. So it is diffi-cult to define a Cretan standard, more so even than to define a Protoattic standard; for Attic eccentricity comes largely from its search for a grandeur beyond its powers, but the Cretans spent themselves on novel or curious detail. There is experiment in technique too. Besides the usual dark on light there is much use, especially for Subgeometric decoration, of white paint on a background of dark paint, and the two methods are sometimes combined on one pot. Both the incising technique of black-figure and outline drawing are mastered. Occasionally (anticipating by a century or so Attic red-figure) there is reservation in a dark ground. At the same time an unambitious Subgeometric continued to decorate pots, mostly small, with sparse concentric circles which are now usually reduced to two or three rings. The few Bucchero pots mostly belong to this period. But Cretan vase-painting, like East Greek in the sixth century, was too capricious and uneven, and the style – or the attempts to form a style – petered out in the early sixth century.

The principal large shape remains, at first anyhow, the pithos; its body tends to lengthen and ends often in three looped feet, occasionally in a pedestal. A dinos with rings through the handles and a sort of hatbox (decorated with figures in white) occur in graves at Arkades. Of the oinochoai, many and various, the commonest is the old small jug with round mouth, still wearing its garland of cross-hatched triangles or instead small concentric circles. The round aryballos, a smarter relative of this jug, is also popular; circles are similarly its usual decoration, but sometimes it Orientalizes. Later there appear ovoid aryballoi, imitating Corinthian. Alabastra, often sagging and with plastic rings round the neck, look nearer Cypriot than Corinthian in shape; they mostly have simple Orientalizing patterns. Kotylai ape Corinthian; and there are the usual cups, mostly Subgeometric in style. Dish and plate are not common. Finally, there are many plastic vases and pots with plastic attachments. In general, Cretan shapes like Cretan decoration often differ from Greek norms. The technique ordinarily continues that of Geometric. Occasionally there is a yellowish slip. The peculiarities of the polychrome group have already been described.

The impulses that aroused the Orientalizing style of Cretan pottery came in part from Cyprus, where there are precedents for some of the ornaments (for instance the form of the lotus), various shapes and the polychrome technique; and some of the plump flasks with a great set of circles on each side are frank copies of Cypriot. Later and increasingly Cretan imitated Corinthian. The doctrine, once widely held, that the Greek Orientalizing style was established first in Crete and from there transmitted to Corinth is for painted pottery untenable, even though some of the Orientalizing forms appear less Hellenized in Cretan than in other schools: the chronology of the ending of Geometric, now worked out in fair detail, is decisive. For metalwork and perhaps for sculpture Crete was more important, but its vase-painting in spite of some engaging originality was not progressive.

Cretan exports, almost all Subgeometric, have a limited range. They are least infrequent in the neighbouring islands of Thera and Rhodes, and there are a few pieces from Gela, founded by Cretans and Rhodians about 690 B.C., Ischia, Cumae and Tocra. Reports of finds in the Peloponnese and Etruria need to be checked. There was a little connection between Cretan and Cycladic. Resemblances in the Italocorinthian of Etruria, as in the shape of one type of alabastron, are probably accidental. A fair amount of Corinthian and some Cypriot were imported and had their effects.

12. Italy

After the Geometric period first Corinth and then Athens dominated the market for Greek pottery. This appears more clearly in the West than round the Aegean, where there was more competition from established local schools. Some Cretan Subgeometric and rather more East Greek of the southern Wild Goat style have turned up at Gela, a joint colony of Cretans and Rhodians, a little East Greek occurs at Catania, Syracuse and Selinus, and in sixth-century Italy there is a sprinkling of Laconian; but other exceptions to the rule of Corinthian and Attic are very rare, unless of course 'Chalcidian' came from Chalcis. In general for their better-painted pottery the Greeks of the colonies imported, those natives who had adopted a Geometric style continued it, and the Etruscans both imported and imitated.

Ischia and *Cumae*, just north of the bay of Naples, are the earliest and most distant of the Greek colonies known in Italy. In their cemeteries have been found not only much imported Protocorinthian but also imitations of Protocorinthian of the late eight and the seventh centuries. These imitations, presumably made locally, can often be distinguished by a wilder or clumsier style and by their coarser clay which is sometimes disguised by a yellowish slip. But the distinction is not always clear. At Ischia the local school appears to have persisted through the seventh century; the evidence from Cumae needs to be examined afresh.

At *Megara Hyblaea, Syracuse, Gela* and perhaps at other sites in Sicily and South Italy local workshops tried the Orientalizing as well as the Subgeometric style. Their models were generally Corinthian.

Most of this local pottery is unassuming, though recognizable by the clay and sometimes by the presence of a slip, but it is only at Megara Hyblaea that – thanks to conscientious excavators – we know much about it. Here manufacture of decorated ware decreased rapidly in quantity after the first quarter of the seventh century, when Sub-geometric was becoming unfashionable, and had finished by its end. For the earlier part of this period Sicilian workshops exploited the Orientalizing style most eagerly on larger pots, in which the parent Corinthian school was deficient, and during the generation around 650 B.C. they produced some figured polychrome work of erratic grandeur. The character of this polychrome decoration is much less dependent on Corinthian but other sources are no more evident and polychromy – that is the addition of a light brown to the range of colours – occurred in several schools of that time. Perhaps we should give most credit to local originality, but anyhow production was too small to allow a coherent style to develop. After this experiment we have nothing better than straightforward and sometimes competent imitation of the Animal style of Corinth. On the present evidence it is reasonable to suppose that the bulk of the colonial wares found at Megara Hyblaea were made there, but we do not know how far other Greek colonies in the West engaged in local production of decorated pottery. The kraters of the Fusco group suggest something similar at Syracuse, where they were found. One of them has on it a couple of tolerable figures, but most are tamely Subgeometric or develop simple Orientalizing motives with heavy-handed incomprehension. Before colonial vase-painting was considered credible, the Fusco kraters were often attributed to Argos; but though there are some resemblances, they could be provincially independent variations on the Corinthian repertory. Their date should be in the second quarter of the seventh century. In the late sixth and early fifth centuries a little poor imitation of Attic black-figure seems to have been attempted here and there in South Italy and Sicily, most notably in Campania. But unless 'Chal-cidian' was made in one of the Western colonies, no important local school took root there before the middle of the fifth century.

The *native Sicilians*, so long as they were not submerged by the Greeks, continued even into the fifth century a weakening Geometric tradition, varied occasionally by more modern borrowings. In south-east Italy the *Apulian* style, though freely taking Greek motives, kept its barbaric independence till the fourth century. The *Lucanian* style is related. Central Italy belonged to the Etruscans.

The *Etruscans* in the seventh and sixth centuries were expanding their dominion, and in spite of local divergences and survivals the culture they imposed was fairly uniform. If they had been settled elsewhere before they emerged in Italy, they brought with them no tradition in pottery but made do with old Italian practices and Greek example. The primitive pots of the native Italians had been made of coarse gritty clay, shaped by hand, and uncertainly fired. Acquaintance with Greek processes – and presumably immigrant craftsmen – introduced better levigation, use of the potter's wheel and control of firing; but the older tradition was not discarded and Etruscan pottery (or pottery made in Etruscan territory) has a remarkable range of technical quality. In the shapes some old favourites continued, often refined under Greek influence, Greek imports were directly imitated or adapted, and there was much unmistakable reproduction of metal forms. For decoration the

FIG. 25. 'Phoenician' palmette

Scale 1 : 2. Italocorinthian: late 7th cent. B.C. Black polychrome technique: the pattern is incised on a dark ground and embellished with added purple (here hatched) and white (here black)

models were mainly Greek, since though the early Etruscans welcomed objects of Oriental as well as of Greek art the pottery was Greek: even so, such ornaments as the 'Phoenician' palmette (FIG. 25) may not have come to them from Greek artists. This Etruscan pottery, which varies from more or less close copies of Greek to clumsy barbarisms, can be roughly divided into fabrics with a light ground (whether produced by a slip or of a ware that is light throughout) and those with a dark ground: the former are decorated by painting which is often careful and ambitious, on the latter incised and relief ornament is more common and painted decoration is generally rough and unskilled. Though our concern is with the finer of the light-ground groups, it would be unkind to pass over the finest of the dark-ground; for the Etruscans were not at their best in pottery, and their one excellence is in their Bucchero.

Light-ground painted pottery first appears in Etruria decorated in the Geometric style and was presumably borrowed with it. This

Etruscan Geometric (mentioned already on p. 39) continued vigor-ously till the middle of the seventh century, and offshoots (often degenerate) survived longer in remote districts. Meanwhile by 700 B.C. the *Italocorinthian* style had begun its prolific copies and adaptations of Corinthian imports. Rather before the middle of the sixth century this in turn gave way under Attic influence to *Etruscan black-figure*, which lasted to the middle of the fifth century. But Etruscan vase-painting was not yet done, and turned to a *red-figure* style that even outlived its Attic parent. Remoteness in space, which made Greek imports expen-sive, and the size of the home market rather than artistic or patriotic appeal are reasons for this remarkable persistence of what is one of the lesser schools of Greek painted pottery. As for *Bucchero*, the most original product of Etruscan workshops, its heyday was from the middle of the seventh to the second quarter of the sixth century. There remain two notable classes of painted pots, '*Chalcidian*' and the *Caeretan hydriai*, one the product of a school, the other of a single workshop: their styles are unmistakably Greek and so many scholars believe that their makers worked in Greek lands, but I think it more likely that here we have Greek vase-painters who were settled in Italy and more precisely – anyhow for the hydriai – in Etruria. There are signs of a few other such settlers.

Although the Etruscans imported a great quantity of Greek pottery their own wares had a market overseas. Italocorinthian was exported to Cumae, Carthage and the Greek outpost of Emporion in Spain. Bucchero deservedly had a wider market and finds – mainly of kan-tharoi – are known also from Greek Sicily, at Emporion, and occasion-ally even from Greece itself and the Aegean. 'Chalcidian' naturally appealed more directly to Greek taste; it was popular in South Italy and reached the western Mediterranean. But it is easy to exaggerate the scale of the Etruscan industry; for though its products are numerous in the museums of western Europe, that is because so large a part of their con-tents have come from the cemeteries of Etruria. Unfortunately, useful contexts have not often been recorded, and so the dating of all these wares depends on stylistic comparisons with Corinthian and Attic. There may sometimes be more lag in the chronology than is suspected.

Italocorinthian

The Etruscans were great admirers and imitators of Corinthian painted pottery so long as it remained fashionable. Their imitations, which are called Italocorinthian, vary widely in technical and artistic fidelity, according to the difficulty of the model followed and the competence of the Etruscan craftsman. Some, especially those in the Subgeometric and Linear styles, are truly Corinthian in character and can be distinguished only by their clay; a large and showy class travesties the Ripe Animal style; others enlarge the repertory with forms unknown in Corinth; and beyond these stretch outlying groups in which Corinthian influence gradually becomes unrecognizable.

The earliest Italocorinthian begins by 700 B.C., since it depends on Early Protocorinthian. Till about the middle of the seventh century the principal shape is the oinochoe of the type of PLATE 8C; here the Etruscan painters sometimes catch the spirit of their models. There are also aryballoi, but for other shapes the Italian Geometric style remains much more usual. This is not surprising, since even in Corinth the Proto-corinthian style had a limited scope. But when in the later seventh century the Corinthians turned towards mass production of an Animal style the Etruscan workshops followed eagerly and for two generations or more did a roaring trade in this and simpler lines. With a little prac-tice it is easy to distinguish by style between genuine Corinthian and most Italocorinthian. Compare the lions of FIGS. 6 and 26, especially their heads. The Etruscan workman is not very sensitive to the logical rules, nor always to the conventions, of his Greek model. So in Italo-corinthian we often find figures grotesquely proportioned, shoulder markings converted into meaningless rings, creatures with three wings, stridently particoloured animals and human legs dangling from a lion's mouth. Greek figures are credibly constructed, Etruscan more often are not.

In the later part of the seventh century the range of Italocorinthian widens. The typical large shape is now the olpe, usually with Animal or black polychrome decoration; in the latter group big overlapping semicircles or 'Phoenician' palmettes [FIG. 25] often replace the more orthodox scales, which themselves are larger than in Corinthian. Oinochoai, with animals or simple bands and tongue pattern, are also common. The amphorae are more erratic. Plates are mostly of the sixth century. The cup is rather deeper than the Corinthian shape; a popular sixth-century group has on the lip the Laconian squares and dots [as PLATE 26B] and in the handle frieze a row of balloon-bodied birds. The pointed aryballos with its heavy foot is succeeded before 600 by an ordinary round aryballos; another variety has a round body drawn out below into a point, much like a lemon. The common alabastron is of Corinthian shape, often rather flatter at the base. There is also a very long alabastron with flat bottom, as if it had been sawn off near the middle. Many of the alabastra are embellished with a bolster round the neck, and bodies are sometimes channelled or ridged. On these small pots Linear decoration remains common: the effect is sometimes indistinguishable from Corinthian, sometimes remote with clumsy banding and (especially on the pointed shapes) a prominent band of herring-bone ornament. Human figures occur on a few late pots. The technique varies as much as the style. Sometimes a fine clay is used, firing from a light cream (which differs from Corinthian in a slightly muddier tone) to a

FIG. 26. *Italocorinthian olpe*
Ht 26·8 cm. Late 7th or early 6th cent. B.C.

dull medium brown; sometimes, especially for larger pots, the ware is coarse and pink with a cream slip. The dark paint is usually duller and thinner than Corinthian; and purple and white are rather more freely applied. Dating is uncertain, since it is mostly by style. This allows a rough estimate of when a foreign model was first imitated, not how long imitation continued. But it does not seem that Italocorinthian, strictly defined, much outlasted the middle of the sixth century.

The dominant factor in Italocorinthian is Corinthian. There is some borrowing from other styles at home in Etruria, a little from Laconian, and a residue not yet explained. Particoloured animals are known earlier in Cycladic, but may be independent. A few resemblances to Cretan are probably accidental. It is not clear whether early Italocorinthian is related to Cumaean directly or by sharing common models. Though several groups and painters have been disentangled, there is so far not much clear evidence for local schools. Artistically trivial, it could not compete on equal terms with Corinthian. So outside Etruscan territory it is found only at Cumae, Carthage and Emporion in Spain; the stray oddments from Provence, Megara Hyblaea and Rhegium are insignificantly few.

Etruscan bucchero

Bucchero (or Grey ware) had long been popular in Aeolis when Etruscan bucchero first emerged. There seems to have been no direct connection in shape and decoration, nor yet in technique. Anyhow in Etruria the development of the bucchero technique can be traced from traditional Italian wares; the clay is refined and the reduction in firing, previously perhaps accidental, is in the end deliberate and complete. Good specimens are in this way fired throughout to a dark grey with a shiny blackish surface, but the colour ranges to a light and sometimes yellowish grey. Though there are, especially in the seventh century, many partially reduced pots (mostly with brown surface and pale core) which differ from bucchero only in the degree of reduction – a difference that is not obvious in photographs – it is fair to speak of a bucchero style, which was compounded for this fine variety of Etruscan dark-ground ware. In spite of the great quantity of Etruscan bucchero its history has been neglected and so the sketch that follows is tentative.

The earliest distinctly bucchero pottery of Etruria appears about the middle of the seventh century. In the first stage, which covers the third quarter of that century, the technique is often excellent, the shapes finely conceived and executed, the decoration (where desired) relies on simple ornaments boldly incised or neatly pricked out. By 600 B.C. increasing Greek influence has modified the shapes, which are now more refined but tamer; decoration has shrunk to groups of bands lightly incised; the technical quality, though still good, is often duller. In the next stage refinement gives way to clumsy ostentation, and before the middle of the sixth century the typical bucchero is a lumpish pot with a roughly incised zigzag or heavy-handed plastic decoration. In another generation the style was dead and the technique of reduction relegated to kitchen ware.

The common shapes are amphorae, oinochoai, olpai, cup, kantharos, kyathos, handleless chalice. In the seventh century the typical amphora (or rather amphoriskos), a little pot related to a Villanovan shape, is remarkable for a high neck wide at the base but contracting to the top and the ribbon handles which reach from shoulder to lip; the body, standing on a rudimentary foot, is at first globular but in time tautens and becomes egg-shaped. During the sixth century a large orthodox neck-amphora is current. Contemporary with the Villanovan amphora is an 'olpe', differing from it only by having a single high handle. Oinochoai with trefoil mouth are very numerous; an early variety with narrow neck tapering upwards (not unlike the Ithacan type) does not last long; more canonical is the jug with a wide, often flaring neck and

FIG. 27. *Etruscan bucchero kantharos*
Ht 11·6 cm. Later 7th or early 6th cent. B.C.

egg-shaped body – this shape is still common about 600 B.C.; overlapping in time with this is a new form with elliptical or barrel-shaped body and a stronger foot; from this develops a high heavy pot, often very large and encrusted with plastic decoration. An olpe of Corinthian type has a short run near the end of the seventh century. The kotyle is only early. The cup, much of the shape of FIG. 4B, is common in the later seventh century. The kantharos with tall upright handles and a highish splayed foot [as in FIG. 27] begins to be popular in the last quarter of that century; late examples tend to be clumsier. The kyathos, which has as long a career, takes many forms. There is also the chalice, a thick-walled handleless pot with high lip and shallow bowl like the kantharos; sometimes it has a long pedestal, more often a splayed foot or a mere ring foot. Some of the bucchero shapes have obvious prototypes in Greek pottery, and others show its influence. The Villanovan amphora is a refinement of a native Italian type. The kantharos has a Greek look, but no Greek kantharos of fired clay and so elegant a shape is as early; the model, wherever it came from, was of metal. The pedestalled chalice evidently copies an Oriental ivory form of which examples occur in Etruria. The tapering oinochoe may originate in Syria. Generally there appears to be much imitation of metalwork, and some early bucchero pots were covered with silver leaf; but it is going too far to claim that the black surface itself imitates metal, unless of course the Etruscans had a perverted taste for tarnish.

Decoration, anyhow till the late stage, is subordinate to the shape and often omitted. In the early period the medium is incision – a bold double spiral on the belly of the amphora, hatched or boxed rays round the shoulder or base of oinochoai, a broad band of vertical striations round the belly. Other incised ornaments are neat horizontal zigzags, rosettes, birds and even the horse. Characteristic too are fan patterns, closed or open, pricked with a notched tool. Sometimes, regularly perhaps if preservation or cleaning had been more kind, the incised line is filled with white or red paint. Late Bucchero erupts too often into heavy relief decoration – thick tongues for instance on the shoulder of an oinochoe and round the belly Orientalizing beasts, pressed into moulds and clumsily modelled; or, especially on chalices, a roller stamp repeats a narrow series of negligent little figures or ornaments. In general the models for bucchero decoration, incised or relief, are Greek and probably from painted pottery; but the fan patterns seem to be original, and some at least of the stamped motives may be Oriental. There was also in Etruria, as in the East Greek region, a little coloured bucchero – that is bucchero with decoration painted in white and purple (and sometimes blue) over the dark ground; this *Polledrara group* takes its name from an ambitious hydria in the British Museum, Corinthianizing work little earlier than the middle of the sixth century and incidentally not itself properly bucchero, since its dark surface is painted over a pink clay.

Bucchero is common throughout Etruscan Italy and was probably made in many places; Caere may have been the pioneer and later Chiusi (Clusium) was perhaps the centre for relief ware. There was some export, especially of the elegant kantharoi. Finding places include Marseilles, Narbonne, Emporion, Cumae, Tarentum, Megara Hyblaea, Syracuse, Gela, Selinus, Motya, Carthage, Corcyra, Ithaca, Corinth and nearby Perachora, Athens, Delos and Rheneia, Naxos in the Cyclades, Chios,

Smyrna, Samos and Rhodes. The quantity is often respectable in the West, very small across the Adriatic, though even there its range is greater than that of the Greek bucchero of Aeolis.

Etruscan Black-figure

In the second quarter of the sixth century Attic imports replaced Corinthian in the Etruscan market and set a new standard for local imitation. The first Etruscan workshop which regularly produced Atticizing ware seems by comparison with Attic to have begun rather before 550 B.C. In general Etruscan black-figure painters were careless draughtsmen and did not fully comprehend the style of their models, nor always the subjects. Floral ornaments are disintegrated and reformed in a more abstract spirit, sometimes [as on PLATE 34] with pleasing results. Inner detail tends to be inorganic. Groups are often made up of stock figures in meaningless relations, and Greek mythology – naturally enough – is sometimes mixed. What we have in the earlier phase of Etruscan black-figure is not so much copying as adaptation.

Pontic is the most attractive and probably the earliest school. The name, given in the hope that the place of making was some Greek colony of the Black Sea, has survived for want of a better and because there is no genuinely Pontic vase-painting to dispute it. The style is based on Attic, as exhibited in Etruria by the Tyrrhenian amphorae. So in Pontic too the staple shape is the neck-amphora, with its principal field on the shoulder. Two more fields on the belly and another on the neck display rows of animals or ornaments. The decoration is completed by long rays round the base and sometimes a band of pattern on the lip. Distinctive motives are single or doubled band of meander and star, net pattern (especially on the lip), partridges, sea-horses and Tritons, and panthers with blank white eyes like headlamps. The drawing of outline and detail is weak, and the effect depends on diffusing the decoration and enlivening it with much purple and white. At its best Pontic has a cheerful gaiety, more often it is passably decorative, and towards the end as recent Attic fashion intrudes and colour becomes sparser it appears monotonous and dull. PLATE 34 shows a fair specimen.

Though Attic is the basis of Pontic, there are other constituents. The neck-amphora is derived from Attic of the second quarter of the sixth century, but the chalice and some oinochoai take their shape from Etruscan bucchero. Etruscan too are the pointed coifs worn by some female figures, the motley animals with legs of different colours and (though not exclusively) such details as boots with up-turned toes. The lanky birds that often attend human figures have a Laconian look, and the partridges apparently come from East Greek. Other motives that are not Attic, as for instance pomegranates, may not be directly imported, since they occur already in native Italocorinthian. The rejection of the Attic male eye could be the painters' whim or indolence, and general resemblances to East Greek are so vague that they may well be accidental. The plants, natural or abstract, that sprout in figure scenes, perhaps reflect Etruscan taste. Towards the end the Caeretan hydriai had a little influence. In short there is very little direct foreign influence besides Attic.

The Pontic workshop flourished for about fifty years. So far as is known, none of its pots has been found outside Etruscan lands. Whether by origin the painters were Greek or Etruscan is unimportant; as painters they were Etruscan. Some of their details are at the time characteristic of Etruria, no intimate stylistic relation has been discovered to any Greek school, and technical proficiency is too low for craftsmen trained in a reputable Greek workshop. The rather muddy clay varies from dirty yellow to pink. Often there is a yellowish slip. The paint, brownish black with some sheen, is applied unevenly and for that reason or because of bad firing is often discoloured.

Other Etruscan exponents of black-figure are more progressive and less successful. They prefer large fields, and any subsidiary decoration is modest. Their figures are in consequence large and few and exposed to undistracted inspection. The animals are more passable than the human types. The *Ivy group*, which apparently belongs to the third quarter of the sixth century, specializes in the one-piece amphora with a mythological excerpt in the panel or a straddling lay-figure swinging monstrous ivy leaves. The painter follows the Attic style with some care and even attempts the Attic form of the male eye. His lumbering short-legged men have a likeness to those of the Affecter. The shapes of oinochoai and some small pots belong to Etruria, but in the drawing it is the general flavour that is Etruscan rather than specific details. The unassuming style, which makes some use of white and purple, has a dry merit. The *La Tolfa group*, running rather later, prefers a neck-amphora with simple ornament on the neck and a single human or animal figure spreadeagled across the panel on the body. Here the Attic influence is more remote, though the painters advance to a more plastic representation of folds. The last few years of the sixth century and the beginning of the fifth are dominated by the *Micali painter*. Prolific and usually negligent, he has a repertory of solid figures and ornaments. Inner detail is inconsequent and sometimes omitted, or white lines may replace incision. White and purple additions are scanty. His favourite shape is the neck-amphora with a main field on the belly and a minor on the shoulder, or with a single field covering both; often the rest of the pot is covered with dark paint. He also makes good use of the hydria. Other painters of this time turn out some respectable imitations of Attic, but their successors, who continue till the middle of the fifth century, become more abject and incompetent. Generally they ape the black-figure and even red-figure fashions of contemporary Athens, so far as that can be done in a technique dependent largely on silhouette with or without inner detail of white lines.

The technical and artistic skill of Etruscan vase-painters is not high. The shapes are often badly proportioned and the painting and firing uneven. The clay ranges in colour from yellowish grey to pink and is not always well refined. Sometimes there is a slip, normally yellowish, but in the Micali group reddish brown. The paint varies in darkness and is rather dull. Differences of this kind appear in the works of each of the major painters and so help little towards locating workshops. But it is anyhow likely that the home of the Etruscan black-figure industry was in one of the large cities near the coast. Later, to judge by distribution and inferior style, there were workshops at Orvieto and Chiusi.

Though much Etruscan black-figure has been preserved, the painters were few. It is not surprising that their products are very rarely found outside Etruria.

'Chalcidian'

The school known as 'Chalcidian' appears suddenly about the middle and continues till the end of the sixth century. Its dating depends on stylistic comparisons with Attic, which are close enough to be reliable to a few years. The founder of the school, the Inscription painter, was an artist with an unusual and decorative sense of mass as opposed to line. The contours of his figures are less important than the areas they contain, inner detail is restricted and overlapping is unwelcome. In composition there is a conscious balance of dark painted and light unpainted surface. Shape and decoration are carefully related. It is not surprising that this painter is more at ease in conversation pieces, of which PLATE 36 gives a good example, adapted to serve as Hector's farewell. The shapes of his pots, their large fields, and the repertory of figures and ornaments come generally from Attic, but he impressed them with his own character. His younger contemporaries and followers observed his standard as best they could, adding from time to time new borrowings from Attic. In the second generation the Phineus painter, who adopted the relief line, retained a feeling for mass in his figures, but combined it with calligraphy in his ornament, especially on the outside of his admirable eye-cups. His repetitive types have a uniform elegance with their chirpy poses, weak profiles and, if female, rouged cheeks. Charming but mannered, he did not inspire successors.

' The system of decoration, as was normal in the modern schools of mature black-figure, displays large figures in a deep field, sometimes bordered by narrower bands of ornament, sometimes panelled in a dark ground. Scenes of heroic and mythical action are less frequent than groups of stock male and female figures, and on lesser works of all painters the animal style often recurs. Two typical subjects are the frontal quadriga (or four-horse chariot) and lions or panthers mauling a deer. In the drawing of the figures detail is usually scanty and sometimes mean. Draped figures tend to reveal their back contour, like the Helen of PLATE 36. The shape of the head exaggerates a widespread trend towards receding foreheads and longer skulls. Female eye-balls are often purple. Of ornaments the most characteristic is the great square of interlaced lotus (or ivy) and palmette, erected in the centre of a main field. The chain of lotus flowers and buds, of the plump type shown on PLATE 36, is popular for subsidiary bands or to fill the neck of smaller neck-amphorae.

The principal shapes are the large neck-amphora, the hydria, the column-krater and later the cup. Of less artistic importance are the smaller neck-amphora and oinochoe. Among other shapes are one-piece amphora, kotyle, pyxis and even the psykter. The modelling of the finer pieces is excellent and corresponds to the best Attic of the third quarter of the sixth century. The clay is fine and its colour ranges from yellowish orange towards a reddish brown. The paint is shiny, and near-black or golden brown according to its density. The use of purple and white conforms more or less to Attic custom. In all this the effect is, deliberately, very like Attic, though the firing is less sure. But there are also differences of technique. In painting figures the 'Chalcidian' practice, at least on more careful works, was first to apply a thinnish coat and then to daub over it a thicker, which does not reach the edges. Sometimes, when a dark neck was wanted, the pot was dipped upside down in a bowl of paint: such dark necks were often embellished with a wavy line of purple.

'Chalcidian' borrows heavily from Attic, but the borrowing was intermittent: this is particularly clear in the folds of drapery, which show no development but jump from one Attic stage to another. In the early phase Corinthian legacies are visible, though most of these probably came through Attic. As the style develops a few details suggest a flavouring of East Greek or Etruscan. But 'Chalcidian' has a positive character of its own, less disciplined and precise than the Attic standard, but more fluent and more decorative. It is the only properly black-figure school of the second half of the sixth century which stands comparison with that of Athens.

The distribution of 'Chalcidian' is unusual. It is relatively frequent in Etruria, a large find of sherds was made at Rhegion, and there are several other pieces from South Italy and Sicily. A very little comes from Marseilles and Emporion in Spain. But in spite of false alarms from Chalcis no example has certainly been discovered east of the Adriatic. Two dependents of 'Chalcidian', the Memnon and the Polyphemus groups, occur in Etruria and, more rarely, in South Italy and Sicily. There is no other plainly discernible influence of 'Chalcidian'.

The home of 'Chalcidian' is disputed. The relevant facts are its style, influence and distribution, and its painted inscriptions which by alphabet and dialect effectively limit the candidates to Chalcis in Euboea (which has been explored only casually), to some Chalcidian colony in the West, or to a Chalcidian or colonial workshop in Etruria. The more valid arguments are for Chalcis that the quality is too good for Western manufacture, for the West the absence of specimens in Greece and of influence on the receptive schools of Eretria and Boeotia. The Western claim seems to me the stronger, but a closer localization is difficult. Numerically Rhegion has the advantage, but the frequency of 'Chalcidian' there – most of them from a single deposit – may be accidental and its extreme rarity at the well-excavated site of Megara Hyblaea suggests a more distant place of manufacture. Perhaps, in spite of its quality, the school was settled in Etruria.

There are similar doubts about some other groups of pottery so far found only in Etruria. The very small *Northampton group* aims at Attic standards, but has a few resemblances to East Greek as well as some kinship with the art of Etruria. Its quality is good, and its date apparently in the 530s. The *Campana group*, clumsier and a little younger, has stronger connections both with East Greek and Etruscan. Both these groups and the Caeretan hydriai (discussed in the next pages) are by some assigned to the east Aegean, though it is difficult to find a place for them there. Again the opinion seems to me more credible that their makers were Greek settlers in Etruria.

Caeretan Hydriai

A group of more than thirty hydriai and fragments of hydriai, most of them found at Caere in Etruria, are known as Caeretan Hydriai. Their painter (or painters, if there were two of them) must be counted among the great archaic masters. An adequate draughtsman with a good eye for colour, he excels by his flair for comic expression: when his subject is conventional, he is often mediocre.

The standard hydria, a sturdy well-balanced pot about eighteen inches high, shows some influence of metal vases. Its shape and system of decoration appear clearly on PLATE 35; inside the lip there is usually a deep band of thick purple and white tongues. The emphasis is on the belly with its large field in front and two shorter fields behind on either side of the vertical handle. On one piece the secondary frieze below also contains figures. The most famous of these hydriai is the Busiris vase in Vienna; Heracles, a hefty nude of little intrinsic interest, massacres the puny white-shirted Egyptians, who are drawn with a venomous ridicule that contrasts with the stolid dignity of the negro slaves coming to their aid on the other side. Other good pieces have Heracles bringing Cerberus to the terrified Eurystheus, griffin and Arimaspian, the battle with the hydra. Besides mythology there are hunts, battles and conventional groups. Generally the figures are solid and fleshy, and their motions rather jerky. The ornaments are drawn broadly but surely, with a gay reliance on added purple and white. No artist better exploits the narrow formulas of Archaic vase-printing.

The clay varies from a light yellowish brown to a warm brown and even to orange-red; such a range is more usual in Etruscan than Greek pottery. Besides the shiny dark paint, purple and white are used freely and arbitrarily; a light buff also occurs on the Busiris hydria for the flesh of some of the Egyptians. The bright colours and ample figures suggest, perhaps wrongly, a connection with free painting.

The Caeretan master was an individualist who belongs to no known school but his own. So it is hard to place him or to date him exactly. The style of his drapery suggests that he was active in the last third of the sixth century. Opinions differ on where he worked. None of his pieces (so far as can be proved) has been found outside Caere and perhaps Vulci, so that some think his workshop was there; others who find it unthinkable that such masterpieces of Greek art could be painted in Etruria settle him on the coast of Asia Minor – at unknown Phocaea, for example – or compromise on a Greek city of South Italy. The argument for Caere is to me convincing. But the Caeretan master was a Greek; if his style and subjects are not proof enough, there is also a Greek inscription painted by him on a hydria certainly rescued from the cellars of the Louvre. The common view is that he was an Ionian, though for the figures at least there are parallels on the contemporary terracotta altars of a Corinthian painter; it is anyhow safe to say that the Caeretan master was not trained in Athens, but we know too little of later sixth-century painting elsewhere to define his connections exactly. The only certain signs of his influence are on some Etruscan black-figure pots, and there are a few connections with wall-paintings in Etruscan tombs.

Campanian Black-figure

A number of black-figure works have been recognized as Campanian, though attributions are not always agreed. ¡The earlier class, of the late sixth and the first half of the fifth century, is related to and in part dependent on Etruscan black-figure – not surprisingly since the Etruscans then held Campania. Though sometimes lively in its effect, the quality of draughtsmanship is very provincial. There seems to be no continuity to the later Pagenstecher class of Campanian black-figure, of which little is known. Here the most familiar shape is a kind of lekythos or bottle, often decorated with a clumsy, plump bird but occasionally imitating red-figure groups with some elegance. White lines may replace incision. The date is roughly the last third of the fourth century and manufacture may have extended to Sicily.

13. The Eastern Fringes

Some of the eastern neighbours of the Greeks were influenced by their art. In *Lydia* and less certainly in *Caria* and further East there was more or less straight though not very competent imitation of Greek styles (cf. p. 125), in Lydia sometimes combined with local patterns. *Phrygia* had an Animal style of its own, which has resemblances to the East Greek Wild Goat style but began earlier. Presumably, because of the striking difference in the filling ornament, the relationship is mainly collateral, though odd instances of Greek borrowing from Phrygia had occurred in the late eighth century. *Lemnos*, an island in the north-east Aegean which probably did not become Greek till the sixth century, drew eclectically on Greek sources for its earlier painted pottery and occasionally developed them adventurously.

5 The Red-figure Style

1. Introduction

In the mature work of Exekias the black-figure technique reached –
and perhaps passed – its limits, and artists interested in the new problems of a more natural anatomy and the expression of mood needed a
freer medium. They found it in the red-figure technique, by which the
figure was drawn in outline on a light ground, inner detail marked by
the brush instead of the burin, and the background filled in with solid
black. Something of the sort was inevitable. Outline drawing with
painted linear detail was a common practice in free painting and an
occasional variation on contemporary black-figure pottery; black-figure
artists were used to dark detail on figures painted in white; and the
black background, desirable in itself to give the drawing prominence
on the retreating surfaces of a pot, had parallels in relief sculpture
(where the background was coloured red or blue) as well as on some
painted slabs. The important question is not how, but why artists came
to choose the red-figure technique; for it was a choice made by artists
to suit themselves and not to satisfy the market, where for another
generation or more black-figure was as popular as ever.

The red-figure style was founded on line drawing, independent of
colour or shading, but (what is not always evident in the familiar black-
and-white reproductions) two kinds of line were very quickly distinguished. One is the flat line, which may be diluted to a light brown.
But to emphasize major details vase-painters preferred a fine ridge of
shiny black that can be felt by the finger – the 'relief line' [see PLATE
37A]. This was not a new invention, since for a generation it had been
popular in black-figure in such humble places as the divisions in bands
of tongue pattern; but its importance is new and gives a peculiar precision to the earlier red-figure work. Incision was not at once entirely
renounced; for about thirty years it was commonly used to outline
black hair against the black background, and it occurs even later.
Accessory colour was for a century very modestly applied. Purple was
convenient for such things as fillets and for the inscriptions in the field
where reserving the letters would have been tiresome; but white is rare,
even for the hair of old men. In the late fifth century an ornate taste

erupted into white-and-gold embellishments, and later still white was used freely for flesh. Occasionally a brown wash of the diluted paint picks out a small area. Other colours appeared now and then, particularly in works influenced by free painting, and became regular on the white-ground pottery of the middle and later fifth century.

The red-figure technique was invented about 530 B.C. in Athens. The earliest exponents had of course been trained in the black-figure style, and their first red-figure ventures are not much more than translations from black-figure. But within ten years the character of the new style is clear, even though many of the red-figure painters of the first generation were working in black-figure too, sometimes – especially for the inside and outside of cups – using both techniques on the same pot. The black-figure technique is an admirable medium for puppets, whose jerky movements and (for white men) unnatural colouring set them apart in a conventional world of their own. The red-figure technique permits a rounder illusion of humanity and the human figure becomes a subject to be studied for itself, not as a component of some scene of action or decorative grouping. The formula inherited from black-figure was that head and limbs should be in profile and the upper part of the body either in profile or frontal, the waist there acting as a simple pivot. By the end of the sixth century the leading artists could show the twisting of the waist and of other parts of the body; so we get three-quarter chests and backs, frontal legs and feet, and in kneeling figures the masking of the lower leg by the thigh. But in spite of the interest in foreshortening and complicated poses the general direction and grouping of figures remains in the plane of the picture. At the same time the details of ribs and musculature were being more closely studied. The next generation of vase-painters, brought up to the new views, was less aggressive in displaying them; their figures have an easy suppleness and grace, and still are at home on the surface of a pot. In this period, the first thirty years of the fifth century, the art of painted pottery reaches its highest level, judged by the accepted standard of Greek beauty. Further development – and Greek art had a long tradition of development – could only be towards fuller modelling of the figure, subtler expression of mood and composition in three dimensions, in fact towards free painting which was at last advancing rapidly. Great artists might perhaps have adapted this new pictorial vision to the requirements of pottery, but vase-painting was sinking to a minor art and soon it no longer produced or attracted great artists. So in the mid-fifth century Attic vase-painters range from mannerists trying to perpetuate the style of their predecessors to the admirers of free painting with their grandiose figures and sometimes grandiose compositions; the best work of this period, calm and refined, tends to be academic. The innovators of the late fifth century are content with prettiness or ape the florid, of which the culmination is the Midian school with its lavish display of white and gold. But a soberer classicism survived, till in the middle years of the fourth century a more loose and pictorial style brought a new spirit to Attic workshops. Even so, by 320 B.C. the red-figure style had come to its end in Athens. It did not adapt itself to being one of the humbler graphic arts.

Another response to free painting was made in the White-ground pottery. From the late sixth century some black-figure vase-painters had had a liking for a white slip as a background to their figures or designs, and by the second quarter of the fifth a few red-figure artists were adopting the white ground for their outline drawings, supplemented – to give contrast to the figures – by washes of colour. The result is a style softer and more pictorial than red-figure, and soon in their white-ground work – for at first white-ground and red-figure were often practised by the same man – painters abandoned the emphatic relief line. Most of the white-ground pots are slim lekythoi which were used especially as offerings to the dead and so did not have to stand ordinary wear; their purpose allowed the use of delicate fugitive colours, their narrow fields encouraged quiet compositions of a pair of figures. The earlier of these lekythoi with their simple schemes have often a classical grace and pathos, which later decline into emotion and clumsiness. The white-ground style did not outlast the fifth century.

Attic red-figure pottery was universal in the Greek world and popular beyond until the later part of the fifth century, when it began to lose its Italian markets to local competitors. Elsewhere Attic was still appreciated, but even before its collapse customers generally preferred the black-painted wares to the largely degenerate survivors of the red-figure tradition.

In time Attic red-figure had its imitators and rivals. A few Clazomenian sarcophagi around 500 B.C. borrow the technique, though the ground is not red but the normal cream of the slip. At Corinth sherds of the outgoing fifth and earlier fourth centuries show a style very like Attic, but the red ground – as in some black-figure Corinthian – is provided by a slip or a thin wash over the yellowish local clay. There is more from Boeotia, where contemporary Attic was followed from the second quarter of the fifth century to the middle of the fourth: the earlier examples were a side-line to black-figure and have a character of their own, the later are little more than travesties of red-figure.

Elsewhere in Greece and even in South Russia local craftsmen occasionally tried their hand at red-figure. But it was in the West that independent schools developed. In the third quarter of the fifth century painters fully trained in the Attic tradition appeared in South Italy and from them there gradually developed local standards, influenced by Attic but also more susceptible to the innovations in free painting. By the second quarter of the fourth century South Italian had split into five recognized schools, of which the Apulian was the largest and most important. It is best known for its elaborate volute-kraters, gaudily but competently decorated with pretentious set-pieces. Etruria too – earlier even than Greek Italy – had its red-figure painters: during the fifth century they were content to follow Attic, often in simplified techniques, but in the fourth century output increased and more homebred Etruscan schools were modestly successful. Both South Italian and Etruscan survived into the early third century. But these competitors, in Italy too, could not exclude imported Attic, which even in its decline still kept some classical dignity. Compared with the well-bred red-figure of Athens, South Italian is parvenu, Etruscan provincial and Boeotian rustic.

2. Attica

Early Red-figure (c. 530–c. 500 B.C.)

The Attic red-figure technique was invented, not evolved. The pioneer of the style (and so far as we know of the technique too) was a painter who worked with the 'maker' Andocides and so has been christened the Andocides painter. He was appropriately a pupil of Exekias and had been trained in the black-figure style, in which (if he is also the Lysippides painter) he continued to work while he was teaching himself red-figure. His work is uneven, varying from a mannered elegance and elaborate patterning to a bold but cheerful simplicity. An amphora in Munich [PLATE 38] shows the red-figure maturity of this painter: Athena is still posed and dressed with a black-figure stiffness, but Heracles is a large and limber figure and the folds of his drapery have a plastic quality. In spite of the scanty anatomical detail (though the collar-bones already show a movement towards an oblique view) the sure outline gives this Heracles some appearance of being in the round. On the other side of the same pot is a similar scene in black-figure, competent but petty; our painter was by now out of sympathy with the old style.

The Andocides painter was an artist of the first rank and he impressed his personality on his successors. Though he himself did not exploit the relief line regularly and a stricter canon rejected the plant life he was fond of, his strong plastic forms and simple expressive groups and his understanding of the new balance of light and dark determined the direction of Attic red-figure. FIG. 28 gives a specimen of the new standard of the human figure, sturdy and supple. Here there is very little inner detail to distract the eye from the compelling clarity of the outline; but often the markings of the belly, ribs and the

FIG. 28. *Attic Rf cup*
Inside: diam. of field 10·7 cm. By Oltos: 520–510 B.C.

muscles of arms and legs are added [some of these details appear on FIG. 29]. In general the red-figure style of the 520s was experimental, in the 510s the new types were consolidated, and in the next ten years the problems of oblique views and foreshortening were seriously considered. The greater realism admitted by the red-figure technique had already made the more sensitive artists uncomfortable at the abrupt swivel from profile hips and belly to frontal chest and they had tried various devices to make the transition more organic. Often the markings of the full belly appear, but pushed away towards the further side of the body and sometimes also set at an angle; or the muscles of the chest or the collar-bones might be shifted [as on PLATE 38] to make the torsion appear less violent; but in general the old principle still held that the body is the sum of its parts, all of which must be represented in a typical view. Now in the last ten years of the sixth century two great masters, Euphronios and Euthymides, proved that other views of the human body were artistically possible. A model though unusually thorough exercise in the treatment of the torso is given by Euthymides on one side of an amphora in Munich [PLATE 39] and a new view of the leg has been adopted by Epictetus for the satyr on a cup in Boston [FIG. 29]; frontal legs and feet seen from above or below are equally

FIG. 29. *Attic Rf cup*
Inside: diam. of field 9·8 cm. By Epictetus: *c.* 500 B.C.

successful. Less happy is the full view of the female breasts, which usually project like a pair of lemons one below each armpit, though occasionally the nearer breast points inwards: female anatomy is still distinguished from male only by its accessories. The eye continues to be drawn full though in a side face, but the almond shape inherited from the light-ground heads of black-figure has been modified and the pupil set further forward. With greater versatility in drawing goes greater freedom of pose; to the satyr of FIG. 29 corresponds for instance the crouching archer seen from behind, and reclining or fallen figures have a wider and more graceful range of movement. Pride in their new achievements tempted artists at first to display them a little incongruously, sometimes even clumsily; but their good sense kept them faithful to the sound principle that the figures should appear to be and move in the plane of the surface of the pot.

A similar interest in the twisting and foreshortening of the human body appears in relief sculpture of the end of the sixth century and in free painting also, to judge by unambitious painted plaques of terracotta and by the common interpretation of Pliny's remark that Cimon of Cleonae invented 'catagrapha'. What precisely 'catagrapha' may mean we do not know, even if Pliny did; but if Cimon was active at this time – and Pliny puts him much earlier – the invention attributed to him was probably in the field of foreshortening. But Pliny is untrustworthy as well as obscure and there is no reason to suppose that all advances were made in a single one of these three branches of art, which were still closely connected, and that the others only imitated. At least the great red-figure painters had the ability and assurance to invent for themselves, and it is likely that they took their part in solving problems common to all two-dimensional art of that time.

Drapery, as well as anatomy, interested artists. The heavy, sleeveless peplos was already in the 530s being replaced by the chiton, a short-sleeved garment of lighter weight. The regular red-figure dress is chiton and the thicker cloak or himation, worn singly or together. Various schemes were inherited from black-figure. The peplos was decorated, if at all, with a pattern of small chequers; for the chiton a set of vertical lines, straight or wavy, was usual; wider oblique lines marked the transverse folds of the long himation, and often the ends were sharply folded back or the hem stepped in series. The red-figure artists with their more fluent lines developed the use of folds, parallel or diverging, and ending in steps; for soft materials the lines are dilute and close together, for heavy in relief and further apart. By the last decade of the sixth century the single set of stepped edges had been replaced by series of steps going alternately up and down with a wider space left between each group of folds, the ends are no longer rectilinear but curved, and the further side of the skirt is shown as a long loop below the nearer. The elegant fall of drapery is becoming a subject that can be represented for itself.

Mythological events and battles are still common subjects, but scenes of more ordinary human and subhuman life are rapidly increasing – youths exercising in the palaestra or before or after their exercise, evening parties, soldiers arming, and so on. The subtler composition that red-figure encouraged in place of the strongly vertical accent of black-figure brought a renewed interest in the circular field of the inside of the cup, and now it is the outside which often is undecorated: FIG. 29 shows how admirably the new freedom can be employed.

Ornament in the Early phase is still largely black-figure, except for the palmettes, enclosed or free, that are large enough to be conveniently drawn in outline. This elastic and often graceful form is sometimes used as part of the standard frame to the panels of large pots, though such arid black-figure relics as the single or doubled chain of lotus and palmette are throughout more common, but it reaches its richest development where it sprouts about the handles of kraters or stamnoi. In contrast to the elaborate framing on large pots the cup is severely simple. Inside the tondo has no surround of ornament; outside a large palmette springing from each handle often flanks the central decoration, particularly on the eye cups which remained popular till near the end of this period.

Shapes are in general simply but rhythmically designed and finely executed. Already in the black-figure work of the mid sixth century a reaction against angularity had begun; so the one-piece amphora had been rising in favour and was more delicately modelled [cf. PLATES 21A and 22] and in the 530s a new standard was established for the cup in which the profile of the bowl makes a single shallow curve from rim to rim. In the red-figure style this tendency grew stronger in harmony with the subtler lines of its composition. The one-piece amphora is the most frequent of the larger pots, and the pelike with sagging belly and the squat-necked stamnos make their appearance. The old hydria is gradually replaced for red-figure by a more fluent form, where the shoulder is rounded and the neck low; but most of the hydriai of this time, as also the neck-amphorae and lekythoi, are still black-figure in decoration. The calyx-krater, used by Exekias, becomes more usual. But the commonest of all shapes is the cup, the early type of which is shown in FIG. 30A: the trend is towards a shallower bowl, taller and narrower stem, and a curving transition between which ousts the masking fillet [FIG. 30B].

The output of red-figure pottery was growing steadily and very soon painters concentrated either on large pots or on cups. Of the painters of the former – 'pot-painters' as opposed to 'cup-painters' – the Andocides painter [PLATE 38], who was active in the first half of this period, had the virtues and faults of the pioneer. His junior contemporary Psiax had a greater delicacy and observation of detail, but lacked his robustness and gusto. Both worked in black-figure too. In the last ten years of the century Euphronios and Euthymides were great and original artists: Euphronios had a grandeur that is not always controlled, Euthymides [PLATE 39] a smoother assurance with a spice of malice. The best of the cup-painters are Oltos, Epictetus and Skythes. Oltos, an early pupil of the Andocides painter, shows a sturdy competence [FIG. 28], but Epictetus [FIG. 29] has an effortless economy of line and a graceful vitality that make him one of the greatest of draughtsmen. Skythes, towards the end of the century, adds to a precise style a taste for the unheroic, but there is no reason for that or his name to suppose

A

B

FIG. 30. A. *Attic Bf cup, type A*
Ht 13 cm. *c.* 530 B.C.
B. *Attic Rf cup, type B*
Ht 11·7 cm. 490–480 B.C.

him a foreigner. In general the work of this period, even when mediocre, is vigorous and cleanly drawn.

The normal technique of red-figure is described elsewhere (pp. 161–2 and 242–3). At the beginning there was some experiment. On a few pots figures were painted in colour over the black background and the detail is incised; there are one or two instances of outline drawing where the background is not filled in; occasionally incision marks not only the outline of hair (as remained normal throughout this period) but also a few other details. Purple – for beards, hair, exceptionally even for outlines – was used more freely than later. The combination on one pot of black-figure and red-figure scenes continued for some fifteen or twenty years, and is most common on eye cups, many of which have a black-figure tondo but red-figure decoration outside. But the superiority, technical or artistic, of the red-figure method easily asserted itself.

Late Archaic Red-figure (c. 500–c. 480 B.C.)

The successors of Euthymides and Euphronios refined their inheritance and where the earlier painters had aimed at strength they preferred grace. There is little innovation in the drawing of anatomy but greater facility, so that though poses are more varied and sometimes more acrobatic than before they do not appear forced. Artists – at least the better among them – had now so thorough a control of their medium of line drawing that they could turn their figures as they wished and view them from any angle, but they did not misuse their control; so though the three-quarter torso is a commonplace, the three-quarter face is extremely rare and even the full face unusual. But there was much improvement in the natural and delicate representation of details: the eye, for instance, becomes less symmetrical and is often opened at its front end, and the female breasts can be convincingly outlined [PLATE 40]. A subtler expression of mood in face or gesture ranges from the ecstasy of the two contrasted maenads of PLATE 42 to the momentary impulses of the carousers of PLATE 43. The isolated figure can [as PLATE 41] justify itself by grace of body or the manifestation of feeling and, since a group no longer requires a physical connection, composition becomes less formal. On the amphora of PLATE 42 the arrangement is centrifugal – in earlier vase-painting that would hardly have been tolerable – and on the outside of the cup of PLATE 43 the loosely radial composition is in large part held together by the personal relations between the figures. Dangers to which such a style is liable are on the one side prettiness and posturing, on the other a statuesque inanity and indifference to formal composition. Already the cup interior of PLATE 40 for all its charm is less attentive to the circular field than the earlier tondo of FIG. 29, and soon a favourite group is two standing figures tilted slightly away from each other: the border of meander which occurs at the very end of the sixth century is becoming a necessary frame.

A parallel change appears in drapery. At first a decorative but artificial elaboration of folds was fashionable, but soon the leading artists were studying the hang of dress to make it conform to the body inside. Contrast PLATE 42 of the beginning of this period with the slightly later PLATE 43: here is a keener perception of the texture of material.

In the sculpture of the first quarter of the fifth century the cheerful and decorative formalism of the Archaic style was being transformed into the severer but more natural discipline of the Classical. Vase-painting, being essentially decorative, admitted the change with more reluctance; the arts were beginning to diverge. Of contemporary free painting we have little idea. Some of the grander vase-paintings may reflect its themes and the occasional use of shading and such rare tricks of foreshortening as the three-quarter face and the oinochoe tilted towards the spectator were very likely borrowed from pictorial art, but vase-painters stuck resolutely to their proper rules of linear drawing and two-dimensional space.

The repertory of subjects is enlarged. Mythology keeps a place but with a wider range of incidents; many of the old favourites were not suited to the new more intimate style of drawing. Among scenes of human life battle-pieces are less common, drinking parties and youths at exercise very numerous: a typical new choice is the school-room. In general the treatment becomes more refined; passion is often there, but it is human and not bestial, and even satyrs are sometimes gentlemen [PLATE 41] or fond parents.

The typical ornament is now a simple meander, usually of the type of PLATE 40; it is often interrupted by squares containing crosses [so on PLATE 42]. Some of the more old-fashioned painters continued the black-figure patterns, and the delicate red-figure palmette – sometimes set obliquely in a band – is used when required. But ornament has a small part in Late Archaic red-figure, smaller than before or after. Inside cups there is usually a border of meander, outside more often there are not even palmettes at the handles. On amphorae the advanced artists normally do without a frame; their figures stand on a band or strip of meander or even, if solitary, float in space. Much the same happens on other shapes, with variations according to their needs.

The one-piece amphora is losing in popularity to various forms of the neck-amphora, particularly those with twisted handles, of Panathenaic shape and of the small kind called 'Nolan'. The pelike, introduced at the end of the sixth century, and the stamnos become very frequent. The new rounded hydria has not quite ousted the old angular shape. Kraters are numerous; the greater masters prefer the calyx-krater, the lesser the column-krater, and the volute-krater survives. The lekythos comes into favour with red-figure painters, and one workshop specialized in long white-ground alabastra which are mostly decorated with a lanky Negro in striped trousers. The cup, with low spreading bowl and an unbroken sweep from top to graceful foot, is now at the summit of its glory and its outside decoration is adjusted to the shape as never before. The average standard of execution is extraordinarily high, partly because so many inferior painters still stuck to black-figure.

The division between painters of large pots and of cups continues, and the painting of small closed pots is becoming a separate trade. Of the painters of large pots two are pre-eminent. The Cleophrades painter, whose name turns out to have been Epictetus (to be distinguished from the earlier cup-painter), was a pupil of Euthymides whom he resembles closely in his earliest work. His own style, grand and expressive, was mature in the 490s [PLATE 42], in the 480s there is less fire but more dignity, and afterwards his powers waned. From his hand are also several Panathenaic amphorae in the black-figure style which the Cleophrades painter was one of the last Attic vase-painters to understand. His contemporary the Berlin painter, in his delicacy reminiscent of the same Euthymides, was a rather mannered draughtsman of unusual grace, particularly successful in the single figures he delighted to put in the unframed fields of slim pots [PLATE 41]. His long career lasted into the 460s, but though his later work is less careful there is little development in his style. His decorative elegance had a wide influence. Myson, an old-fashioned mediocrity whose taste was for column-kraters decorated with large figures, had a following in the Early Classical mannerists. Among cup-painters Onesimos (the Panaitios painter), already active in the closing years of the sixth century, kept up with the times [PLATE 40]; his drawing is usually vigorous and always fresh. His pupil the Brygos painter refines on his model and at the best combines delicacy with passion [PLATE 43], but later he grew tamer and more correct. Duris, another long-lived artist, began as a colleague of the young Onesimos, who both influenced and was influenced by him; his style has a youthful affected charm till he settled into an academic propriety, receptive of the new classicism. Makron was a lesser artist, remarkable for the flow of his women's clothes. The most influential of these cup-painters was the Brygos painter, and next to him Duris. The end of the period sees the growth of an academic trend and other signs of flagging imagination.

In red-figure technique there is little change. The outline of hair is now commonly reserved and not incised. Purple is used very modestly. Dilute washes appear a little less rarely, exceptionally even as shading to model inanimate objects. A few red-figure painters still did passable work in black-figure too. The white-ground technique of outline drawing against a light background had yet hardly interested red-figure artists outside the workshop that turned out the Negro alabastra, and their thick summary style cannot be reckoned as true red-figure.

Early Classical Red-figure (c. 480–c. 450 B.C.)

In the second quarter of the fifth century the Attic red-figure style splits into schools that aim at different ideals. The reasons lie in the gradual establishment of the classical standard with its emphasis on a calm and reflective humanity and in the related advance of free painting towards pictorial art, for neither classical figures nor spatial depth could easily be suited to the scale and scope of vase-painting. So red-figure vase-painters divide according to the degree and manner in which they reject or accept the old and the new. There are the frank imitators of the

FIG. 31. *Attic Rf cup*
Outside: ht of field 9·5 cm. By the Penthesilea painter: 470–460 B.C.

grandeur of free painting [FIGS. 32–33], the moderate classicists who thoughtfully adapt the new types and groupings [PLATE 45], minia-turists preferring charm and prettiness [FIG. 31] and mannerists who continue or reinterpret archaic forms [PLATE 44]. There is about much of the work of this period an air of study rather than of spontaneity and a feebler sense of the relation between shape and decoration so that it is easy to enjoy the drawing and forget the pot. Admirable individual figures are often set in casual, static compositions, for which the high fields of tall pots offer the best chance of success: the decoration of cups, especially of the long narrow frieze of the exterior, becomes less attrac-tive. Though its technical tradition of line drawing saved it from collapse, the art of painted pottery is beginning to decay and sink grad-ually to a minor rank.

Greek free painting has been mentioned several times in this book, but now its influence becomes more evident. Little is known of its early history. Murals and large wooden panels, presumably its main forms, have vanished completely in Greece though some works painted by or for Etruscans and Lycians survive in their tombs, and we are left with a few painted slabs of terracotta and marble which served as architectural decoration, gravestones or dedications, with uncertain statements

FIG. 32. *Attic Rf calyx-krater*
Detail: scale *c.* 2 : 5. By the Niobid painter: *c.* 460 B.C.

of ancient writers, and with the reflections to be glimpsed or guessed in vase-painting and sculpture in relief. Probably free painting began in the seventh century, since the Geometric style as we know it can hardly bear enlargement. Our earliest examples are the painted terracotta metopes from Thermon and Calydon, coloured drawings in the Corinthian style of around 630 B.C.; the technique is outline drawing with simple linear detail and the enclosed surfaces filled with flat washes of various colours, but the style, poses and types resemble contemporary vase-painting. The square field of the metope forbids elaborate composition, but that there were more ambitious paintings is deduced from some polychrome Corinthian pots of the mid seventh century [such as that of PLATE 9C, discussed on pp. 51–2]; here the composition is more largely conceived and colours are used freely though incision is retained. So far as can be inferred, free painting continued till the end of the sixth century the technique and general standards of the Thermon metopes; its scope may have been wider than that of vase-painting, but both were governed by the same ideals and perhaps often practised by the same artist. The difference in technique was not important, for though the black-figure style of vase-painting was conventional, so too was the outline and wash of free painting. It is tempting to imagine in the more monumental or elaborate of black-figure vase-paintings the influence of free painting, but there were among the vase-painters artists of the first rank who could themselves be original, and on the other hand the influence of vase-painting is seen on some sizeable clay plaques which are decorated in the black-figure technique. Later, when vase-painters needed a more expressive medium than black-figure and turned to line drawing, they did not adopt the colour schemes of free painting. Vase-painting, free painting and relief sculpture were parallel but independent manifestations of the two-dimensional archaic art, and their differences were the differences that come from the medium used, not from the status of their artists. It was not till the end of the sixth century, when the archaic restrictions were being broken, that free painting started on its pictorial development. The first step, the mastery of foreshortened views of the human figure, was perhaps not – or anyhow not wholly – its invention; intimations of obliquity (though rare and unsystematic) had begun to appear in sculpture and vase-painting some fifty years before their general acceptance. There is more reason to suspect the influence of free painting in certain novelties that occur in a few vase-paintings but were generally rejected. So in the pretentious tondo of a cup by the Sosias painter, where Achilles bandages Patroclus's arm, the eyes of the two heroes are drawn in profile, a rendering that does not become regular in vase-painting for another generation, and the teeth of Patroclus are clenched in pain; and on the slightly later Vivenzio hydria of the Cleophrades painter the sack of Troy is depicted with a grandness of composition that is very rare in contemporary vase-painting. But though the cup with Patroclus may owe details it does not simply copy free painting, since the scene has been specially composed to fit a circular field. In fact the earlier red-figure masters were self-confident and original, the equals in all probability of the free painters of their day, and if they borrowed it was with discrimination. But in the second quarter of the fifth century the position changed. Red-figure vase-painting in its turn was reaching its proper limits and there was little more even to refine. So it ceased to attract or breed artists of the first quality and the achievements of free painting, which now under Polygnotus and Mikon was attempting in earnest the problems of three-dimensional figures and space, set a higher standard for lesser craftsmen to admire and for the imprudent to copy.

Some influence of free painting may be suspected also on the white-ground vases, where outline drawing – later regularly supplemented by colour – is set against a background of white or whitish slip [PLATE 49A]. A pale slip, yellowish to cream, had been used on some Attic pots from Protogeometric to Early Geometric, and again in Protoattic, but was probably not connected with the whiter coating which towards the end of the sixth century became popular in some black-figure work-shops for their lekythoi. But red-figure artists made very rare use of this technique till the Early Classical period. Their earliest ventures in white-ground work – by a sensible convention the term excludes black-figure pottery with a white ground – are in effect red-figure drawings the background to which has not been blacked in; now a distinct manner begins to establish itself, though for a generation most painters of white-ground pots painted orthodox red-figure pottery too. The sharp clarity of red-figure line drawing gradually gives way to softer effects, as the flush line of dilute paint replaces the strong relief line, even for the out-line, and the flat washes of purple, browny red and yellow that often cover the drapery take a bigger part in the design. The finest of the early white-ground paintings are on the inside of cups and there are also white-ground alabastra and pyxides, but by the middle of the fifth cen-tury the lekythos has become the normal shape. The reason is hardly the example of the miserable black-figure lekythoi, even though these sometimes offer drawings that are partly in outline; the lekythos is not at first the white-ground shape most preferred in red-figure workshops. More important was the demand for lekythoi to dedicate at graves, where they had not to stand daily use. So white-ground painters could indulge in new and perishable colours and a whiter friable slip – on some earlier pieces, though the slip is whitish, a purer white paint was thought necessary for the flesh of women – and the white-ground tech-nique became unsuitable for anything except funerary ware. But the full development does not come till after the Early Classical period.

Though the red-figure style declines in artistic quality, there is no decline in skill. The drawing of the human figure is more accomplished than before and drapery more accurately studied. Archaic artists had made clear the structure and working of the body, their classical suc-

cessors were interested in its surface and bearing. Detail follows nature
more carefully: the profile eye is now regularly drawn in profile, and
the separate strands of hair are sometimes suggested by a streaky use of
dilute paint. With this more sensuous anatomy appear more graceful or
dignified poses and gestures, subtly expressive of purpose or feeling;
so the tempting of Eriphyle with the necklace [PLATE 45] has a well-
bred reticence that is fully classical and even the sentimental boys and
pony of FIG. 31 palely reflect the same spirit. As drawings the best of
these works are admirable, but it is less certain that they are in place
as the decoration of pottery. Even so the plane of the surface of the
pot is still generally respected, though three-quarter faces and shading
are rather less uncommon and feet are sometimes planted above the
baseline. A few ambitious pieces go further and exhibit figures tiered
in a sort of Oriental perspective or partly concealed by cardboard
hillocks, and there are battle scenes where combatants seem to be
bursting out of the picture [FIG. 33].

Drapery, except in mannerist works, abandons the old formal
systems of decorative folds. Instead we find sketchier impressions of
the fall and pull of material across body or limbs [PLATE 45] or dry
close-set corrugations as on the half-concealed Amazon of FIG. 33. The
uncompromising clarity of the traditional line drawing is being sur-
rendered. In the 460s the peplos again becomes fashionable. Ornament
is rather less restricted than in Late Archaic. Some painters repeat older
– even black-figure – patterns, others try to improve the plant forms:
so lotus and palmette are in borders contorted into novel elaborations,
and when used independently break into rank, straggly growth.

Shapes continue in general to become slimmer and as in the drawing
of human anatomy the transition from one part to another is less sharply
defined. The one-piece amphora is now very rare; neck-amphorae, both
large and the small Nolan, are common, as are the pelike, the stamnos
and the hydria. The column-krater is the favourite of the mannerists;
other painters prefer the bell, calyx and volute forms. Oinochoai are
fairly numerous. The stemmed cup is losing popularity, the stemless
cup and the kotyle gaining. Besides the regular lekythos, red-figure or
white-ground, the squat lekythos and the alabastron are frequent.

Most of the greater artists of Late Archaic, though past their best,
were still working in the Early Classical period. Their now old-fashioned
style was continued more or less faithfully by many lesser painters.
Among these mannerists the Pan painter stands out, an original artist
with an individual taste for elegance and oddity, who knew to a nicety
how to put new wine in old bottles [PLATE 44]. The Pistoxenos painter

is a pioneer of the new classical style; his sharply drawn, staring figures have a dramatic quality. More fully classical is a younger artist, the Villa Giulia painter, whose subtle harmony does not need vigorous or sensational movement: his school is represented here by the work of a pupil, softer but equally correct [PLATE 45]. The Achilles painter, in the third quarter of the century the greatest painter of white lekythoi,

FIG. 33. *Attic Rf volute-krater*
Detail: ht of field 21·5 cm. By the painter of the Woolly Satyrs: *c.* 460 B.C.

resembles them in character. A more watered classicism is evident in much of the work of the Penthesilea painter – in his day capable of grandeur – and of his colleagues: FIG. 31 offers a mediocre specimen, sketchily pretty and sugared. The Sotades painter also belittles his human figures, but is redeemed by an unusual sense of space and even of nature; the white-ground inside of a cup in the British Museum with a girl picking apples is one of the most surprising masterpieces of classical art. Of the adherents of the grand style, who went far in their imitation of free painting, the most notable is the Niobid painter: FIG. 32 shows one of his competent but frigid figures, FIG. 33 – from a krater painted by a member of his group – a section of one of the elaborate compositions to which he aspired.

Classical Red-figure (c. 450–c. 425 B.C.)

The full classical ideal of effortless human dignity now became dominant and in the third quarter of the fifth century permeated Attic vase-painting. The red-figure style, based on emphatic line drawing, found it difficult to translate into its traditional technique the easy harmonious poses in which organic unity of the figure was attained by subtle transitions between its parts, and the result often looks strained or inappropriate. But white-ground was already less dependent on line and perhaps still offered artists the attraction of novelty, and it is in this period that it reaches its finest achievement. There is in some vase-painting now a spirit that recalls the sculptured decoration of the Parthenon, the greatest work of this period and the best preserved; but it is hard to judge what direct influence it had on the painters of pottery.

In their drawing of figures vase-painters had at their service a sound knowledge of the appearance of the human body in a wide range of views and positions, but this knowledge is used with classical restraint. Quiet standing or sitting poses are typical, subtly varied to prevent monotony and scenes of action, even battles, are for decency toned down: the drunken return of Hephaestus, for example, becomes a respectable procession, and satyrs finding sleeping maenads think first of not disturbing them. Groups are often unified solely by bearing or glance, which some painters make more expressive by shortening the lower lid of the profile eye. So the musical tableau becomes popular, with performer and hearers fixed in varied attitudes of rapture [PLATES 46A and 48B]. Careful scenes are now usually kept for the front of the pot, while the back – for economy or contrast – is summarily filled with a few stock figures standing aimlessly by. Perspective, of which painters are now more conscious, is confined generally to the legs of tables and chairs [PLATE 46A], though some ambitious sets have also half-open doors. In advanced workshops rocks and a variable standing line are used freely but discreetly [PLATE 48B]. This restraint in representing depth suggests that vase-painting was influenced as much by relief sculpture as by free painting. The relation of shape to decoration is no longer given much thought, and the principles for the composition of groups tend to be based on a rectangular field. The body of the lekythos happily provides such a field; the inside of the cup does not, but the composition is rarely planned to suit the tondo. The effect now is not so much painted pottery as pottery with painting on it.

The repertory of ornament remains much as in Early Classical. Where there is room, the tendency to abstract elasticity increases. By now most shapes have their characteristic ornaments, as for instance the double row of leaves below the lip of bell-kraters [PLATE 48A]. In technique the relief line is less regularly used and for outlines is by now largely abandoned. Washes of dilute paint, for shading or modelling minor objects, are no longer so rare.

In red-figure the Achilles painter, whose finest work is on white-ground lekythoi [PLATE 49A], is the most important of the painters who develop the quiet classicism of the period just past. Polygnotus, a master with a still larger following, who shares his name with two other contemporary vase-painters besides the famous mural painter, is the heir to the grand style, though his forms are fleshier and more rounded and his spirit is fully classical: the amphora of PLATE 46A and the kraters of PLATE 37B and 48B were painted by his companions. But now that the admirers of free painting had outgrown their early wildness the schools of this generation differ less in their ideals than in the way they express them. Of other vase-painters the Eretria painter had most influence: his style, mature about 430 B.C., rejects classical severity for a finicky prettiness, tricked out with ornaments raised in gilded clay [PLATE 47]. A comparable lowering of ideals appears on the white-ground lekythoi. Red-figure is a declining art; good work is becoming rarer, trivial or bungling more common.

The white-ground style was now almost confined to the very numerous lekythoi. Here the standard was set by the Achilles painter, the last of the great Attic vase-painters. This artist began his career about 460 B.C., spent ten years or so in finding his idiom and then changed very little. His slender, fine-boned men and women stand or sit with easy dignity, looking at one another in silent, often melancholy understanding. There is no purer expression of classical art than the mature white-ground work of this master [PLATE 49A]. His followers in the 430s and 420s preferred something more tender or unreserved. Characteristic of the new human touch are children, now pathetically childish. The tall narrow field of the lekythos was admirably fitted for classical figures, at first usually two, later often three. Funerary subjects had become common during the second quarter of the fifth century and now they are regular: the favourites are the lady and her maid, the soldier's farewell to his wife, the visit to the grave where often the dead man or woman appears, and sometimes such scenes are conflated; or, especially later, there are incidents from the other world – Charon and his boat, Hermes guiding the dead, two winged attendants carrying the body away. The progress of the white-ground style was helped by changes in technique. Already by the 460s the relief line had been generally replaced by a flat line of shiny dilute paint, and now this gives way to matt paint, black or red. The staring 'second white' used for female flesh does not last long into this period. To the purple, browny red and yellow pigments that were moderately fast, there are gradually added less stable shades – rose, vermilion, sky-blue and a light purple. The present nakedness of many figures on white-ground lekythoi is a consequence; the flat washes of colour that clothed them have perished.

The shapes of this period often show a new, but mistaken sense of curve. So the amphora of PLATE 46A slurs the transition from neck to shoulder and develops an unpleasant concavity at the base of the body. Of neck-amphorae the Nolan is most common, but the pelike is commoner still. The krater remains in favour; first comes the bell-krater, then the calyx and column forms. Stamnos and hydria keep, oinochoai increase their popularity. The stemmed cup is still frequent enough, the stemless cup comes a respectable second to it, the kotyle a poor third. Squat lekythoi are fairly, tall lekythoi (mostly white-ground) very numerous. There are a good few loutrophoroi of one kind or another; these were ritual vases, specially designed for weddings or funerals.

In the earlier part of this period the red-figure style was transplanted to South Italy. The Polygnotan group and less so the Achilles painter were the earliest models of this new school.

Late Classical Red-figure (c. 425–c. 400 B.C.)

During the last quarter of the fifth century some painters of Attic red-figure were again attracted to the ideal of pictorial depth and volume. In the past the figures had generally in their direction and arrangement conformed to the surface of the pot. Now they may emerge or recede obliquely from the field or be set at different levels: the decoration no longer needs to have regard to the shape. Similarly the drawing is more diligent in the modelling of rounded forms, on naked bodies by subtler curves of the contour and of the sparse anatomical lines, on drapery by series of folds, often hooked, which cross a thrusting limb. The emphatic relief line and the lucid outline are correspondingly neglected. For hair a curly mass of separate strands is regular. Accessories of white and gold become more common. Dresses are often spangled with crosses or other simple patterns. At the same time poses tend to be theatrical and expressions – partly because of the shortening of the profile eye – vapidly intense. Some of these novelties were probably prompted by free painting, but the tradition of red-figure was too strong for any systematic imitation.

The use of ornament is discreet. Floral forms are drawn out more finely. The acanthus leaf becomes common on the last white-ground lekythoi.

The Polygnotan school, now in its second generation, remained dominant; and its most influential artist, the Dinos painter, was a cautious pioneer of the new style [PLATE 48A]. His figures, plumper and sinuous but still solid, are economically modelled by firm lines. Though he knows the new tricks – such as the shadowing of a fold by a streak of dilute paint – he uses them discreetly. The work of his prime has sometimes a touch of fire and normally a dignity and sober grace above the average of the school; there are other members, equally competent, who achieve no more than a classicizing elegance.

A different spirit is exuded by a celebrated contemporary, the Midias painter, who developed the style of the Eretria painter. Here is the world of the boudoir, respectably sensual, peopled by feminine women and effeminate cupids. The Midias painter is a delicate draughtsman who lovingly analyses draped forms into a multitude of fine lines. He had also a taste for the florid and indulges in white and gilded details. There is great charm in his smaller scenes [PLATE 46B]; the larger, heavily ornate and weakly composed, have been admired. Though he had his imitators and some wider influence, his style was in its way too exquisite to leave a lasting tradition.

In minor works the standard falls. The drawing is often negligent and perfunctory, and the effect though plain deplorable. Some unambitious classes of small pots have a whimsical charm – for instance the flat askos with a conventional animal and the small jug called the chous on which a favourite figure is a chubby child.

White-ground lekythoi were turned out in great quantity. Though the medium was more suited to the style of free painting, the field gave little scope; anyhow, decay is rapid [PLATE 49B]. The white-ground specialists – for white-ground and red-figure were no longer painted by the same man – went their own way. In the standard scene of mourning at the tomb classical restraint often gives way to passionate grief, or what the painter intended for it. Lines are often sketchy, and the choice of colours now includes green and mauve. A few lekythoi of group R come from a draughtsman of exceptional quality, whose sensitive contour needs little inner detail to show how volume can be suggested by pure line. He had no following, and the white-ground style was dead by the end of the fifth century.

The shapes of large vases become more swelling, and mouldings of foot and lip grow richer. The neck-amphora is following the one-piece amphora into disuse. The pelike flourishes. The bell-krater is very popular, the calyx-krater moderately popular. The stamnos is obsolescent. The hydria is temporarily less important. Oinochoai, especially of the small chous variety, are numerous: the body is now nearly globular. The common form of cup is stemmed. Squat lekythoi [PLATE 46B] are frequent, as are tall lekythoi, some of which reach a height of eighteen inches. Loutrophoroi continue. A shape new to favour is the lekanis of the Midian school.

Fourth-century Red-figure (c. 400–c. 320 B.C.)

Red-figure had by now become a minor art of a special character. The gap had widened decisively between vase-painting and free painting, which was at last progressing beyond line drawing towards a systematic use of shading. From early in the fifth century, to judge by occasional examples in red-figure, such minor details as metal objects, pelts and rocks were sometimes shaded; but at its end the revolutionary innovation was made of shading drapery and the male body – the white female body remained unshaded for two generations longer. This new aid to illusion was after a little experiment rejected by vase-painters, whether because the new technique was difficult or the old seemed more pleasing. Even so, new ideas seeped in and in late red-figure works there is often an uneasy compromise between modern expression and traditional style.

Attic vase-painting of the fourth century is less well explored than of the fifth. But the classical tradition, transmitted by the Dinos painter and his colleagues, persisted with modifications for fifty years or more. Shortly before 400 B.C. it had put out an offshoot, the so-called Ornate style, ambitious and short-lived. Later, in the 370s, some workshops succeeded in harmonizing composition in depth with line drawing and respect for the surface of the pot. Though this new style at its best is skilful and effective, it did not long outlast the classical tradition which it denied. Red-figure had ended at Athens by 320 B.C.

The novelties of the Late Classical painters have become commonplaces to the next generation. The silhouette of the figure is no longer studied. Modelling by curving lines is regular, and fully profile figures are rare. Though shading is exceptional, the quality of lines is softer or weaker and some painters vary the breadth of their strokes. Patterning of drapery becomes heavier. Whole figures, especially in the centre of the composition, may be painted white for emphasis or to distinguish the layers of a group or just from habit: details on these white figures are done in the yellowy brown of dilute paint. Buildings, when they are put in, may be tilted or recede in a sort of perspective. These characteristics are more dominant in the Ornate school; the classical wing is more restrained and modest; and the growing mass of hackwork, on cheap pots or the backs of expensive pots, has the simple but irredeemable badness that comes when sophistication is hurried and careless.

The Ornate style begins about 420 B.C. and trails on for some forty years. Here we meet again after a generation of disuse grandiose compositions in which the figures are tiered above each other to mark their distance from the spectator or (since free painting had discarded that form of perspective) as a device to fill a high field. In the often crowded scenes one or two figures are marked out by their white flesh, white and yellow accessories are spattered around, and drapery is loaded with borders of large hooks, stars, stripes and even little animals, some of them still Orientalizing. One of the most successful of the Ornate confections is the name-piece of the Talos painter, a volute-krater in Ruvo, on which the bronze giant Talos falls back limply into a throng of bystanders. His white flesh, exceptionally modelled by shading in dilute paint, contrasts significantly with the red of the other figures. The small Bacchic scenes on the neck of this krater are more conservative.

At the other extreme the Jena painter is perhaps the best and – through the excavation of his workshop – certainly the best-known of the classicists of the early fourth century. He is in the tradition of the Dinos painter, but quieter and more refined. His composition – at least on cups – is uncrowded and avoids depth; his heads are regularly in profile; and he is attentive to the silhouettes and to the balance of light and dark in his pictures. For inner detail he makes sparing and skilful use of thin lines, which effectively suggest the plastic forms of the body: on PLATE 50 may be noted the doubling of the lines across the naked belly and the blank surfaces and cross folds which neatly express the thrust of draped breast or thigh. So lucid a draughtsman had little use for patterns on his dresses and less for added colours, except in the garland of leaves and berries round the inside of cups. At his best the Jena painter is graceful; but sometimes, especially in his later cups, he is as bad as the contemporary hacks who turned out work that for its lack of other character may be called traditional.

Between the Ornate masters and the classicists there stretches a row of intermediate painters with more pretensions than perception. The standard of Attic red-figure is low in the first quarter of the fourth century, and it deservedly lost ground everywhere to black-painted ware and in Italy also to the local red-figure.

From about 380 B.C. a few competent artists gave a new twist to red-figure. In their line drawing they followed the Jena painter, though they preferred softer and weaker strokes, abandoned the relief line (which is rare after the middle of the century), and made free use of white to give prominence or contrast to particular figures. But their major innovations were in composition. Although on examination the picture often proves to have considerable depth, its depth does not appear obtrusively. This effect is obtained partly by the rejection of perspective tricks, but more by the poses of individual figures, which seem to lean against the curving wall of the pot and so to be on its surface. The grouping too is loose, with the outer figures often turning away from the central action, and the poses have the grace and languor that were then fashionable in sculpture and – no doubt – in other arts. The pelike of PLATE 51, about 350 B.C., shows the new red-figure at its best. Peleus surprises Thetis: Aphrodite seated on the left and the fugitive nymph to the right each in her way exploit the curvature of the pot. The new style is at home on the pelike, hydria and calyx-krater; the bell-krater generally has rougher or less modern decoration. The final generation of red-figure painters grows clumsy and fumbling: figures are often elongated, lines become sketchier or harsh, experiments in colour and relief (which had begun in the first half of the century) are abandoned.

By the beginning of this period Dionysus and Aphrodite were the favourite gods of the vase-painters, and where other immortals appear the setting is likely to be Dionysiac. There is too a growing taste for Oriental costumes; and by the middle of the century Amazons, Arimaspians and griffins are familiar. The backs of bell-kraters and pelikai are throughout disfigured by the inevitable trio or pair of cloaked youths, always (if possible) more degenerate than before (FIG. 34]. On smaller pots there is a fondness for heads.

The use and forms of the ornaments are much as in Late Classical. Palmettes trimmed almost beyond recognition to make a low triangle fill the lower border on some late calyx-kraters. The band of spiral hooks is common.

The principal shapes are kraters of the bell and also of the calyx variety, the hydria and – commonest of all – the pelike. They suffer a continual elongation of neck, body and stem. The lekanis is frequent in the first half of the fourth century. The cup, stemmed and stemless, disappears in the second quarter. The heavy cup-kotyle has a vogue from the end of the fifth century till about 380 B.C. The kotyle continues popular. The squat lekythos, small jugs and askos do not last much beyond 350 B.C.

This dwindling range of shapes was supplemented by black-painted ware (or, as it is usually but wrongly called, black-glazed ware). There had always been some pottery of fair quality that was decorated simply by a coat of dark paint, and about the middle of the sixth century Attic workshops began to produce admirably finished black pots. Before the

FIG. 34. *Attic Rf bell-krater*

Detail of back (three draped youths): scale 1 : 2. By the Filottrano painter: mid 4th cent. B.C. The upper part of the figure on the left is uncertain

middle of the fifth century impressed decoration had been admitted, particularly for rosettes and soon for bands of short strokes and small palmettes in the centre of cups, some of which have red-figure decoration outside; and from the later years of the century the bodies of pots are sometimes ribbed. It is difficult to estimate the relative outputs of red-figure and black wares, but by the fourth century black ware – plain, impressed and ribbed – must have been the staple product of Attic workshops.

The end of Attic red-figure came not later than 320 B.C. Why it ended is not obvious. The style till the 330s had vitality and inventiveness, the market for Attic pottery was still large, the taste of customers did not jib at decorated wares. Perhaps artists accomplished enough to reach and maintain the standard of the Thetis pelike [PLATE 51] could find more congenial and profitable employment than painting pots.

3. Corinth

Just as there are Corinthian imitations of mature Attic black-figure, so there are Corinthian pots in the red-figure style. Though the exposed surface is given a more or less correct colour, they can be distinguished from Attic by their yellowish clay. The finer variety has an orange slip, sometimes supplemented by a red wash on reserved areas, and uses the relief line freely. The poorer variety has the red wash, but no slip, and the quality is generally inferior. The finds are too scrappy to allow a history of this school, but it looks as if it began just before 400 B.C. and might have been established by Attic craftsmen: the finer ware, which remains close to Attic, may have lasted through the first quarter of the fourth century, the poorer rather longer. Though Corinthian red-figure had only a small share in its home market, it was exported to Aegosthena (to judge by the excavators' report) and occasionally to the Argolid, Sicyon, Anticyra and Olympia. More may well turn up at other sites westward of Corinth.

Outline drawing on a light ground was used for the Haloa group of small pots, decorated with figures of rustic charm and simplicity. Their date is in the second half of the fifth century. Some are said to have been found in Boeotia.

4. Boeotia

Boeotian vase-painters remained faithful to black-figure into the fourth century, but there was a little red-figure too. It begins slowly in the second quarter of the fifth century. The style is current Attic in intention; but the drawing of inner details, which often misunderstands the folds of drapery and even the human anatomy, tends to flat and inconsequent patterns of lines without a suggestion of modelling. Perhaps the painters, some of whom certainly worked in black-figure workshops, were themselves primarily black-figure painters and had not enough practice in red-figure. Boeotian taste is to be seen in some of the subjects, for instance the banqueting hero, and among the shapes in the importance of the kantharos. In the years around 400 B.C. one group shows a little independence: its typical product is a smallish bell-krater with a large female head on the front, a large palmette on the back and another female head on the lid. But the formula is arid and grows clumsy with repetition. During the fourth century such other painters as there are turn out work of more distinctive incompetence. Boeotian red-figure at its best has a dry and simple merit, the worst is inept. It ends probably about the middle of the fourth century.

The colour of the fired clay is usually paler than Attic and the paint is less even. According to the distribution Thebes was the place of manufacture, at least of the better groups. Occasionally a piece of Boeotian red-figure found its way to some other part of Greece, but even at home it was less frequent than imported Attic.

5. Etruria

In Etruria the red-figure style of Athens was at once admired and after a while imitated. Apart from the Praxias group the earlier imitations are more or less isolated. It was not till the fourth century, when production increased and the influence of South Italian (particularly Campanian) was added, that positively Etruscan schools developed. This sluggishness in style is matched by uncertainty in technique: at the beginning and again towards the end painting in applied colour competes with the true red-figure process of reservation, and where reservation is preferred the painters did not consistently use the relief line. The cemeteries of Etruria have been ransacked vigorously, but though the place of finding is often recorded the context usually is not: so dating depends mainly on stylistic comparison, which till the early fourth century is satisfactory. For the location of the Etruscan workshops our evidence is distribution and inscriptions. There is also some variety in the clay, which is generally fired to a lightish brown, noticeably paler than Attic.

Most of the earliest Etruscan essays in red-figure belong to the Praxias group, which begins in the early fifth century and lasts for about a generation. Here the decoration is done in red paint over a background of the ordinary dark paint and details are normally incised through the red so that they show in the colour of the background; the effect resembles that of true red-figure, especially in reproductions. This technique of applied colour had already been tried in Athens and found wanting, but its simplicity recommended it to Etruscan craftsmen. In style and subjects the Praxias group followed various Attic models and, unless perhaps the shapes owe something to the contemporary black-figure school of Etruria, the deviations from Attic standards have no common quality except incompetence. But though one of the later painters of this group wrote Greek – in the Euboean alphabet – there is no reason to suppose that it was in a Greek city that he learnt to paint. The home of the group was probably Vulci, where so much of their work has been found.

Red-figure in the proper reserving technique began only a little before the middle of the fifth century and did not become frequent for fifty years more. Curiously the Etruscan painters did not generally accept the relief line till the end of the century and then not usually in such secondary places as the outside of cups. Till the early fourth century Attic was imitated or copied more or less faithfully – sometimes indeed the expert can detect the painter of the Attic model. So far there is little that is constantly or peculiarly Etruscan: the relief line is used hesitantly and some of the figures have a sturdy homeliness, but it is easier to recognize Etruscan because it is not Attic nor of any of the other provincial schools. Vulci seems again to be the chief place of finding, and a cup in the Musée Rodin in Paris offers another argument for manufacture in Vulci, since it evidently copies an Attic cup that has been found there. But if the painters were all working in one city, in style they were remarkably unconscious of each other.

At the beginning of the fourth century a new group – the Faliscan – suddenly appears at Falerii, a Latin-speaking town in the south-east corner of Etruria. Here the style is at first so purely Attic that it may even have been brought by emigrants from Athens. But fairly soon, as now at Vulci, the painters become more eclectic and independent. South Italian red-figure, and particularly the school of Campania, provides forms of floral ornaments, of which the flower seen in perspective is the most obvious [FIG. 35], and less regularly other notions; themes, in a few instances brutal, are taken from Etruscan tradition or chosen for Etruscan taste; workshops cultivate their own mannerisms, and in the second half of the century give up the relief line. The Faliscan school, in its prime graceful and refined, preserves a flaccid elegance, still Greek in style though Greek with a South Italian flavour. Minor but convenient peculiarities of Faliscan are on large pots the band of full tongues, each in its rounded compartment, and – though less constantly – the trefoil leaf. Cup, stamnos and calyx-krater are the important shapes. The school of Vulci (if Vulci it is) has a clumsier vigour and is less self-effacingly Greek: its favourite shapes are calyx-krater and stamnos. In the late fourth century both these schools add to their repertory scenes from the Etruscan netherworld with demons hideous or grotesque. The third main division of later Etruscan, which occurs in central Etruria, is more conventional in its themes. This is the school which in its first phase is called the school of Clusium, in its second of Volterra; but it is more credible that its home was throughout at Volterra than that the painters migrated. Its period is from the third quarter of the fourth century to the first quarter of the third. A characteristic of this school is the form of the palmette, in which the leaves have decayed into a simple fringe. The drawing of figures is at first weak, but modest; then, as the relief line is forgotten, the painters tend to use broader brush strokes, hatching and shading. These devices of free painting are known in the late school of Vulci – the purer Faliscan school was more resistant – but the Volterrans exploited them more boldly. The typical shapes are in the early phase the cup, the head-kantharos (a sort of Toby jug) and the askos in the form of a duck; and in the later phase a high-necked kind of column-krater. These kraters are notable for the large heads painted on them, especially cowled women in three-quarter view and profiles sketched in clever caricature. Ordinary profile heads of women in a frame of spiral hooks decorate many of the miserable Genucilia dishes and plates, one of the later red-figure groups of southern Etruria and the Faliscan district, where they are common in the second half of the fourth century.

During the fourth century there was a revival of the technique of applied colour, but now it is increasingly white or yellow and soon details (if there are any) are done in dilute dark paint. Here Gnathian has its effect. Good work in applied colour still appears in the second quarter of the third century. There is also in the fourth century a reversion to a sort of black-figure, especially in the chain of scraggy palmettes and flowers drawn in silhouette. These simpler techniques are most often used on smallish pots, such as the particularly Etruscan beaked oinochoe, a narrow jug with high neck that ends in a long scoop.

Though the Etruscan versions of red-figure were made for fully two centuries, the output was remarkably small. Vulci appears to have been the first place of manufacture, and after it Falerii and Volterra. Caere and Tarquinia, more open to Greek trade and taste, did not fancy the local product as long as there was anything better, though they may have had small workshops in the later fourth century. At its best Etruscan red-figure is provincial, though it has the merits of good provincial art and does not aspire to the magnificence that spoils much South Italian. There was a little export beyond Etruscan lands to the Gallic settlements of northern Italy.

6. South Italy

Since the first big finds of painted Greek pottery were made in Campania and the Basilicata, most of the older museums have a surfeit of the South Italian version of red-figure. Its availability, the many theatrical scenes it exhibits, and perhaps their stronger stomachs made it popular with an earlier generation of scholars. Now it is neglected, except by a few specialists.

The Greek cities along the coasts of Sicily and South Italy had for up to three hundred years regularly imported their better painted pottery, first from Corinth and then from Athens. But in the middle and later fifth century a few craftsmen, presumably (except in the Owl-Pillar workshop) trained immigrants from Athens, began to manufacture red-figure ware in South Italy and Sicily. Their products are known generically as South Italian (or Italiot) since, though in Greek history the two regions were distinct, the name South Italian was fortunately too firmly established to be changed when the Sicilian workshops were recognized. Perhaps less fortunate is the established division, based on places of finding, into regional schools – Apulian, Lucanian, Campanian and Paestan (to which Sicilian has now been added): painters seem to have moved about much more freely here than in other parts of the Greek world, so that differences between schools are often blurred. Apulian, the largest and most influential grouping, has some unity and so for a time has its provincial neighbour Lucanian: but Sicilian, Campanian and Paestan, if a fresh start was made, might be lumped together or divided in some other way. A more serious trouble is the unsteady or sluggish development of personal styles, so that it is sometimes difficult to determine the relationship of one painter to another. New finds are still liable to upset some currently accepted propositions.

The first venture, apparently in Campania, is the so-called *Owl-Pillar group*, which apes Attic of the second and third quarters of the fifth century, though with a strong Etruscan flavour. The commonest shape is the neck-amphora, decorated with a couple of figures on each side. These figures are robustly ill-proportioned, their feet often sink into the frame below the picture, and their interpretation is sometimes curious or obscure. The technique is adequate, and the style though clumsy is clean. Its ingenuous assurance recalls good peasant craftsmanship. The Owl-Pillar workshop, which (like the Campanian black-figure of its time) is perhaps better classed with Etruscan than Greek, was short-lived and had no following or influence.

More successful were two establishments on the southern coast of Italy, the progenitors one of the Lucanian and the other of the Apulian school, and formerly designated as group A and group B of Early South Italian. Early Lucanian [PLATE 52B], domiciled – so finds suggest

– somewhere west of Tarentum, began about 440 B.C., the time when the Athenians colonized Thurii, and perhaps the two events are connected. Early Apulian [PLATE 52A], which became much more important, appeared in the 420s and probably had its home in Tarentum, the principal city of south-eastern Italy. Early Sicilian starts a little later, but before the end of the fifth century, and on a smaller scale. These three schools were based, independently of each other, on Attic models and their resemblances in style to particular Attic workshops make it probable that the founders of the new schools had trained in those workshops. Sicilian, being geographically remote, remained apart from the other two, but Lucanian was affected by Apulian; and all diverged from Attic. The painters, few and often isolated, were able to indulge personal mannerisms, which their pupils copied; here, in contrast to Athens, there was not a vigorous and critical standard. Even so, local manufacture increased, whether this was an effect or a cause of diminishing Attic imports, and by the 370s (when the Early stage of South Italian ends) four or five regional schools are recognized. The largest, showiest and most influential is Apulian [PLATE 53]. Lucanian [PLATE 54] was now becoming provincial. As for Sicily, some enterprising painters left about this time to set up workshops in Campania and Paestum; of the three schools, which keep up some connection with each other, Campanian [PLATE 55A] is the most varied and prolific, Paestan [PLATE 55B] more steadily compact and Sicilian – the smallest – shows greater originality towards its end. South Italian red-figure outlived Attic and a few workshops survived into the early years of the third century.

It is not easy to describe in words the peculiarities of South Italian red-figure. The technical competence of the best work is equal to Attic, of the poor work generally inferior: the paint, for example, tends to flake away or – in Campanian – to blister. The fired clay varies in colour and texture. Sometimes it looks like Attic; more often it is duller or paler, ranging as far as a yellow which may be mistaken for Corinthian; and in some Campanian examples it is chocolate. But where the colour is far from the Attic standard, the visible surfaces are usually improved by a reddish wash. The paint often appears muddy or greenish, with a sheen that suggests a metallic harshness rather than the glassy transparence of Attic.

The style, starting as second-rate Attic, soon takes its own road or rut. The ordinary work becomes monotonous and impoverished, and in the fourth century repeatedly lapses towards barbarity. Pretentious pieces attain a self-conscious and uncomfortable classicism, often admirable in detail but heavy or stupid in composition. The more original essays in parody or the subhuman are much happier. The red-figure of South Italy is often as accomplished, rarely as successful as that of Athens, where even in the fourth century the classical tradition was supply tenacious. There was not the same restraint on South Italian painters, who continued practices considered freakish by the Athenians and also were more susceptible to the novelties of free painting. In

FIG. 35. *Apulian Rf volute-krater*
Detail of neck: scale *c.* 1 : 2. By the Darius painter: *c.* 330 B.C. Black areas represent white paint

Attic vase-painting towards the middle and again around the end of the fifth century there was a limited vogue for grandiose compositions where depth is indicated by tiering and the remoter – that is higher – figures may be partly concealed by conventional hillocks: this device remained acceptable in South Italy. A bolder perspective is freely used in architecture (especially for ornate structures viewed obliquely from below) and even in floral ornament [FIG. 35]; and, as the style progresses, forms – except those of the female body – are sometimes modelled by shading and even high lights. Minor aids that become popular are the lines of white dots on which figures stand and the filling ornament – rosettes, bunches of grapes and the like – which bestrew the field. Judged by Attic standards – and their work shows a recurrent though remote awareness of Attic standards – the South Italians are heavy or vulgar or dull.

The stock subjects are Dionysiac incidents and increasingly Eros attending women. The perfunctory draped youths are of course normal on the backs of bell-kraters. On more ambitious pieces mythology is illustrated, and there is a persistent taste for tragic scenes, chosen perhaps from a love less of the theatre than of the theatrical. More lively are the so-called Phlyax vases [PLATE 55B], with their stubby burlesque actors and stage scenery: the South Italian series begins about 400 B.C., apparently developing an experiment made in Athens, where similar figures occur very rarely but earlier. In the later fourth century female heads embowered in gross palmettes bedizen small pots or in more careful settings the necks of large ones.

The early shapes come from the Attic repertory; but some flourish in South Italy when discarded in Athens, some develop on their own, and there are a few local or native inventions. The bell-krater remains the commonest of the larger shapes. The column-krater is restricted to the Apulian and Lucanian schools, which also exploit the volute-krater for their ornater efforts. The neck-amphora, rare in late Attic, continues popular in Campania and Paestum; and in Campania a new variety – the bail-amphora – substituted an arched handle across the lip. The pelike is mainly Apulian and Lucanian. Hydria and oinochoai are fairly numerous. The so-called nestoris, a jar with high, knobbed handles above ordinary side handles, is characteristic of Lucanian. Smaller vases multiply in the fourth century; notable are the askos (shaped rather like a toy duck), the squat lekythos, the handleless bottle and a clumsy kantharos. The cup is rare, but not the kotyle. A curious speciality of later Apulian and Campanian is the fish-plate, a large saucer with a hollow in the middle and a turned-down rim: it comes from Attic, though there the decoration with edible fishes is not usual. In general the shapes gradually become longer and more angular, and towards the end the ornatest of them are liable to break out into plastic ornament.

On some Apulian works of the second quarter of the fourth century subsidiary ornaments or even figures are not reserved, but painted in colour on the dark ground. This technique becomes commoner in later South Italian red-figure, and is also extended to be the sole decoration of the so-called Gnathian ware [PLATE 56B], which begins around 360 B.C. and lasts for perhaps a hundred years. The Gnathian formula, usually consisting of simple decoration and applied to small pots, remained most popular in Apulia but was adopted in other regions too.

Although so many South Italian pots survive, very often complete, the records of finding and of context are not yet sufficient, except for Sicilian from around 340 B.C. For the rest we still have to rely on stylistic criteria – sequences within schools, connections of one school with another and parallels with Attic. This last criterion, on which our absolute dating depends, has the extra hazard that the intermittent Atticisms in South Italian may well be retarded.

The South Italian workshops produced mainly for their local markets, and indeed the definition of the local schools depends partly on distribution. During the fourth century Campanian and, perhaps indirectly, Apulian influences are evident in Etruria, and in Spain some ornaments of the native Iberian pottery seem to come from South Italian. Later Apulian has been found here and there along the Dalmatian coast, but other certainly identified exports are very few.

Apulian

The founders of the Early Apulian school settled in the 420s at Tarentum, to judge by the distribution of their products, the importance of that city, and the wasters (admittedly of later date) that have been found there. They started with a version of Attic of the Polygnotan school and followed Attic developments closely for the first generation, then intermittently. But they quickly formed a standard of their own, classical and grandiose; individual figures are well drawn in statuesque poses, but the composition is tiresomely clumsy. This inability to compose large groups continues throughout Apulian, so that its more ambitious pieces look better in fragments than complete. Of the pioneers the Sisyphus painter [PLATE 52A], active through the last quarter of the fifth century, was a decisive personality: the two classes of the subsequent Apulian school, the Ornate and the Plain, both descend from him. His competent figures have a studied nobility, and on large volute-kraters pose self-sufficiently in two or three registers. The successors of the Sisyphus painter specialize as Ornate or Plain painters, but do not reach his level.

For the Plain manner bell-krater, column-krater, amphora, pelike and of course smaller shapes were preferred. The normal repertory of subjects is limited – Dionysiac groups or women at their toilet (sometimes attended by Eros), and on the backs of kraters the familiar young

men in cloaks. Towards the middle of the fourth century this Plain
manner began to merge with the Ornate, adopting its richer colouring
and ornament; and though some of the old austerity persisted for a
time on column-krater and pelike, the term 'Plain' ceases to have much
meaning.

The Ornate manner, exhibited first on such large pots as volute-
krater, amphora and hydria, reaches its full bloom after the middle of
the fourth century. An earlier example is shown on PLATE 53. For
ambitious pieces the regular subjects are scenes from mythology, notably that of tragedy, and gatherings around a funerary shrine, often one
on the front and the other on the back of the pot; the cast is deployed
at as many as three levels round the central feature, and vacant spaces
are filled with sashes, flowers or rosettes. The abundant subsidiary
decoration is notable for the rank vegetable ornament, which is
developed with a metallic crispness and displays flowers in three-
quarter view – a trick found very rarely (though earlier) in Attic; and
there are even meanders modelled by shading. White and yellow had
been growing popular from the beginning of the fourth century. In
the fully Ornate style they, and purple, are used generously and broadly,
and sometimes applied over the dark paint: the effect is gaudily overwhelming in spite of the fluent competence of the draughtsmanship.
On lesser works, particularly after the decline of the Plain manner,
the subjects are more trivial and the style often more effeminate, and
in the second half of the fourth century there is a glut of small vases
with palmettes and large female heads. The style, simpler and more
negligent than that of the more important productions, is generally of
a dreary uniformity. The output was correspondingly immense.

The Apulian school lasted perhaps into the first years of the third
century. Its headquarters probably remained at Tarentum; but there
may have been workshops in some of the native towns, for instance at
Canosa, seventy-five miles to the north-west. There was some export
to other parts of South Italy, to Sicily and to the Dalmatian coast.
Apulian influence became strong in Lucanian, and both Campanian
and Paestan had a late Apulianizing phase. Canosa ware, it seems clear
is derived from Late Apulian.

Lucanian

Lucanian, though the oldest, is the worst of the four South Italian
schools. It begins as a respectable second-rate offshoot of Attic – of
the school of Polygnotus and the followers of the Achilles painter –
but with more stiffness and angularity in draughtsmanship and less

expression [PLATE 52B]. Contact with Athens is weaker than in Early Apulian and the painters, isolated and unaspiring, grow mannered and provincial. The ideal nobility of Attic eludes this school, but it is sometimes amusing in conscious and unconscious parody. Subjects and types are monotonous. On bell-kraters, the commonest shape, the stock formula for the front is a three-figure group – especially women pursued or satyrs with maenads – and for the back two or three draped youths. During the fourth century Lucanian tags more or less wearily behind Apulian till in the third quarter a stronger dose of that style is injected by the Primato painter [PLATE 54], who had been trained in one of its Ornate workshops, and by the Roccanova painter, who had studied what was then its Plain manner. But they in turn succumb to the environment, and the style of their successors can at last hardly be described as Greek. Characteristic of developed Lucanian, apart from clumsy distortions and simplifications of Apulian, are a doubled dark stripe down women's skirts, palmettes with serrated edges, Z pattern, and an old-fashioned taste for thick rays. Next to the bell-krater the hydria has some importance; and there is the nestoris, an unpleasant shape of native Messapian origin but in red-figure almost confined to Lucanian. The school shambles to its end rather before 300 B.C.

It is likely that at first the workshops were in some Greek city on the southern coast of Lucania, Thurii for instance or Heraclea. Later, according to the distribution of the finds, they shifted into the barbarian interior, to Armento and perhaps Anzi and other towns. In the earliest generation there is export to Apulia and even influence there, but by 380 B.C. both have become negligible.

Sicilian

In eastern Sicily, so it appears from the presence and absence of finds there and in Campania, a local manufacture of red-figure began near the end of the fifth century. Initially it followed Attic models of the time, particularly of the style of the Pothos painter (a rather florid and second-rate artist), and then continued on its own. Though in the 370's leading painters of this small school moved off to Campania and Paestum, a few lesser colleagues continued at work in Sicily. Then around 340 B.C., presumably as a consequence of the prosperity imposed by Timoleon, the output of red-figure pottery increased and for some forty years several workshops were active, influenced by Campanian models and perhaps immigrants and also showing acquaintance with Apulian, but independent enough to develop (especially in the Lipari group) an unusually polychrome technique.

The style of Early Sicilian, the product perhaps of only one work-shop, is floridly tame. In subjects there is a preference for draped women and satyrs; and the favourite shapes are bell-krater and calyx-krater, but amphorae are not yet known. The middle period, between 370 and 340 B.C., is still obscure, but later workshops show a more sensuous taste. Their commonest subjects are now half-naked women, indo-lently posed and often inspected by an effeminate Eros, and – even more than in other South Italian schools – solitary female heads; there are also some Dionysiac and even a few phlyax scenes. Composition is simple. Among frequent shapes are the krater of the calyx (but not the bell) variety, the skyphoid pyxis (like a kotyle with a lid) and the bottle. More remarkable is the trend to polychromy; to the traditional white and yellow are added first various gradations of red, then blue, and towards the end green, pink and mauve as well, so that if it was not for the dark background the more colourful pieces would not be recognized as red-figure. From here it was a logical step to the more fully pictorial style of Centuripae ware.

Campanian

After the false start of the Owl-Pillar group no red-figure was made in Campania till the 370s, when followers of the Dirce painter and per-haps that painter himself moved across from Sicily. Campania was mixed in its population and by now under Samnite rule, but affluent enough to appreciate Greek civilization, and the venture flourished. By the 350s the new Campanian school had three branches, located – according to distribution – one at Greek Cumae and one or perhaps two at Italian Capua. Though there continued to be relations between these branches, their development differed. In particular, Apulian influence was much stronger at Cumae, where it looks as if one or two of the earlier painters had trained in Apulia; and one of the Capuan painters may have worked at Paestum and certainly left his mark on its later style. By the end of the fourth century all branches of Campanian were in decay and the school petered out probably just after 300 B.C.

The quality of Campanian is rather provincial but has, compared with Apulian and Lucanian, the merit of modesty. There is great play – especially at Cumae – with white and yellow both on figures and to model floral ornament, which is usually stiff and often unduly straight. Palmettes tend to hatched stems or white-rimmed leaves. Women, whose flesh is often white (in contrast to Apulian practice), may have capes fastened at the neck. Soldiers sometimes wear armour of an Oscan type [PLATE 55A]. The shapes, mostly smallish, include bell-

krater, neck-amphora, the peculiar bail-amphora with its one handle
arched across the mouth, hydria, kotyle and squat lekythos.

Paestan

Paestum, another Greek city under Italian rule, lies at the north-west
corner of Lucanian territory but has better access to Campania. It too
has been given its red-figure school. The founder, Asteas, whose
activity began in the 360s, came from an Early Campanian (and ultimately Sicilian) workshop and, if he had not signed some of his works,
perhaps Paestan would now be counted as another branch of Campanian. His personal style has a stodgy dignity with its solid figures
and compact but heavy composition – for this PLATE 55B is not a good

FIG. 36. *Paestan Rf bell-krater*
Handle ornament. Later 4th cent. B.C.

example – and his followers remembered his style though they coarsened it. Other late Paestans, from about 330 B.C. on, turned to
Campanian for their models; and before the end, which came at the
beginning of the third century, there was much imitation of decadent
Apulian.

The school of Paestum, small and concentrated, has till the last
quarter of the fourth century an unusual unity. The typical product is
the bell-krater, from the time of Asteas straight-sided and decorated
with a square picture framed at the sides by a reserved line or the
characteristic Paestan volute and palmettes [FIG. 36]. Dionysiac subjects
are popular, and there are showier scenes from Phlyax plays and
mythology: the back normally carries a couple of cloaked youths.
Drapery often has the so-called embattled border, a row of squares or
dots that follow an edge. There is no Ornate manner, though the more

elaborate pictures are richly coloured. Besides the bell-krater the main shapes are neck-amphora, hydria and squat lekythos.

Gnathian

Gnathian, which may eventually have been made at Gnathia as well as other places, is a style which for its decoration uses applied colour on a dark ground. The technique had occurred intermittently in one Greek school or another since the late eighth century, but here the main impulse probably came from its subsidiary employment in Ornate Apulian red-figure, which by the second quarter of the fourth century was extravagant with white and yellow colour, not only to embellish its red figures, but also on some elaborate pieces for adding laurel wreaths or, later, heads and foliage on lip or neck. It was an easy step to make this secondary decoration in added colour the sole decoration of smaller pots.

Besides white and yellow there is some purple. Incision is not very common, even for stems of leaves. Typical ornaments are wreaths and scrolls of ivy and of vine, horizontal or vertical, bands of laurel, necklaces and ribbons. More pretentious are the female head, the full figure of a woman or Eros, an actor's mask, and as fillers musical instruments, votive tablets, birds and various properties. The decoration is spread often over much and sometimes over all of the available surface. Some early works in Gnathian technique, for instance those of the Konnakis painter, display more important scenes or studies of human figures, but stylistically they are better reckoned with red-figure. The Gnathian style proper [PLATE 56B], though it occasionally employs advanced tricks of shading, is deliberately restricted in scope. Its ideal was decorative prettiness, and its course inevitably downhill.

The shapes, many and varied, come from the red-figure tradition of South Italy, but tend to be more elegant. Among them are kraters (especially the bell-krater), pelike, oinochoai of several types and sizes, kotyle, kantharos, squat lekythos, a still squatter lekythos, bottle, and small bowls and cups. Ribbing of the body becomes common in the last quarter of the fourth century. A narrowish reserved band is usual near the junction of body and foot.

Gnathian pots are very numerous and some have useful contexts. Comparison of shapes shows that the style was established by the middle of the fourth century. It was probably over by the middle of the third, though outlying workshops may have lasted another generation. Early connections with Apulian red-figure argue that Gnathian began in Apulia, perhaps—since it was then the dominant city of the region –

at Tarentum. But to judge by differences in clay and sometimes differences in style, manufacture was diffused over Apulia and as far as Campania, where the dark paint and the white are duller and ribbed decoration was more popular. In Sicily in the late fourth and early third centuries a local variety is distinguished by its use of blue and fondness for vine sprays. Related wares, using white or yellow on a dark ground, appear in Latium and Etruria, which had also its own tradition of painting in added colour. Gnathian is most frequent in Apulia, but is found throughout Greek Italy and Sicily, in Etruscan and Latin lands, and even in the Mediterranean settlements of France and Spain. In the eastern half of the ancient world it seems to be very rare, except perhaps at Alexandria.

6   Hellenistic Pottery with Painted Decoration

1. Introduction

By the late fourth century the red-figure style was dead or dying, and with it ended the main tradition of Greek vase-painting. In the period that followed, the ordinary pottery with painted decoration was for the most part content with a few simple ornaments, simply arranged and drawn either in light paint on a dark ground or in dark paint on a light ground. Whatever the reason, painted decoration was no longer important, and even the more numerous and often more elaborate wares that have designs in relief or impressed are rarely original works of art. The Hellenistic standard of pottery was set by metalwork.

The favourite ornaments of Hellenistic vase-painting are wreaths and festoons of ivy and laurel (in which are included myrtle and olive, if they can be distinguished) and also vine. These are supplemented by a few abstract patterns, dolphins and such oddments as round garlands [as on FIG. 37], ribbons and musical instruments. It is a limited repertory, taken mostly from established convention, and the forms have no positive development. The effect too is trivial. The decoration appears no longer to be a considered part of the finished pot, but rather to be applied to its surface, as very obviously in the festoon of ivy of PLATE 56A. The new vase-painting needed neither the skill nor the imagination of an artist.

The *dark-ground* class divides into two principal schools, West Slope ware in Greece and Gnathian in Italy. Each had imitators and local varieties. Gnathian [PLATE 56B and pp. 200–1], established by the middle of the fourth century, is a byproduct of Apulian red-figure and tends to a similar extravagance. This confectioner's style was probably extinct by the middle or at latest the end of the third century. The West Slope school [PLATE 56A] was more restrained and sturdy. It appears in Athens at the end of the fourth century as a humble successor of Attic red-figure, and persisted in much of the Greek East till the second or even the first century B.C.

In the *light-ground* class, though hardly of it, are the veteran Panathenaic amphorae, which till the late second century or even longer exhibit on one side a current interpretation of the Archaic style and on the other modern anatomical drawing painfully executed in the black-figure technique. This black-figure manner was during the third century imitated in South Russia and echoed on some of the Hadra hydriai of Alexandria. But the light-ground class proper consists of various groups of pottery decorated with the common Hellenistic ornaments in a brown to blackish paint on a white or pale slip or surface. The most widespread group – east of the Adriatic – is that of the Lagynoi [FIG. 37], squat jugs with tall thin necks and a modicum of ornament: their home is unknown, their date probably from the late third to the middle of the first century B.C. More imposing is the larger of the two groups of the Hadra hydriai, with which a modest South Russian group has some affinity. In Rhodes, where a provincial light-ground (though unslipped) ware had survived in the Classical period, a few local pots have a perhaps delusively Hellenistic look. Cyprus pursued its own deviations, yielding reluctantly to the fashions of the times; and central Anatolia had its 'Galatian' ware, with a desiccated version of the familiar flora. In Italy the native Daunian tradition of northern Apulia incorporated contemporary motives in its spidery late style. Across the sea Carthage, Hellenistic though not Greek, produced modish oinochoai that have a charmingly casual air, and in eastern Spain the decoration of some Iberian pottery would not have looked strange to Greek visitors. In general the light-ground method belongs to the fringes and backwaters of the Hellenistic world; in metropolitan Greece the taste for a dark ground was ingrained.

Hellenistic pottery has been neglected, and deservedly. The dated Panathenaic amphorae are occasionally useful by way of comparison for the chronology of higher arts. But there were now few intrinsic merits in the painting of pottery, and as time went on production became sparser and feebler. Though West Slope ware and the Lagynoi continued probably into the first century B.C., most of the other groups that have been mentioned did not outlast the third. But the technical methods of this vase-painting were invitingly easy and the stock of conventional motives simple enough, so that unpretentious essays in dark on light or light on dark decoration were liable to recur in one place or another throughout antiquity, as for example on some poor Athenian bowls of the third century A.D. and the Yorkshire Crambeck ware of the late fourth.

Hellenistic shapes range from the clumsy to the elegant. The general tendency of careful pieces is to flowing curves and arbitrary angles. There is much more imitation of metal than in the past, and plastic ornament is applied more freely. Since the manufacture of painted pottery, though small, was less concentrated than in the preceding centuries variation in clay is more marked. The paint is less regularly black and shiny on the dark-ground ware, and on the light-ground is more often streaky and dilute.

Besides these useful wares there are a few Hellenistic groups of *polychrome* pots. At various times since the end of the Geometric period some pottery intended for funerals had been painted with colours that did not and did not need to wear. Examples have already been mentioned in the early Orientalizing of Crete (p. 142) and in Protoattic of the third quarter of the seventh century (p. 71), and there are the sometimes more durably coloured Attic white lekythoi. In the scattered Hellenistic groups the normal procedure was to coat a fired pot with a chalky white solution and to paint on it in tempera. Largish hydriai and amphorae decorated with heavy coloured festoons are known in the Hadra ware of Alexandria and from Cyrene and South Russia, and a few similar urns have come to light in the Aegean region. Figures are more usual in the West – at Canosa in Apulia, where their flat treatment recalls the red-figure tradition, and at Centuripae in Sicily, where the style exploits the illusionist tricks of free painting. But these curiosities, which are mostly of the third century, can hardly be reckoned as vase-painting. That art was dead.

2. West Slope Ware

West Slope ware, which takes its name from a site facing the Acropolis at Athens, may be defined as pottery made during the Hellenistic period east of the Adriatic and decorated with simple ornaments painted in white and yellow over a dark ground. The definition is loose and at its borders shadowy, but in our present ignorance it is useful. Painting in colour over a dark ground had been tested in both early and late red-figure, but a more important precedent are the wreaths and festoons of added white and yellow (or gold) that before the end of the fifth century sometimes encircle the field inside cups or modestly embellish the necks of hydriai and other pots. Though this last class survives into the third century and merges into the West Slope style, there is a distinction between them. In one the ornament is subsidiary, in the other it occupies a principal place.

The character of the West Slope style is exhibited most clearly on its amphorae, such as that of PLATE 56A. The decoration is limited to the upper part of the pot, and other shapes have similar restrictions.

The repertory of ornament is small and impoverished. Of naturalistic patterns the favourites are ivy and hanging buds, and there are also laurel and vine, necklaces with pendants, and the row of spiral hooks. The stock abstract patterns are chequers, alternately plain and coloured, and boxed rectangles; later there appear cross-hatched rectangles. A rosette or rough star is usual in the centre of bowls and other open pots. Animal and human figures are rare. A few early pots include in their decoration the painted names of deities. The style degenerates rather than develops, with at Athens a growing preference for abstract ornaments; the drawing steadily coarsens and is supplemented and increasingly replaced by incision.

Though some kantharoi have the excessive refinement of the more elaborate black-painted ware, the typical West Slope shapes are un-compromisingly solid. They include the squat neck-amphora with twisted handles, kantharoi (some resembling the Cabiran type), saucer, plate, small bowls or cups of various kinds, lids, kraters, and oinochoai with broad or narrow neck. There is some use of plastic ornament – for instance, the heads at the base of the handles on PLATE 56A; and sometimes a band of moulding is borrowed or the lower part of the body is ribbed or knobbed. In general the shapes grow clumsier and worse proportioned. The amphora, for example, starts with a cylindrical neck and rounded shoulder: that of PLATE 56A, of the first half of the second century, has an angular shoulder and a flaring neck.

The clay varies from place to place, but is rarely as fine as in red-figure pottery. The dark paint is from the first duller and muddier, and to these faults are added streaky application and careless firing. The thick yellow often stands out in relief. The white, thick or thin, is flush. At first white is subordinate to yellow, but gradually it becomes at least as important.

At Athens West Slope ware begins towards the end of the fourth century. It lasts till the end of the first century B.C. Its quality and connection with red-figure, small though both are, suggest an Attic origin. But it was also made at Corinth and, it is claimed, in Pergamum, Gordion, Tarsus, Samaria, Alexandria and South Russia. Indeed most sizeable Greek cities may have had West Slope workshops. The local versions differ in standard and perhaps in style, if the term may be so debased. There seems to have been some export, at least of Attic. Though nowhere very frequent, West Slope pottery is found through-out the lands of the eastern Mediterranean.

3. The Lagynos Group

The most widespread and, not only for that reason, the most characteristic of the Hellenistic wares with decoration on a light ground is the group of small jugs which have with fair reason been dubbed lagynoi. The normal shape and system of decoration is shown on FIG. 37. The ornaments, restricted to the shoulder, are sometimes continuous – ivy, laurel or less often festoons looped across the field – and sometimes such isolated objects as wreaths, musical instruments, lagynoi, dolphins and even fighting cocks. Occasionally some convivial word is added as a motto. The style is hasty but adequate.

FIG. 37. *Light-ground lagynos*
Ht 19 cm. Later 3rd or 2nd cent. B.C.

The standard shape of FIG. 37 with squat angular body occurs also in dark-ground and relief wares. A few lids and cylindrical pieces – some pyxides and others described as incense-burners – belong to the group. But it is tidier to exclude the kraters and other pots of vaguely similar decoration but coarser quality which occur in Hellenistic contexts. The clay, often micaceous, is moderately fine and in colour varies from light brown to reddish. The slip is normally hard and white. The paint is sometimes fairly black, but more often diluted to brown and even yellow-brown. There is some sheen. The wall of the pot is often very thin. Fragments of lagynoi are sometimes mistaken for Chiot of the sixth century.

The Lagynos group is thought to continue, but not develop, from the later third to the mid-first century B.C. and perhaps longer. Though the style is generally uniform, the clay is said to vary significantly. It is not known where the principal factory or factories may have been, but comparison of clay rules out Athens and Corinth. In Athens, Cyprus and, it is said, South Russia inferior and presumably local imitations have been recognized. Lagynoi occur throughout the Greek world east of the Adriatic, though less frequently in Greece itself. In the West they are very rare.

4. Hadra Ware

The name Hadra ware is given to two groups of hydriai which were frequent in the Hadra and other cemeteries of Alexandria where they were used to contain ashes.

The first and larger group is distinguished by its technique of dark painting on a yellowish slip or surface. Normally the decoration is in two minor fields on the neck and the shoulder and in a major field (interrupted by the handles) at the top of the belly; the rest of the body is reserved, and the foot is dark. The commonest ornaments are laurel and ivy wreaths, and there are also volutes, scrolls, wilting palmettes, garlands, dolphins, long-necked birds and simple abstract patterns. Often a rosette is inserted in the middle of foliage on the neck, and on the body the front field is bounded by narrow panels with rough cross-hatching or even opposed triangles. Occasionally this field contains figures – confronting animals or monsters, or such ambitious scenes as Erotes hunting, Nike between tripods, and a race in armour. Though some of the figures are in silhouette, the more careful or elaborate – presumably emulating Panathenaic amphorae – revive a niggling black-figure technique of incision. Outlined figures are rare. A little white is sometimes used for ornaments. The quality of the painting varies, but is generally sober and at its best neat. There appears to be no development, but only the rehashing of traditional motives.

The second or polychrome group generally has a chalky white coat on which the decoration was painted in tempera. The colours, which of course are not fast, are principally reds and blues and also yellow and green, besides of course brown and black. The usual decoration con-sists of thick festoons slung across neck or belly. Sometimes the belly displays insignia of sex, arms for the man and articles of toilet for the woman. The painting is rather crude, except for a skilfully shaded head of Medusa. A few intermediate hydriai use colours and dark paint on a yellowish slip.

The two groups should be contemporary, to judge by their

similarity of shape and the evidence of graves. That they were, sometimes at least, made in the same workshop is supported very strongly by
a specimen of the first group which after firing was painted over in
polychrome. A frequent use of the hydriai was funerary, as containers
of ashes; and this was clearly the purpose of the polychrome group, in
which subjects and technique were suitable only for the grave.

The shape of the hydria varies within the limits of carelessness, but
tends with time to become slimmer. It is a tallish pot of simple profile,
with neck more or less distinct from the body, rounded shoulder and
splaying foot: sometimes the floor of the pot is well down inside the
foot. There are a few examples of other shapes. Plastic decoration is
uncommon. The clay is light brown to reddish, the dark paint brown
to black according to its thickness.

It would be hard to date Hadra ware by style alone, but fortunately
some hydriai of the first group have written or incised on them not
only the name of the dead but occasionally the regnal year as well.
The most credible identification of reigns gives dates from 271 to 209
B.C. Though the hydriai are numerous, they need not extend much
earlier or later.

To the first group may be added several hydriai from Crete and
there are also similar or connected pieces from Cyprus, Rhodes,
Thera, Athens, Eretria and South Russia. In Crete smaller hydriai of
the same species are not uncommon, and some oinochoai and other pots
from South Russia show a tamer but comparable character. Relatives
of the polychrome group have been found in Rhodes and reported from
Cyrenaica, South Russia and perhaps Cilicia; and odd pieces – more
loosely connected – come from Thera, Myrina, Tanagra and Apulia.
From comparison of clay and because of the friable technique of the
decoration it is likely enough that the polychrome hydriai found in
Alexandria were made there, but the hydriai of Rhodes may well be
Rhodian. For the first Hadra group the place of manufacture is generally supposed to be Alexandria again, but the clay – for what that is
worth – does not look particularly Alexandrine and Crete on present
evidence is a possible alternative. Of pieces found elsewhere those from
South Russia have a fair claim to be local, but decoration so simple and
familiar could be managed by any moderately competent workshop.

5. Canosa Ware

At Canosa (or Canusium) in northern Apulia a well-known group of
pots also displays decoration in colours put on after firing. Here the

favourite motives of the vase-painter were human and animal figures, especially winged or wingless horses, and vegetable patterns are subordinate. Often there are rosettes as filling ornaments in the field. Outlines are drawn in dark paint and filled – at least sometimes – with a yellowish wash; inner detail is done partly by a few dark lines, partly by modest touches of colour. The white background is usually painted over in pink or blue. The style, flat and without modelling, resembles red-figure in its linear draughtsmanship and some of its motives. It develops out of the later Apulian school.

The best Canosa vase-painting has a decent charm. This is more than can be said of the shapes. The *chef d'œuvre* is the old Daunian askos, now crowded with figurines and other plastic ornaments, between which there is sometimes space for a little quiet vase-painting. Other, less eruptive, shapes are oinochoe with long, slender neck and kantharos. The clay is fairly fine and light brown. The white slip, added after firing, does not always reach to the base of the pot. The colours used are yellow, pink, red and blue.

The connection with red-figure and some vague contexts show that this group of pots belongs to the very late fourth and early third centuries. Most of them have been found at Canosa. A few pieces in the same or a very similar style come from Cumae.

6. Centuripae Ware

Centuripae, a native town in the interior of Sicily, remained independent of the Greeks politically, but admitted their culture. Indeed the polychrome pottery that from time to time is found in its graves offers what in their way are the most accomplished of Greek vase-paintings or, to be more exact, paintings on vases. The favourite shape is a sort of bell-krater with high lid and pedestal but no handles. On the deep field of the bell large figures, mostly women, are spaced in studied poses that usually avoid fully frontal or fully profile views. The figures are modelled by shading and high lights, the colours simulate nature. The background is a flat pink or, on some early pieces, black. The style appears familiar from wall-paintings at Pompeii and elsewhere.

The shapes show a heavy good taste in profiles and even in the plastic ornament which, genteelly florid, on some pots of this group leaves no space for painted decoration. Besides kraters there are lowish bowls with tall conical lid and also a kind of kotyle. All are big pots, not intended for ordinary use; for sometimes the lid is fired in one piece with its pot and the colours are very friable. The clay, red to brown, is not fine. On this, after the pot had been fired, the painter applied a chalky white undercoat, then outlined the figures in black and filled in from an unusually wide choice of colours – yellows, browns, reds, blues and black. These colours are often mixed, as for instance to make the pink of the background.

This group of pots was probably made at or near Centuripae, since they have been found only there and at Morgantina and are unhandy to transport. Their date is probably early in the third century: it is unlikely that so compact and peculiar a group was made over a long period, fragments have been found at Morgantina in a deposit of the fourth and third centuries, and the polychromy suggests a connection with Sicilian red-figure though the style borrows much from free painting. This borrowing explains the resemblances, which misled some earlier students, to Pompeian and other murals of late Hellenistic or Roman date but following older models.

7 *Black-Painted and Relief Wares*

1. General Comments

The pottery described in the preceding chapters is characterized by its painted decoration. At the same time there was also much pottery of comparable quality which was simply covered with the standard dark paint. Such pottery has little artistic merit till near the middle of the sixth century, when Attic workshops were refining their standards of shape, paint and finish. For the next century and a half the new Attic *Black-painted* ware (or, as it is commonly miscalled, Black-glazed ware) is often technically and aesthetically excellent. There follows a steady fall in quality, but not in output. Meanwhile the less exacting requirements of black-painted pottery had encouraged local imitations in many, if not most, Greek cities and in Etruria. But the Attic product, because of its better clay or tradition, was still exported widely, even in the Hellenistic period, though it gradually lost its western markets to black-painted Campanian and to Gnathian. At last, apparently in the later years of the third century, a needed revolution began. The native peoples of parts of nearer Asia had been used to pottery with a red surface, and perhaps for that reason as much as technical convenience some potters of the Hellenistic East chose to fire their paint to an even, slightly shiny red. This kind of red-painted pottery is generically and imprecisely classed as *Sigillata*, and its Hellenistic version is – or used to be – particularized as '*Pergamene*'. Though Red wares became normal in Greek Asia by the end of the second century, a degenerate black-painted ware persisted at Athens and perhaps in the rest of European Greece till at least the beginning of the first century B.C. and in Italy till about its end. Italian Sigillata, of which *Arretine* is the principal representative, began in the third quarter of that century, and its universal success justified imitation throughout the Roman empire. During the next two centuries, which were the heyday of Sigillata, the manufacture of *Early Roman* wares spread as far as Syria and Britain. The later Sigillata of the eastern or Greek half of the ancient world, the so-called *Middle* and *Late Roman* wares, prolonged their decline from the second to the seventh or eighth century A.D., when a true glaze was at last adopted generally. So the last flicker of the tradition of Greek vase-painting was snuffed out.

From the middle of the fifth century B.C. these black-painted and, later, red-painted wares become very frequent and so are most useful to excavators for dating their sites. Knowledge of Western Sigillata is well advanced, thanks in part to the many makers' stamps. In the East the Attic black-painted pottery and the 'Megarian' bowls have been studied; of the other black-painted wares we are still more or less ignorant, but the Sigillata has provoked some careful investigation.

The shapes of Attic black-painted pottery of the sixth and fifth centuries have the elegance to be expected of their period. In the fourth century hydriai and kraters and oinochoai still show a considered refinement, sometimes (as in the later fifth century) enhanced by ribbing of the body, but cups and kantharoi and kotylai often suffer clumsy distortions, and the many little bowls are trivial. Later the regular shapes grow fewer and mostly small – bowls, saucers, plates, and for a while kantharoi and dumpy jugs with round or trefoil mouth – and though the imitation of metal forms at times produced an angular or brittle precision, the modelling is more often careless as well as inert. 'Pergamene' invents or introduces new profiles, cleaner though looking more mechanical, but the repertory of Sigillata remains in general limited to plates, saucers and open bowls.

The clay and paint vary from one place and time to another. At Athens the deep and rich black of fifth-century paint tends later to become thinner and duller, and the Hellenistic ideal is a glassy bluish grey though the average approaches a muddy brown. Misfiring is increasingly frequent, so that on many pieces the paint is partly or wholly oxidized to red. At Athens this red comes through negligence, but in 'Pergamene' the darkish and not very shiny red is deliberate. The red of Arretine and its successors is more vivid, and so is its sheen: occasionally a yellow of equal quality is preferred. In the Middle Roman period decay sets in, and Late Roman paint is usually matt with a pink or even a brown tone. The clay much more than the paint depends on the place of manufacture. Attic in the Hellenistic period is generally a little browner and coarser than before, Campanian is a rather lighter brown, and Corinthian is of course very pale. The typical 'Pergamene' clay is yellowish, Arretine redder and Late Roman generally more pink.

Few of these monochrome wares are regularly plain. The most characteristic decoration was impressed, the most imposing in moulded relief, and especially during the earlier periods there was a modest allowance of reserved or painted ornament.

2. Reserved and Painted Decoration

Much of the dark-painted ware that was current before the black-painted canon was established relieved its monotony by reserving or by adding in white or purple one or two narrow stripes in some emphatic position, for instance on the lip of cups or round the belly of taller pots. Some examples of this banding have been mentioned earlier, and indeed it is not always easy to distinguish logically between decorated and dark-painted pottery. The black-painted practice was stricter. At Athens there are sometimes ovules of red-figure type on the deep lips of pelikai and hydriai, and a group of squat aryballoi of poorish quality and later fifth-century date have a band of paltry ornament round their middle. In the late fifth and the early fourth century a slight wreath or festoon in added white or yellow often crosses the neck or shoulder of hydriai and other careful pots; but this discreet usage soon coarsens and merges with the related West Slope style. The Hellenistic black-painted and the Sigillata wares only rarely indulge in added colour.

3. Impressed Decoration

In the seventh and sixth centuries simple incision or impressed stamping was commonly used in Etruria on bucchero and some coarse wares. In Greek lands at that time the main use of these techniques was for stamped bands of repeated patterns on large rough-surfaced pots, of which the best-known is a group of great amphorae found in and near the island of Rhodes. But such predecessors have no relevance to the new system of impressed decoration which developed in classical Athens and lasted for over a thousand years.

This new system first appears just before the middle of the fifth century as a modest embellishment of the black insides of some Attic stemless cups, a few of which have mediocre red-figure decoration outside. The Sotades painter, as might be expected, was among the pioneers. The units of ornament, incised or impressed before the surface was painted, were and remained small and simple. In the earliest examples a familiar arrangement is a rosette of tongues surcharged with a star and enclosed in concentric circles: these ornaments are incised freehand (with some aid of the potter's wheel and perhaps of a ruler), though the stamped palmette was in use about the middle of the fifth century. During its third quarter the style was fresh and inventive and the effect often rich; but before its end Attic workshops accepted for the various shapes of drinking vessels easier formulas, based on the chain of linked palmettes, ovules and also tongues. They now abandoned the more elaborate motives, such as the meander regular on a group of miniature pointed amphorae, and made the detail of stamps coarser and more durable. Even so, the Attic standard is superior in design and execution to its new competitors in Corinth, Boeotia, Campania and elsewhere. Early in the fourth century impoverishment and deterioration were accelerated by the introduction of chains of strokes produced by rouletting or rather chattering – since the impressions come not from a cutting wheel but by the jumping of a thin metal strip held against the rotating surface of the pot – and with this easier technique the stock decoration for most shapes soon became the chain of palmettes with links drawn out into long points and the serried band of chattered strokes. On Hellenistic black-painted plates and saucers impressed decoration became less frequent and more feeble – careless chattering and scattered palmettes, usually not linked and often without volutes at their base. This tradition was taken over in 'Pergamene', but there seems to be no connection to the Sigillata wares of three hundred years later, when we still recognize vestigial palmettes, shaped like fans and ferns, among the more popular stamped rosettes and sets of little concentric circles.

4. Relief Decoration

There are a few good examples of decoration in relief on coarse Greek pottery from the late eighth to the sixth centuries, and many poor examples in the late bucchero of Etruria. During the later fifth and the fourth centuries at Athens figures in relief occasionally supplement or replace the normal red figures. But a regular use of moulds to decorate and even to shape what may be called fine pottery was an innovation of the Hellenistic period, when vase-painting had decayed and metal ware set the ideal.

The so-called '*Megarian*' *bowls*, commercially the most successful relief ware of the Greeks, extend through most of the Hellenistic world and age. The shape is roughly hemispherical with or without a low ring foot. The decoration, which covers all the outside except the lip, ranges from abstract and vegetable ornaments to animals and human figures, usually arranged more or less symmetrically. The finer and more elaborate examples are mostly early. The process of manufacture was first to make a mould and – normally – to impress the patterns in it by stamps. Next, after firing, the mould was centred on the potter's wheel, the bowl of the pot thrown inside the mould and the lip added freehand.

Then the pot was left to dry and shrink enough for removal from the mould, coated with the ordinary dark paint, and fired or misfired in the same way as the plainer black-painted wares. 'Megarian' bowls were made in many Greek cities, though it is likely that the stamps were often imported. The Attic variety has a deep bowl and outcurving lip, across the Aegean the bowl is shallower and the lip turned in, and in Boeotia scenes from Homer were a speciality. Some authorities claim that the 'Megarian' bowls originated in Egypt, though the quality of the Attic products suggests autocthonous invention or rather adaptation from metal. On dating too opinions vary: perhaps the earliest bowls go back to the beginning of the third, the latest reach well down the first century B.C. A heavier form of moulded relief, popular for appliqué medallions in the centre of cups and open bowls, is best-known from the *Calene* ware of Campania, made at about the same time in Campania and perhaps other parts of Italy. Here impressions were taken from older metalwork, and some of the potters had Latin names.

The 'Megarian' technique of moulded decoration was taken over into Sigillata. 'Pergamene' examples are few and mostly undistinguished, but in Arretine the neoclassical groups are often of surprising and delicate excellence. Its successors of the first two centuries A.D. continued the use of moulds, more commonly in the West than in the East, but standards of design and execution were increasingly neglected.

8 Shapes

1. General Comments

Most Greek pots were made for domestic use, even those which were dedicated to the gods or deposited in graves. The chief exceptions are the great amphorae and kraters of later Geometric, the Attic white-ground lekythoi, the volute-kraters of red-figure Apulian, the Hellenistic polychrome wares – all of which were made specially for burials – and the innumerable miniature pots turned out for dedication at sanctuaries. But though these differ in scale or the fastness of the decoration, their shapes generally follow those current in useful pottery.

The principal uses for which Greek fine pottery was designed did not vary much in time or place. They were first drinking and secondly toilet. In drinking the Greeks mixed their wine with water; so there were wine jars and water jars, bowls for mixing, jugs for pouring and cups. Toilet oil and perfume needed flasks with narrow necks. But though the main categories of shapes remained fairly constant, there was room for variety in proportions and details. Generally the shapes of any one time or school are in harmony with each other. In Proto-geometric they are loose and full, in Geometric more sharply defined and tautly compressed. In the succeeding period the local schools differ in shape as in style, but the trend is to higher, generous bellies with more taper below, and at Corinth a new refinement appears, especially for smaller pots. A rapid advance was made at Athens rather before the middle of the sixth century; shapes, large and small, are modelled with precision and elegance, and foot and lip receive increasing attention. With red-figure comes a wider appreciation of rhythmical, uninterrupted curves, already practised in the one-piece amphora. During the later fifth and the fourth centuries subtlety degenerated into cleverness or is replaced by a clumsy solidity; the worst excesses are in South Italian. Hellenistic pottery, which has lesser pretensions to art, is mostly dull or lifeless in its profile. This evolution can be followed in details too, most obviously in the horizontal handles of cups and hydriai: for long they are simple loops, in the later sixth century the crook grows squarer and begins to turn up, by the end of the fifth century handles are fanning out and the upward curve is bending over and back, and in the fourth century these contortions are sometimes exaggerated for their own sake.

The most distinctive quality of Greek shapes, when compared with those of other civilizations, is the conscious articulation of the parts of the pot, even though precise symmetry may be neglected. This articulation often offends modern critics, who prefer a more fluent use of the plastic character of clay. The Greeks might have retorted that the potter's wheel also invites turnery. Some have seen in Greek shapes the influence of metal ware, rarer and more expensive than pots of clay. But there is nothing peculiarly metallic about the shapes of pottery before the middle of the seventh century, and not much for two or three centuries afterwards apart from certain details of handles; a clear example is visible in the rotelles of PLATE 30B, which in metal serve to clip the handle to the lip. In the later fifth century the ribbing of black-painted ware was presumably borrowed from metal ware, and much Hellenistic pottery is frankly imitative. It is sometimes forgotten that the early Greek processes of metal-working were simple and that sharp mouldings and projections [such as those of the stand of PLATE 18] were more natural in the turning of wood and stone. Even so, clay is tractable and Greek potters were inventive.

The exquisite forms of the best Attic pots have lured some students to believe in a construction calculated according to geometrical rules of proportion, and they have broken down selected shapes into complex systems of two-dimensional rectangles. That the shapes show a sense of proportion is evident. It is also evident that their makers did not bother about exact symmetry. But the modern investigators must be thanked for the only set of measured drawings of fine Greek shapes.

The names now given to the various Greek shapes are mostly conventional. For many of these shapes there are no modern equivalents, so that it is natural to look for ancient names, of which the largest assortment is offered by the late miscellanists and encyclopaedists. Unfortunately literary contexts and dictionary definitions are usually ambiguous, even if the writer knows the shape he is describing. A few names explain themselves or are explained by being inscribed on or against the shape to which they refer, but even these names were not all applied uniformly at every time and place, and it is besides possible that the vocabulary of the trade and of the public differed. So, for example, in the inventories of the Mycenaean tablets the names of vessels are sometimes accompanied by a sketch of the shape, but of these names only 'amphoreus' can be said to have been currently used in historical times of a pot of similar shape. More significantly, Aristophanes uses 'hydria' and 'calpis' of the same water pot. Again, 'poterion' is written as a description both on a deep cup of Geometric type and on a lip cup, 'cylix' on both lip cup and Chiot chalice. There are other names, such as 'pelike', which are currently used without and even in contradiction of ancient authority. Earlier archaeologists were very ready to adopt Greek names, but in the course of time their more extravagant or unnecessary foundlings have been abandoned and when new definitions are needed the general practice is to invent (as for instance 'lip cup'), to use symbols (such as 'kantharos type B'), or – more whimsically and, because of the difficulty of translation into other languages, inconsiderately too – to revive vernacular archaisms such as 'pitcher' and 'chalice'. Though usage has not yet been completely standardized – witness the confusion between 'kotyle' and 'skyphos' – it is unlikely that radical changes in nomenclature will be accepted: utility and habit are more compelling than pedantry. So the student must still remember that where an ancient author names some shape there is no presumption that he means the shape so named by modern archaeologists.

For convenience in sorting sherds, shapes are divided into 'closed', that is with a narrowish mouth, and 'open', if the inside of the pot can easily be seen. Normally, except at the mouth, the inside of closed pots is rough and unpainted. Of large closed shapes the principal are amphora (including pelike), oinochoe and hydria; of large open shapes the krater, and well after it the dinos. The commonest of the smaller closed shapes are oinochoe, lekythos, aryballos and alabastron. Of the smaller open shapes the cup in its many forms is pre-eminent; and from the end of the fifth century black-painted plates and small bowls become numerous.

The paragraphs that follow attempt a summary account only of the more important shapes of the more important schools. So rarities like the psykter are left to the *Glossary*, the peculiar shapes of Laconian and Cretan are neglected, and black-painted pottery – as much from ignorance as contempt – does not receive its archaeological due. Coarse pottery, which has a different and sometimes more fluent range of shapes, is outside the scope of this book. Two more limitations must be emphasized. First, since knowledge of shapes is still based largely on complete pots, complete pots come mostly from graves, and graves have their own fashions in offerings, the shapes with which we are familiar are not always a fair sample of the shapes current in any school: if, for example, our knowledge of Attic pottery in the sixth century

came only from graves in Attica the amphora would rank lower than
it does and the phormiskos would have more fame. Secondly, a shape
may disappear or be absent from the repertory of fine pottery, but
flourish in humbler wares. The study of Greek shapes has been laggard.

2. Amphorae

The amphora is a high two-handled pot with a neck that is considerably narrower than the body. Coarse amphorae were the standard
containers for transporting oil and wine, and they survive in great
numbers. Fine painted amphorae, which have mouths too wide to be
easily plugged, were used as decanters. Between these two classes comes
the Panathenaic amphora, of fine quality because it was presented at a
public festival and narrow-necked because it contained oil. Outsize
amphorae were at times made for funeral use, and a special narrow
amphora – the loutrophoros – had a place in the ritual of weddings.
Amphorae are very frequent. A normal height is about eighteen inches,
but some are larger and many are not more than a foot high.

The name 'amphora' or rather, since that is Latin, the Greek form
'amphoreus' was certainly applied to this shape.

There are two main classes, the neck-amphora [PLATE 23] in which
neck meets body at a sharp angle and the one-piece amphora [PLATE
22] in which neck and body merge in an unbroken curve. Some
authorities choose to limit the simple term 'amphora' to the one-piece
shape, although it does not appear till the late seventh century and is
never more common than the neck-amphora. The Villanovan and
Nikosthenic amphorae form a class apart. The pelike, though a derivative of the one-piece amphora, is regarded as a distinct shape. The
stamnos is similarly distinguished from the neck-amphora. Very small
amphorae are sometimes called amphoriskoi.

Neck-amphora

Protogeometric. The neck-amphora is inherited from Mycenaean [PLATE
2A], but is now remodelled to become a leading shape. Of the two main
types one has a plump body, concave flaring neck and handles set
horizontally on the belly [PLATE 2B]; the other, with vertical handles, is
the more spreading ancestor of the common Geometric type.

Geometric. The shape is narrower and straighter, with a taller neck
and higher belly [PLATE 3A and B show the development]: the handles
usually reach vertically up to the neck, except on very large works such
as that of PLATE 4A. At the end of Attic Geometric the progressive

group produces a still narrower amphora in defiance of the contemporary tendency to spread. Notable examples of this spreading are in Theran, where the neck too is very wide, and still more in the Cycladic Wheel group [FIG. 3].

Orientalizing and Black-figure to c. 550 B.C. Several forms of amphora are current. (1) A more spreading version of the Geometric standard continues in Attic and appears in 'Melian' and the Pontic group of Etruscan: many amphorae towards the middle of the sixth century have an almost ovoid body [PLATE 20B]. (2) Still wider amphorae are found in the Cycladic Ad group; and the much later Fikellura amphora is very wide [FIG. 21]. (3) The narrow form of Late Geometric is adapted by the Heraldic group of the Cyclades, and recurs in the Attic Polos group of the early sixth century and later in the loutrophoros. (4) The amphorae of the Linear Island group of Cycladic [PLATE 29A], and of Boeotian, Eretrian and 'Melian' begin at the end of Geometric, but are much commoner in the seventh century. The amphora was very rare in this period in Corinthian and, it seems, in Laconian.

Mature Black-figure and Red-figure. About the middle of the sixth century the old neck-amphora of form (1) is remodelled and refined at Athens, especially in the workshop of Amasis; and later there are further innovations. (1) The new standard amphora of black-figure, which lasts till the first quarter of the fifth century, has an egg-shaped body with a flattish shoulder [PLATE 23, though that, like many early examples, is wider and more elaborately moulded than the norm]: the shape is adopted in 'Chalcidian', in Clazomenian, where also a very narrow form is derived from it, and in Etruscan black-figure. (2) A smaller version, with simple foot and usually about twelve inches high, is known – after a prolific site – as the Nolan amphora; this is a red-figure shape, common in the first half of the fifth century and a little after. (3) The characteristic neck-amphora of red-figure is a much slimmer pot, which at first often has twisted handles [PLATE 46A]; it begins at the end of the sixth century and continues in Attic till the early fourth century, in South Italian red-figure till its end. (4) The so-called pointed amphora, with wide belly and knob-like foot, is a large and rare shape of red-figure of the early fifth century, and narrow miniature versions with impressed decoration become common in the black-painted ware of the third quarter of the fifth century.

Amphorae of this period were sometimes provided with flattish, knobbed lids.

Hellenistic. The neck-amphora is important only in West Slope ware, where it is from the beginning squat [PLATE 56A]. Development is towards an angular profile.

Panathenaic amphora

The purpose of this variety of amphora is explained by its familiar legend, painted before firing, 'a prize from Athens'. Examples stretch from about 560 B.C. to the second century B.C. or later, and are conservative in shape as well as in their black-figure decoration. Characteristic are the large body and narrow neck and foot [PLATE 21B]: gradually neck and stem grow attenuated and concave, till by the fourth century the shape is no longer strictly a neck-amphora. Many full-sized amphorae of Panathenaic shape, and of course all the miniatures, were souvenirs rather than prizes. The shape was borrowed for red-figure by some Attic painters of the fifth century and was elaborated by many South Italians of the fourth [PLATE 54].

One-piece amphora

This shape, which is rare outside Attic, appears humbly in painted pottery in the earlier part of the seventh century, but is very rare till its last quarter [PLATE 21A]. It is remodelled and becomes important about the middle of the sixth century [PLATE 22] and is a favourite of the Archaic red-figure painters. It dies out in the last quarter of the fifth century. Three types are distinguished by certain details. In type B, which continues the early shape, the lip is straight or slightly concave, the handles are round in section, the foot is simple [PLATE 21A]; in type A the lip is again concave, the handles are flanged, the foot is complex [PLATE 22]; in type C the lip is convex, the handles and foot vary.

Nikosthenic (and Villanovan) amphora

The Villanovan amphora is a native Italian shape, which is adapted and refined by Etruscan bucchero. It is characterized by the conical neck, which at the base is nearly as wide as the body, and – in its bucchero form – by the vertical handles that join on to the lip. In the late sixth century an unhappily revised version with black-figure decoration was produced at Athens in the workshop of Nikosthenes, perhaps as a speciality for the Etruscan market [FIG. 38].

Loutrophoros

This is a necked pot, tall and very narrow, reminiscent of the progressive Late Geometric amphora. It was used in the ritual of weddings and at the funerals of unmarried persons.

The name 'loutrophoros' is rightly used, to judge by the references in ancient literature, representations in vase-paintings and the subjects of the decoration of many loutrophoroi.

There are two varieties, which differ only in their handles. The commoner, a neck-amphora, is called simply loutrophoros; the other is the loutrophoros-hydria. A steady series of loutrophoroi continue from the late sixth century, when the special form is first distinctly

FIG. 38. *Attic Bf Nikosthenic amphora*
Ht 31 cm. *c.* 530 B.C.

recognized, until the later fourth century. The shape, which becomes very spindly, is confined to Attic and to South Italian red-figure.

Pelike

The pelike is a one-piece amphora with a sagging belly [PLATE 45].

A Greek word 'pelike' exists, but was not applied to this shape.

The shape first appears in Attic red-figure rather after 520 B.C. and remains very popular till the end of red-figure. Small pelikai are common in Gnathian. The tendency is for the mouth to grow broader, till in the fourth century it is wider than the belly [PLATE 51]. Gnathian pelikai are slimmer and more fanciful.

3. Hydria

The hydria is primarily a pot for fetching water. It has a vertical handle at the back for dipping and two horizontal handles at the sides for lifting. In size hydriai correspond to amphorae.

The name 'hydria' is satisfactorily attested for this shape. So too is 'kalpis'. Some modern writers conventionally use 'kalpis' for the rounded hydria of Attic red-figure.

Most hydriai are broad pots with a character of their own. But in wares in which the hydria is exceptional the shape is often that of the amphora with a different set of handles [for example PLATE 14A, which is one of a short-lived group of Attic hydriai around the end of the Geometric period]. Similarly the loutrophoros hydria is only a three-handled loutrophoros. There are also, especially later, many small and miniature hydriai.

FIG. 39. *Attic Rf hydria* (*'kalpis'*)
Ht 27·75 cm. 450–440 B.C.

Hydria

Outside Cretan, where the form is mean and peculiar, the hydria rarely appears in fine pottery till the end of the eighth century, and then only in some schools. There are in succession three or four main forms. (1) The typical early hydria has a wide belly, broadly rounded shoulder and offset neck. It is common in Cycladic from Subgeometric to 'Melian', and a stumpy variety appears in Ripe Corinthian and the Polos group of Attic. (2) Rather before the middle of the sixth century the shape is modernized in the same sort of way as the neck-amphora; the new standard [PLATE 35] has a flatter shoulder that joins the belly in a sharp curve or even at an angle. This form appears in Corinthian, Laconian, Attic, 'Chalcidian', Clazomenian, Caeretan and Etruscan.

(3) In Attic a modified version, slimmer and with a more angular shoulder, becomes normal for black-figure in the last quarter of the sixth century and continues into the second quarter of the fifth. (4) Another shape [FIG. 39], which seems to have antecedents in coarse pottery, is discovered and immediately preferred by red-figure painters towards the end of the sixth century. Here the neck is small, and belly passes into shoulder and shoulder into neck in a continuous curve. The new hydria (which is sometimes called the 'kalpis') is a broad pot, but gradually it contracts, and in the red-figure and black-painted wares of the fourth century achieves a slim elegance. A less sensitive version of this shape, which usually has an offset neck, survives in the Hadra ware of Hellenistic.

4. Oinochoai

The oinochoe is a jug. It is one of the commonest and the most variable of Greek shapes. Larger sizes are a foot or more high, and till the early sixth century there are many oinochoai that in scale are comparable to amphorae and in some schools seem to have taken their place. But smaller oinochoai are always numerous. The artistic importance of the shape is roughly proportionate to its size.

The name 'oinochoe', which means 'wine-pourer', fits a frequent use of this shape. The precise meaning of 'chous', now used often of one type of oinochoe, is not altogether certain.

The range of shape is wide. For instance, the mouth may be trefoil, round or beaked; the neck broad or narrow, straight or curved; the body slim, squat, truncated or angular. In Attic red-figure alone ten varieties have been classified. Here only a rough distinction of major forms is attempted. Three varieties – conical oinochoe, olpe and lagynos – are generally classed apart.

Standard oinochoe

This has a more or less ovoid body, widish neck and trefoil mouth. The Protogeometric norm is represented by PLATE 1D. With Geometric the body becomes stumpy, at least in the metropolitan schools; later there is a tendency to lengthen it again. This shape is taken over by Protocorinthian [PLATE 8C], where the belly grows steadily broader. In the second half of the seventh century the Corinthian belly spreads yet wider, the neck becomes meaner and concave, and the handle is high [PLATE 11B]. A compacter version of this shape is inherited by Attic about the middle of the sixth century. This necked shape con-

tinues with modifications throughout the fifth century, and a sturdier
relative with a broader base remains popular in the fourth. This is the
main line of development, but some other forms deserve notice. In
Etruscan bucchero an early Protocorinthian shape persists till the end
of the seventh century, gradually giving way to a heavier oinochoe with
barrel-shaped or oval body. Attic in the first half of the seventh century
is fond of a miniature jug, with narrow body and neck tapering upwards [FIG. 9]. More important is the East Greek sequence, which can
be followed back to the end of the Geometric style, probably in the
second quarter of the seventh century [PLATE 7A]. From this comes the
canonical oinochoe of the Middle Wild Goat style [PLATE 30B]: the
oinochoai of the Late Wild Goat style and of Fikellura are more solid.

One-piece oinochoe

This type, which has its predecessor and perhaps ancestor in the Attic
olpe, has a generously curving belly, a short neck that merges into the
body and a trefoil mouth. It appears in Attic towards the end of the
sixth century, grows in popularity till the end of the fifth century and
then gradually drops out of the repertory of Attic red-figure, though
not of black-painted ware. The name 'chous' is often given to a numerous class of oinochoai, mostly small, of this shape. A tallish variant
remains common in Gnathian, where there is also a slimmer, sagging
alternative.

Bell-mouthed oinochoe

(1) A peculiar shape [PLATE 4B], sometimes called 'pitcher', is popular
in Attic Late Geometric. It can be very large. A reduced model of
medium or small size and with a lower body persists in Protoattic till
the middle of the seventh century, but is usually described as a mug (or
sometimes, if the lip is very high, as a tankard). (2) Another and distinct
oinochoe with wide neck (the 'round-mouthed oinochoe') occurs in
East Greek from Late Geometric [PLATE 7A] till the end of the Middle I
phase of the Wild Goat style [PLATE 30A].

Oinochoe shape 5

Another shape, which appears in Attic at the end of the sixth century,
has a narrow body rising steeply to the shoulder and returning in an
unbroken curve to the round, wide mouth; sometimes there is an angle
at the shoulder; the handle is high. The shape is abandoned by Attic
red-figure painters before the end of the fifth century, but persists in
Apulian.

Broad-bottomed oinochoe

This is a low, broad oinochoe with nearly vertical sides, a lowish and soon narrow neck, and a trefoil mouth. It becomes common in Corinthian in the first half of the seventh century and outlasts the Animal style. It appears to have Geometric antecedents, and in the later fifth century there is a trivial oinochoe that is perhaps its descendant. This new type, which prefers a concave profile to the belly, an angular shoulder and a beaked lip, persists into Hellenistic and presumably influenced the lagynos.

Small globular oinochoe

A humble but common type of Geometric is a small pot with short, narrow neck and globular or even depressed body. The mouth is trefoil or, less often, round. This is the ancestor of the aryballos and perhaps of the conical oinochoe.

Oinochoe shape 7

This is a tallish footless jug with widish offset neck and the lip usually pulled up into a large beak. It appears in Attic during the fifth century, and with an inward curve to the lower part of the body is a great favourite of Etruscan throughout the fourth century.

Conical oinochoe

A minor Geometric shape is a little oinochoe with trefoil mouth, narrow neck and a body that consists of little more than a broad shoulder. In Early Protocorinthian the contour of the body is straightened till it approaches a more or less shallow cone, and the neck becomes taller: this conical oinochoe remains popular in Corinthian till the early sixth century. Later there are some slight black-painted oinochoai of truncated type, though the slope of the body is curved.

Olpe

This name is given to some tall jugs with sagging belly.

The Greek word 'olpe' is used of jugs or flasks, and is inscribed on a Ripe Corinthian round aryballos and perhaps also on a Protocorinthian pointed aryballos. There is no authority for its restricted modern use.

Two main forms go by the name of olpe, and a few oddments are sometimes lumped in. (1) The olpe of PLATE 11A (which does not show the handle) is frequent in Corinthian from the middle of the seventh to the first quarter of the sixth century and, often debased, for rather longer in Italocorinthian [FIG. 26]; the shape occurs also in Etruscan bucchero. (2) A shorter pot, in contour something like a pelike, has lip and body continuous, high handle, and often trefoil mouth. This appears in decorated Attic ware early in the seventh century and is common throughout the sixth. Etruscan imitations run later.

Lagynos

This is a Hellenistic form of broad-bottomed oinochoe with a sharp or, less often, curving shoulder and a round mouth [FIG. 37].

The use of the word 'lagynos' is well supported. It was a kind of wine-flask.

The shape is best known in the light-ground Lagynos group, and appears also in contemporary black-painted and relief ware.

5. Kraters

Big deep bowls with a wide mouth were used for mixing wine. A frequent range of size is from twelve to eighteen inches high, the stem (if there is one) excluded, but generally the earlier shapes are broader and more capacious than the later. Very large kraters were sometimes made for funerary use, and a special variety – the lebes gamikos – for marriage ceremonial.

The ordinary Greek word for these mixing-bowls was 'krater'. 'Lebes' sometimes, 'dinos' perhaps never has that sense. The restriction of 'krater' to the footed shapes is a modern convention. The application of 'dinos' to the less common bowl with rounded bottom is unreasonable, though there is some evidence for using the alternative 'lebes'.

Mixing-bowls are frequent and important pots from Protogeometric till the fourth century. The varieties are readily distinguished. In all the trend is to narrower forms.

Simple krater

The Protogeometric shape is sturdy and wide, with low belly and modest or later conical foot. The handles, as is regular in this type, sit horizontally on the belly and often are doubled. The ordinary Geometric shape is tenser and curves in strongly to the simple lip, its foot is either low or stems into a flaring pedestal, and the handles are often joined to the lip by a sort of strap. This shape, which with some modification survived humbly well down the seventh century, appears to be the ancestor of the column-krater. A byform of Attic Late Geometric and

earlier Protoattic is the egg-shaped krater, in which the body is taller
and narrower. The very big funerary kraters of later Geometric add a
short vertical neck to the ordinary shape, and consequently the handles
do not reach up to the lip.

Kotyle-krater

The kotyle-krater, a giant kotyle usually attached to a high flaring
pedestal and covered by a lid, is an Attic invention. Its period is the
middle and second half of the seventh century. A kotyle-krater without
a pedestal appears also in the Aeolian Wild Goat style.

Column-krater

Though once anticipated in Attic Late Geometric, the column-krater
is a Corinthian novelty of the last quarter of the seventh century [PLATE
12C], and there is some evidence that it was known as the 'Corinthian
krater'. The shape appears to be adapted from the simple krater of
ordinary Geometric type with the strap from handle to lip. Now the
lip is broader and extends at each side in a rectangular plate supported
by the handles: their columnar effect gives the shape its modern name.
A more advanced form is shown on PLATE 36. Widely adopted, the
column-krater reaches its greatest popularity in inferior Attic of the
first half of the fifth century. In Attic red-figure it dies out early in the
fourth century, but continues in the ordinary style of Apulian and has
a curious revival in the latest red-figure of Etruria. Development is to
a narrower body and higher neck.

Volute-krater

The volute-krater [PLATE 19A], so called from the form of its handles,
comes from the column-krater. Though not very common, it is an important shape. It appears perhaps before the end of the seventh century
and continues till the late fourth. The example illustrated is early,
before the canon was fixed. Soon the volutes are tightly rolled and the
lip is capped with a moulding, and gradually the whole pot becomes
narrower. Very big and elaborate volute-kraters, with scenes suggesting
a funerary purpose, are the most ornate confections of Apulian red-
figure. Possibly the ancient name 'Laconian krater' belonged to this
shape.

Calyx-krater

The krater which by a modern conceit is called the calyx-krater is in
its structure not unlike the Chiot chalice [FIG. 20]. It appears in Attic

black-figure soon after the middle of the sixth century and becomes a favoured shape till the end of red-figure. It grows steadily narrower, more concave in its upper part and more stemmed at the base. Small calyx-kraters continue for a short time in Hellenistic black-painted and West Slope wares.

Bell-krater

The bell-krater [PLATES 44, 48A and 56B] is established in the repertory of fine pottery by the beginning of the fifth century, rises in frequency till the early part of the fourth century and though rejected by the progressive painters of red-figure remains the most common type of krater till its end. It too in the fourth century often grows an incurving stem. Sometimes, especially in early red-figure and in Gnathian, lugs take the place of handles [PLATE 44]. The shape recalls that of a Protogeometric krater, but if there is a connection it must be through coarse ware, unless perhaps – because of the lugs – the prototype was of wood. A sort of bell-krater survives in Centuripae ware.

Stamnos

The stamnos is a wide-mouthed pot with the neck reduced to a collar and the handles consequently set horizontally on the belly [FIG. 40]. Sometimes at least it was used as a krater.

In Greek 'stamnos' seems to be more or less equivalent to 'amphora'. The modern distinction is arbitrary.

FIG. 40. *Attic Rf stamnos*
Ht 33·1 cm. *c.* 450 B.C.

The shape, which properly belongs to red-figure, establishes itself during the last quarter of the sixth century and in Attic is popular throughout the fifth, in Etruscan throughout the fourth. It grows taller and thinner, especially towards the base. The name is sometimes loosely and unwisely applied (as on p. 139) to plainer pots of roughly similar body ending in a low rim.

Dinos

This shape, probably misnamed, is a big round-bottomed bowl that curves in to a more or less emphatic mouth [PLATE 18]. It is normally handleless. Sometimes there is a matching stand, which may be elaborately turned [PLATE 18]. The dinos occurs in fine pottery from the middle of the seventh till the late fifth century, but is frequent only in the later Wild Goat style.

Lebes gamikos

The lebes gamikos or nuptial lebes, which is probably correctly named and is certainly connected with weddings, has the shape of a small, deep dinos with two high handles, a lid and a simple attached stand (or, more commonly later, a short foot). It first appears early in the sixth century. In Attic red-figure it lasts beyond the middle of the fourth century, in South Italian till its end. Perhaps the kotyle-krater, which also has a lid and an attached stand, is its predecessor.

6. Lekythoi, etc.

Flasks for toilet oil and perfume, and also for some condiments, are distinguished by their narrow aperture and are normally small or smallish. The Attic white-ground lekythoi are larger, but they are pots made specially for the ritual of the grave. Many small oinochoai and the miniature pointed amphorae also served as toilet flasks, but it is convenient to classify them by shape rather than function.

The Greek word 'lekythos' could describe several kinds of flask; there is evidence that it was used for what are now called the ovoid aryballos, the round aryballos, the lekythos of white-ground shape and the squat lekythos. 'Aryballos' (or rather 'aryballis') is defined by Hesychius, rightly or wrongly, as a Doric equivalent of 'lekythos'. The painter of one Ripe Corinthian round aryballos called his pot an 'olpe', as perhaps did the painter of an earlier Corinthian pointed aryballos. 'Alabastron' is presumably valid for the second and third of the types that now go under that name, since there are alabaster pots of the same shape. But there is no evidence that 'askos' was ever used by Greeks of a pot. The current distinctions between these words are conventional.

Lekythos

Two main types are given the simple name of lekythos: (1) The Proto-geometric lekythos [PLATE 1C], normally about five to eight inches high, replaces the Mycenaean stirrup vase (except in Cretan) and is itself replaced by the small globular oinochoe of Geometric. (2) A new shape of Attic and Corinthian in the early sixth century is a pot about six inches high with oval body, plastic ring round the short neck, narrow round mouth and one handle. This lekythos soon develops an angular shoulder and a stronger lip, loses its ring, and grows narrower. By the end of the sixth century the canonical proportions have been reached and the shape is very popular with lesser black-figure painters. During the second quarter of the fifth century red-figure painters adopt the lekythos and it becomes the characteristic vehicle of the white-ground style [PLATES 49A–B]. Since the white-ground lekythoi were made for funerary use, their decoration could be in evanescent colours and their size was not limited by handiness. Some sizeable specimens have thriftily a small inner container attached to the neck, so that they could appear full without much expenditure of oil. The shape disappears at the end of the fifth century.

Squat lekythos

This shape [PLATE 46B], familiar in red-figure and black-painted wares, appears at the end of the sixth century and is popular in the later part of the fifth and the early part of the fourth. The shape gradually becomes narrower and more elongated. The usual range of height is three to six inches.

Aryballos

The ancestor of the aryballos is the small globular oinochoe that appears in Geometric and continues after, and indeed one variety of this shape is often called 'jug-aryballos'. But the first true aryballos (according to the conventional definition of the term) is in Early Protocorinthian. The Corinthian evolution from 'round' through 'ovoid' to 'pointed' can be followed on PLATE 9A & D and FIG. 5A–B: these forms are sometimes confusingly named 'lekythoi'. At the end of the third quarter of the seventh century a new round form [PLATE 10B] becomes regular, and there is also a flat-bottomed version: the round shape continues till the fifth century. These aryballoi are very common in

Corinthian and in Italocorinthian, which adds some original variants, and round aryballoi are fairly common in Laconian of the sixth century. A new type develops in Attic in the last quarter of the sixth century and lasts till the early fourth: this has a bell-shaped mouth rather like the contemporary lekythos, two handles or later no handle, and a flat or rounded bottom. A common height for aryballoi is around three inches, but in Ripe Corinthian there are larger sizes too.

Alabastron

Of three types of alabastron the second and third have justification for their name. (1) The Corinthian alabastron [PLATE 10C] comes in about the middle of the seventh century, is enormously popular in the last quarter and dies out about a generation later. A usual height is three to four inches, though from the end of the seventh century larger sizes are common enough. Italocorinthian imitations are numerous and include flat-bottomed variants. (2) A long, pointed alabastron without handles occurs about the same time in East Greek bucchero, Etruscan bucchero and Italocorinthian. (3) Another alabastron with rounded base and sometimes two small lugs has exact parallels in alabaster. This type, usually from four to eight inches long, is fairly common in Attic from the late sixth to the early fourth century.

Askos

The name is given to various flasks wider than high, with a narrow orifice set at one side of the top, and a handle reaching across to the other side. Four |types can be reckoned as fine pottery. (1) In East Greek related to Clazomenian there is a lumpy flat-bottomed askos as much as six inches across. (2) A very low neat askos, with flat bottom and about four inches wide, is popular in Attic red-figure and black-painted wares of the fifth and early fourth centuries. (3) The bulky 'deep askos', with a body like a brooding hen, flourishes in later Apulian red-figure and other Italian wares, but is known earlier in plainer pottery. (4) A still larger askos with round bottom is a staple shape of the Daunian school of native Apulian and is elaborated in Canosa ware.

7. Pyxides

Round, mostly handleless boxes with lids were used by women to hold cosmetics or trinkets. This is evident from the favourite subjects of their decoration, their occurrence in graves and the rare survival of their contents. The commonest size is perhaps four inches across.

The Greek 'pyxis' (which gives the English 'box') may or may not have been extended in our period to boxes not of boxwood. But the modern usage is fair enough.

Shapes vary without much logic. Some (agreeably to etymology) seem to show the influence of the wood-turner. Here only the principal types are mentioned. The Protogeometric fashion is for a globular body with out-turned lip and low foot. In Early Geometric (at least in Athens) this gives way to two derivatives: the pointed pyxis (which ends below in a point) hardly outlives the ninth century, but the flat pyxis (which begins later) flourishes till the end of Geometric, growing still flatter and larger and soon elaborating the knob of its lid [PLATE 6A]. In Corinth a straight-sided pyxis of more modest proportions is at home from the late eighth century; during the seventh century the modish profile is increasingly concave, and in the sixth century convexity is favoured. Attic from the mid sixth century prefers concave types, with flat bottom or low recessed base. But the simple round box persists and in the fourth century is left as the normal pyxis of Greece, though Apulian red-figure preferred a hemispherical bowl with moulded foot completed by a hemispherical lid with big knob.

8. Cups

In fine Greek pottery cups usually have two handles. The normal size varies according to the shape. Cups of one sort or another are very common in all periods.

Of the many Greek words for cups four are now in fairly common use. These are 'skyphos', 'kotyle', 'cylix' and 'kantharos'. The name 'kotyle' and 'kotylos' is written on shapes that we call cup and kantharos; and 'cylix' appears on cups of shapes ranging from Geometric type to lip cup, on the kotyle (as defined below), the cup-kotyle and also the Chiot chalice. 'Kotyle' was too a standard measure of volume. But there is no ancient authority for limiting any of these words to a particular shape of cup. Nor is the modern terminology consistent. What some call 'skyphos' others call 'kotyle', and their 'skyphos' is the 'kotyle' of the contrary faction: fortunately one of the disputed shapes can be called simply 'cup'. With 'kantharos' the uncertainty is whether or not to include some unassuming types. As for 'cylix', the current fashion is to replace it by 'cup', variously qualified. The special forms known as lakaina and phiale have respectively vaguely plausible and good title to their names.

Cup

The cup in its restricted sense may be defined as a drinking pot with lowish bowl and handles set horizontally. It remains popular till the fourth century, when the kantharos overtakes it. Sizes vary. In Protogeometric a diameter of six inches at the lip is fairly normal, by the mid sixth century the standard cup is about eight inches across, and some of the red-figure show-pieces are much wider. But there are always many smaller cups. Of the types listed below (1) and (2) are often called 'skyphos' (or 'kotyle'), and (3) and (8)–(11) 'cylix'.

(1) The typical Protogeometric cup is unmistakable [PLATE 1A]. (2) Its Geometric successor [PLATE 8A] renounces the high foot and is squatter in the body: at the end of Attic Geometric an improved version occurs with an oblique and longer lip, but the old shape persists through the seventh century. (3) In Corinthian of the seventh century a modernized cup also is current, neater in proportions and more definite in its narrow foot [FIG. 4B]: this type of cup continues on the Greek mainland into the second quarter of the sixth century [cf. PLATE 24A], and rather longer in East Greek and Italocorinthian. (4) Another innovation of Attic Late Geometric has a wider but shallow body and a vertical lip of about equal height, flat instead of rounded handles and often a tall stem ('stemmed bowl' or 'standed bowl'): its descendants last into Middle Protoattic. (5) In Laconian before the end of Geometric a similar glorification of the lip led to the lakaina [FIG. 11]: this shape, peculiar to Laconian, survived (anyhow in miniatures) till the Hellenistic period. (6) The Chiot chalice [FIG. 20], which appears in the late seventh century and lasts at least till the fourth, develops a conical foot as well as a high lip. (7) The East Greek Bird bowl [PLATE 29D], which with its descendants is popular throughout the seventh and long into the sixth century, is a back formation from a broad kotyle current in East Greek Late Geometric. (8) To return to the main course of development, the standard shape (3) is during the second quarter of the sixth century refined by Attic potters through the Siana cup [PLATE 24B] into the lip cup [PLATE 25A] and into the band cup [PLATE 25B] and Droop cup: the lip cup flourishes from the 560s to the 530s, the band cup rather longer. (9) In the 530s Attic masters were turning to another shape, the eye cup: here the lip is abolished, as in the rarish merrythought cups of the previous generation, and the stem quickly shrinks to a heavy flaring member surmounted by a broad fillet [FIG. 30A]. This, the type A of Attic red-figure, is old-fashioned by the end of the sixth century. (10) In type B [FIG. 30B], which is the most exquisite

accomplishment of Greek pot-making, the curve from rim to edge of base is checked only by a low step on the foot, the stem grows tall and slender, and the bowl is shallower still: its period is from the last quarter of the sixth century to the middle of the fourth. (11) Type C is a humbler cup, which prefers a concave offset lip and interposes a fillet to mark off foot from stem: it too begins in the late sixth century, but continues – especially popular in black-painted wares – till the second quarter of the fourth century. (12) The 'stemless cup', in which foot is separated from bowl by no more than a groove, appears in Attic red-figure at the beginning of the fifth century, becomes very frequent in black-painted wares and dies out in the fourth century. (13) The so-called bolsal is a small shallow bowl with low foot and horizontal handles, frequent in less pretentious black-painted pottery: in the fifth century its profile is usually a simple curve and the foot light, in the fourth century the foot is heavier and often the rim curves outwards.

Cup-kotyle

This is in effect a much narrowed and deeper form of the cup, with foot directly joining bowl. It is common in inferior Attic during the fifth and fourth centuries.

'Tea cup'

A small deepish cup with one vertical handle and three to four inches in diameter may for convenience be called a 'tea cup', though those who use 'skyphos' for what here is called 'cup', use 'cup' for this one-handled shape. In Protogeometric this 'tea cup' has a high conical foot and is often decorated [PLATE 1B]. Afterwards it loses its foot and the decoration is restricted to reserved stripes on the lip, but it is unobtrusively frequent in Geometric and Protoattic.

Kotyle

The kotyle (or, according to the opposite terminology, the skyphos) is a deep two-handled cup with no distinct lip [FIG. 4A]. Though there are earlier Geometric cups with little or no lip, the evolution is not completed till the Late Geometric phase of Corinthian. At first often the bowl is wide [PLATE 8B] – and it is from such a kotyle that the East Greek Bird bowl diverges – but in Corinthian a standard is soon fixed and the kotyle with its remarkably thin wall becomes the finest of Protocorinthian shapes. In Corinthian the kotyle remains very common into the Hellenistic period, in Attic its popularity begins in the

fifth century. Two principal types of kotyle, conventionally distinguished as Corinthian and Attic, now compete. The Corinthian type is
truer to tradition, but curves in more at the top. The Attic type curves
outward at the rim and has a heavier foot. A byform of the fifth century
has one of its handles set vertically and is called owl-kotyle or 'glaux'
from the owls that decorate many red-figure examples. During the
fourth century both types, the Attic since it lasts longer more so than
the Corinthian, grow narrower and more concave in the lower part
of the pot. The kotyle does not survive long into the Hellenistic
period.

Kantharos

The kantharos, which in its early stages is closely related to the cup,
has its two handles set vertically. Except in Etruscan bucchero and
after the seventh century in Boeotian it does not become a widely frequent shape of pottery until the fourth century, when it is supplanting
the cup. In the Hellenistic period it loses importance to the 'Megarian'
bowl. A normal size is four to six inches across, but there are very
many smaller kantharoi and some larger.

The Protogeometric kantharos has low handles and of course a
conical foot. In Geometric this foot is rejected, soon the handles may
rise high above the rim and sometimes there is no distinct lip. A
modified version, narrower in the body and higher in the lip, is fairly
common in minor Protoattic and later in the Boeotian Bird-cup group.
Comparable deep-bowled kantharoi with high or low handles occur
in the contemporary black-painted ware of Boeotia.

What may be considered the characteristic and perhaps the finest
form of the kantharos appears in pottery in Etruscan bucchero [FIG. 27].
Here the bowl is subordinated to the lip and the foot is emphatic. In
the sixth century this type is adopted by Attic and Boeotian. It soon
develops an inward curl of the top of the handles and taller and more
upright stem and lip [PLATE 38 – the kantharos grasped by Heracles].
The final stage, familiar in later Apulian red-figure as well as in black-
painted ware, is much higher and narrower, with a concave profile to
the lip, often a strut and a spur to each handle, and a plastic ring half-
way up the stem. Smaller versions of the high-lipped kantharos, with
low handles and little or no stem, are very common in black-painted
pottery of the fourth and third centuries.

The opposite principle of deepening the bowl and suppressing the
lip may be recognized in some little Corinthian pots of the late eighth
and early seventh centuries: this shape, which has low handles and no

foot, is by some confusingly designated 'kyathos'. Something similar but without decoration recurs in Chiot of the sixth century. More significant is the favourite kantharos of the Cabiran style of Boeotian, a sturdy pot about as wide as high, with rotund body, wide low foot and a spur projecting outwards from the ring handles. A closely related shape popular in black-painted and West Slope wares has a narrower, often moulded foot, and tends to be slightly concave in the upper part of the bowl (so giving a vestigial appearance of a lip). This type of kantharos is still found at the end of the Hellenistic period.

Mug

The name, though not in regular use, is sometimes given to small pots with a wide round mouth and one vertical handle, for example the small bell-mouthed oinochoai of Attic Late Geometric and Protoattic and the squatter oinochoai of shape 8 of red-figure and black-painted wares.

Hemispherical bowl

Roughly hemispherical bowls without handles and with or without a ring foot are common in Hellenistic black-painted ware. The most elaborate of them are the so-called 'Megarian' bowls, which have a good lip and sometimes a small ring foot. A normal diameter is five to six inches. The shape may have been called 'hemitomos' in Athens.

Phiale

A phiale is a wide, shallow saucer, often with a hollow boss rising in the centre (the phiale mesomphalos). 'Phiale' was applied by the Greeks to pots for pouring libations and vase-paintings show this shape so used; but the name was given to the rhyton too. The phiale appears in Chiot and Corinthian pottery at the beginning of the sixth century and afterwards in Attic too, but it is not common except in miniature. To judge by finds the shape is taken from Oriental metalwork.

9. Plates and Dishes

Plates and dishes to hold food are unusual in pottery of good or moderate quality till the late fifth century. Presumably the ordinary platter was of wood, as the Greek name 'pinax' suggests.

'Pinax' evidently could describe a plate, but is ambiguous and unnecessary and happily obsolete. The authority for 'lekane' and 'lekanis' is not conclusive.

The distinction between plate and dish and lekane and saucer must be arbitrary, but what is called the lekanis has a lid.

Plate

The plate is a flat or flattish disk with a rim and often a low ring foot. It is fairly common in the latest Corinthian and Laconian Geometric: the Corinthian shape has a straightish oblique rim which may be prolonged below into a low foot, the Laconian a more horizontal lip from under which extends a pair of handles. In the Late Wild Goat style of the early sixth century a footless plate is a main shape (at least in graves): here the disk rises slightly to the centre and the short lip curls outwards. About the same time plates become more frequent again in Corinthian, and appear also in Attic and in Italocorinthian: their lip curls out and over, and the ring foot under it is sometimes double. A flatter lip and foot is usual in the next considerable batch of plates, which are Attic of the late sixth century. From this form develop the black-painted plates that become frequent from the late fifth century, though the subsequent variations of the lip are perhaps prompted by metal ware: the trend is to a more centrally placed foot and a more curving section. Large plates, as much as fifteen inches across, are frequent in the earlier groups; later plates are mostly much smaller.

Fish-plate

The fish-plate, which takes its name from the fishes that so often decorate its surface, is a sort of plate with down-turned rim, disk sloping inwards to a central hollow and a ring foot. A normal size is eight to ten inches across. The shape appears in black-painted Attic at the end of the fifth century and flourishes in Campanian and Apulian red-figure in the fourth.

Dish

The name of dish is given to almost any sizeable shallow bowl. A few groups have some importance. (1) In the Wild Goat style around 600 B.C. there are many large dishes, some with simple rim and high stem, others with flat wide rim and high stem or ring foot. (2) A large shallow basin with narrow ring foot, flattened vertical lip and two recurving handles is fairly common in poor Attic and in Boeotian black-figure around the middle of the sixth century, and with the lip more and more assimilated to the bowl is popular again in later red-figure: it is to this shape that the name 'lekane' is confusingly assigned.

Lekanis

The lekanis is much like the lekane (or second type of dish) except that its rim has a ledge to receive the lid. Though it has predecessors, the lekanis proper comes in during the second half of the sixth century and flourishes in the red-figure and black-painted wares of the late fifth and fourth. In Sicily it may have been called 'sipyis'.

10. Lids

Some shapes – pyxis, lekanis, lebes gamikos, the large Geometric bell-mouthed oinochoe and the kotyle-krater – regularly had a lid which was made to fit. Other shapes sometimes had careful lids – in Attic, for example, many fine amphorae of mature black-figure and earlier red-figure – and rough lids for trefoil-mouthed oinochoai are very common in the Orientalizing stage of Corinthian pottery. But there is no reason to suppose that most pots of closed shape had their own lids.

9 Technique

1. The Standard Processes

There is of course no ancient account of how Greek pots were made. What we have are the remains of several kilns, some terracotta plaques and vase-paintings with brief illustrations of potters at work, comparative technology and the pots themselves. But most of the processes are obvious enough, and for those that are not explanations have been proposed that are at least generally probable. Since Greek pottery reached its highest technical refinement in Attic workshops of the later sixth and earlier fifth centuries, it is convenient to take for summary description the making of a typical red-figure pot.

Presumably the potter dug his clay locally, piled it in his yard and left it to weather. Next he washed – or levigated – it; that is he mixed it with water, let it stand till the coarser and heavier particles had sunk to the bottom and the finer were still in suspension, and ran off this refined solution. In the Greek climate it was not long before evaporation left a paste of the right stiffness for kneading. After kneading the clay was ready to be worked. Like most Greek potters' clays, it contained ferric oxide (Fe_2O_3) and so was reddish in colour. It was also, as can be judged from such shapes as that of FIG. 30B, very plastic. Whether or not the Greeks mixed their clays is unknown.

The potter next took a lump of his prepared clay and centred it on his wheel, which was spun directly, often by an assistant. Most sizeable pots were made in sections; sometimes neck and body were thrown separately, the body (if large) might be in two parts, and the foot was often attached later. Such sections were put aside to dry to a leather hardness. When they had dried the potter assembled them and luted the joins with a thin solution of clay, and then, turning the pot on the wheel, pared down the surface with a knife, cut mouldings and hollowed out the foot. Lastly he added the handles. Greek potters had no taste for mechanical precision, anyhow before the Hellenistic period, and their products are by modern standards often decidedly asymmetrical. So far there is nothing unusual about Greek technique.

Before describing the next processes, those of decoration and firing, some explanation is wanted of two curious features of fine Attic pottery (and in lesser degrees of most other Greek pottery with painted ornament). One is the conjunction of red and black (or reddish and blackish) colour. The other is the sheen, stronger on the black paint and weaker on those reddish surfaces that were meant to be seen. These effects were obtained not by using basically different materials, but by the nature of the clay, its preparation and the firing. Since modern practice is here quite different, at least in Europe, students for a long time could not understand the ancient methods and there are still some points not altogether elucidated by chemists.

Both the red and the black colour of Attic pottery are due, as analyses have proved, to the presence in the natural clay of a fair quantity of ferric oxide, which can be fired red or black according to conditions in the kiln. If the atmosphere is oxidizing, the ferric oxide is unaffected and the fired clay will keep its red colour. But if the atmosphere is reducing – that is, short of oxygen – then oxygen is absorbed from the ferric oxide (Fe_2O_3) which thereby becomes one or other of the iron oxides that show black (FeO or the blacker Fe_3O_4). Conversely, if a black oxide is exposed to an oxidizing fire, it will absorb oxygen and become the red Fe_2O_3. So Attic clay – and the painting medium was clay too – can be fired red or black. What is at first puzzling is that it was fired both red and black on the same pot. This can be managed in two ways. First, since both oxidation and reduction are retarded if the particles of the clay are finer and so more compact, the paint which is more refined than the clay of the rest of the pot changes colour more slowly. If then a pot so painted is exposed in the firing first to a reducing atmosphere – till the paint as well as the rest of the pot is black – and then to an oxidizing atmosphere, a time comes when the rest of the pot is red but the paint still remains black. There was besides an initial oxidizing stage, necessary for good firing. This sequence of oxidation, reduction and partial reoxidation was the normal method of producing the contrast of black and red till the early sixth century and, as can be imagined, the last stage was tricky; indeed a very large proportion of the pots so produced show some reoxidation of the paint, whether through unequal exposure of different parts during the firing or because the thickness of the paint varied.

Secondly, in the same sequence of firing, reoxidation of the black oxides can be prevented by sintering, a partial vitrifaction which in the clays used by the Greeks results at temperatures between 825° and 950°C. Here the particles of iron oxide become enclosed within crystals of quartz, present in Attic clay, and so – if already reduced – they are insulated against reoxidation until the temperature is raised to 1,050°

and the quartz softens. Sintering, to be effective for protecting the black colour, requires a considerable refinement of the clay and, though the paint remains black, the rest of the pot can be reoxidized; presumably in its coarser constitution the particles of iron oxide and quartz are too scattered for much enclosure. This fixing of the black paint by sintering occurred from time to time in earlier wares, but perhaps as much by accident as intentionally; the controlled use of the sintering method was a discovery of Attic potters soon after the beginning of the sixth century.

The explanation of the sheen is rather less certain. This used to be called 'varnish' and is still often called 'glaze', but it is not any kind of varnish nor yet one of the familiar silicate or lead glazes. On pots made of some natural illite clays of fine quality it is said that the plate-like particles tend simply through evaporation to align themselves with the plane of the surface, smoothly enough to reflect light; but this effect is improved by careful preparation. First, the clay can be refined by levigation till the particles are of colloidal dimensions. Secondly, an electrolyte (or peptizing agent) can be added to break down excessive coagulations of particles: potash, which was usually at hand in potters' yards, is a good electrolyte and has the further advantage that when added to a solution of clay it makes it thinner and more fluid. Thirdly, burnishing of the surface helps to compact and align the outermost particles. Fourthly, the partial vitrifaction produced by sintering increases the reflective quality of the surface. At present it is not clear how much each of these improvements contributed to the Greek sheen. The higher sheen that becomes regular in Attic work of the early sixth century evidently makes more use than before of controlled sintering and burnishing.

The constitution of the clays used in Greek pottery and of those available in Greek lands has not been much studied, but it is clear that what was used for fine Attic ware was a secondary iron-bearing clay of the illite variety, perhaps – because of the quartz – containing celadonite. This clay was used both for the pot itself and in a more refined colloidal solution for the paint and the thin shiny film over other exposed surfaces. Since refinement of the clay eliminates the coarser particles and the particles of iron are finer, this solution has a higher proportion of iron than the less refined clay and therefore a deeper tone, both before and after firing. Before starting his work the painter needed supplies of the finer solution in two or more concentrations.

A first, though not obligatory, stage in decorating the leather-hard pot (if it was to be painted in the red-figure style) was to make a rough preliminary sketch. This sketch was made with some hard instrument, since in many red-figure paintings, if they are turned to catch the light, the preliminary lines are visible as slight depressions in the surface. If, as may be expected, the sketch was reinforced by some pigment, it was a pigment (such as charcoal) that disappeared in firing; not only does no trace of it survive, but also the final drawing does not exactly follow the preliminary sketch, as with the collar-bone of PLATE 37A. In black-figure painting, whatever the reason, these depressions are much rarer, though they are known as far back as the middle of the seventh century.

Next the visible surface of the pot was coated with a thin film which dried quickly and often with a slight sheen. Opinions differ on whether this film was a weak solution of the more refined clay or a wash of ochre or a mixture of the two. Ochre (probably the ancient 'miltos') is anyhow the constituent of the deep plummy red of which there are traces here and there on many pots of the red-figure period and especially on the underside of the feet of kotylai. This ochre has not worn well and the period and extent of its popularity are uncertain, but it is not likely that it was used before the sixth century.

For the best results the surface was burnished before and after coating. The painting followed. Its medium was the clay solution in the strong concentration, stiff enough not to run, and the instruments were for the broader surfaces a brush – the marks of its strokes can very often be seen – and for the line-work a fine brush or quill or a syringe, though the fine groove that runs down the middle of some relief-lines does not depend on the instrument used. The painter first marked out carefully with a broad thick outline the areas that were to be painted black [see PLATE 37B], following more or less closely his preliminary sketch. Then he filled those areas in with an even coat of his solution and added details according to the style in which he was painting. Incised lines were engraved with a sharp point, relief-lines were drawn with a thick concentration and lines intended to fire brown with a thinner, and purple and white enhancements were put on. The painting of bands round the pot was preferably done on the wheel.

At this stage the colour of the pot, or at least of the surfaces coated with the finer solution of the clay, varied only in tone, according to the density and nature of the solution. As has been said, the final contrast of reddish surface and black paint resulted from firing, not from the addition of any special pigment. Of the subsidiary colours, which showed more or less their final tone, the purple seems to come from red ochre, powdered and mixed in a fine solution of the ordinary clay; and the white is probably a primary clay with very often slight traces of iron – enough to produce in an oxidizing fire an ivory-yellow tone. The purple regularly and the white frequently has no sheen. Neither of these colours adheres very firmly to the pot. As for yellow, used occasionally in some Greek schools, a satisfactory recipe is to dilute the white with a solution of the ordinary 'paint'.

The Greek kiln was a small and simple structure of clay, but its details are uncertain. The reconstruction shown in FIG. 41 is based on the plaques from Penteskouphia (see p. 337), some excavated remains and modern analogy. The kiln proper was domed and may have been sunk partly in the ground; the size varied. It contained a lower fire-chamber and an upper larger chamber in which the pots were stacked; the floor separating the two was perforated to allow the circulation of air and gases, which could escape through a vent in the top of the kiln. In the wall of the upper chamber there was a door, plastered up with clay during firing, and in it a spy-hole through which the potter could watch the progress of his pots. A low tunnel for stoking about two feet long ran into the fire-chamber: the opinion that it was divided into two channels is unfounded and improbable. The draught could be regulated by closing the mouth of the tunnel and the vent at the top. In a kiln of this type, if wood or charcoal is used as fuel, a temperature of 900°–1,000°C is practicable. This reconstruction is not beyond criticism. First, all Greek potters' kilns were not of circular plan; the earliest kilns yet found at Corinth, which are said to be (like the plaques) of the sixth century, were probably apsidal, and at Athens Classical kilns are becoming rectangular at their far end. Secondly, though some sort of door with spy-hole is regular on the plaques, its size seems too small for inserting very large pots or even for stacking small ones, though it would have been useful for withdrawing test pieces; perhaps the roof of the kiln was not always permanent, but a temporary crust of straw and clay, put on after the unfired pots had been arranged in the kiln and demolished when the firing was over. Thirdly, by analogy with Romano–British practice, there may not always have been a raised (perforated) floor. Fourthly, the floor of tunnel and fire-chamber may have sloped upwards from the mouth at an angle of 5–10 degrees.

After they had been decorated and left to dry out the pots were put in the kiln. Since neither the paint nor the rest of the surface became fluid at the temperature reached, there was no regular need of spurs or stilts and the pots could be stacked one on another without danger that they would stick together, though such stacking might sometimes prevent even firing. A fire was now lit of dry wood and a strong draught admitted, and the temperature was gradually raised to about 800°C.

SIDE ELEVATION

SECTION AT C D

PLAN AT A B

SECTION AT E F

RELATION OF KILN TO GROUND LEVEL.

FIG. 41. *Conjectural restoration of a Greek kiln*

In this oxidizing atmosphere the pots fired red, deeper and more shiny on the painted parts. The second stage required a reducing atmosphere. This can be produced simply by damping the fire and closing the stokehole and the vent; it may also have been convenient to use green wood for fuel. The temperature was now raised to about 950°C. So the pots turned towards black, the intensity of the colour depending again on the density of the concentration of iron oxide, and some sintering occurred, especially in the paint. Finally, when the heat had dropped to about 900°C, oxidizing conditions were restored by admitting some draught, and the pots started turning back from black through brown to red; but well-prepared paint, because of its compacter structure or sintering, did not reoxidize during this stage of slow cooling and stayed black. When the cooling was complete, the pots were taken out of the kiln, ready after wiping to be sold. Ancient potters could probably judge the critical temperatures fairly well by eye, though some test pieces have been found.

All these processes required delicate and accurate craftsmanship. The writer of the Homeric epigram to the potters named five devils who plagued them, and there were mistakes. The commonest fault is that areas intended to be black have fired brown or deep red; this may be the result of misfiring, but often the paint had been laid too thinly on the affected parts [as probably on PLATE 37B] and so was more susceptible to reoxidation. Sometimes indeed the contrast of red and black paint was deliberate, as on many Corinthian Late Geometric pots and in the Wild Goat style of Aeolis. Sagging of the shape is also common, though generally slight. But the average technical standard was high. Greyness of the unpainted surface is more often the result of a subsequent reduction, especially when pots or sherds were burnt in a funeral pyre.

These technical processes of preparing the clay and of firing are subtle, but simple. They could easily have been discovered empirically and independently. Pottery with a sheen and the contrast of reddish ground and darker brown-black paint, which seem to have been similarly produced, has a wide distribution in time and space. The earliest known is the Tell Halaf ware of northern Mesopotamia, which goes back to the fourth millennium B.C. In Greece the first appearance of these techniques – whether independently invented or derived from Asia is not known – is in Neolithic in the later fourth millennium: in Crete it was adopted a little later. During the Bronze Age it was the normal Greek practice, except for the matt-painted wares of the Middle Helladic period, and the Iron Age inherited it. But the refinement of the sheen and the regular achievement of a black colour were the work of Attic potters in the sixth century, and their successors and imitators carried on the tradition into Hellenistic times. Arretine and some other sigillata wares made full use of the shiny property of their clays, though the sifting of the particles was less fine; but, perhaps to simplify factory production, only a single oxidizing firing was employed. Later the sheen in its turn was gradually neglected.

2. Other Processes

Bucchero, unlike the black-painted wares, is dark all through. It too used a very fine illite solution, though in its dilute form, so that the surface has only a faint sheen. But the firing ended with the reducing stage. The dirty yellowish tinge of some bucchero pots comes from incomplete reduction.

The *red wares*, of which Sigillata is the most notable, have undergone only a single stage of oxidation.

The varying technique of *relief wares* has already been mentioned (pp. 214–15), and the methods used for *impressed decoration* (pp. 213–14) are obvious enough.

The white-ground wares with friable *polychrome decoration* have not all been investigated satisfactorily. The Attic lekythoi and their relations were evidently fired in the normal three stages, but some at least of the colours were put on afterwards – this is why the bodies of figures were sketched in the ordinary paint before the firing. In the early Orientalizing of Crete and the Hellenistic Hadra ware there are instances of polychrome painting over the ordinary decoration; here too the second painting presumably followed firing.

A few Attic pots of the later sixth and earlier fifth centuries make play with a deliberate contrast of black and 'coral red'. The simplest explanation is that ochre was mixed with the standard paint and, since even after sintering the mixture is oxidized easily, it turned red in the third stage of firing. The drawback was that the 'coral red' does not adhere firmly.

3. Local Clays

It is difficult if not impossible to describe clays and paints in ordinary language, though catalogues rightly attempt their description. In particular the colour may vary on the same pot through uneven firing or application, and few students have a precise and consistent vocabulary for distinguishing shades. So, for example, 'red' is variously used of the subsidiary colour which this book loosely calls 'purple', of the brownish unpainted clay of Attic pots (hence the term 'red-figure'), of the ruddier miltos, and – more justly – of the surface of sigillata wares. In the paragraphs that follow the brief descriptions aim more at consistency than precision.

Mycenaean pottery is remarkably uniform in its technique. Specimens from the Argolid, Attica and Rhodes have a similar light brown surface, dark brown paint and good sheen. The use of clays with a fair content of iron oxide and illite and the process of firing in three stages are regular, though through uneven application of the paint or bad arrangement in the kiln the colour of the decoration on one pot often ranges from dark brown to dark red. In Submycenaean there is a decline in technical accomplishment, most obvious in the weaker sheen, and neither the Protogeometric nor the Geometric craftsmen recover the Mycenaean standard.

In the Geometric period there is rather more divergence between local schools. But the differences in style are not much more than parochial and the technical ideal is generally to produce a lightish brown surface painted with a brownish black. The unpainted surface is rather darker than is regular in Protogeometric. The paint varies in depth of colour according to its concentration – in the hatching of meanders the paint is often intentionally dilute – and the browns often shade into reds. Before the end of the Geometric style wares with a whitish slip appear to be regular in Laconia, some Cycladic and Euboean workshops, and Chios. By 'slip' Greek archaeologists mean a coat of clay of a different constitution from that of the pot to which (after the turning) it was applied. Greek slips are generally primary clays with a very low iron content, and so fire to tones ranging from white to yellow. Some local clays were perhaps such that they could not practicably or profitably be refined; or there may have been an aesthetic preference for a lighter ground, as presumably later induced East Greek potters to change their technique when they adopted the Wild Goat style.

The break-up of Geometric increases the local variety of technique as well as style. Athens, the metropolis of the old style, continues the old technique, occasionally (perhaps in emulation of Corinthian effects) reviving the yellowish slip that had been known in its Protogeometric and early Geometric; about 580 B.C. the colour of the surface deepens from buff to orange, and this with the rich black of the paint sets a new standard for Greek potteries. Corinth on the other hand had in the late eighth century produced a very smooth pale clay, fired at first a yellowish to pinkish tinge, but in the Ripe period more often faintly green: about 575 B.C. the new Attic tone provokes the painting of an orange background to the principal field of elaborate works. Few other cities used such fine clay for making pots. The Boeotians had access to a clay scarcely inferior to Attic, but also made slipped pottery. Laconia preferred a pink clay with a cream slip. In Crete the clay is generally brownish with or without a pale slip. The Orientalizing schools of the Cyclades have usually a yellowish slip over rather coarse, brownish clay. Most East Greek fine wares after Geometric are slipped. The clay is coarse and varies from buff to pink, the slip ranges from the white of Chiot through cream to yellow, and the paint is generally brownish and streaky. But the Subgeometric Bird bowls continue the Geometric technique; and during the sixth century there is imitation of Attic, often palish, by the Ionian Little Master cups and by Clazomenian and other black-figure ventures. In Italy the abler makers of painted pottery copied with varying success first Corinthian and then Attic clay and finish. The red-figure style of Athens carries on the black-figure technique of clay and paint. At the end of the sixth century a thin white slip sometimes occurs, especially on small black-figure lekythoi. From this develops the very white but friable slip of the white-ground lekythoi. During the fourth century Attic clay tends to be yellower than before. The red-figure of South Italy uses various clays, mostly pale, and often, as at Corinth, the potter felt obliged to cover the surface with a reddish wash.

The technical decline of the fourth century continued in the Hellenistic period. Attic potters for some while remained superior to their rivals, but even Attic clay is less regularly fine and deep in colour, and the paint takes a bluish tinge or becomes streaky. A little more has been said on p. 212.

Students of Greek vase-painting are very ready to assign pots and sherds to local schools on the appearance of the clay or paint to the unaided eye. In this they are within limits successful. Corinthian clay, for example, is pale and clear, Italocorinthian pale but slightly muddy; and Attic clay is unusually free of what is called mica. From time to time chemical analyses have been attempted, but their scope may be limited. For the local beds of clay are not necessarily homogeneous in themselves, the prepared clay used for much fine pottery has been not only rid of its grosser impurities but also perhaps mixed with other substances, and there is always the possibility that some clay may have been imported. It is, perhaps, the slipped wares with a coarsish body that offer most hope to the analyst.

4. Mending

Many Greek pots were mended. Mending was usually done with lead or bronze rivets for which holes about the diameter of a matchstick were drilled along the edges of breaks. Usually only the holes are left. Often even inferior small pots were repaired, and an early Protoattic krater of moderate size has over forty pairs of rivet holes. Occasionally a piece of another pot was inserted as a patch, or a tall foot cut down.

10 *Inscriptions*

1. General Comments

Inscriptions first appear on Greek pots in the later eighth century, but do not become at all numerous till the sixth and even then are relatively few. They may be painted or incised, or even written in ink or stamped. A more significant distinction is whether they were executed before or after firing, by the painter or by the merchant or purchaser. As it happens, nearly all painted inscriptions other than merchants' marks were put on before firing and nearly all incised inscriptions after firing. The exceptions can easily be detected, since incision before firing (when the pot is leather-hard) leaves a clean and not a ragged edge to the cut, and painting after firing is usually under the foot and – if the test is permitted – can be removed by methylated spirit or some other solvent.

The main classes of inscriptions painted before firing are captions, signatures, mottoes (for all of which nonsensical groups of letters sometimes serve), and fourthly dedications. Inscriptions incised after firing mostly record dedication or ownership. Many of the inscriptions painted after firing and some of those incised are the marks of merchants; normally they are under the foot. Writing in ink is an alternative to incision for the bare epitaphs added to some Hadra urns. Stamping, of course before firing, appears on some Megarian bowls and many Calene phialai, and also on many Classical and Hellenistic coarse amphorae and on sigillata wares of the Roman period. All these inscriptions were put on whole pots. There are also 'ostraka', sherds already broken and casually picked up to make jottings on or inscribe with a vote. But though ostraka have their importance, it is not for the study of Greek pottery.

Till the fifth century inscriptions on pots, though brief, are both more numerous and more securely dated than most other inscriptions that survive. So they offer much of the evidence for the date when the Greeks adopted their alphabet, for some of its local varieties and their development, and for early orthography. They offer something too to the knowledge of Greek dialects, especially if the origin of the writer is known. Conversely, the forms of a painter's alphabet and dialect may help to decide where he worked. But some of the results are perplexing;

for example, around the middle of the seventh century the Polyphemus painter, a notable Attic vase-painter, wrote like an Aeginetan, and the painter of the Chigi vase, a leader of the Corinthian school, was not a Corinthian, if judged by his writing. There is also much for prosopographers and for those who can reconstruct social history from personal names.

2. Inscriptions before Firing

Inscriptions put on a pot while it was being decorated are usually painted. Where the ground was light, they were done in the ordinary dark paint. Where the ground was dark, as normally in red-figure, first purple and later white was the obvious medium, though occasionally a signature might be incised in some remote place like a handle or the edge of the foot. But most of these inscriptions belong to the principal field.

In the placing and lettering of an inscription painters took more or less pains to conform to the decorative scheme of the vase, but there is one class of Attic pottery in which it has become a regular and integral part of the decoration. The lip cup, created in the 560s, is remarkable for its rejuvenation of old artistic forms and it uses inscriptions with equal virtuosity. A fairly typical specimen is illustrated on PLATE 25A (though inscriptions on the lip are rare). Here, as also on some band cups, the handle frieze contains between the terminal palmettes a neat row of fine letters, which spell out sometimes a signature, sometimes an invitation to drink and sometimes – for the sense does not really matter – what is partly or wholly nonsense. Since the proportions of the field are fixed and the inscription should have an appropriate length, signatures are often padded out, and so we know (less from piety than because his name was a short one) that the prolific maker Tleson was the son of Nearchos. There are also some curious instances of the misspelling or muddling of words, such as Χσενοκλες εποκλεσεν and ενεοινοιοιεν, which are best explained if the painter could not himself spell but was drawing from a text set before him or his memory of such a text.

Captions

Names written against figures first appear during the second quarter of the seventh century. In the second quarter of the sixth they suddenly become excessive; on the François vase in the scene of Troilus the wellhouse, Polyxena's water pot and Priam's seat are labelled superfluously κρενε, ʰυδρια, θακος – a fashion vaguely known to Aelian (*VH* x. 10) – and on Tyrrhenian amphorae there are often meaningless blobs to simulate lettering. In the fifth century these names grow much fewer. It is usually individual figures that are named, rarely objects or groups of figures, and very rarely whole scenes. The captions are written against the figures to which they belong, forward or backward, and at whatever angle space and convenience recommend. Occasionally the words of a speaker issue from his mouth as on an amphora of Exekias in the Vatican where Achilles calls 'four' and Ajax 'three'. A few red-figure pots of the end of the sixth century express the ebullient feelings of the vase-painter; so in the remarkable anatomical study of PLATE 39 Euthymides appends the comment ʰος ουδεποτε Ευφρονιος – 'as never Euphronios', and he in turn is toasted by Phintias with σοι τενδι Ευθυμιδει in a scene that makes the compliment ambiguous.

Since captions are an addition to scenes of human and especially mythological figures, they are not to be expected in all groups of Greek pottery. They are comparatively frequent in the more ambitious products of Corinthian, Attic and 'Chalcidian'; in Laconian around the middle of the sixth century there were two painters who could write; in Boeotia the naming of figures is least rare in the Cabiran style; and some red-figure Etruscan and South Italian workshops follow the Attic example. In other schools of vase-painting examples are few and isolated. The naming of figures appears also on plaques, free paintings and sculptures in relief, lingering on into fully illusionist pictures such as the Odyssey landscapes from the Esquiline and on mosaics continuing till the end of antiquity. But there is no rule for captions. At first, when mythological scenes were a novelty, names may have been thought necessary to explain who the characters were, but often the scene is self-explanatory or in its action or spirit anonymous, and more often still – at least in vase-painting – the artist does without names. Nor does the placing of the letters usually improve the decorative composition. In general captions were a convention of Archaic and Early Classical art, which Greek taste did not feel unpleasant or obligatory. They add some new names to the catalogue of mythical persons, usually supplied by the painter's invention or faulty memory.

The legends of official Panathenaic amphorae form a special class of captions. On these conservative monuments the formula τῶν 'Αθήνηθεν ἄθλων ('a prize from Athens') continues till the end, though the names of magistrates that begin in the fourth century are painted in the modern style. Some of these magistrates can be dated, and so their inscriptions have a little value for the chronology of vase-painting.

Signatures

In number much fewer, signatures rank first in interest for the student of Greek pottery, since they give an insubstantial existence to its personalities. These signatures – the term is loose, since not all can be autographs – are of two kinds, one naming the painter, the other the maker; Σοφιλος εγραφσεν and Αμασις μ εποιεσεν are typical. The oldest certain signatures are of the first half of the seventh century and come from unexpected places. The earliest – a name ending in . . inos – is on a krater found on Ischia and apparently local work in a Euboean style of about 700 B.C.; and a generation or more later there follow a banded aryballos imitating Protocorinthian and signed by Pyrrhus in a Euboean alphabet, a krater probably made in Italy by Aristonothos (or Aristonophos), and a 'candlestick' of the Ithacan school by Kalikleas. All these were makers. The first Corinthian to leave us his name is the painter Timonidas, who was working in the 580s, and in the next generation Chares painted a miserable pot and Milonidas a plaque. Sophilos, a contemporary of Timonidas, begins the long line of Attic painters and makers whose names we know. Attic signatures reach their peak about 500 B.C. and are rare again by the end of the fifth century. A few Boeotians thought themselves worth recording, two Paestans, Praxias in Etruria and some late manufacturers of relief ware.

Ἔγραψε and ἐποίησε are the two normal verbs of signature – 'so and so painted (me)' and 'so and so made (me)'. It is plain that the painter and the maker were not always the same person, since for example the pots that Andocides signed as maker are painted by more than one hand and on the François vase the joint signatures distinguish between the painter Clitias and the maker Ergotimos. 'Painted' is clear enough, but 'made' is ambiguous in Greek as in English and whether on Greek vases it means maker in the narrow sense of the man who shapes the pot on the wheel or in the wider sense of the master of the workshop can be debated for ever. Little is known of the organization of Greek potteries except that they were often small, and so one man might combine two or all three of the roles of master, shaper and painter. Those who hold that 'made' refers to the shaper claim first that the Greeks valued shape as much as decoration, and secondly that vases signed by the same maker were in fact shaped by the same shaper. The opposite school asserts that the owner of a workshop would sometimes at least have insisted that he should be advertised rather than his employees, that two men cannot have combined to shape a band cup though in a couple of instances two combined to 'make' one, and that it is lexically irrational to limit 'making' to shaping. None of these arguments is beyond question. We do not know how the ancient Greeks rated the shape of a vase and the painting on it, though it does not seem likely that shape was closely valued before the refinements of the second quarter of the sixth century. The claim that all pots signed by one maker are by one shaper has been tested extensively only for Attic cups of the later sixth and earlier fifth centuries, and not many of these are signed. Two relevant results are that cups signed by one maker are or may be by the same shaper and that cups painted by one man are very often shaped by one man: if then painter and shaper were separate persons, they worked together faithfully, and it is no harder to believe that painter and master of the workshop stayed together. That the master should neglect to advertise his products by putting his name on them is by modern notions absurd, but so few Greek pots are signed that such advertisement cannot have been valued – an exception should be made perhaps for Nikosthenes. Even so, it is worth noting that the signatures of makers are more than twice as common as those of painters – an unnatural instance of unselfishness if the painter (who wrote the signature) was advertising a colleague and not a master. There are two minor arguments that point opposite ways. A few Attic pots have the signature of one man as both painter and maker; of these men Duris also painted pots made by Python both before and after those he made himself. Euphronios is the name of an Attic painter of the end of the sixth century, of a maker of the early fifth and of a potter who before 480 B.C. made an expensive dedication as a tithe on the Acropolis at Athens; unless we accept coincidence, it appears that Euphronios began as a painter and then became a maker and, since he was or grew wealthy, that he was owner of a workshop. So three conclusions are possible. First, 'made' means 'shaped'; this is now the orthodox opinion, with the two optional provisos that 'making' was occasionally extended to other manual processes and that the shaper was usually the master of the workshop. Secondly, the 'maker' as such was the master. Thirdly, the term 'made' did not necessarily have the same meaning at different times, or even at the same time. The second and third solutions seem to me the more likely.

Mottoes

Convivial phrases like χαῖρε καὶ πίει εὖ, though appropriate to drinking cups, are not common. They occur principally on Attic lip cups where an inscription of any kind was useful, and round the lip of some

Hellenistic kantharoi. There are also a few oddities like καλόν εἰμι ποτήριον – 'I am a good cup'.

More curious are the καλός inscriptions (or love-names) of the pattern of Λεαγρος καλος or more cannily ho παις καλος and simply καλος. These inscriptions, which record more than two hundred names, are fairly frequent on Attic pots from the third quarter of the sixth to the third quarter of the fifth century, after which the fashion quickly disappears. The range of the Greek καλός includes the English 'beautiful', and the accepted interpretation of these phrases is that they celebrate the homosexual charms of the popular aristocratic youths of the day. This fits with the short currency – normally five to ten years – of individual names, some of which after a proper interval recur among leaders of the Athenian state. Thus Leagros, the most celebrated of the καλοί, should have been in his teens within the years 510–500 B.C. and could well have grown up to be the general Leagros who died at Drabescus in 465. These inscriptions are an interesting commentary on fashion, since they were not bespoken solely (if at all) by the intimates of the beautiful youth, but were put on pots for public sale, many of which were exported to Etruria where young Leagros and the rest can have had no admirers. Occasionally a woman's beauty too is celebrated, and there are instances where the epithet is applied to a god or a hero. The normal καλός inscriptions are useful for chronology; pots with for example the legend Παναιτιος καλος should have been made about the same time.

Dedications and owners' names

Inscriptions recording dedication or very much less often private ownership are usually added after the firing. But a few bespoke pieces received such inscriptions in the workshop.

Dedications painted before firing are preserved on Chiot chalices, kantharoi, and phialai around the 570s. The formula is of the type of Ζωιλος μ ανεθηκε τηι Αφροδιτηι – 'Zoilos dedicated me to Aphrodite'. Many examples have been found at Naucratis in Egypt, some in Aegina and a few in Chios. It seems that outside Chios these pots were dedicated by merchants, since the same dedicators recur too often to be casual visitors, and that some merchants had regular connections with certain potters, since the inscriptions for each dedicator are usually written by one painter. Outside this class of Chiot pottery fired dedications are very rare.

Fired inscriptions of private ownership are rarer still. The earliest is perhaps an Attic cup not much after the middle of the seventh century with . . . *υλο ειμι* – 'I am . . yl(l)os's' – on the rim. Only one known painter, a Corinthian of the second quarter of the sixth century, made anything like a regular practice of adding customers' names; he has left four specimens on simple quatrefoil aryballoi.

3. Inscriptions after Firing

Inscriptions put on pots already fired are mostly incised. These vary greatly in carefulness of planning and execution, but even the best are a little ragged along the edges of the cut or scratch. Inscriptions painted after firing are usually in purple or white. Of these unfired inscriptions most were added by or for the ultimate purchaser, and their obvious place is on the lip or shoulder. A few are merchants' or dealers' notes, scribbled usually under the foot. Generally, it may be presumed, these inscriptions were incised or painted while the pot was still fairly new, but some may be considerably later, and a few are modern, to be detected only by the forger's negligence or faulty knowledge.

Dedications

Formulas of dedication vary, but regularly give the name of the recipient deity and not so regularly the name of the giver, occasionally supplemented at international sanctuaries by his ethnic. The commonest formulas are of the types of *Ερμησιφανης μ ανεθηκεν τηφροδιτηι* and *Απολλωνος εμι* and, especially in Hellenistic times, *Αφροδιτης* and *Υγιειας*, though this is often a toast or invocation rather than a gift. These dedications are useful principally for identifying the deities of sanctuaries and shrines and sometimes their cult titles.

Owners' names

A number of pots, mostly from graves, are inscribed with the name of a private owner, for instance *Χαριλεο εμι* or *Ευθυμο*. Sometimes the assertion is expanded, as in *Θαριο ειμι ποτεριον*, and a very few longer inscriptions add the occasion when the pot was acquired or a curse on anyone who should steal it. At Athens pots which were public property might be marked *δημοσια* or in abbreviated ligature *δη*, but these are coarse ware.

Mottoes and captions

Unfired convivial inscriptions would perhaps be less uncommon if excavators had picked through more dumps from private houses and taverns. There are also some obscene comments on friends or enemies.

Titles designating a pot as a prize are very rare apart from the fired inscriptions of Panathenaic amphorae, but they provide what may be the earliest incised text; this is on the so-called Dipylon jug, an Attic oinochoe of Late Geometric style offered as a prize for dancing – ηος νυν ορχεστον παντον αταλοτατα παιζει it reads in a good hexameter, and then tails off into incomprehensibility.

Epitaphs

Some of the Hadra hydriai from the early Hellenistic cemeteries of Alexandria give in ink or incision the name of the dead person and the date of death or burial.

Merchants' marks

Merchants' and dealers' marks, incised or painted after firing, are as nowadays mostly cryptic. A few longer texts give prices, but not usually of the pot on which they are inscribed.

11 *Chronology*

1. Introduction

Chronology may be absolute or relative. Absolute chronology is tied accurately to calendar years. Relative chronology states more or less loosely the relation in time between one event and another, which may or may not itself be absolutely dated. But for convenience, if nothing worse, it is usual to express relative dates in absolute terms. For example, the pots illustrated on PLATES 2B, 3A and 3B are in the captions dated to the tenth, the second quarter of the ninth, and the middle or later ninth centuries B.C. but it would be truer to say that the first was of the beginning of the Greek Iron Age, the second appreciably later than the first and the third rather later than the second. In studies concerned with Greek pottery it is often important to remember which dates are absolute and which relative, and also how secure those dates are.

2. Relative Chronology

In many schools of fine Greek pottery, anyhow before the Hellenistic period, style and to a smaller degree technique developed more or less consistently, and the study of these developments (which requires a good eye and the judgement and knowledge to pick out the significant characteristics) has enabled specialists to determine sequences of pots in various schools and is in fact the basis of what we know or think we know of their courses and ties. It allows also more subtle inferences if the pieces compared are connected closely. But where there is no close connection, as for instance between the Boeotian Bird cups and other Orientalizing schools, the internal evidence provided by style is inadequate or even misleading.

The external evidence comes mostly from graves and stratified deposits. In a stratified deposit – that is a deposit which accumulated gradually or in successive layers – the depth at which an object is found should show how early it was deposited. But stratification usually deals in periods of not less than fifty years, and the excavators of Greek sites have not reported many strata of any sort. Graves are more frequent and informative, if they were used only once. The ancient Greeks and their neighbours regularly put pottery in graves, so that we have many groups of pots that were buried at the same time. Though it does not follow that they were made at the same time, comparison suggests that the range of the pots in any one interment is usually not more than twenty or perhaps thirty years. So grave groups are excellent for synchronisms between different schools or trends within a single school. But it is dangerous to argue from a single instance; to allow for heirlooms and the negligence of excavators several similar contexts are wanted before a synchronism or its absence can be accepted.

By combining these two methods, the stylistic and the external, a system of parallel sequences may be obtained. Such a system is essentially relative. Occasionally there may be hints of the absolute intervals between various points in a sequence. If style allows the recognition of individual painters, the period of their works is limited by the span of human life. A close series of grave groups might perhaps excuse a rough reckoning in steps of some twenty years, and the ingenuous student can try to divine the annual rate of deposit in a stratified site. For Attic vase-painting in its prime the καλός names seem normally to have been current for not more than ten years, though they are most useful for synchronisms and sequences. But such checks hardly become available till they are no longer needed.

The results so far reached by these methods are set out perfunctorily in FIGS. 42 and 43. The two principal sequences are the Attic, which runs from the beginning of Protogeometric to the end of red-figure, and the Corinthian, which is clear from Late Geometric till the end of the Animal style. These sequences are fairly well tied to each other by connections in style and by grave groups, and other schools are linked to them. Some of the links are weak. For Protogeometric and Geometric the synchronisms, depending mainly on stylistic resemblances to Attic, are not much more than tentative till near the end, when first Attic and then Corinthian influence became strong. Of the Orientalizing and black-figure schools Laconian III is tied mainly to Corinthian by style and grave groups. For Boeotia grave groups have dated the Bird cups and style its Archaic black-figure. The connections for Cycladic are stylistic, loose for the early schools and close for 'Melian'. Of East Greek wares the Bird bowls are tolerably fixed by grave groups and other contexts; the Wild Goat style appears in useful grave groups about the Early phase of Ripe Corinthian; Chiot still depends mostly on uncertain stylistic parallels, Fikellura on grave groups, Clazomenian black-figure on style and one context, and the Clazomenian sarcophagi on style and three grave groups. For Crete there are a few insufficient items of internal and external evidence. In Italy grave groups and lax stylistic links are at hand for Geometric, Italocorinthian and Bucchero; and for Etruscan black-figure, 'Chalcidian' and the Caeretan hydriai stylistic comparison with Attic is good enough. In red-figure Attic till its late stage influences and dates the other schools. For Hellenistic, where style is no longer coherent, contexts are necessary. But even in the well-explored periods of mature black-figure and red-figure new discoveries may be surprising.

3. Absolute Chronology

Greek and Oriental literature and records offer a large number of dated events. The Greek sources are accurate enough from the fifth century onwards, when historical study had begun and public archives became extensive. The period before 500 B.C. is more obscure. Greek events are few and dates less certain, since it does not seem that there was much official recording, anyhow before writing was introduced, nor did the ancients themselves agree on the very bare chronologies that they constructed in Classical and later times; and though in the older civilizations of the East there are many accurately dated events, only rarely have they been linked to Greece. Besides, not all events are relevant to pottery, and all that are relevant are not equally valuable. In general the most valuable fixed dates are those given by the sealing of a rich deposit, as in a communal grave or a destroyed settlement. The foundation of a settlement is not so definite, since the earliest deposit may be poor, escape notice or have been cleared away. Parallels with sculpture and free painting are mostly delusive in the Archaic period, since the dating of those arts is almost always dependent on pottery, and afterwards the arts no longer proceeded in step. Nor is there much help from small independently dated objects, such as coins, which often prove much older than the context in which they are found; so an isolated object of this sort is usually suspect, though if the association is repeated it becomes more trustworthy.

The useful dates for Archaic and earlier pottery, few and regressively more unreliable, must be considered critically. For later times a statement of the more important dates is enough.

Late Bronze Age

At Amarna in Egypt, in contexts of the second quarter of the fourteenth century – the date is safe to ten or fifteen years – there has been found Mycenaean pottery of the Late Helladic IIIa stage; and two centuries later there is a less secure and less direct synchronism for the Late Helladic IIIc1 style in the new settlements of the Philistines.

Protogeometric and Geometric periods

The next five or six hundred years have so far no good fixed points. The Dorian invasion (whatever that was) is disappointing; its date is uncertain and its traces have not been recognized in pottery. From Tell Abu Hawam in Palestine there are three pieces of imported Greek ware, which look contemporary with Attic Early and Middle Geometric and were found in a stratum thought to be no later than the end of the ninth century. From Megiddo, in a stratum thought to end no later than 850 B.C., we have two Attic sherds of the beginning of Middle Geometric and two other sherds that appear to imitate Greek work of much the same time. From Samaria come seven Attic or Atticizing sherds of Middle (or very early Late) Geometric style and sealed in a stratum thought to end no later than 750 B.C. At these three sites the dates given above depend on the contents of the strata and their relative chronology according to the system constructed by Palestinian archaeologists, but unfortunately there is no agreement yet on their absolute values. It is different with Hama, which was destroyed by the Assyrians – as their records tell us – in 720 B.C.: so the one example of Attic Middle Geometric II and the three Late Geometric fragments must be earlier. Al Mina is delusive, since its beginning is dated only relatively by comparing the earliest Oriental finds with those from other Syrian and Palestinian sites, and there is no certainty that its earliest Greek finds are as old.

Archaic period

With the Western colonization of the Greeks we are approaching their historical times. For the Sicilian foundations Thucydides gives some relative dates in two distinct series and Eusebius absolute dates which tally very roughly with Thucydides and a chance remark of Pindar's. Modern students generally combine Thucydides and Eusebius, though the ancients were less agreed. At four of the colonies so dated – Syracuse in 733, Megara Hyblaea in 728, Gela in 688 and Selinus in 628 B.C. – there has been enough excavation to raise the hope that the plentiful Corinthian pottery goes back to within a few years of their founding, though where the earliest pieces are from graves a few perfectionists profess to allow a longer lag for the first settlers to grow old and die. The relative order of these foundations is confirmed by the sequence of the pottery, Syracuse and Megara Hyblaea of course appearing contemporary. For the earlier absolute dates two contacts with the East give some support. In a grave at Ischia which contained three Corinthian pots little later than the earliest from Syracuse and earlier than any from Gela there was a scarab with the cartouche of the Egyptian Bocchoris, whose reign can be fixed with a margin of a few years to 718–712 B.C. If the scarab is Egyptian (as has been asserted) it was probably made during and not after the reign of that inglorious king, but the context can be used to suggest a more precise result. It is obviously improbable that all three pots should be much older than the time of the burial and therefore than the scarab; but, to judge by the generations of Attic Geometric painters, the interval between these pots and those from Samaria cannot be more than some sixty years; if then the latest date of the Samaria pots is 750 B.C. and the earliest date of the Ischia pots is 718 B.C. (since the scarab of king Bocchoris cannot be earlier than the beginning of his reign), then the range of error in the absolute dating here should not be more than twenty-five years and the chronology followed in this book cannot be raised or lowered by more than ten or fifteen years. The importance of this Bocchoris scarab is exceptional; other scarabs found in Greece have not been helpful.

Selinus is troublesome. Till 1958 it was believed that its earliest finds were Early Ripe Corinthian, and the beginning of that stage was related to the fixed date of 628 B.C. which Thucydides gives for the foundation of the colony. It now appears that Transitional or even Late Protocorinthian too was excavated there. But simply to lower the dates of these phases by fifteen or twenty-five years seems impracticable: the development of style and the sequence of painters in Middle Proto-corinthian would be spread over too long a time, and the compression of the subsequent period is equally difficult. So it is more likely that Thucydides was wrong in his date for Selinus. To accept Eusebius's date of 650 B.C. would be convenient, if Eusebius was generally reliable. Though archaeologists will no doubt continue to harmonize the statement of Thucydides with the chronology that is currently accepted, it is wiser for the present to retain that chronology but recognize that Selinus does not provide any fixed absolute date. It is also wise to consider that Thucydides' earlier dates may be no more reliable.

For another colony, Aziris in Cyrenaica, dates can be obtained by a combination of statements of Herodotus and Eusebius. This puts its beginning in 637 and its end in 631 B.C. If the site has been identified correctly, the Archaic objects found there should be of, or not much before, that time. The very few finds recorded include fragments of

Protocorinthian pots and examples of East Greek Bird bowls and banded cups.

In the East the sources of our tradition may be different. At three colonial sites there has been much excavation – Naucratis, Istria and Olbia; Eusebius puts their foundations in 749, 657 and 647 B.C., but to judge by the finds they should all be a good generation later than Selinus. Perhaps the earliest pottery of Naucratis, Istria and Olbia has not been revealed, or more likely they were founded later than Eusebius thought. Certainly the earliest finds so far made at those colonies are no earlier than the latest from Old Smyrna, which Herodotus says was destroyed by king Alyattes of Lydia, that is on his reckoning not before 613 B.C., since Alyattes was occupied elsewhere in his first five years. It is easiest to conclude that though Eusebius's dates cannot be trusted consistently, the western series is more or less right. But Greek history in the early Archaic period is so shadowy that an absolute error even of thirty or forty years should not be disturbing.

A little absolute evidence comes from Oriental sites. Tarsus was destroyed by Sennacherib in 696 B.C. and Protocorinthian and East Greek Bird bowls were found there; unfortunately it is not yet agreed whether they belong before or after that destruction. There is also Meṣad Ḥashavyahu near Askalon, where a small fort which was in use only a short time contained pottery of the Middle II Wild Goat style – not, I think, the earliest – and also several Hebrew inscriptions. Since the inscriptions are Hebrew and this area was occupied by the Egyptians in 609 B.C., it is reasonable to suppose that the pottery too is earlier and consequently that the Middle I Wild Goat style and, since it seems contemporary, Early Ripe Protocorinthian did not begin later than 620 B.C. Yet Early Ripe Corinthian, so the finds at Old Smyrna show, was not yet at its end when that city was sacked and so can hardly have ended earlier than 605 B.C. If then, as is likely, Early Ripe Corinthian lasted for some twenty-five years, its absolute dating can be fixed within ten years and the system generally accepted by archaeologists should not, so it happens, be over five years out. Suspicious though this result is, the main framework for the chronology of Archaic pottery seems reasonably sound, though when applied to lesser schools the error may be considerably more.

The next fixed date is 566 B.C. when, according to Pherecydes and Eusebius, the Panathenaic festival or its games were instituted, and with them – it is assumed – the officially inscribed Panathenaic amphorae: so the earliest surviving amphorae, one near Lydos in Halle and Burgon's in the British Museum [PLATE 21B], are dated in the later

560s. There is also the famous Laconian cup that shows a man labelled Arcesilas presiding over the weighing of wool: if this is a contemporary record of a king Arcesilas of Cyrene, then to conform with our other fixed dates he must be the second of that name and the cup was made in the 560s or not much later. Some students also hold that since, as Herodotus and inscribed fragments say, king Croesus of Lydia gave columns to the new Artemisium at Ephesus, the surviving sculpture from columns of that temple can be dated about 550 B.C.: but the Artemisium was a very big building, and work, even on the pedestals, may have been spread over many years.

Herodotus also records that, after the building of the Siphnian treasury at Delphi, Siphnos was attacked by Samian exiles who had taken part in the Spartan expedition against Polycrates, and that that expedition took place while Cambyses was invading Egypt in (as we know) 525 B.C.: though the story is probably in part false and the interval between the building and the attack is not stated, archaeologists assume that it was only a year or two and so roundly date the sculptures of the Siphnian treasury about 525 B.C. Another fixed point at 525 B.C. may come from the same invasion of Egypt by Cambyses. According to Herodotus Daphnae was the frontier fortress to the east of Egypt and there were Greek mercenary troops in the Egyptian army that was defeated by the Persians: if, as seems likely, Daphnae is the modern Tell Defenneh, then the latest Greek pottery from that site may be not later than 525 B.C.

The last three Archaic dates are owing again to the Persians. Miletus was sacked in 494 B.C., but the finds are largely lost or unpublished. At Marathon in 490 B.C. the Athenians raised a mound over their dead and duly furnished them with pottery. On the Acropolis of Athens, sacked in 480 B.C., rich pockets of debris have been recovered; admittedly there is contamination from later periods, but it is very small.

Classical period

With the fifth century, dates in Greek history become exactly reliable. After the sack of Athens in 480 B.C. the next useful peg is the refounding of Camarina in 461 B.C. In 426–425 B.C. the Athenians purified Delos, digging up the graves and removing their contents to Rheneia; there the Purification deposit has been found and only slightly (so it seems) contaminated by later objects. After the battle of Delion in 424 B.C. the Boeotians buried their dead and local pottery in the Polyandrion at Thespiae. A little later is a grave of the Lacedaemonians in Athens of 403 B.C. Motya was sacked in 397 B.C. Olynthus came to an end in

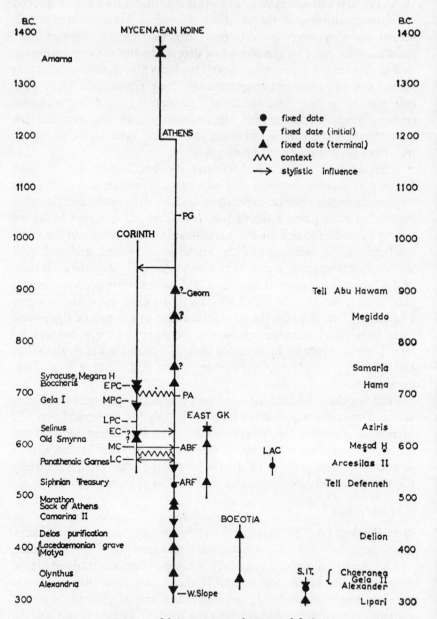

FIG. 42. *Main structure of system of dating*

348 B.C. Gela, destroyed in 405, was refounded about 340 B.C. and destroyed again some sixty years later: the second settlement is now being useful for South Italian wares. At Chaeronea the Thebans killed in the battle of 338 B.C. were buried in a communal grave, which is not yet published properly. Alexandria was founded in 331 B.C., and an early cemetery has been unearthed at Chatby (or Sciatbi). The effect of Alexander may be seen also on some Apulian red-figure pots, which show a Greek attacking a Persian king; if rightly interpreted, these must

FIG. 43. *Cross-dating of some archaic schools*

have been painted after 334 B.C., but probably not long after, since the vase-painters had not yet learnt that Alexander had no beard. There are also from 379 till 312 B.C. Panathenaic amphorae painted before firing with the name of an annual archon.

Hellenistic period

Alexandria offers not only its foundation, but also a number of funerary dates inscribed on Hadra hydriai; these dates give the year of the reigning Ptolemy and if the identifications are right (as seems likely) they extend from 271 to 209 B.C. The Panathenaic amphorae continue to show names of officials, but after about 310 B.C. archons are replaced by treasurers and agonothetes, and very few of these can now be identified. Lipari was wasted in 304, to the benefit of South Italian specialists. An excavated fort at Koroni in Attica, occupied only from 265 to 261 B.C., is useful for black-painted ware. The destruction of Carthage in 147 B.C. has little, of Corinth in 146 B.C. much value. The keen student of Hellenistic pottery can probably find other good dates that are fixed more or less precisely.

Other absolute chronologies

Besides dates based on historical records there are physical methods of computing time. Calculation of the decay of radiocarbon, by now indispensable to prehistorians, is not precise enough to help students of Greek vase-painting. Measuring thermoluminescence has the convenience that the material is provided by the pottery itself, but for the first millennium B.C. a hundred years is an optimistic limit to its accuracy. As for the thermo-remanent magnetization of fired clays, there is the advantage that the point of reference is not the present but the nearest ascertained magnetic date; but it is uncertain how far it will be practicable to fix such dates, and even then the margin of error is not likely to be less than fifty years. For the time being it looks as if Classical archaeologists, with resignation or relief, had better stick to their old methods.

4. The Reconciliation of Relative and Absolute Chronologies

Once a relative chronology has been established, it is easy to peg it to the relevant absolute dates. But in spacing the sequences between pegs some assumption must be made, either that the output (or rather the surviving output) of pottery or that the development in style continued at a uniform rate. Usually development in style seems more scholarly and is preferred, though students tend to consider it as proceeding not continuously but by stages. So, till small shifts were made to accommodate Samaria and Gela, Attic Geometric was often presented in four parts, to each of which fifty years was allotted, and the Orientalizing style of Corinth was marked out in phases of twenty-five years. On the other hand the early phase of Attic Protogeometric has been made short to fit the rarity of its products.

The absolute dating of early Greek pottery is precarious. Towards the middle of the fourteenth century there are good contacts with the secure chronology of Egypt, and in the late eighth the Sicilian colonies provide dates that may be correct to about fifteen years. Between these two pegs lie over six hundred years and rather more than the Submycenaean, Protogeometric and Geometric styles. To assign dates to those styles is convenient, to rely on them foolhardy. During the seventh century the normal range of error should not be more than ten or twenty years. By the end of the sixth century the fixed dates should be strictly accurate.

FIGS. 42 and 43 summarize very roughly the structure of the relative chronology and its attachment to the absolute dates.

12 The Pottery Industry

Greek writers show little interest in economics, perhaps because their economy was simple and obvious. Anyhow, the few literary references to pottery say nothing useful about the industry. What we know or guess comes from the pots themselves and a few inscriptions set up in public by potters.

Excavation of a potters' quarter at Corinth and the name Ceramicus at Athens show that in those cities potters had their workshops close together. Fine pottery was not their only product. Others were coarse pottery, tiles, architectural revetments, plaques, figurines and larger statuary; and till the fifth century vase-painters may well have painted in other media too. How far workshops specialized in one or more of these lines we do not know, but it is natural to suppose that the coarser products were more suited to larger establishments.

For the size of workshops or parts of workshops that made fine pottery there are a few scraps of evidence. Several Corinthian plaques and Attic pots of the sixth and fifth centuries illustrate potters at work. Most of these have room for only one or two figures, but a black-figure hydria of near 500 B.C. shows the manager, one painter, one man shaping a pot and five assistants, and on a red-figure hydria of about 460 B.C. four painters (or perhaps metalworkers) are being honoured by celestial visitants. Round the middle of the fifth century a group of Attic painters associated with the Penthesilea painter occasionally collaborated two together on the same cup, so that plainly they worked in the same shop; there are more than a dozen of these collaborators, spread over a period of perhaps thirty years. Yet in the early fourth century the Jena painter, one of the leaders of his generation, was the only regular painter in his workshop, to judge by the debris found in its ruins. Stylistic analysis gives similar results. The hackneyed sameness of the Penthesilean group is fair proof that its members worked together; so this workshop during its forty years had over twenty painters. But in several decent red-figure establishments there were, it seems, not more than two or three qualified painters at one time. The study of shapes also points in the same direction. There is not much sign of factory methods, at least till the Hellenistic period. In the great period of Attic fine pottery, the later sixth and earlier fifth centuries, it appears more or less often (according to the interpretation taken of the 'maker's' signature ἐποίησε) that cups and presumably other pots were shaped by one man and painted by another, but division of the painter's labour remained very rare.

The status of potters need not have been uniform. At Athens during the last quarter of the sixth and the first of the fifth centuries several potters including Andocides and Euphronios, who are reasonably identified with the makers and painter of fine pottery, were able to erect impressive dedications on the Acropolis. In the later fourth century the brothers Kittos and Bacchius, potters and Athenian citizens, were honoured with the citizenship of Ephesus and an inscription to record it; and another potter Bacchius, probably their father, has left a respectable gravestone in Attica. The family of Bacchius may have been owners who did not work with their hands, since though by the fourth century literary Athenians looked down on manual work, they admitted the propriety of owning a workshop. But in an earlier age Euphronios as a painter used his hands, and yet was prosperous and presumably reputable. These men were masters. Of their workmen we know less. A Boeotian kotyle perhaps of the earlier fourth century shows a potter's workshop in which one of the men is suffering servile punishment. But the mobility of such a painter as Oltos, who painted for at least six makers, argues that he was a free agent. There is nothing in inferences from names, that for example Skythes and Brygos were Scythian and Phrygian slaves; foreign ethnics and personal names were naturalized in Archaic Greece.

It has been alleged that vase-painters and other potters migrated freely within the Greek world, and in particular from Ionia to Athens. But though in most schools of pottery foreign influences are visible at one time or another, there are not so many signs of painters trained and matured in a foreign tradition. The Italocorinthian style is technically so novel in Etruria that Corinthian or at least Greek teachers must have been necessary. The Eretrian black-figure of the mid sixth century, the South Italian red-figure of the later fifth and perhaps some Faliscan red-figure of the early fourth all start in a style too Attic to have been learnt outside an Attic workshop, and some Boeotian painters may have trained at Athens. But normally the vase-painters of any city appear to have been brought up in the local tradition of that city, and the odds are that they were born there. Signatures very rarely help. In the third quarter of the sixth century Lydos signs two Attic pots ho Λυδος, of which the simple meaning is 'the Lydian'. The contemporary painter of a wooden plaque from Pitsa is Corinthian in style and calls himself a Corinthian. In the fourth century there are two pots of Attic style inscribed as made by the Athenian Xenophantos. As for the generality of inscriptions painted before firing, the painters of any school usually follow the local alphabet and dialect, and though sometimes these may not have been their own, the cumulative effect is telling. It might perhaps be expected that, as a local school of fine pottery declined, unemployment would drive its craftsmen to emigrate; but fine pottery was only a part of the production of potters, and its decline was usually gradual.

The general character of Greek industry makes it very unlikely that potters themselves engaged in merchanting. Presumably they sold in the workshop to ordinary purchasers and to dealers or merchants, who in turn sold to other merchants and dealers overseas. Even a regular connection between a potter and a merchant or market was unusual, if we may judge by the dispersal of the works of individual painters. There are a few probable or possible exceptions. Some Chiot workshops around the 570s appear to have had close ties with particular merchants; at least Chiot cups found at Naucratis and on Aegina have dedications painted before firing, the dedications of the same man are too numerous for a casual traveller, and each dedicator has usually his own painter. The Attic Tyrrhenian amphorae run a little later, a showy class of pots almost all found in Etruria; perhaps then they were made specially for the Etruscan trade. Towards the end of the century the Attic maker Nikosthenes may also have studied the Etruscan market, since his peculiar variety of amphora not only occurs principally (if not exclusively) in Etruria, but also looks suspiciously like a native Etruscan shape. It has been argued that the griffins and Arimaspians of many Attic pelikai of the mid fourth century were chosen to appeal to the Greeks and Scythians of South Russia, but they are as common at Spina in Italy.

For the Chiot pottery just mentioned it may be inferred from the painted dedications that export from Chios to Naucratis and Aegina was direct; it may also be inferred that the exporters were Chiots, since in four or five instances the dedicator adds his ethnic and that ethnic is o Χιος. For exports from the Aegean to Italy and Sicily the route was more difficult, requiring transhipment at the Isthmus or the hazardous rounding of the Peloponnese. Who handled the western trade we do not know, but the merchants' marks on Attic pots imported into Italy during the later sixth and early fifth centuries suggest that at some stage the trade was not in Attic hands.

For the prices of pottery we have a few scribbles on the bottoms of pots mostly found in Italy. They are not all certainly intelligible, and those that are do not show in what currency or at what point in the journey the price was given, nor always what was included in the lot. We read, for example, on several Attic bell-kraters of the later fifth century that six kraters were offered or sold for four drachmas, and on two Attic hydriai of much the same date the letters νδιδραχποι and νδτριδραχποι presumably signify that ὑδρίαι ποικίλαι (or decorated hydriai) cost three drachmas and two drachmas. A practical potter might perhaps estimate the cost of production. But evidently in most of the Greek world it was over long periods cheaper to import fine and moderately fine pottery than to produce it at home, and even in distant Italy the advantages of local manufacture were not overwhelming.

The industry making painted pottery was small, even when it was flourishing. This can be demonstrated from J. D. Beazley's *Attic Red-figure Vase-painters* – I use the first edition since I have not made detailed counts for the second, though generally this gives similar results. In *ARV*[1] close exploration of Attic vase-painting of the fifth century assigned two-fifths of the known pots to some five hundred painters and workshops. Balancing new painters still to be detected against old painters to be combined, one may reasonably conclude that the true total (casuals excluded) is not likely to be far from five hundred. Since the average working life of a painter was evidently not more than twenty-five years, the average number of vase-painters working at any time should not be more than a hundred and twenty-five. Another and perhaps sounder method gives a comparable result. Some red-figure painters have been more closely studied and are more widely known, so that it is likely that most of their extant works have been identified. Lekythoi and cups had, of course, better chances of survival than large pots; but on average it seems that the number of extant works of these painters, as listed in *ARV*[1], is equivalent to not less than three for every year of their working lives. The number of red-figure pots that had been examined competently when *ARV*[1] was written may be estimated at not more than forty thousand or, on this calculation, the equivalent of thirteen thousand painting years. Since the period over which these pots extend is something like one hundred and thirty years, the average number of painters at work throughout this period should be about a hundred. To the number of painters must be added a complement of shapers, which can hardly have been larger even if the painters rarely shaped the pots they painted, and also various assistants and labourers. So the total of workmen, skilled and unskilled, required to produce the decorated and the fine black-painted Attic pottery of the fifth century is likely to have been in the order only of hundreds. Yet the Attic potters of the fifth century supplied the greatest part of the fine pottery used throughout the Greek world. It is because pottery survives that its industrial importance has appeared great.

13   Uses for Other Studies

Greek historians have usually learnt little about archaeology and Greek archaeologists have thought little about history, so that the historical conclusions they draw from archaeological evidence are often discreditably naïve. But pottery has a limited usefulness for historians.

1. Dating

Greek pottery is plentiful and can be dated with some precision, according to the system explained in Chapter 11. Briefly, that system is reliable from the end of the sixth century, but before then depends on stylistic sequences that are at a few points pegged to dates taken from the literary tradition. But the intervening stretches are not necessarily measured out correctly nor are all the literary dates necessarily of comparable validity. So it is one thing to say of the oinochoe of PLATE 4B that it was made about twenty-five years before the earliest finds from Syracuse, but something of a different kind to say that it was made about twenty-five years after the institution of the Olympic Games.

The theory of stratification is well known. Objects found in the same stratum are of the same date as the stratum and – within its limits – as each other, and a lower stratum is earlier than a higher stratum. These bald statements are true only in general, and a single association or dissociation is not very important. But at some Greek sites enough has been found to date various stages of their development, usually by deposits connected with levels of destruction or rebuilding. Other sites have been only partially explored or casually inspected, and there is a special difficulty in determining when a settlement was founded, since small beginnings (especially on a new site) may easily have been destroyed or missed. Before using pottery to date a site it is necessary to consider how complete and efficient was the excavation, how reliable the report, and how frequent the pottery on which conclusions are to be based. It is helpful to remember that it was more than fifty years before the excavators of Corinth struck a Mycenaean deposit.

2. Trade

The more relevant facts until the Hellenistic era are roughly these. All Greek cities used Greek pottery, and so did some other peoples of the

West and of Anatolia, but not the older communities of the Orient. Greek cities used only Greek pottery. Most Greek cities, anyhow from the seventh to the fourth century B.C., imported rather than made fine pottery. The favourite imports in that period were till the early sixth century Corinthian and afterwards Attic, but a few other wares have a considerable distribution in limited areas. The importation and the quality of fine pottery were both declining from the later fifth century onwards.

The reasonable inferences from these and more general facts are disappointing. First, the presence or absence of Greek pottery has different meanings in different places. In Europe an urban settlement using an appreciable quantity of pottery that was not Greek was itself not Greek; if it also used Greek pottery it traded with Greeks, and if it did not use Greek pottery it did not trade with Greeks. But in the East an appreciable quantity of Greek pottery is evidence of Greek residents, commercial or military, and the absence of Greek pottery does not preclude trade with Greeks. Secondly, though pottery made up a part of Greek trade, it was presumably a minor and inconstant part, so that the total value of trade cannot be estimated from pottery. Thirdly, the comparative value of the exports of different cities cannot be related to the pottery they made, since most Greek cities made no pottery to export. Fourthly, Greek trade was not organized strictly or elaborately. If pottery of one of the less important wares was exported in some quantity from the place where it was made to some other place, the likeliest explanation of its export is direct trade between the two places. But the universally admired wares may often have been traded indirectly. These last two assertions have a little support in merchants' marks on a few Attic pots and perhaps in the painted dedications on Chiot chalices; on the other hand the Attic Nikosthenic amphora may have been designed particularly for the Etruscans.

It should always be remembered that the total quantity of pottery that happens to have been found varies greatly from one site to another, and so it is not the absolute as much as the relative quantity of a ware that is important. Few archaeological aids have been more delusive than those distribution maps which mark where specimens of a particular class of objects have been found, but not in what frequency. An isolated find is of very little importance.

3. Political Relations

There is no evidence that private purchasers of Greek pots regularly let political reasons impair their tastes. If politics had effects on the distribution of pottery, it was through the promotion or restriction of trade and especially direct trade. Such effects should be visible, if at all, in the exports of those minor wares which depended on direct trade. Two possible examples will serve. East Greek pottery is less rare at Gela than at most western sites; Gela had an East Greek mother-city. Laconian pottery of the mid sixth century appears to be less rare on Samos than at other East Greek sites; according to Herodotus Laconia interfered in Samos a little later. But whether the proportions of those wares is significant may be doubted.

4. Prosperity

It is likely enough that at any one time the Greeks were uniform in their uses, domestic and dedicatory, of painted pottery. So it should be possible to compare the prosperity of contemporary settlements and sanctuaries by the amount and quality of the pottery found in them, if the finds are representative. That condition is not often satisfied. It is true that some sanctuaries, like that on Mount Hymettus, appear from the character of the pottery to have been poor, but such conclusions can usually be proved more clearly by the architectural remains. For comparing sites of different periods there is the extra difficulty that from the fifth century onwards fine pottery was losing in importance.

In most Greek graves pottery was the principal part of the furniture, and very often this pottery is complete. But local fashions and individual piety make comparisons less reliable. In general early graves vary more in lavishness than later graves.

5. Daily Life

From the eighth to the fourth century B.C. scenes with human figures are regular on Greek pottery. Some are based on ordinary life, and even in those that are mythological many details are contemporary. A few artistic conventions must be discounted, notably the representation of youthful males as naked in almost every context: this convention, which is sometimes explained as 'Heroic nudity', was a dominant characteristic of Greek art. Another convention, demanded as much by pictorial composition as by epic tradition, was the resolving of a battle into separate duels. But paintings on pots offer valuable illustrations of much of Greek life – at home, parties, exercise, ceremonies, work and war.

6. Mythology and Religion

Mythical and divine occasions provided the favourite themes of Greek painting. Most are orthodox, and of the rest some deviate through negligence. Scholars of the eighteenth and nineteenth centuries were much concerned with the interpretation of rare myths and cults, often to fit the religious theories then fashionable; their spirit is kept alive by the zealots who look for illustrations of lost epics or sense 'daimonic' forces. But generally the moderns prefer statistical studies of particular incidents, though when they come to explain changes in form or popularity they occasionally forget that artistic capacity and the shape of the field have some connection with the choice of subjects.

14   *Practical Comments*

So much Greek pottery survives that most students have occasion to handle or acquire examples. Experience is learnt by trial and reflection. But some unsystematic hints may be helpful to the beginner.

1. Handling

Pottery is fragile, especially if like many old pieces it has been cracked or broken and repaired. So continuous care is expected in handling Greek pots, and no strain should be added to the weaker parts. An amphora such as that of PLATE 32A ought not to be picked up by the handles or lip but by putting both hands under the belly, and in the same way the cups of PLATE 25 should be supported below the bowl. When set down again, a pot should be lowered gently to avoid jarring. It is prudent too, when lifting a pot off a shelf or putting it back, to watch the bottom of the shelf above, since often there is little clearance and if the shelves are of glass they are easily overlooked.

2. Examination

Many pots have been restored, some misleadingly. Sherds may be inserted in the wrong places, parts of different pots combined, a fragmentary shape wrongly completed in plaster, lost or damaged decoration repainted, and occasionally there are more creative forgeries. The character and extent of restoration varies from one collection to another and even within the same collection. At present the approved practice is to distinguish original and restored parts of a pot by leaving the plaster white or (more considerately) tinting it to a colour not too near that of the clay, and the painting in of missing decoration is done, if at all, with unobtrusive faintness. But earlier ethics, still observed by some dealers, preferred complete restoration or improvement. Plaster repairs and damaged surfaces were coloured to match the original parts. Missing pieces of the decoration were supplied faithfully or imaginatively, and occasionally indecent parts were painted out. Damaged or vanished paint and colours were renewed. Often too the whole surface, ancient or modern, was treated to a coat of varnish that has since become

279

opaque. A variant method, especially inside cups, was to apply a skin of plaster over a damaged surface and on that to paint in the original or some novel design. In some arrant forgeries the decoration, painted or incised, is wholly modern. Though elaborate restoration or forgery is relatively uncommon, any pot should first be examined for signs of modern work.

Where parts of a pot (especially the base, handles or neck) have been wholly or largely reconstructed in plaster, the profiles and proportions of those parts may be wildly wrong and are rarely quite right. This is a truism, though sometimes forgotten. But it is much less easy to determine whether genuine fragments come from the same pot – feet are the commonest intruders – or whether they have been put in the right place. For the thickness of the wall may vary greatly at different levels and slightly at the same level, and colour of clay and paint may range widely because of some fault in the making or a later accident. But the quality of the clay should be uniform, and the agreement of the decoration and of wheel-marks should help. Here practice and a knowledge of style are the quickest guides.

Wheel-marks are worth attention. When a pot is being thrown on the wheel, the pressure of the fingers on the moist clay produces a series of grooves and ridges of varying sizes but all approximately horizontal, and though the later process of turning may remove these wheel-marks the removal is not always complete and such parts of a pot as are not meant to be seen are usually not turned. If a sherd with wheel-marks is held up at the level of the eye and twisted about till the chosen wheel-mark appears as a straight horizontal line, the sherd must then be at its correct angle to the horizontal plane of the pot. It may, of course, be upside down, but that can usually be decided by experience or common sense. Bands of paint also often run horizontally, but are less reliable than wheel-marks. Once the angle of the sherd is fixed its curvature, unless the sherd is very small, allows a calculation of the diameter at its level and a surmise about the profile. Further, the finish of the inside generally shows whether the pot was open or closed, and the decoration too may be suggestive of the shape. Wheel-marks may also have a pattern sufficiently distinctive to decide whether sherds come from the same level of the same pot, or even to allow an estimate of their distance from each other: FIG. 44 should make this clear.

Where restoration is thorough and tries to conceal itself, the commonest clues are some fault in style or a messy appearance. Plaster tends to have a rough or flattened surface without wheel-marks, the dark paint may be dull or thick, the white rather coarse. Such differences in texture show best in a glancing light, though if the whole pot has been varnished the underlying texture is usually invisible. Sometimes the inside of the pot reveals what is plaster, but often the plaster has been smeared too widely for any precision. A few museums have ultra-violet equipment, which distinguishes clearly between clay and plaster. But it is best if the restorations can be cleared away.

Forgeries so far have not given much trouble. Occasionally genuine ancient pots have been provided with new painting in their blank fields or with black-figure decoration cut out of a dark band; but the new and unfired paint usually dissolves in spirit, incision on a pot already fired is ragged and scratchy, and a surface from which paint has been scraped is implausibly rough. As for wholehogging imitations of Greek pots,

FIG. 44. *Inside of sherd showing wheel-marks*
The section on the right gives the angle at which the wheel-marks on this sherd appear horizontal

ignorance of ancient techniques has made them rare and mainly unconvincing, at least till the 1960s, when recent research could be assimilated: even so, thermoluminescence tests should discourage the more ambitious frauds, unless somehow a convenient method can be devised for irradiating newly fired pottery.

If, as is more usual, a pot has not been restored, its decoration may be badly worn. The standard dark paint is very, the purple colour moderately durable, but the white disappears easily and other colours are worse. Yet even the dark paint may be destroyed by prolonged damp or exposure. In general surfaces once covered by paint lack sheen, and if the only damage is the loss of the paint they show distinctly, especially in a glancing light. Similarly, dull patches and lines in the shiny dark paint often betray the loss of purple or white additions. In Attic and some other black-figure work, where detail on white was done by incising through it, faint incisions on the dark paint are another indication of lost white. Occasionally the whole surface has been equally worn away, so that the parts once reserved have become rough while the paint survived long enough to protect the smooth ground beneath it.

3. Taking Notes

In taking notes it is convenient to follow some system. Models may be found in most of the recent catalogues of active museums. For objects in a museum the inventory number ought always to be quoted, whether or not there is a catalogue number too; for the inventory is a permanent record, but catalogues may be replaced or forgotten. Measurements, usually of the height though idealists demand the diameter too, should be on the metric system.

The shape and decoration of a pot or sherd may be learnt by inspection but its provenance often cannot be checked. If an object in a reputable collection is said to have been found in an authorized excavation, the statement can generally be trusted. So too with objects attributed to some of the less official enterprises. Even so, if sherds are left uninventoried for a long time, they are liable to become mixed with aliens. Dealers' provenances have always been suspect, perhaps more so since the Greeks and Italians enacted laws to control the exhumation and export of antiquities; sellers wish to protect the source of their supply or oblige a customer with information to his taste. But in general purchases made in Athens have been found in what at the time was Greek territory. The market in Rome has been supplied principally from Etruria and Latium, that in Naples from South Italy. Smyrna till 1912 attracted clandestine finds from western Anatolia and the nearer islands off its coast. Cairo and Alexandria drew and perhaps still draw much of their stock from across the Mediterranean. Elsewhere in Greek lands there has been no established trade in antiques, and objects bought for example in Rhodes or Cyprus or Boeotia have almost always been found in those parts.

4. Drawing and Photographing

In tracing or sketching the decoration of a pot there are recognized conventions. Solid areas of dark paint are simply outlined, incision is distinguished by a darker or heavier line, purple is shaded or hatched: PLATE 9B is exemplary. White too is outlined, if its position is obvious; but if there might be confusion, some sort of hatching or shading is permitted. For direct tracing from pottery the more transparent the material the better, and so such plastics as Kodatrace are preferable to paper.

In photographing for study the aim is a clear, sharp and clean negative, suitable for publication without any retouching. The illumination should be evenly distributed over the object, avoiding heavy shadows or high lights, and the background should be neutral, of uniform tone, and plainly distinguished from the pot. High lights, which are dazzling if the paint is shiny, can be evaded by lighting a pot only from the sides, so that there is no strong reflection from its surface to the lens of the camera. Oblique lighting is useful also for bringing out faded or damaged details. These and other reasons recommend artificial lighting in a darkened room or a portable tent. Some experts have a dirty habit of dulling high lights by smearing the spot with plasticine. There is no particular difficulty about complete pots which can be photographed upright, though some thought should be taken to find the best eye-level. Sherds are usually laid out flat and photographed from above. To avoid shadows it is best to arrange them on a sheet of ground glass not less than eighteen by twelve inches in size and supported at the corners some six inches or more above a sheet of white paper: to reflect the light evenly onto the glass above it the paper may have to be tilted or curved, and if artificial light is being used an extra lamp may be needed to shine on the paper. If several sherds are being photographed together, they should be arranged in a sort of grid so that each sherd is in a separate rectangle: then, if the prints are chopped up, each sherd is properly framed, and there is no temptation to the discreditable makeshift of cutting round the edges of a sherd or masking out its background. When photographing sherds it is useful to include a scale, but the scale should be placed in the right alignment and towards the edge of the field so that it can at will be trimmed off the print. In spite of what some authorities declare, scales are valueless for complete pots which have depth of perspective. Photography needs practice, but the amateur who knows what he wants is more likely to succeed than the professional who does not.

Copying the shape of a pot (which the eyes see only in perspective) can be done in several ways. The quickest should be photographing with a long-focus lens from a distance of thirty or more times the longer dimension of the pot; at that range distortion is negligible. Polarized light and sand boxes have not yet proved successful. Templates are unwieldy and expensive for large pots, though useful for sherds. A copying frame, with one arm touching the profile of the pot and another tracing an outline on a vertical board, is practicable and exact. Lead wire is handy and useful: a suitable length of it is rolled flat on a board, moulded against the profile of the pot till it takes its shape, then carefully removed and laid flat on a sheet of paper, where it must be held in position while the inner outline is traced with a sharp pencil; since the wire springs back a little the ends of each section should be fixed by measurement with dividers, and sharp angles must be corrected by eye. But most students, who only rarely need a precise shape, rely on measured drawings: the height of the pot is noted and its diameter at lip and foot, other points are transferred by the combined use of a vertical ruler and of a horizontal ruler or calipers, and intermediate contours are sketched by eye. FIG. 27 is a measured drawing, showing on the left a profile and on the right a section (though current fashion prefers to black in the wall of the section). But for complete pots it is often impracticable to calculate a complete section. Profiles and sections are demanded much more now than in the past, especially for undecorated pottery where shape is a principal criterion of date.

5. Cleaning

When a piece of pottery is dug up from the ground, it is usually incrusted with mud or some other deposit. This incrustation should not be picked off nor immediately scrubbed, since it is liable to take the paint with it. The proper preliminary is to soak the specimen in water for some hours or days; this may dissolve the deposit or loosen it so much that it comes off with light brushing. If water is not enough – and it rarely is – a more efficient solvent is dilute hydrochloric acid. Though neat hydrochloric acid does not damage well-made and well-preserved Greek pottery, one part of acid to twenty parts of water is normally ample. The specimen should be saturated with water before it is put into the solution of acid. If it fizzes or bubbles there is no cause for alarm. After twenty-four hours or so it may be taken out and brushed lightly. If a deposit still remains, it can be steeped longer or in a stronger solution of the acid. When finally removed the specimen should again be soaked and rinsed in water, and then put aside to dry. Incrustations that survive this treatment are best left to experts. But there are many pieces in collections which have not even been washed.

Pottery that has been cleaned sometimes develops whitish crystals on its surface, caused by salts that have penetrated the clay. The cure is soaking in plain water.

The removal of restorations may be troublesome. Varnish and unfired paints can be more or less slowly dissolved by wiping them with methylated spirits. Plaster usually loosens in water and breaks up in a weak solution of hydrochloric acid. The treatment of the adhesives used to join sherds is mentioned in the next section.

6. Mending

Before joining sherds the order in which the joins are to be made needs to be thought out. If the join between any two sherds is not immediately obvious, it helps to hold them together in their correct position and to draw a pencil stroke on the inside across the join; then, when the adhesive is applied, no time is lost in fumbling for the fit. Of adhesives there is a choice. In the past the favourite has been shellac dissolved in hot or cold methylated spirit and brushed onto the edges to be joined. But some menders now prefer the proprietary adhesives made specially for repairing domestic china. Whatever adhesive is used, it should not be put on too thickly and the join should be made when it is tacky. Then the two fragments should be pressed tightly together for a little while and when they are holding left to set without any strain, as for instance by standing them with the join upright in a box filled with sand. Any surplus adhesive that may ooze out of the join should be removed before it dries hard. Shellac can be loosened again by heat and may give through prolonged dampness, but it is very difficult to break down the china adhesives, though methylated spirit may weaken them slowly. Durability is not always an advantage.

To fill a gap with plaster a strip of plasticine should be put at the back of the gap and the plaster pressed in from in front. When it is set, any roughness can be cut or sandpapered away and smears or splashes wiped off with water, though it may be difficult to remove plaster from incisions. Plaster is easily tinted with water-colour.

More complex mending may need some sort of form to ensure that the circuit of the pot is made regularly and that the final sherd joins on both sides. For weak joins a plaster backing may be advisable. But anything elaborate is best left to an expert.

7. Collecting

In Geneva, London and Paris there are dealers who specialize in Greek pottery, and since the market is free – that is, since purchasers are not thwarted by laws restricting export – the prices are high. Ordinary antique shops in northern Europe and America rarely have

Greek pots. In Greece and Italy, the principal sources of supply, the unlicensed export of antiquities is forbidden by law and at present only poor or mediocre pieces receive a licence. So in Athens prices are relatively moderate, and in the rest of Greece low. In Rome and Italy generally prices are higher, perhaps because evasion of the law is more regular. Even so, to judge by the pottery on sale in free markets, there must be some smuggling of good pieces from Italy (especially Etruria) and Greece.

Sherds can be picked up by any visitor to Greek lands (if the police do not object), and unless they are exceptional the authorities usually permit their export, though official permission may be slow. It is worth emphasizing that much of the interest of sherds is in where they were found, and so any sherd intended for a collection should be promptly marked with its provenance, preferably in Indian ink on a clean patch of the clay.

The History of the Study of Vase-Painting

Though ancient sherds are always turning up and the rarer complete pots are likely to be preserved, if only for re-use, they were for long ignored. The Middle Ages have left few records, but Arretine relief ware is mentioned from the late thirteenth century on. Ristoro d'Arezzo in his *della Composizione del Mondo* of 1282 wrote that artists supposed its maker divine or the fragments fallen from heaven. Giovanni Villani who died in 1348 also thought it superhuman in his *Cronaca Fiorentina*, and in the mid fifteenth century Giorgio Vasari (according to his grandson, the biographer of painters) succeeded in imitating it. Giulio Romano in 1524 possessed an ancient cup of terracotta and M. Negri in 1557 in his *Commentarium Geographicum* mentioned pottery from Adria, but neither said anything of decoration. A few pieces, no doubt, could be found in the cabinets of the time, as for instance the painted vases of Cardinal Carpi, praised for their garlands by U. Aldroandi in L. Mauro's *Antichità della Città di Roma* of 1558, and there were the black-figure pots found about 1565 in a chamber tomb at Orbetello by a Spanish engineer who was building fortifications there for Philip II. But such specimens were hardly noticed, and Thomas Dempster, a Scots papist who read and remembered everything, did not include vase-painting in the ceramic accomplishments of the paragons of his encyclopaedic and uncritical panegyric *de Etruria Regali*, compiled while he was professor of Law at Padua from 1616 to 1619. Avid though they were for other kinds of antiques, it is clear that writers and collectors, at least till the middle of the seventeenth century, had generally no interest in ancient painted pottery and, since it was available and its material not despised, this must have been from some stylistic repugnance. What that repugnance was may by elimination be inferred. After the end of antiquity, though technical standards had sunk, formulas survived for oblique views of faces and modelling by shading, so that to inquisitive painters of the late Middle Ages and still more so of the Renaissance the drawing of figures on the Greek pots commonly found in central Italy would have appeared primitive. For the same reason the earliest known facsimiles of Greek red-figure vase-painting mostly

correct their originals by supplying heavy shading. These facsimiles –
now at Windsor Castle or lent to the British Museum – are part of a
large collection of drawings procured in the mid seventeenth century
by Cassiano dal Pozzo (or perhaps his brother) and reproduce a dozen
Attic and South Italian figured pots accurately enough to allow the
identification of their schools and in some instances of their painters.
About the same time the French sculptor F. Girardon, who studied in
Rome around 1650, possessed two examples of South Italian red-figure;
and it was perhaps through him that C. A. du Fresnoy, in his versified
de Arte Graphica of 1668, listed vases among the examples of ancient
art to be noticed. The next honour, that of first publishing an ancient
vase (to be distinguished from an 'urn', which at that time meant a
cinerary casket) belongs, it seems, to M. A. de la Chausse (or Causeus),
a French resident in Rome and the author of the *Romanum Museum*. In
this enlightened folio, which first came out in 1690, there are tolerable
drawings with commentaries of a Calene phiale and of an Attic black-
figure pelike (on sale again in Rome in the 1930s). A few years later,
probably in 1701, L. Beger produced the third volume of the *Thesaurus
Regius et Electoralis Brandenburgensis*: among the items, most of which
had recently been bought from the estate of G. P. Bellori in Rome and
were soon after traded from Berlin to Dresden for a regiment of dra-
goons, there are illustrated one piece of Attic and one of South Italian
red-figure as well as an Italocorinthian alabastron. In another context
and so unnoticed for more than a hundred years was the publication
of a Panathenaic amphora from Benghazi, which Lemaître, French
consul at Tripoli, contributed to P. Lucas's second *Voyage* of 1712. In
1719 and 1724 B. de Montfauçon, in his *l'Antiquité Expliquée*, added
several red-figure pots, mostly bought in Naples, but was as much interested in shape and use as in decoration. Then from 1723 to 1726
F. Buonarroti inserted in Dempster's work, at last being published,
drawings of over thirty vases and appended a long disquisition about
them.

Buonarroti had an advantage over his predecessors; there were more
pots for him to see. In Rome and Tuscany, where the vocal antiquaries
lived or sojourned, it appears that in spite of the statements of la
Chausse and Montfauçon painted pots were still rare in the early years
of the eighteenth century. In Naples they were commoner, since the
graves of Campania were already being exploited, but Naples was in
another realm. We know very little of the early Neapolitan cabinets
apart from that of the lawyer Joseph Valletta, whose heirs about 1720
sold to Cardinal Gualtieri what became the first Roman collection of

Greek vases. By 1725, as Buonarroti's captions show, there were several connoisseurs in central Italy who owned a few specimens, mostly of South Italian red-figure. Gualtieri's collection, which also contained an assortment of bucchero and other local finds made by Bargigli, the bishop of Chiusi, passed to the Vatican, where in 1744 Cardinal Quirini furnished a separate vase room, though according to a precept still honoured in certain museums visitors were not permitted – so Uhden and Millin say – to make close examination or drawings of the exhibits. Thus the taste for painted vases was becoming acceptable; they were convenient in size and not too scarce or expensive.

The antiquaries also indulged their fancy. Of these the most eminent were A. F. Gori, G. B. Passeri and the Count de Caylus. Gori, whose Tuscan patriotism (so he boasts) impelled him to publish his *Museum Etruscum* from 1737 to 1743, illustrated and expounded several ancient painted pots and one modern forgery. Passeri, best remembered for his *Picturae Etruscorum in Vasculis* (1767–75), devoted three hundred plates to specimens from forty collections throughout Italy and even beyond the Alps. Caylus was more critical and observant, though there is not much pottery in his *Recueil d'Antiquités égyptiennes, étrusques, grecques et romaines*, which began to appear in 1752.

All these writers believed that the painted vases were Etruscan. The reason is probably not, as is usually asserted, that the earliest examples had been unearthed in Etruria; in fact most of them were made and so probably found in South Italy. But the Etruscomania that still visits the credulous was virulent in the seventeenth and early eighteenth centuries. It goes back to the forged Etruscan histories which began in the late fifteenth century and, though recognized as impostures by critical scholars, fed the prejudice, convenient to contemporary Tuscan pride and politics, that in the past the Etruscans had been a great and creative people. In effect all ancient monuments that were not obviously Roman or Greek (then barely known) nor yet Egyptian were likely to be classed as Etruscan. Antiquaries, as Paciaudi remarked of Gori, found something Etruscan everywhere, and the frequency of painted vases in South Italy was a proof only of Etruscan suzerainty. This attitude was strong enough in Rome and Tuscany to dub Greek vase-painting Etruscan, and Rome and Florence were then the homes of antiquarian curiosity and speculation. But the collectors of Naples and Sicily were less disposed to accept the incidental notes of Servius and supposedly Philargyrius that the Etruscans were once masters of almost all Italy, and besides the painted vases were found chiefly in their own territories. However that may be, the Etruscan addicts soon felt obliged to defend their attribution. La Chausse had used the term 'Hetruscan' casually and loosely, since he dated his Attic pelike to the epoch of the Roman emperors. Beger simply followed la Chausse, and Montfauçon identified the pot as Martial's Arretine. But Buonarroti gave ampler reasons, that painted vases were found throughout Etruria and that their Bacchic scenes – his repertory was largely South Italian – had details alien to both Greeks and Romans. Gori, a more fanatical Tuscan who concluded that Homer was taught in Etruria, deplored the error of those who claimed vase-painting for the Greeks, and where Pliny says that most of mankind uses earthenware pots he would have liked to emend *terrenis* to *Tyrrhenis*. But by 1749 even Gori had to concede to the Sicilian Benedictine Blasi that some of the painted vases then being found in Sicily had been made by the Greeks of Sicily, a claim repeated two years later by the Theatine G. M. Pancrazi in his *Antichità Siciliane*. Still Caylus next year resisted, and even proposed that owl-kotylai were made in Etruria to suit Athenian customers. Gradually logic prevailed. In 1754 A. S. Mazocchi argued from painted inscriptions on some red-figure pots that their painters were Greeks. A. R. Mengs, the most respected artist of his day and a judicious critic, was converted by 1759; and in 1764 in the first edition of the *Geschichte der Kunst des Alterthums* J. J. Winckelmann gave his sanction to the Greek origin of painted vases, though three years later he conceded to the Etruscans those found in Etruria, not that he had seen any. Passeri in 1767 still tried to compromise – vase-painters may mostly have worked in Campania, but despite Winckelmann Campania was then Etruscan – and in 1769 the learned potter Josiah Wedgwood christened his new factory Etruria. But serious students were soon agreed that most painted pottery was Greek – Greek, that is, of South Italy and Sicily – though the old name persisted on the fringes of scholarship and is not yet quite extinct.

About this time a new and much more influential personage was busying himself with painted vases. William, later Sir William, Hamilton had been appointed at the age of thirty-three as British envoy to the king of the Two Sicilies, a post he occupied from 1764 till 1800. Hamilton was a man of parts – diplomatist, amateur and collector of objects of virtu, natural philosopher, promoter of manufactures and scholar of some acumen. Within two years of his establishment in Naples he had amassed his first remarkable collection of vases, part bought and part excavated by his own enterprise. Till then the principal interest in painted pottery had been the scholarly interpretation of its subjects, and the drawings published (with few exceptions) had been of an improbable crudity or carelessness; and though Winckelmann preached the study and appreciation of style, his own illustrations were bad enough. Hamilton was impelled by the new idea, apparently more practical, of providing correct models for the designers of his own time and in particular of his own country. He resolved to publish his collection worthily, and when Winckelmann refused enlisted the quick-witted adventurer P. F. Hugues or, as he chose to call himself, the Chevalier P. V. d'Hancarville. D'Hancarville's *Collection of Etruscan, Greek and Roman Antiquities from the Cabinet of the Honble Wm Hamilton* issued in four volumes in 1766 and 1767, is the first great work on Greek pottery. The drawings of the decoration, large and coloured, are recognizably close rather than pedantically accurate, and the novel diagrams of the shapes have a precision that is not usually equalled today. The text too, a mixture of shrewdness and negligence, had its value. Soon after the British Parliament bought Hamilton's collection for £8,400, convinced of its utility to contemporary potters and artists, and so in 1772 the British Museum became the first public gallery to exhibit Greek pots. But though Wedgwood, with whom Hamilton corresponded, painfully copied the ornate Apulian red-figure and John Flaxman formed his gentle style from Classical models, the trade which most benefited was that of the dealers in antiques. Ancient vases became a requisite of the connoisseur's outfit and prices rose infinitely higher, as Hamilton lamented when he built up his second collection. This too was published handsomely, though incompletely, by Wilhelm Tischbein in the *Collection of Engravings from Ancient Vases mostly of Pure Greek workmanship*, four volumes of which came out from 1791 to 1795. Hamilton himself wrote the introduction, Italinsky interpreted the subjects, and Tischbein and his pupils prepared the illustrations. These illustrations, which established the current practice of outline drawing that ignores the contrast between dark and light areas, set a standard worthy of an art master, officiously correcting such inelegancies as the archaic eye to conform with perspective and good taste. Twenty years later J. B. Millingen published the first honest reproductions; and later generations have accepted that ideal, even if they have not always bothered to achieve it.

The students of the eighteenth century did two services to vase-painting; they discovered it and they recognized it as Greek. In their other inquiries they were handicapped by want of material, of general evidence and of sound method. The pottery they knew was mostly red-figure, South Italian of the fourth century but also Attic of the fifth. There was next some Attic black-figure and a little Corinthian. Black-painted ware and Etruscan bucchero were fairly plentiful, Italogeometric cannot have been rare, and native Apulian appears occasionally. This at least is the effect of the publications, though it must be remembered that the interests of the time were in subject and politeness of style and so naturally concentrated on red-figure. The material was very soon divided into three main classes – red-figure, black-figure and what was called Egyptian – and their order was deduced rightly from the sophistication of their style. The Egyptian class corresponded roughly to what we know as Orientalizing, though it might include Geometric too. The reasons for its name were the belief, clearly formulated by Caylus, that art had originated in Egypt and the observation that this class of painted pottery was the most primitive; it was then easy to discover a resemblance between Orientalizing animals and Egyptian hieroglyphics, though the closest parallels were supplied by the forgers. It is hard to say how seriously students took the name Egyptian: Caylus for instance, in 1752 was sure that the Egyptians did not paint their pottery, Passeri in 1767 was sure that (unlike the Phoenicians) they did, and F. Münter in 1790 in his *Nachrichten von Neapel und Sicilien* contended that the style, though crude, was not at all Egyptian. But even in the middle of the nineteenth century some reputable scholars believed that Geometric pottery was imported into Greece from the East. The distinction between vases with black figures and vases with red (or yellow) figures is obvious.

The earlier writers supposed that both black-figure and red-figure vases were Etruscan. When about the middle of the eighteenth century it was admitted that most of them were Greek, antiquaries turned to the reasonable assumption that pottery was made in the neighbourhood where it was most commonly found. The chances of discovery seemed to confirm this assumption. Attic red-figure was best known from Nola, Apulian from Apulia, black-figure from Sicily, bucchero from Etruria and the experts soon learnt to see subtler local differences. But generically red-figure was regarded as Italian Greek and black-figure as Sicilian Greek, and such terms as Sicilian, Campanian and Italo-Greek became current. ·

The accurate dating of pottery proved impracticable. It was natural to rely on the Greek and Roman authors, and they said little about pottery and almost nothing about painted pottery. A few events from historical records appeared to be relevant and there were rare clues in inscriptions or comparisons with coins, but the choosing of evidence was chancy and its use incidental. La Chausse's dates are so strange that they can hardly have been based on any system. Montfauçon, relying on Athenaeus, fixed the end of pottery made from clay in the time of

Alexander. Gori, to suit his theory of Etruscan priority, could put painted vases before Homer. But generally it came to be accepted that there was a connection between the Dionysiac scenes of South Italian red-figure and the Senatus Consultum de Bacchanalibus of 186 B.C. and that Demaratus about 660 B.C. introduced vase-painting into Etruria. From these and other faulty data it could be concluded that the period of painted pottery was from the eighth to the second century B.C. Only d'Hancarville, taking advantage of the general neglect, examined dating in much detail and his results were not orthodox: characteristically he appreciated and neglected the evidence of the coins of Sybaris, destroyed about 510 B.C., to provide a fixed date for archaeologists.

The erudite found a readier and more congenial exercise in the subjects of vase-painting. La Chausse patently did not yet know the rules. But Buonarroti had observed how popular Dionysus was in the red-figure he studied, and discerned in its pictures the rites and mythology of the Bacchic mysteries. This mode of interpretation, or rather intuition, was popular for more than a hundred years. A second and lesser school, founded by Passeri, held that the paintings on vases symbolized the major events of their owners' lives: so draped youths denoted success in the gymnasium and Heracles (to the Etruscomaniacs) the assumption of the toga virilis. It is at first startling and then depressing to read the descriptions that accompany the illustrations in the works of this period and of the early nineteenth century. But the connoisseurs were not blind to artistic quality and admired Attic red-figure (or Nolan) more than South Italian, even if their eyes were not yet opened to the modern merits of the primitive.

With the nineteenth century the German scholars arrived, to impose a new discipline on archaeology. The French for a time still held second place. The British contributions, few and amateurish, had the virtue of considering the pottery found in Greece and so admitted to have been made there. Hamilton, it seems, had been the pioneer. In the introductions to his volumes of 1791 and 1795 he pointed out that though a particular variety might be commoner on one site than another, in general vases found in Greece and the Two Sicilies were in all respects so alike that they might be supposed of the same manufacture; either then there was one centre of manufacture or, as he thought more likely, an established method was brought to the Western colonies by emigrants from Greece and presumably from Athens, since he recognized that many of the subjects were Attic. E. Dodwell added that duplicate vases, evidently copied from the same original, were found on both sides of the Adriatic. Dodwell was one of the travellers and had visited Corinth: there in 1805 he bought his pyxis, a work in the Egyptian style with Greek – in fact Corinthian – inscriptions, and this he published admirably in 1819. Thomas Burgon is famous for the Panathenaic amphora [PLATE 21B] which he excavated at Athens in 1813 and Millingen illustrated in 1822, dating it correctly enough a little before 562 B.C. Some Geometric pots also turned up in Athens and Melos, but though examples were displayed in the British Museum and Leyden they were ignored elsewhere for at least forty years. During the first quarter of the century publications of collections became frequent, though the text was often restricted to describing and interpreting the subjects. The sanest of the broader students of vase-painting was J. V. Millingen, who suggested that the misnamed Egyptian class originated in Corinth (citing Athenaeus's etymological derivation of Thericlean from θηρίον), denied that black-figure was specifically Sicilian, and though he still preferred to classify painted vases by subjects rejected their symbolical interpretation.

The second quarter of the century was dominated by Eduard Gerhard. This indefatigable scholar settled in Rome in 1822 and six years later succeeded in organizing the Instituto di Corrispondenza Archeologica, which regularly published reports of new discoveries and other papers in its *Bullettino*, *Annali* and *Monumenti*. The timing was happy. In the past Etruria had yielded little painted pottery, but during the spring of 1828 the necropolis of Vulci was found and by the end of 1829 over 3,000 painted vases had been unearthed. The lucky proprietors (of whom the luckiest was Napoleon's slippery brother Lucien, the Prince of Canino) were soon selling off their booty to European collectors, but not before Gerhard had seen most of it. In the years that followed other sites in Etruria were tapped and there was renewed discovery in South Italy, although the Nolan landlords at first left their fields fallow till the markets should recover. But Vulci was the richest of all the sites, providing especially Attic black-figure from the second quarter of the sixth century onwards and red-figure of the earlier phases, as well as some 'Chalcidian', Pontic and Corinthian. It is surprising how many of the famous examples of those classes come from this one obscure Etruscan city.

Gerhard perceived at once the importance of the new finds and prepared himself for their study by a tour of South Italy and a paper on the local red-figure manufactures, especially those of Nola, Avella, Sant' Agata de' Goti, Capua, Basilicata, Apulia and Lucania. Accustomed to such neat taxonomy he was able in his *Rapporto Volcente* (in

Annali 1831) to detect three contemporary schools at Vulci – the Nolan, the Tyrrhenian and the Etruscan. The Nolans were Greeks or Italo-Greeks and their work was the finest; the Tyrrhenians, Greeks permanently settled in Etruria, were coarser and more old-fashioned and fonder of inscriptions; the native Etruscans betrayed themselves by negligent style and Etruscan details and dipinti. Gerhard also kept the three familiar classes or (as he preferred) manners, naming them the Egyptian, the Archaic and the Perfect; the Egyptian began before the Archaic and the Archaic before the Perfect, but all three continued together. Though vase-painting was invented a little before 660 B.C., when Demaratus landed in Etruria, the finds from Vulci were more advanced in development and for historical reasons should be dated between 480 and 280 B.C.: Apulian and Lucanian lasted another century until the Romans suppressed Bacchanalia. On the black-figure and red-figure pottery from Vulci the subjects and inscriptions were undeniably Attic; they must then have been painted in Etruria by Greeks of Attic stock, and perhaps Vulci was an Athenian colony. Gerhard's classification shows keen observation and some of his distinctions are valid, but he was misled by his choice of evidence and his love of system.

Most of Gerhard's colleagues were impressed by his enthusiasm and authority. They accepted the coexistence of the three manners, not realizing that many of the tombs at Vulci were family vaults in use for a long while; besides, Heinrich Meyer, C. A. Böttiger and Millingen had already declared that the periods of black-figure and red-figure overlapped. To support this theory it had to be assumed that much vase-painting was 'affected' – that is, consciously archaizing – as, for example, the Affecter's group in Attic black-figure. But though the Duc de Luynes laid down the rules by which later imitations could be detected, they proved too subtle for general application. The dating also was acceptable and evidence was chosen to support it, especially from ancient notices about the development of the alphabet, parallels in sculpture, and historical records and silences. So C. O. Müller in 1831 identified the Leagros of the Archaic καλός names as the butt of the comic poet Plato, and de Luynes in 1833 recognized the fourth Arcesilas on the famous Laconian cup, which otherwise he interpreted admirably. The comparison between black-figure and the coins of Sybaris, which Böttiger had stressed in 1811, was dismissed by Bunsen as valid only for Sybaris. In general the early pottery, in so far as it was not considered affected, was dated with fair accuracy; so Müller put the Dodwell pyxis about 580 B.C., though others went a century further back. But black-figure was usually dated too late, so that some students assigned even the Burgon amphora to the fifth century, and the beginning of red-figure was commonly fixed about 450 B.C.

What most puzzled the archaeologists of the 1830s was the great quantity of the painted pottery found at Vulci. Canino with his claque at once insisted that it was Etruscan and with the virtuous indignation of the monopolist threatened by competition clamoured that the vases being found in Greece were planted by agents who had stolen them from his Tuscan estate, or else were ancient exports from Etruria. But the majority of students were resolute in believing that black-figure and red-figure were Greek. Either then Greek vase-painters worked at Vulci or the Vulcentines imported Greek painted vases. Gerhard's first explanation was an Attic colony at Vulci, his second an isopolity of Athenians and Etruscans. F. G. Welcker postulated a hereditary guild of emigrant Attic potters. L. Hirt thought of Athenian refugees from Thurii. Millingen more simply made the Etruscans Greek. Those who preferred import were troubled by distances. D. Raoul-Rochette chose South Italy or Sicily for his factories. C. O. Müller risked Athens, but quickly switched to Cumae. The scholarly diplomat C. K. J. Bunsen, later Baron von Bunsen, after neatly dissecting his predecessors, allotted most black-figure to Athens and most red-figure to South Italy, since the import of pottery was not necessarily more expensive than local manufacture, particularly when trade was not yet restricted by governments. These Greek theories and their historical consequences may now seem extravagant, but their authors were honest and reputable students and, granted their premises, they argued with tolerable logic. Their statements are mostly printed, in full or in summary, in the early volumes of *Annali* and *Bullettino*.

A more radical solution was published in 1837. Gustav Kramer was a textual critic, still respected for his edition of Strabo, but in 1835 he visited Italy and on his travels examined the collections of painted pottery. His conclusions, lucidly and courteously expressed in the pamphlet *Über den Styl und die Herkunft der bemalten griechischen Thongefässe*, were founded on stylistic observation and epigraphic forms, since chemical analysis of clay and paint had proved useless or impracticable. He began by denying the multiplicity of local fabrics. The Egyptianizing style (which Bunsen had recently dubbed Doric) was at least in part Corinthian. The Old style – his name for black-figure – was Attic, as he had seen. But Bunsen's argument could be extended to red-figure, which also must be Attic, even– and here he deserted his epigraphic principle – the late group commonly called Apulian. What is now named Gnathian was connected with Apulian, but perhaps later in date and Italian. In his chronology Kramer was conventional, comparing for instance his Severe (our Archaic) red-figure to the Aegina pediments and his Free (our Classical) red-figure to Praxiteles' female nudes and so dating them respectively from 460 to 420 and from 420 to 380 B.C. But he could not see archaistic imitations, except in some Panathenaic amphorae. Kramer's argument was too fundamental to be accepted at once; seven years later C. Lenormant and J. de Witte wrote that the problems of vase-painting had seemed nearer to solution before Vulci was exhumed, and in the fifties Gerhard would concede only wandering guilds of Attic potters.

The publication of painted vases was continued busily, notably by Gerhard after he had moved on to Berlin. But almost all that was published came from Italy. In Greece discovery was slow and not well known. L. Ross, who was in charge of the antiquities of the kingdom, observed in 1835 that there were red-figure sherds in the debris from the Persian sack of the Acropolis of Athens; but Ross was difficult and often wild, and his observation was at the time ignored, if indeed it became known before his paper in *Allgemeine Monatschrift* in 1852. The most promising work was on the Orientalizing and Geometric styles. Even before 1830 the Sicilians had preferred to speak of Phoenician rather than Egyptian, and as knowledge of Oriental art grew de Witte and Müller and Raoul-Rochette pointed to parallels in Phoenicia and Babylonia. Geometric was slowly being suspected. In 1837 Gerhard commented on the big Late Geometric amphorae from Thera and Baron O. M. von Stackelberg published a couple of Attic Geometric pots; since the beginning of the century travellers had been noting Geometric and Mycenaean sherds at Mycenae; and there was, of course, Geometric and Subgeometric from Italy. The tendency now was to distinguish Geometric as genuine Phoenician, and Orientalizing as Greek imitation. While the experts were groping towards a solution, the veteran Burgon published in 1847 the results of observations he had made in Greece nearly forty years before. He saw that Geometric (with which he mixed a few Mycenaean sherds) was a separate, earlier and probably universal stage of Greek pottery, dated it from the twelfth to the tenth century, and included it with the subsequent Orientalizing in his Pelasgian or Heroic class, which preceded true Hellenic. Burgon's paper was printed in the *Transactions of the Royal Society of Literature* and escaped the notice of continental students.

The study of subjects was waning, in spite or because of T. Panofka's brilliant follies. Panofka also supplied ancient names for the shapes of Greek pottery in his *Recherches sur les véritables noms des vases grecs* of

1829, and Gerhard in *Annali* 1831 proposed a rival system that was no more veritable. More than a century before Montfauçon had seen that such researches were futile, and A. Letronne rightly attacked both Panofka and Gerhard. But their new nomenclature was thought more reputable than the current Italian names, which were attributed to the Neapolitan dealers. Later students have proposed various modifications and additions, and the more fanciful names have gradually lost favour, though 'stamnos' and 'olpe' for example still survive. A convenient key to the three early systems is given in note 619 of the introduction to O. Jahn's *Beschreibung der Vasensammlung*.

Jahn's book, published in 1854, makes a good epilogue to the early epoch of the study of Greek painted pottery. He accepted the three classes and analysed them neatly, in general recognizing Kramer's attributions, except for South Italian, and retaining and refining some of Gerhard's juster distinctions. So he derived black-figure from Orientalizing (a term that he used incidentally) and marked the transition just after the Attic François vase, and he had a notion (though misplaced) of 'Chalcidian' and was sound enough on later Etruscan black-figure. He denounced the symbolic interpretation of subjects, and recommended that the place where a pot was found should be recorded at the time and not invented to suit its supposed style. In dating he was more judicious and accurate than his predecessors. The Oldest style began at a time not yet ascertained and lasted at least till 460 B.C.; black-figure was established well before the Oldest style ended and, except for some Panathenaic amphorae, ended in the 430s; in Attic red-figure the Severe phase was current from before 480 till 436, the Fine phase from 436 till the end of the fourth century; Etruscan red-figure, such as it was, belonged mainly to the third century; South Italian flourished from the third to the first century B.C. The most important chronological pegs were Ross's report of red-figure in the Persian stratum at Athens, the Pronomos krater, a grave at Panticapaeum (or Kerch) containing a coin of the early fourth century, and the Panathenaic amphorae from Benghazi inscribed with the names of Athenian archons of the late fourth century. Jahn had a cool and shrewd intelligence and his survey was thorough and systematic, so that it deservedly became the primer of the next generation. It also lays bare how little had been achieved by the first four generations of students. They had, of course, the excuse (so often trotted out by their successors) that published illustrations were few and bad, and there was the further hazard that till 1859 all plates were engraved by hand. Yet the successful specialists of the 1920s, when photography was still cumbrous and expensive, made do for the most part with the old – and irreplaceable – aids of careful notes and tracings.

Soon after the middle of the nineteenth century a new spirit was transforming the study of vase-painting. It can be glimpsed even in S. Birch's *History of Ancient Pottery*, published in 1858, only four years after Jahn's *Beschreibung*. Birch was an Orientalist, who approached Classical antiquity with an open, if not empty, mind; and in his Greek chapters, ignorant and grossly careless as they are, the emphasis is towards stylistic evolution. It was the specialized study of style that marked the new epoch, encouraged and supported by excavation in Greek lands east of the Adriatic. Greece itself was becoming more attractive than Italy to foreign students and welcomed them more generously. So new schools and periods of Greek pottery were soon discovered.

Within the modern epoch the First World War, or rather the publication of E. Pfuhl's *Malerei und Zeichnung* in 1923, is a convenient point near which to halt. The excavations undertaken in this period varied greatly in standard, but on most there was some interest in sherds and even in contexts. Of those significant for Hellenic pottery the first occurred in what was then Turkish territory. In 1859 A. Biliotti and A. Salzmann, the British and French consuls at Rhodes, were encouraged by C. T. Newton to exploit the cemeteries of Camirus and Ialysus, where their most novel finds were Mycenaean, Rhodian Geometric, Wild Goat style and Fikellura; this new material became available very quickly, since like good patriots they sold the greater part to the British Museum and the Louvre. In Greece, where the export of antiquities was restricted by law, it was more necessary for excavators to publish what they found, and some of them did. New Prehellenic wares were revealed in Therasia and Thera in 1866–7, when among others the geologist F. Fouqué struck Middle Cycladic remains below the deposits of an unrecorded eruption; in Cyprus especially in 1868 and the next few years, while General L. P. di Cesnola was ransacking sites of all periods; and at Troy and Mycenae in H. Schliemann's campaigns of 1871–3 and 1874–6. More directly important was the Geometric cemetery near the Dipylon gate of Athens, where J. Palaiologos and G. Hirschfeld delved in 1871–2. New East Greek of the sixth century came in 1884–6 from the operations of W. M. Flinders Petrie and E. A. Gardner at the Egyptian sites of Naucratis and Tell Defenneh. The turn of Cycladic was later; H. Dragendorff in 1896 and E. Pfuhl in 1902 excavated much Theran Late Geometric and Linear Island wares on Thera, and D. Stavropoullos in 1898–9 exhumed other groups from the Purification enclosure on Rheneia, though the release of the bulk of his finds did not begin till 1934. For Protocorinthian and Ripe Corinthian the key sites were the western colonies, for which ancient authors offered fairly consistent dates. Here L. Mauceri in *Annali* 1877 published a small and P. Orsi in *NSc* 1893 and 1895 a large sample of recent finds at Syracuse; for Megara Hyblaea Orsi in *MA* in 1892 could offer little, but his account of work just done at Gela, published in *MA* in 1906, was full; E Gàbrici in 1913, also in *MA*, surveyed the results of the last thirty-five years at Cumae; and from the 1880s onwards some information slipped out about Selinus. Laconian was augmented by R. M. Dawkins at Sparta in 1906–10. In Attica and Boeotia the local wares turned up constantly; of sites regularly excavated the most relevant were for later Boeotian the Theban sanctuary of the Cabiri in 1887–8 and for Submycenaean Salamis in 1893. An important find of Middle Protoattic was made soon after on Aegina, but mostly concealed. For Attic of the fourth century South Russia had been providing material since about 1840, some of it admirably published by L. Stephani, and for early Hellenistic Alexandria from about 1885. In Turkey excavation was politically difficult and in its outcome unlucky, though after 1882 the dealers of Smyrna could lay their hands on Clazomenian sarcophagi. The chronological order of these excavations and finds gives a clue to the course of study.

In surveying the work of the specialists it is simpler to follow one style at a time. Geometric is conveniently taken first. In 1870 in the *Sitzungberichte* of the Vienna Academy A. Conze produced *zur Geschichte der Anfänge der griechischen Kunst*, where he catalogued some sixty Geometric pots. Generally he elaborated and improved Burgon's notions, giving a clear, though incomplete, analysis of the style. Two years later in *Annali* G. Hirschfeld published many of the new finds from the Dipylon graves and added human figures to Conze's repertory. The students of this time necessarily concentrated on Attic Geometric, though they recognized more or less close relatives in Thera and Italy and tended to include what Mycenaean they knew as well as some early Orientalizing. Mycenaean was abruptly detached in 1879 by A. Furtwängler and G. Loeschcke in their *Mykenische Thongefässe*, and gradually local Geometric schools were distinguished. Furtwängler, in particular, from 1879 to 1886 could refer understandingly to Rhodian, belated Apulian, Italogeometric and Cypriot, and in 1888 he discovered the Geometric which preceded Protocorinthian. J. Boehlau in *Jdl* 1887 recognized Protoattic and its position, so finally establishing against Furtwängler and Loeschcke that the dominant Geometric school had its home in

Athens: in *Jdl* 1888 he studied Boeotian; in 1895 in *zur Ornamentik der Villanovaperiode* he gave reasons for deriving the earliest Italian Geometric from Greek. Then in *Jdl* 1899 and 1900 the diligent Sam Wide roughly summarized the present state of knowledge: he collected examples of the Theran, Melian, Cretan, Boeotian, Laconian, Argive and Attic schools, noted the Mycenaean connections of some Protogeometric pots, and saw, but refused to believe, the stages of Attic development. H. Dragendorff in *Thera* II, which appeared in 1903, was less timid: he outlined the coarse of Attic and Theran, transferred Linear Island from Boeotia to Euboea, commented on the Protocorinthian school which inspired Italogeometric, and made a division between the vigorous Geometric style of mainland Greece (with Melos and Thera) and the weak and arrested Geometric of Cyprus, Crete and the East Greek region, though Rhodes slowly submitted to western influence. F. Poulsen, two years later, in his *die Dipylongräber und die Dipylonvasen* gave an admirable conspectus of earlier work, supplemented Wide's lists, and made a close and sensible examination of Attic development. There was still a gap between Mycenaean and Geometric; this was partly filled by the Submycenaean finds from Salamis, cited by Dragendorff and published in *AM* 1910 by Wide, though he named them Protogeometric. A fuller study of Argive Geometric followed in 1912, contributed by W. Müller and F. Oelmann in *Tiryns* I. Finally, in 1918, K. F. Johansen in *Sikyoniske Vaser* gave a clear account of Protocorinthian (that is, Late Corinthian) Geometric, and B. Schweitzer in his *Untersuchungen zur Chronologie [und Geschichte] der geometrischen Stile in Griechenland* (of which the first part was printed separately and the second in *AM*) at last defined Protogeometric, though more broadly than is accepted now, noticed the existence (which by now could not be denied) of other East Greek schools besides Rhodian, and with the aid of some new metaphysical terms made a brave and generally successful analysis both of Protogeometric and Attic Geometric. Schweitzer's was almost the last major work to speak of the Dipylon style. 'Dipylon' had superseded 'Pelasgian' about 1880 as a general name for what we now call Geometric, but within twenty years was normally restricted to the Attic school. 'Geometric' itself had been mentioned by Semper and was afterwards always current, if only as a term of description.

The dating of Geometric (including Protogeometric) could hardly be far wrong. From the first it was seen that Geometric came immediately before Orientalizing, and the Dipylon graves showed that it still belonged to the Iron Age. So it was easy to reject Conze's choice of the second millennium B.C., based on a mistake over Theran geology, and when Mycenaean had been recognized and dated most students put the beginning of Geometric in the tenth or else the eleventh century. But in fixing the end of Geometric they found two extra difficulties. First, they did not agree on what was Geometric and what early Orientalizing. Secondly, they presumed that some Greek regions were little affected by Geometric and so Orientalizing could be its contemporary rather than its successor. So Furtwängler, who included the S.O.S. amphorae, maintained that Geometric was widespread in the seventh century and in Athens was current in the mid sixth. Boehlau reclassified some of Furtwängler's Attic Geometric as early Protoattic, and the second half of the seventh century became the limit of his own Geometric Attic. Wide tried in vain to compress the period of Geometric generally. Dragendorff made progress, he took account of the finds from Italy and Sicily and inferred that the Protocorinthian and Attic schools of Geometric must end with the eighth century. Müller and Oelmann for the same reason went back to the middle of that century. It was left to Schweitzer to examine the evidence thoroughly and to conclude that his Protogeometric belonged mainly to the eleventh and tenth centuries, Geometric to the ninth and eighth. There still was, and is, some doubt on how long the lesser Geometric and Subgeometric schools persisted or lingered.

The earlier students found more interest in the origin of Geometric and its relation to Orientalizing than in the development of its style. In 1860 and 1863 G. Semper in his influential treatise, *der Stil in den technischen Kunsten*, had observed that geometrical ornaments were widespread among primitive peoples and by the principle of the spontaneous evolution of art derived them from textiles and wickerwork (as indeed Burgon had suggested for his Greek pots, though with less ado). This derivation, which some still maintain, had the convenience of allowing a geometric pottery to appear suddenly and unheralded. Semper also observed a close similarity in the Geometric style of the Greeks (of which he had a vague notion from Birch) and that of other early Europeans. In 1870 Conze developed this theory: the Geometric of Greece (and Italy too) originated in the primitive style of northern Europe, brought by the Indo-German invaders and then adapted to pottery. This explanation accorded with notions becoming prevalent among philologists and in one form or another has had a long life. An older theory was refurbished by W. Helbig in *Annali* 1875: in Greece and Italy the Indo-Germanic Geometric (which he conceded) was a rough, incised ware, but the painted Geometric had a highly developed system and came through the Phoenicians from the

East. The problem shifted with the isolation of Mycenaean pottery. Little notice had been taken of the finds from Rhodes in the Louvre and the British Museum and none of a collection from Cephallenia exhibited since 1836 in Neuchâtel; a few sherds from Mycenae had been noticed, but classed with Geometric. Then in 1876 A. Milchhöfer, reporting in *AM* on Schliemann's excavation of that site, hinted at a local ware with vegetable ornament that was not Orientalizing. Three years later this new Mycenaean style was clearly displayed in the *Mykenische Thongefässe* of Furtwängler and Loeschcke. It was now apparent that though Geometric resembled Mycenaean in technique and perhaps in some ornaments, it differed greatly in style, the more so since the intervening stages had not yet been discovered. It was also apparent that the change from one style to the other coincided more or less with the traditional invasion of the Dorians. Yet the Geometric pottery found at Athens, where traditionally the Dorians did not penetrate, was the most richly and thoroughly Geometric. Furtwängler and Loeschcke, adapting Conze, saw in Geometric the combination of Mycenaean technique with the European style of the Dorian invaders; this began perhaps at Argos, but spread elsewhere; Athens imported her Geometric. But in 1887 Boehlau demonstrated that Protoattic, undeniably Attic itself, developed out of the Geometric of Athens. In his solution, offered eight years later in *zur Ornamentik der Villanovaperiode* and elaborated by Wide in *AM* 1896, the Geometric style had its origin in the peasant style of Middle Helladic, which was suppressed by Mycenaean, but reemerged with a modern technique after the collapse of Mycenaean rule and art. Thus the contribution of the Dorians was negative, and in his *Dipylongräber* of 1905 Poulsen (inspired perhaps by E. Curtius and K. J. Beloch) denied even this, arguing that the Mycenaean kingdoms were overthrown by aristocratic revolution. But the theory that the Dorians brought the Geometric style, though the hardest to support, remained the most popular and was given a new prop by A. J. B. Wace and M. S. Thompson in their *Prehistoric Thessaly* of 1912. Continuity from Mycenaean to Geometric was asserted by Dragendorff in 1903, demonstrated by Schweitzer in 1918 and afterwards slowly accepted. This new view can be, or rather is, reconciled by diehards with the Dorian theory and perhaps something may be salved even from Helbig's, if (as some of his opponents admitted) such Geometric types as the recumbent goat have Oriental ancestors.

Orientalizing, black-figure and red-figure were still the regular divisions of Greek vase-painting at the middle of the nineteenth century. For Orientalizing there was then no upper limit, except to Burgon and his intimates. But when after 1870 the separate character of Geometric was recognized generally, a natural zeal at first gave it much of what we call early Orientalizing and a little more. To the students of the mid-century, familiar mainly with Italian finds, the core of Orientalizing was Ripe Corinthian, to which were appended the Tyrrhenian class of Attic, Pontic, 'Chalcidian' and a few strays of other groups in which rows of animals were frequent. Black-figure as a stylistic term was reserved more or less to the mature and late phases of the Attic school and to late Etruscan. As earlier Attic became known, the boundary of black-figure was slowly and unevenly pushed back and by the First World War was near its present vague position. But since at the same time interest had been shifting from styles to schools, the definition between Orientalizing and black-figure, always rather arbitrary, became unimportant as well.

The term 'Orientalizing' did not establish itself till the 1870s. 'Egyptian' was already condemned as misleading before 1850 and the other veteran, 'Phoenician', had not become reputable when the Assyrian discoveries of the 1840s suggested that it too was inaccurate. An improved name, 'Asiatic' or 'Asianizing', had some currency in the third quarter of the century, but was perhaps thought too narrow. 'Oldest' or 'Ancient' became absurd when a still earlier style was admitted, though in Germany the derivatives 'altkorinthisch' and 'altrhodisch' survived till the end of the century to denote Ripe Corinthian and the Wild Goat style. 'Dorian' and 'Corinthian' had seemed reasonable to the adherents of Kramer, but as new schools of Orientalizing were discovered could no longer be accepted as generic descriptions. There was no difficulty over 'black-figure', which had always been used as a sort of sub-title and soon after 1850 began to replace 'Archaic' and its variants as the proper name of a style.

Most of the Orientalizing studied in the 1850s was rightly considered to be Corinthian or in its later stage Attic adaptation of Corinthian. The first new school detected was 'Melian', represented by three large amphorae in Athens and a sherd in Berlin. Conze, who published them in his *Melische Thongefässe* of 1862, the earliest and most lavish of special studies, concluded from their place of finding that they were made in Melos by Greeks still influenced by their Phoenician predecessors, and he compared their style to the so-called Corinthian. The excellence of Conze's illustrations made 'Melian' familiar and the size of his amphorae enlarged its reputation, since archaeologists are too often impressed by size. It was commonly supposed that 'Melian' was the earliest of the Orientalizing schools and the transmitter of the new style to Corinth and Athens. J. Boehlau in *JdI* 1887 argued that 'Melian' (as then known) was short-lived and slavishly imitative of the Wild Goat style; and H. Dragendorff in *Thera* II, which was published in 1903, dated it from after the middle of the seventh century till some time in the sixth. But such radical criticisms could hardly be accepted completely, and even now 'Melian' is sometimes over-valued. In part that is because it has not yet been studied closely. The main find of that ware, from the Purification enclosure on Rheneia, still waits for publication. Only one other study needs mentioning, J. H. Hopkinson's in *JHS* 1902, which gave a summary but useful analysis of the style of the Rheneian finds: Hopkinson believed that 'Melian' influenced European Greece, but found it difficult to fit into the evolution of Greek vase-painting. His suggestion that it was made at Delos had some effect.

Among the finds from Vulci were several 'Chalcidian' pots, notable for their subjects, quality and painted inscriptions. Gerhard had put them in his Tyrrheno-Egyptian school, Kramer in the appendage to his Corinthian and Jahn among Attic imitations of Corinthian. But the inscriptions were puzzling. Kramer noted that their dialect was not Doric, Jahn that they were neither Corinthian nor completely Attic. The answer came from the epigraphist, A. Kirchhoff, who in 1863 in the first edition of *Studien zur Geschichte des griechischen Alphabets* (in the *Abhandlungen* of the Berlin Academy) showed that their alphabet was that of the Chalcidian colonies of South Italy and in his third edition fourteen years later that of Chalcis too. The group was at once called Chalcidian, though for a time it was defined more by its inscriptions than its style. The style was first examined, not very satisfactorily, by W. Klein in his *Euphronios* of 1879, and then more accurately by F. Studniczka in *JdI* for 1886. In the same year G. Loeschcke announced a comprehensive study of 'Chalcidian', but though he lived another thirty years did little more than deter other students from attempting it. The task was at last executed in 1927 in A. Rumpf's *Chalkidische Vasen*. A close relation between 'Chalcidian' and later Corinthian had always been perceived, and at first 'Chalcidian' was seen to be the borrower. But Chalcis was 'ethnically' Ionian, and so believers in Ionian pre-eminence tended for historical reasons to make Corinth dependent. This was Klein's opinion, endorsed by Loeschcke in *AM* 1894. But Studniczka resisted in *JdI* 1887 and by the First World War the priority of Corinthian was usually admitted, although 'Chalcidian' was still dated about a generation too early. 'Chalcidian' influence on Attic was accepted by Pfuhl as late as 1923. It was, of course, generally assumed that 'Chalcidian' was made in Chalcis, though the ambiguity of the evidence was shown in 1883 by A. Milchhöfer in *die Anfänge der Kunst in Griechenland* and by A. Dumont (who proposed Cumae) in *les Céramiques de la Grèce propre*: it was not till the 1930s that serious doubt reappeared.

By an unlucky chance the Phineus cup, the chief representative of the later stage of 'Chalcidian', had suffered restoration and its painted inscriptions, originally Chalcidian, had become misleadingly Ionic. So from the first the Phineus group was separated from 'Chalcidian'. Furtwängler in 1880, in *der Satyr aus Pergamon*, naturally diagnosed the style of the Phineus cup as Ionian; J. Endt in 1899 in *Beiträge zur ionischen Vasenmalerei* more moderately proposed Naxos. The style was now recognized as dependent on 'Chalcidian', with of course a more easterly flavour. The collection of a Phineus group began in the 1890s. The first considerable list of cups was that of J. Boehlau in *AM* 1900, though it included much that was alien. Two years later Furtwängler in FR made some sensible corrections, and R. Zahn in *BPW* added several amphorae. Finally in 1921 the Phineus cup was cleaned down to the genuine inscriptions and Rumpf in *AM* proved it and them 'Chalcidian'.

Laconian too emerged from Vulci, and one hydria and half a dozen cups (including the Arcesilas cup) were published before 1850, but their similarity had not been noted. J. de Witte in the *Gazette des Beaux Arts* for 1863 connected five of the cups and in 1871 H. Brunn made a list of seven in his *Probleme in der Geschichte der Vasenmalerei* (from the *Abhandlungen* of the Bavarian Academy). Brunn, an otherwise able student, was the last notable adherent of the theory of 'archaism' and the most extreme, and till he died in 1894 maintained with a perverse logic that most of the best pots found in Etruria were painted in the third or second centuries in imitation of much earlier styles. So some of his Laconian cups were early and some archaistic. An eye trained to imaginary distinctions did not miss true ones, and Brunn observed that on style the Arcesilas cup should be contemporary with the second Cyrenaean king of the name. So far the group had not been located: the dialect of the inscriptions of the Arcesilas cup was evidently Dorian, but the alphabet was unknown. In 1879 in the first edition of his *Euphronios* W. Klein showed that this was Laconian and drew the unpalatable but correct conclusion. Next year G. Loeschcke appended to his *de Basi quadam prope Spartam reperta* a list of two dozen Laconian pots; he noted that the group was provincial enough for Sparta, but would not commit himself till the alphabets of Cyrene and other places were known. This evasion was accepted by O. Puchstein, who claimed in *AZ* 1880 that the Arcesilas cup must be Cyrenaean: after all its subject was set in Cyrene and adapted from the neighbouring art of Egypt. Puchstein also, in *AZ* 1881, enlarged Loeschcke's list to twenty-nine, dated the school from the mid sixth century to the beginning of the fifth, found it more closely connected to the Wild Goat style and 'Melian' than to Corinthian, and traced its development no more accurately than Loeschcke. Most students accepted Cyrene, especially after Studniczka in his *Kyrene* of 1890 had revealed Cyrenaean interpretations of other cups, and they regarded the style as dominantly Ionic. This was still Dugas's position in 1907, when he listed in *RA* over eighty examples, dating them between 600 and 525 B.C. But the excavations at Sparta were now finding that Cyrenaean was the normal pottery there and could be followed back to Geometric. So after a short hesitation J. P. Droop in *BSA* XIV, published in 1909, demonstrated that Cyrenaean was Laconian, and in *JHS* 1910 he proceeded to classify the style in six stages, some of which are still valid. Though a few recalcitrants insisted on a branch factory at Cyrene, the Laconian origin was soon established and Corinthian influences were once again admissible.

Corinthian of the Ripe style was the base of the first of the old three divisions of Greek vase-painting, and by the middle of the nineteenth century most students had accepted at least in part Kramer's argument that it was made in Corinth and fathered the black-figured style of Athens. It fell easily into two parts, the Animal style and the Redground style (to which were attached other pots with human scenes): the Red-ground style was considered late Corinthian, even though some laggards attributed it to Corinthian emigrants in Etruria. When in the 1860s 'Melian' and the Wild Goat style and soon after Geometric came to light, the technical sequence – silhouette, reservation, incision – and the degree of sophistication suggested that Ripe Corinthian was not the earliest version of the Orientalizing style. During the seventies its relations to Attic were probed more exactly, and in *Annali* 1878 Loeschcke asserted that the Red-ground style, which appeared when the Animal style was dying, showed a reverse influence from Attic. About the same time Protocorinthian was discovered. But this early promise was blighted by the new orthodoxy which saw Ionian models everywhere, and so replaced Corinthian influences by 'Chalcidian'. The only bold study of the next generation was that of E. Pottier in 1899 in the second part of the *Catalogue des Vases antiques du Louvre*: Pottier had some imperfect notions of the development of Ripe Corinthian, included an abnormal quantity of Italocorinthian, recognized Ionian traits, and dated it from the early seventh to the middle of the sixth century.

Such early datings were general and not clearly explained, since the refusal to consider Ripe Corinthian as the continuation of Protocorinthian was as much an effect as a cause. It was rather that 'Melian' and East Greek were also dated too early, and they were linked to Ripe Corinthian by style and the contexts of graves in Rhodes; perhaps also the finds at Syracuse were misunderstood. In the twentieth century these early dates were gradually reduced and the present chronology was established in 1931 in H. G. G. Payne's *Necrocorinthia*, a thorough and impressive analysis of the Ripe Corinthian style. Though its main stages were more or less perceived, as catalogues show, it is surprising that a special study of the school had been undertaken only once before, in 1892, and that had been immediately and justly condemned. In spite of the Panionist perversion, Ripe Corinthian had remained important as the parent or foster-parent of the black-figure technique, so that even in the 1890s the incising Late Wild Goat style was without much opposition accepted as an imitation of Corinthian, and before the First World War Corinthian was again seen to have a strong influence on Attic and 'Chalcidian'. Possibly the great number of Corinthian pots overfaced earlier students.

Protocorinthian excited much more speculation, once it was discovered. First W. Helbig in *Annali* 1877 noted the uniformity of some simple aryballoi found in Italy and Sicily, and by historical reasoning suggested that the group was made by Chalcidians. Two years later in *die Italiker in der Poebene* he published Loeschcke's information that similar aryballoi occurred in Athens, Corinth and Aegina, favoured distribution in the West by Chalcidian colonists, and claimed that this was the first group of Greek pottery imported into Italy: as evidence he could cite finds beneath the Servian wall at Rome and Mauceri's useful contexts at Syracuse, which also had been published in *Annali* 1877. Then Furtwängler took over. In 1879 in *die Bronzefunde aus Olympia* he observed that Helbig's group was intermediate between Geometric and Ripe Corinthian, and dated it (according to the low chronology then regular for Geometric) to the seventh and sixth centuries. About the same time he privately invented the name 'Protocorinthian', for want of a better as he explained when others had established its use. In *AZ* 1883 he added two aryballoi with polychrome figures, commented acutely on the Protocorinthian style, and while maintaining that it was older than Ripe Corinthian and closely connected to it could not yet decide on its home: in spite of Ionian traits it was presumptuous to give judgement for Chalcis. He further recognized Italian imitations, which Helbig had not distinguished. In his Berlin catalogue, published in 1885, Furtwängler made a partly successful division between early and late stages; in *die Sammlung Sabouroff* in 1886 he asserted manufacture in Corinth; and finally in *Jdl* 1888 he identified correctly the local Geometric from which Protocorinthian developed. Other students did little more than dispute about origins. Although all agreed that Ripe Corinthian was in the main derived from Protocorinthian, many thought that the two schools were largely contemporary and, if transitional pieces were discounted as imitations, there were obvious differences in style and shapes: since, then, Ripe Corinthian was made at Corinth, Protocorinthian must have been made in some other place or places, preferably not far away. Even so, Corinth always had some supporters, of whom P. Orsi and L. Pallat must be mentioned. Orsi in *NSc* 1895 used his finds at Syracuse to show the development of Protocorinthian, and especially of its aryballoi, and he regarded Ripe Corinthian as a subsequent stage. Pallat had worked on Corinthian sherds at Aegina and his demonstration in *AM* 1897 of the unity of Protocorinthian and Ripe Corinthian is hardly less complete than Payne's more than thirty years later. Chalcis, which seemed to have as good a historical claim as Corinth to trade with the West, had fewer backers: if Ripe Corinthian was hard to reconcile to Protocorinthian, 'Chalcidian' was harder. In the nineties some students rashly proposed Ionia and Boeotia, and others Aegina, Argos and Sicyon, which Johansen supported in his *Sikyoniske Vaser* of 1918. But opinions were still divided between Sicyon and Corinth till in 1931 Payne's *Necrocorinthia* crushed the dispute. On the development of Protocorinthian and its importance for the black-figure style knowledge came slowly. Pallat's was the most notable contribution before Johansen's thorough and exemplary study. As for chronology, the colonies in the West fixed the beginning of Protocorinthian in the mid eighth century, but before Johansen its end was still often prolonged into the sixth.

Very little East Greek was known by the middle of the nineteenth century. Jahn in 1854 could describe a good dish of the canonical Wild Goat style only as an unusual example of Orientalizing, and eighteen years later L. Urlichs ingenuously published two Chiot chalices of the corresponding phase under the title *Zwei vasen ältesten Stils*. The first considerable finds were made by A. Biliotti and A. Salzmann in Rhodes in 1859 and the following years, to the immediate benefit of the British Museum and afterwards of the Louvre. But except for the Euphorbos plate, unique for its painted inscriptions, heroic subject and polychromy, they were not much noticed by active students, who like Conze in *AA* 1864 classed the Wild Goat style vaguely with 'Melian'.

The first important step was A. de Longpérier's *Musée Napoléon III*, published in 1868 and the earliest album of vase-paintings to exploit photography. His plates included examples of the Wild Goat style, Fikellura and Chiot, and his text shows intelligence. Other pieces were illustrated with haphazard captions in Salzmann's *Nécropole de Camiros* in 1875. From now on various classes of East Greek began to be considered separately.

At this stage the new theory of Panionism perverted the study of Orientalizing and particularly of East Greek. As far back as 1833 Millingen had casually suggested the priority of Ionian pottery and in 1864 C. Bursian in Ersch and Grulow's *Allgemeine Encyclopädie* asserted that Greek art originated in Ionia, in much the same way as literature. These untimely claims were ignored. But in 1879 Furtwängler and Loeschcke made clear the existence and character of Mycenaean pottery. Furtwängler at once observed an affinity between Mycenaean and Orientalizing, and the same year in *die Bronzefunde aus Olympia* declared that Rhodian (by which he meant the Wild Goat style), 'Melian' and Boeotian, though borrowing something from Oriental sources, yet evolved directly out of Mycenaean without any Geometric interval. Boeotian was anyhow negligible, and Furtwängler's theory was interpreted as setting the origin of the Orientalizing style in Ionia, an Ionia usually expanded to take in not only the whole East Greek region from Rhodes to Lesbos, but also the Cyclades and Euboea. By another sleight of logic the dominance of this Ionia was extended to black-figure too. The Panionian theory when first propounded was not demonstrably wrong, and it was quickly and universally accepted: after all, the Ionians were historically Mycenaean refugees, Homer and other poets and thinkers testified to the early primacy of Asiatic Greece, and Ionia was in Asia and that much closer to the sources of Orientalizing art. So the students of vase-painting were disposed, even against the evidence, to date East Greek too early, to hail as East Greek any unidentified group of pots, and to see East Greek influence wherever it could not certainly be disproved. At first new discoveries seemed to confirm Panionism. In 1882 Clazomenae began to disgorge its enormous sarcophagi with their curious mixture of Wild Goat, black-figure and even red-figure styles: Clazomenae, some believed, was destroyed by the Persians about 540 B.C. Elsewhere too in Ionia the Persian conquest must have driven creative artists to emigrate. In the later eighties there came the excavations, roughly but quickly published, of Naucratis and Tell Defenneh in Egypt, the first introducing to students Bird bowls and their derivatives, the Late Wild Goat style and the more striking phases of

Chiot, and the second its Situlae and Clazomenian black-figure: by an arbitrary interpretation of ancient writers, the period of Tell Defenneh was fixed as the first third of the sixth century and the foundation of Naucratis about the middle of the seventh, though a few dissenters preferred a date about 570 B.C. without closely considering the consequences. Some students, notably F. Dümmler, turned to Etruria and claimed much of the local manufacture as Ionian, whether imported or made by emigrants: again a terminal date was found about 540 B.C., when the battle of Alalia ousted the Greeks from Etruscan lands. So by a series of prejudiced errors the chronology of East Greek was set some thirty or forty years too high, and perhaps for that reason Biliotti's records of his graves appeared unreliable and though consulted several times in the eighties were never published. But even when dated so early Ionian art did not provide the models that Panionism required, and in the nineties some students began to restore to Corinth the credit that had been transferred to Chalcis and more easterly Ionia, while others searched desperately for the elusive proof. Of these the most distinguished was Boehlau, who in 1898 in his *aus ionischen und italischen Nekropolen* contended that the black-figure style began in Aeolis and culled from Italocorinthian a sample for his original Aeolian school. In 1902 he bravely tested his theory on the site of 'Larisa' in Aeolis, and then from disillusion or some other cause retired into silence for the last forty years of his life. Boehlau's Aeolian claim had few supporters and by 1900 Panionism, though generally professed, was on the wane. Studniczka in *AA* 1899 attacked it radically, but Hopkinson in *JHS* 1902 expressed the moderate attitude most logically: Ionia provided the models for the vase-painting of European Greece, but those models were not painted vases. Even so, the old reverence for East Greek pottery and especially for the Clazomenian sarcophagi was sometimes noticeable till the 1930s, and traces can still be found in studies of Italian material. The chronology, of course, survived independently and was not comprehensively set right till Rumpf's paper in *Jdl* 1933.

The students of the sixties and seventies hardly noticed the Wild Goat style except to assign it to Rhodes, where almost all their examples had been found, and to date it rather later than 'Melian'. Puchstein in *AZ* 1881 listed fifteen pieces and Dumont in 1883 in *les Céramiques de la Grèce propre* made the first analysis. In 1885 in his Berlin catalogue and the next year in *Jdl* Furtwängler showed that he understood the general development. So far only the reserving 'Rhodian' was known, but now Naucratis provided a mass of incised sherds. At first some students claimed the incised Wild Goat style as Naucratite, and a few thought it a Corinthian copy of 'Rhodian'. Another heresy was propagated by Dümmler in *AM* 1888 and *Jdl* 1891. The Euphorbos plate had the only text by a 'Rhodian' painter and its alphabet was Argive. This had been noted in 1867 by Kirchoff, who inferred that the Argive alphabet was current in Rhodes before the epichoric Rhodian. Dümmler, with his flair for the wrong conclusion, claimed the Euphorbos plate for Argos and with it all 'Rhodian' except a few poor plates. More serious was Loeschcke's assertion in *AM* 1897 that the Wild Goat style belonged to Miletus. The exports veered first to 'Milesian', then back again to 'Rhodian'; and Pfuhl compromised with 'Rhodian-Milesian'. A wiser solution, that the Wild Goat style was made in several East Greek cities, had perhaps been glimpsed by Dumont in 1883 and was clearly proposed by R. Zahn in *AM* 1898: its acceptance was slow. So too was stylistic study. Pottier in his *Catalogue* of 1896 and Boehlau in his *aus ionischen und italischen Nekropolen* of 1898 made some useful comments. Prinz in 1908 appended to his *Funde aus Naukratis* a long list of 'Milesian' pottery, but gave a muddled development of the style, which in 1912 in *der Orient und die frühgriechische Kunst* F. Poulsen supported by an ingenious misuse of Oriental parallels. The same faulty system was elaborated by K. F. Kinch two years later in *Fouilles de Vroulia*, which contained the first well-illustrated and detailed, though unsatisfactory, account of the Wild Goat style. Most of these students agreed on their dates: the style ran from the beginning of the seventh century till the early sixth, the younger contemporary of 'Melian' and the older of Ripe Corinthian. The main problems of the Wild Goat style are still far from solved.

A poor Fikellura amphoriskos had been illustrated by Gerhard in 1831 as Orientalizing made by Greeks, but the school to which it belonged could not be recognized before the excavations in Rhodes that began in 1859. The best examples went to the British Museum, where the keepers saw that they represented a distinct and late class of Rhodian Orientalizing and named them Fikellura. Though this was stated by A. S. Murray in *RA* 1882, the Germans, less amateurish but here worse informed, still lumped Fikellura in the Wild Goat style; and Murray's notes of stylistic and stratigraphical connections with mature Attic black-figure and even red-figure were soon forgotten. In the late eighties new groups of Fikellura were found at Naucratis and Tell Defenneh by Petrie, who dated them in the first half of the sixth century. Still more turned up in 1894 in Boehlau's cemetery on Samos, admirably published four years later in his *aus ionischen und italischen Nekropolen*. Here Boehlau gave a catalogue and a careful study of the school, which (following

Loeschcke) he assigned provisionally to Samos; observed a direct influence of Mycenaean that was absent in 'Milesian' (as he called the
Wild Goat style); and concluded that 'Samian', datable in the first half
of the sixth century at Tell Defenneh and in the second at Samos, was
a school parallel and not subsidiary to 'Milesian'. His successors discarded the Mycenaean survivals and tended to raise the dating, so that
it could overlap more plausibly with the Wild Goat style. But no
important advance was made till the Italian campaigns in Rhodes in
the mid and late 1920s confirmed the observations that Biliotti had
recorded nearly seventy years before.

The Chiot school was revealed suddenly in 1886 in Petrie's *Naukratis*
I. Although three chalices had been published by the seventies, their
peculiarities were not evident till compared with the new and rich haul
of sherds from Naucratis, which still provide so much of our evidence.
Petrie naturally argued that this new school must be Naucratite and
dated it according to his stratigraphy from 620 to 530 B.C. Though
Boehlau in 1898 did not distinguish 'Naucratite' from 'Milesian', Prinz
ten years later in his *Funde aus Naukratis* found a neat compromise:
'Naucratite A', the reserving style, was made at Naucratis but derived
from 'Milesian' (and from Boehlau's 'Aeolian' too), and the black-
figure 'Naucratite B' remained a late derivative of 'A'. A new uncertainty was introduced in *A Delt* 1916 by K. Kuruniotis, who had found
'Naucratite' on Chios and suggested that it was made there, at least in
part. Pfuhl of course hankered after 'Chiot-Naucratite' and summed up
competently from his predecessors. E. R Price in *JHS* 1924 denied
manufacture in two places and preferred Naucratis to Chios: she also
made the only detailed study of the school, dividing Prinz's 'Naucratite
A' into the earlier Wild Goat style influenced by 'Rhodian' and the
later Chalice style influenced by Clazomenian. Price it seems was the
only student since Petrie and his collaborators who had looked closely
at the finds.

Bird bowls, Eye bowls and Rosette bowls were other groups
which first caught students' attention at Naucratis in 1885. On Bird
bowls *Naukratis* I, published the next year, candidly offered two opinions. Petrie thought they were made at Naucratis, approximately between 620 and 530 B.C. C. H. Smith more shrewdly saw that the group
was partly Orientalizing and was already finishing when Naucratis
was founded, as he thought, about 650 B.C. But if Smith was right –
and this was generally agreed – Bird bowls must have been made in
some other place than Naucratis. The Geometric motives suggested
Rhodes, though Pottier in his *Catalogue* of 1896 denied the attribution.

Pallat in *AM* 1897, following Dümmler's bad example in *Jdl* 1887, claimed that the Bird bowls belonged or were closely related to Protocorinthian; and Dragendorff in 1903 in *Thera* II thought them probably Cycladic, yet correctly recognized their ancestry. But these heresies, surprising in students who were expert in the wares to which they assigned the Bird bowls, made few converts. The solution of widespread manufacture in the East Greek region was left to Price in her paper in *JHS* 1924. The Eye bowls too had been assigned by Petrie to Naucratis, and neither style nor distribution was against him. Pfuhl in 1923, connecting them again with the Bird bowls, assumed a Rhodian factory in Naucratis, and Price agreed. The Eye bowls were regulary dated in the sixth century and had some repute as the ancestors of black-figure eye cups. The Rosette bowls, numerous but uninteresting, were probably considered, when considered at all, as poor relations of the Eye bowl.

Since the eighties at the latest Vroulian has usually been credited to Rhodes, and till after the First World War was dated in the seventh century as an immediate successor of the local Geometric. The only study of the group was that of Kinch in 1914 in *Fouilles de Vroulia*, where the name 'Vroulian' was first given. G. Karo in 1896 in his *de Arte Vascularia Antiquissima Quaestiones* had related it to Italocorinthian, and Boehlau two years later in *aus ionischen und italischen Nekropolen* labelled Karo's mixture 'Aeolian' and recommended it as the first Greek black-figure style. But these aberrations had no wide effect, though Kinch still fancied that Vroulian might have taught Protocorinthian potters to incise.

The Clazomenian sarcophagi brought out the worst in most of their many students. A poor late example from Rhodes had entered the British Museum in 1863 and received several harmless mentions, but the rot began with the discoveries in Clazomenae in 1882 and the thirty years that followed. These offered, separately or in conjunction, a reserving Wild Goat style and an imitation of a developed black-figure style, a few specimens even attempted red-figure, and there were others with wholly linear decoration. The size of the sarcophagi, their variety of style; the prevailing mood of Panionism and the lack of datable contexts combined to inflate the credit of these deplorable monuments. A favourite principle of study seems to have been to date each sarcophagus by the most primitive element in its decoration: those supposed the earliest were put back to the middle of the seventh century or before, and the end of the school was connected by the more credulous with a Persian destruction of Clazomenae about 540 B.C.

This chronology granted, it was logical to make the Clazomenian painters the first great masters of black-figure and the inventors of red-figure, and the judicious Zahn even turned Pliny's Cimon of Cleonae into a Clazomenian. Equally ingenious were the interpretations of subjects and the recognition that the shape and the ritual of the sarcophagi were derived from Egypt. Sober students, though not denying the premises, ignored the consequences, but there were also a few radicals. In particular F. Studniczka in *JdI* 1890 dated some of the elaborate scenes in the later sixth century, F. Winter in *AA* 1898 insisted that the black-figure style was inanely decorative and that the example from Rhodes could not be much earlier than the middle of the fifth century; and Hopkinson in *JHS* 1902 observed that the Wild Goat style too was a degenerate relic. Zahn also in *AM* 1898, though greatly over-rating the sarcophagi, saw that their period was short and not before the middle of the sixth century. But it was not till the 1930s that the old fantasies were abandoned, whether through Rumpf's insistence or the death of his adversaries.

For Clazomenian black-figure the only important find was at Tell Defenneh, and Petrie though not a Greek specialist saw quickly that this was a new school. In his report of 1888, which was bound up in *Tanis* II, he gave some useful drawings, claimed local manufacture and fixed the date (according to his notions of the history of the site) in the first third of the sixth century. Though A. S. Murray, also in *Tanis* II, observed that the style of this pottery could be later, Petrie's dating was accepted by most students till the 1930s. Zahn in *AM* 1898 added some sherds from Clazomenae and showed a connection with the sarcophagi, and his conclusion that Petrie's group too must be Clazomenian was disputed only by Endt. Prinz in 1908 in *Funde aus Naukratis* listed the pots and sherds he knew. As the only certain school of East Greek black-figure Clazomenian soon attracted a number of strays and small groups, East Greek and Etruscan. The most notable of these, the Campana dinoi and the Northampton group, were still loosely attached to Clazomenian as late as the 1930s, if not later.

The East Greek Situlae too were first recognized at Tell Defenneh, and again Petrie in 1888 in the supplement to *Tanis* II published them sketchily and argued that they were made locally in the early sixth century. This dating was thought if anything too low, till Rumpf's paper in *JdI* 1933. Zahn in *AM* 1898 noted Rhodian connections and Kinch in 1914 in *Fouilles de Vroulia* argued for manufacture in Rhodes. But the home of the Situlae is still disputed.

At the middle of the nineteenth century the Attic school of vase-painting had been traced back to the François vase, and the next generation went little if any further. The Attic black-figure style was still thought to develop out of Ripe Corinthian and the known pieces from the seventh century were treated as sports. Of these there were a fair number, notably from earlyish Protoattic, the Burgon dinos and the small jugs from Phaleron, of which Dumont had illustrated a sample in *RA* 1869, and at the other end the Nessos painter's late bowl in Berlin. But they were not considered as a series, so that even Furtwängler in *AM* 1881 maintained that the 'Dipylon' style (which was not yet linked to Attic black-figure) could not be an Attic school of Geometric. Only C. H. Smith in *JHS* 1884 showed some glimmering of the truth. Then in *JdI* 1887 Boehlau published a remarkable paper that was not superseded for fifty years. Boehlau took some thirty pots and fragments, arranged them in early and late groups, explained their position in the Attic sequence, and called his new style 'Early Attic' – a name soon translated into 'Protoattic'. His dating – around 600 B.C. – was sound according to the low chronology still current when he wrote, and his recognition of an originally Ionian impulse was only to be expected. In 1898 in *aus ionischen und italischen Nekropolen* Boehlau returned to Protoattic, listing late pieces in which he saw the effects of Protocorinthian: but his sequence was faulty, since he took the extent of incision as his index, and his dating, tied now to an unduly high dating of Protocorinthian, was not generally accepted. Other students detected a 'Melian' influence. But the Ionian theory also persisted; it was openly affirmed by G. M. A. Richter in *JHS* 1912, where Protoattic was more subtly deployed in three stages, and had Pfuhl's guarded blessing as late as 1923.

Of early Attic black-figure Jahn in 1854 was aware only of what are now called the Tyrrhenian amphorae and the François vase (which had been found in 1844). Following Kramer he regarded them as the Attic transition from Corinthian. There was little or no progress till the seventies when Brunn and Loeschcke published observations based on style rather than epigraphy. Brunn, whose peculiar belief in archaistic imitations obliged him to examine style more closely than was then usual, put the François vase at the head of Attic black-figure and about the middle of the sixth century. This was in 1871 in his *Probleme in der Geschichte der Vasenmalerei*, and in 1877 in T. Lau's *die griechischen Vasen* (intended like d'Hancarville's album a century earlier to provide models to working potters) he noted that the François vase was both more advanced and more old-fashioned than the Tyrrhenian group. Loeschcke in *AZ* 1876 emphasized the dependence of Attic on Corinthian for its early types, but in *Annali* 1878 recognized that the one-piece amphora with decoration in a reserved panel was invented at Athens and that here Corinth was the imitator. The new Panionist theory of course persuaded many students that it was not Corinthian, but Ionian and especially 'Chalcidian' influence that they saw in early Attic black-figure. Others were more resolute and in 1890 even invented the term 'Attic-Corinthian' to describe the Tyrrhenian group and the new Animal style of the first quarter of the sixth century; this Animal style, made known by V. Stais in *AM* 1890 in his publication of graves at Vurva, soon itself acquired the name 'Vurva'. In the late nineties two important studies show how stylistic perception was improving. P. Wolters in *JdI* 1898 divided early Attic into a coarse series that proceeded from the Vurva group through Sophilos to the Tyrrhenian amphorae and a fine series leading from Clitias to Exekias and the Amasis painter: Clitias, he insisted, was a younger contemporary of Sophilos and his François vase was therefore not so old as was commonly believed. H. Thiersch's '*Tyrrhenische*' *amphoren*, published in 1899, was the first thorough analysis of any group of Greek pots and much of it is still valid. Thiersch, who fixed the name 'Tyrrhenian' in its present meaning, refined Wolters' scheme by inserting the Polos group as the immediate precursor of Tyrrhenian and Nikosthenes' workshop as its successor. It is perhaps a tribute to Thiersch's lucid presentation of the material that his successors rejected his extravagant claims of Ionian influences. Of other Attic pottery of this period the Burgon Panathenaic amphora was from the eighties regularly dated about 560 B.C. (as it still is), but its stylistic connections were not obvious. The Siana cups were first noted by C. H. Smith in *JHS* 1884: he hinted that they were Attic and this opinion became dominant after 1900; but others made them Rhodian or 'Chalcidian' or Corinthian, and Pfuhl in 1923 could describe them as 'Attic-Chalcidian' and perhaps of Cycladic manufacture. That the Comast cups were Attic had been suggested by P. Orsi in *MA* 1909; but till A. Grefenhagen's demonstration twenty years after they were usually reckoned Corinthian or Boeotian. In their dating some of these students tended to go too high, putting the Vurva style in the last quarter of the seventh century and stretching Tyrrhenian over the first half of the sixth. The present chronology was first clearly stated by Payne in 1931 in his *Necrocorinthia*.

Mature and later Attic black-figure had always interested students because of the subjects and the occasional signatures, but the detailed consideration of its style hardly began before the last quarter of the nineteenth century. An important landmark was Loeschcke's assertion in *AZ* 1881 that Exekias was the painter of the Memnon amphora in the British Museum, although one of its inscriptions gave the name 'Amasis'. The three great, because known, masters were Exekias, Amasis and Nikosthenes, and in the late eighties their dating was fixed more or less as it is now. Here too Panionism intruded, the more strongly as it was expelled from earlier Attic: plainly the Persian conquest of the 540s must have driven many Ionians overseas. Since the red-figure style was admitted to be essentially Attic, Exekias as its predecessor could be ranked a true Athenian. But Amasis was betrayed by his name as well as the details and decorative character of his style: Studniczka in *EA* 1886 revived C. O. Müller's innocent suggestion of 1831 that Amasis came from Egypt, Loeschcke in 1894 in his article for Pauly-Wissowa preferred Samos, and the conservative Pfuhl in 1923 still thought he might be an Ionian immigrant. The Affecter smacked even more of Ionia, if indeed he did not live there. Nikosthenes was notable for his special shape of amphora and the white-ground technique that he was supposed to have introduced into Athens. His origin and quality were disputed. Loeschcke in *AZ* 1881 before his conversion to Panionism believed that the Nikosthenic amphora was adapted from Etruscan, but afterwards Ionian metalwork seemed more plausible; Pottier in his *Catalogue* of 1893 made Nikosthenes the chief apostle of the Ionian influx; Thiersch in 1899 degraded him to the unprogressive side of Attic black-figure. The Little Master cups, which were at first dated too late, and the Attic eye cups also showed East Greek or 'Chalcidian' tutelage, and after Droop's paper in *JHS* 1910 the cups since called after him were often said to imitate Laconian. Pfuhl's synopsis in 1923 collected the general opinions held in the twenty years before the First World War, but he did not comprehend the fine distinctions and attributions which were a more important achievement of that time.

Boeotian became known in the late 1880s. Besides true Geometric, four later classes were especially distinguished. The big Subgeometric and Orientalizing amphorae received some attention in the nineties, and were at first confused with the Linear Island group; but after 1903, when Dragendorff in *Thera* II separated the two schools, it became usual to see here a Cycladic influence on Boeotian. Boeotian Bird cups had been shown to Furtwängler in 1878, and in *JdI* 1888 they were studied by Boehlau with exemplary thoroughness: to him and his successors they were transitional between Geometric and Orientalizing, that is of the late eighth and early seventh centuries. The next advance was made in 1909 in *BSA* XIV by R. M. Burrows and P. N. Ure, two representatives of the new, more scholarly generation of British students: from their excavation at Rhitsona they concluded that the Bird cups, now divided into an earlier and a later group, were mostly of the sixth century. This dating, unexpectedly low, was accepted with reluctance. Examples of Boeotian black-figure of the sixth century were published occasionally: their general dependence on Attic was obvious. For the Cabiran style H. Winnefeld's paper in *AM* 1888 was an able introduction: he dated its human scenes to the early and middle fourth century, and so tempted others to find a connection with the Hadra hydriai.

Cycladic other than 'Melian' is still a puzzle. Conze in 1870 in *zur Geschichte der Anfänge der griechischen Kunst* listed in his Geometric a few examples of Theran Late Geometric and added the late stage of the Linear Island group for the transition to Orientalizing. In 1903, Dragendorff published much new material in *Thera* II: he divided Theran into a Geometric phase of the ninth and eighth centuries and an Orientalizing of the seventh and very early sixth, suggested that the Heraldic group might be the style of Melos before about 650 B.C., and distinguishing Linear Island from Boeotian assigned it to Euboea and the seventh century. Pfuhl added many pots and few comments in *AM* 1903. F. Poulsen and C. Dugas in *BCH* 1911 gave a foretaste of the more varied finds from Rheneia, but their classification was not satisfactory.

A few Cretan Orientalizing pots were illustrated by Orsi in *AJA* 1897 and some more by Pfuhl in *AM* 1903. Pfuhl in his thoughtful commentary noted influences from Cypriot and parallels in Protocorinthian. Hopkinson, publishing the Praisos plate in *JHS* 1902, denied that there was any Orientalizing style in Crete, and Poulsen in *AM* 1906 considered that Cretan art of the seventh and sixth centuries was sterile. But as Panionism declined some students, notably E. Löwy in *ÖJh* 1909 and 1911, attempted to substitute Crete as the creator and first teacher of the new Greek art that replaced Geometric. So E. Buschor in 1912 in his perceptive handbook, *Griechische Vasenmalerei*, gave Crete and Rhodes the original schools of Orientalizing and asserted Cretan influence on Protocorinthian. Though as finds increased it became still clearer that Cretan vase-painting was generally dull and the few good pieces were eccentric, its primacy was accepted by Johansen and Payne and was not challenged before the Second World War.

Etruscan pottery was continually produced in the spoliation of Etruria; and although for the maintenance of prices the Princess of Canino ordered her workmen to smash all the plainer ware they found,

most collections were soon well stocked. But its study was left to a few
conscientious excavators and curators and to some devoted Panionists.
Bucchero, as it came to be called in the seventies, was generally admitted to evolve from the native impasto though influenced by Greek
shapes and ornaments, and in the later part of the century the stamped
red ware was often cited for its subjects. A few students maintained that
Etruscan bucchero was inspired from Aeolis and red ware from Rhodes,
or that they were produced in Greek colonies in the West; and till the
1930s it was still sometimes claimed that the finer bucchero kantharoi
were made in Sicily, where several had been found. The most important
publications were S. Gsell's *Fouilles dans la Nécropole de Vulci* of 1891,
which is still valuable, and Pottier's half-informed discussion in his
Catalogue of 1899. Italocorinthian, though mentioned earlier, was not
clearly distinguished from Corinthian before Furtwängler's *Beschreibung
der Vasensammlung* in 1885. Karo in 1896 in his *de Arte Vascularia*
transferred much to Greek workshops in Sicily, and two years later
Boehlau in *aus ionischen und italischen Nekropolen* almost made the black
polychrome and Animal groups Aeolian. These vagaries were rejected,
and so too though less immediately was the corollary that the Animal
style of Italocorinthian owed more to Ionia than Corinth. The best
collection of material was by J. Sieveking and R. Hackl in 1912 in *die
königliche Vasen-Sammlung zu München*: this helped greatly to define the
school, but there is still no complete study. Of Etruscan black-figure
the best and most colourful pieces were in the seventies still included in
the Tyrrhenian group of Attic; the rest, as Jahn had seen, were un-
equivocally Etruscan. Dümmler's Panionism gave them a new aspect.
In *RM* 1887 he collected two dozen of the earlier pieces and by detailed
but shaky argument satisfied himself that they were made around 600
B.C. by Ionians, probably working in the Pontic colonies. In *RM* 1888
he applied the same methods to the later black-figure, detected the influence of the Caeretan hydriai, and unable to ignore the provincial
sterility of his 'Italo-Ionic' school assigned it (or most of it) to Greeks
in South Italy. Dümmler's notions were readily believed, but with some
modifications. For the first group Pontic manufacture was too absurd
to be misleading and so the name was adopted. But gradually the Ionian
originators of Pontic were shifted to Etruria, barbarization of the style
was admitted and the date brought down to the first half of the sixth
century. In the later group of 'Italo-Ionic' the Etruscan character was
undeniable and Dümmler's successors made less of its Ionic origins
and even recognized that in the end its models were Attic. Endt's
Beiträge zur ionischen Vasenmalerei of 1899 had added many new pieces,

but Sieveking and Hackl in their Munich catalogue of 1912 not only illustrated a large collection but classified it with intelligence. The next clear advance was not made till the later 1930s.

It is easy to guess the course of opinions about the Caeretan hydriai. The first illustration was published in 1842, but interest was confined to subjects, and it was not till 1863 that Helbig in *Annali* put together three Caeretan and two Corinthian pots and pronounced them Etruscan archaistic versions of Corinthian. Jahn in 1870 in *die Entführung der Europa* (from the Vienna *Denkschriften*) listed six hydriai and recognized the group's independence. Furtwängler in *AZ* 1882 still thought them Etruscan, but saw a kinship with 'Chalcidian'; and till the 1950s the Ionian character of the hydriai was accepted without question, though its home was less obvious. After the discoveries at Naucratis the Busiris hydria suggested to some students that the Caeretan group was made in Egypt, but the usual choice was and still is between northern Ionia and Etruria as the situation of this probably East Greek workshop. That the group was short-lived has never been disputed. In the 1880s progressive students dated it around the middle of the sixth century, in the 1920s to the third quarter, and in the 1930s to the last third. The Campana dinoi, first studied by Pottier in *BCH* 1893, and the Northampton group, which Studniczka collected in *JdI* 1890, were loosely annexed to Clazomenian by Zahn in *AM* 1898: but though dated too early and often cited, the claim that they were important soon proved incredible.

Red-figure pottery was very frequent in the early finds and invited study by its curious range of subjects as well as its accomplished draughtsmanship. It is not surprising that in the hundred years that followed the opening of Vulci more than twice as much was written on this style as on all others. The main development was plain, since there were no big gaps in the sequence, and Jahn's account (which was adapted from Kramer's) is still broadly instructive. But detailed investigation of schools and painters began only in the last quarter of the nineteenth century: till then, as might be inferred from the illustrations of the time, students put subjects and inscriptions before style. For Attic red-figure the signatures seemed an easy key. It was reasonable to claim that all works signed with the same painter's name were painted by the same hand; and it was further claimed, without much reason, that if a pot was signed only by a maker, then making included painting. So stylistic interest was usually confined to lists of signatures and the forms of letters, though occasionally some students looked further. For instance in 1837 Kramer had thought that it would be instructive to compare the signed works of Epictetus and de Witte that his unsigned works could be recognized; but as late as 1873 R. Kekule in *AZ* was reserved in claiming that Èuthymides had a character of his own. Brunn's archaistic heresy, though generally denied, provided another distraction.

A new stage began with W. Klein, whose *Euphronios* and *die griechischen Vasen mit Meistersignaturen* were first published in 1879 and 1883 in the *Denkschriften* of the Vienna Academy and afterwards were revised and issued separately. Klein's service was rather in collating and refining current opinions than in correcting them. He argued that the founder of the red-figure style was Epictetus, since black-figure and red-figure were often used together on his cups; he insisted that normally the maker was the painter too, even boasting that without this aid Euphronios's development could not have been comprehended; and he felt safer dating by the lettering of inscriptions than by the drawing of figures. But he had some grasp of the relations between his Archaic vase-painters, gave a good account of their new shapes and noted that the incising of the outline of the hair was a mark of early date. In attributing unsigned pieces to their painters Klein was no more successful than others of his contemporaries, though C. H. Smith in 1883 in *JHS* IV pointed to the Charmides painter. Even Furtwängler, whose *Beschreibung der Vasensammlung* of 1885 intimated a clearer understanding of the red-figure style, was right in only a third of some fifty attributions. Much more ambitious was P. Hartwig's *die griechischen Meisterschalen*, published in 1893, which tried to identify the major and some minor painters of Archaic cups. Hartwig's analysis was detailed and subtle, and many of his conclusions were just, especially when he trusted to style: unhappily he also thought makers painters and assumed too readily that each καλός name was peculiar to one painter. His many illustrations, or the best of them, were notably accurate. Furtwängler's review next year in *BPW* made some corrections: the pioneer of red-figure was not Epictetus but the Andocides painter (as Jahn had hinted and de Witte proposed), 'made' did not mean 'painted' nor even 'shaped', and Euthymides must be ranked a great master. Classical and later red-figure were now being neglected. The first important study was F. Winter's *die jüngeren attischen Vasen* of 1885, which Milchhöfer with less perception supplemented and tried to correct in *JdI* 1894.

It was now Furtwängler's turn and in 1900 in partnership with K. Reichhold he began the serial *Griechische Vasenmalerei*, which flourished before the First World War and lingered on till 1932. The object was to publish the most important vase-paintings, especially of the red-figure style, in accurate, full-size drawings and an authoritative text. The exemplary drawings were Reichhold's, as were the technical observations. Furtwängler's commentary illumined the whole range of Attic red-figure; among much else he detached the Panaitios painter from Euphronios, added substance to the Niobid and Eretria painters, and fixed the period of the progressive school of the fourth century. Lesser students too were busy.

Furtwängler died in 1907. The next year J. D. Beazley, the other great exponent of Classical Archaeology, published the first of his many papers. Beazley rejected the hardy prejudice that the isolation of red-figure vase-painters must start from their signatures, and he very soon showed an unrivalled eye and memory. So in *JHS* 1910 he trebled the dozen known works of the Cleophrades painter, and in *JHS* 1911 revealed an unsuspected master, the Berlin painter, to whom he at once assigned nearly forty pieces. In 1918 *Attic Red-figured Vases in American Museums* besides more such lists gave what is still the best and subtlest survey of red-figure, and in 1925 *Attische Vasenmaler des rotfigurigen Stils* was a general catalogue of the painters and their works. This comprehensive progress shocked some older students, who felt it improper to attribute unpublished pieces so freely; even in 1923 Pfuhl's *Malerei und Zeichnung*, though useful for its detailed analyses and references, betrays a puzzled reluctance in accepting the new orthodoxy. But others, notably Buschor in his *Griechische Vasenmalerei* of 1912 and his later continuation of Furtwängler and Reichhold's great album, were converted to Beazley's method, and to the next generation it seemed fundamental. In his *Attic Red-figure Vase-painters* Beazley has scrupulously noted the good attributions of other students, but only made it plainer how many more are his own. It is pleasant to reflect that his unique achievement was honoured by a knighthood.

Attic white-ground lekythoi with black-figured and with outline decoration were familiar from Sicily and South Italy, and acquired the name of Locrian vases. But the later, more polychrome lekythoi are very rarely found outside Greece and so were neglected till 1870 when O. Benndorf published fair drawings of thirty examples in the second part of his *Griechische und Sicilische Vasenbilder*. In the next generation much was written about the lekythoi, but only R. C. Bosanquet in *JHS* 1896 and 1899 showed stylistic insight. A. Fairbanks in his *Athenian White Lekythoi* of 1907 and 1914 compiled a credulous and too methodical catalogue; W. Riezler's *Weissgrundige attische Lekythen*, sensible and well illustrated, though timid in its attributions, also appeared in 1914, as did J. D. Beazley's account in *JHS* of the Achilles painter. When Pfuhl wrote his summary in 1923 the personalities of the white-ground painters were still obscure: afterwards they were explored by Buschor and Beazley.

The Panionist theory did no harm to the study of Attic red-figure, which was beyond doubt Attic and alone. Zahn in *AM* 1898 had logically but unconvincingly derived the red-figure technique from Clazomenian sarcophagi. Some stalwarts, Pfuhl included, thought the Andocides painter an Ionian immigrant, though more followed Loeschcke's assertion made in 1879 that he was a dependent or pupil of Exekias. Duris had a Samian namesake and must be a Samian too, for Dümmler and even Furtwängler and Langlotz. B. Schröder in *JdI* 1914 suspected Ionian influences in the early Classical period. But no one concocted a red-figure school that worked in Ionia. Boeotia had more luck, being often credited with poor Attic works of the fourth century: the distinction is perhaps not yet entirely sure.

In the later fifties there were three systems of dates for Attic red-figure besides the fantasies of 'archaism'. Ross, who had found red-figured sherds on the Acropolis of Athens in the debris of the Persian sack of 480 B.C., fixed its span from the early sixth century to the early fourth, but Birch was his only notable adherent. Jahn admitted Ross's evidence so far as to start red-figure a little before 480 B.C., and he let it continue in Athens till the late fourth century. But some students, incredulous of Ross's observation, still put the invention of the new technique about 470 or 460 B.C. These lower chronologies were based principally on the forms of letters painted on red-figure pots: it was not guessed that private inscriptions might be a generation or more ahead of the official script. Although U. Koehler corrected this error incidentally in *AM* 1885, it was the new excavation of the Acropolis, cited by Studniczka in *JdI* 1887, that stirred students. Not only had red-figure begun before 480 B.C., but its severe (or Archaic) stage was by then almost over. In a few years 530 B.C. was agreed to be the date when the style began, and Furtwängler's chronology of the Archaic phase stood the test of E. Langlotz's thesis of 1920, *zur Zeitbestimmung der streng-rotfigurigen Vasenmalerei*. Once the beginning of red-figure had been pushed back, there followed inevitably the attempt, led by Milchhöfer in *JdI* 1894, to push back its end and cram all Classical and later Attic into the fifth century. But Furtwängler's authority established the general dating that remains current. A few painters were still misplaced and some of the white-ground lekythoi dated too late, but gradually assurance has become more precise. For all these various chronologies connections in sculpture, painting and history were found and accepted: the educated eye and mind are very accommodating.

South Italian red-figure has never been scarce, and since the 1760s the experts have generally been right about its origin. This was at first because they presumed that pots were made where they were found, and most red-figure pots were found in South Italy. Later, when (thanks to Kramer) Attic red-figure was recognized, the residue (in spite of Kramer) remained South Italian, except for a few obvious Etruscan products. Gradually the many supposedly local fabrics were condensed into three schools, though still very impure and hazy round the edges, and by Jahn's time the terms Apulian, Lucanian and Campanian meant more than the place of finding. Because of the subjects much South Italian was published, notably in Gerhard's *Apulische Vasenbilder* of 1845, but its style (as de Luynes had once observed) was not attractive. The Paestan painter Asteas had signed several of his works and so was particularly noticed: in 1890 in *Bonner Studien* H. Winnefeld carefully analysed his style, six years later in the *Catalogue of Vases in the British Museum* H. B. Walters made a special class for the style of Asteas of Paestum, and in 1897 G. Patroni extended his school and named it simply Paestan. Meanwhile in 1893 Furtwängler in his *Meisterwerke* had detected the early stage of South Italian, noting its relation to Attic, with which till then it had been confused, and arguing for manufacture in the Greek coastal cities of Thurii, Heraclea and Tarentum. This was too much for Patroni, who saw in these schools of vase-painting an Italian genius which could have flowered only in the native towns of the interior. But his *la Ceramica antica nell'Italia meridionale* (which appeared in 1897 in *Atti dell' Accademia di Archeologia, Lettre e Belle Arti di Napoli*) was the first broad study of these red-figure schools, and important. Furtwängler, Hauser, Buschor and Zahn made good additions and corrections in the text to FR; B. Macchioro in *RM* 1912 and elsewhere perhaps included no useful observations among his fantasies; and in 1923 in *The Hope Vases* E. W. M. Tillyard offered a sane and intelligent summary. Tillyard also discovered the early stage of Paestan and abolished the so-called Saticulan fabric, seeing that it was not Campanian but Attic. More recently the detailed search for painters has gone far. The dating of South Italian was difficult. After the 1830s it was regarded as the successor of Attic, taking over more or less where the other left off. For its end the evidence seemed conflicting. Many students held the old opinion that figured vase-painting was suppressed in 186 B.C. through the Senatus Consultum de Bacchanalibus. Others had it continue till the next century, deluded by the report of red-figure at Canosa in a grave of 67 B.C. There were also those who thought the third century late enough, finding a cause – if one were wanted – in the Second Punic War. A fairly sound chronology began at last to emerge from the observations of Furtwängler, Patroni and Furtwängler's successors.

Etruscan red-figure has had still fewer investigators than South Italian. That it existed was allowed even by those who first claimed painted pottery for the Greeks, and Jahn in 1854 had a rough grasp of its character and development. But the earliest close study, of the late school of Clusium and Volterra, was C. Albizzati's in *RM* 1915. Since then progress has been considerable.

Of Hellenistic pottery knowledge is still vague. Though its Italian schools were soon observed, the first and often the only special studies came mostly in the early twentieth century. Gnathian, which by its showy elegance appealed to some collectors, was evidently related to Apulian red-figure and often considered its successor: the name, given by Neapolitan dealers, was accepted reluctantly by archaeologists around 1880. The Pocolom group with its early Latin inscriptions exercised epigraphists; stylistically it was attached to Gnathian, and its place of origin was often put in Campania. The polychrome ware of Canosa, becoming known towards the end of the century, was studied with moderate competence by M. Jatta in *RM* 1914. The still more polychrome products of Centuripae had turned up as early as 1830, but obtained only passing mentions. It was of course seen that both these groups were late. A Calene phiale had been one of the first two Greek pots published; here too students were preoccupied with Latin inscriptions, but Benndorf in 1883 in *Griechische und Sicilische Vasenbilder* illustrated several pieces and R. Pagenstecher in *die Calenische Reliefkeramik* of 1909 was thorough, though not always right.

West Slope ware was cited casually as Gnathian till and even after 1901, when C. Watzinger defined and analysed it excellently in *AM*; since then it has been found regularly in excavations and museums. The Hadra hydriai, noted already in the 1850s, offered inscribed dates to be determined; their style was first considered, with too much reference to Cabiran, by R. Pagenstecher in *AJA* 1909 and four years later in *Expedition E. von Sieglin* and also by E. Breccia in *la Necropoli di Sciatbi* in 1912. Zahn in 1904 in *Priene* made a few sound observations on the light-ground lagynoi, and G. Leroux in 1913 in *Lagynos* assembled the group and examined it with care and judgement. The 'Megarian' bowls, as they came to be called in the 1880s, were soon attributed in part to Athens, though many supposed that at least the technique of moulding came from Alexandria; their dating, within the Hellenistic period, was and is not altogether certain.

The Black-painted wares had always been exhibited in collections, but they remained too plain and difficult for students. The credit for the first thorough inquiry should go to P. N. Ure for his *Black Glaze Pottery from Rhitsona* of 1913, a work noteworthy as much for its devotion as its precision.

Since the First World War progress has been remarkable. New excavations, when published or made available, have contributed something. But the main reason is that students, taught by the example of Beazley and others, have seen that the examination of style can be pushed much further than it was before and they expect that in any figured school of painted pottery they will probably find some painter. Much more can be done by this method. 'Melian', if the finds from Rheneia are set free, and some of the earlier Etruscan groups are easy enough. Advances can be made in East Greek Orientalizing, Boeotian and Hellenistic. For most of the Protogeometric and Geometric schools other than Attic – at least till their latest phases – and for the earlier Orientalizing wares of the Cyclades new evidence is the first need. But whether all these subjects are worth probing is a question that may well be asked.

The history of the study of vase-painting, like the history of all studies, offers entertainment to the curious or cynical mind and is sometimes useful for understanding older books and papers. But it is also instructive. Although there are rare students of genius, most are clever only in detail, normally uncritical of their methods or presumptions and blind to the further consequences of their arguments. So such fashionable theories as the Etruscan origin of painted vases, the representation of the ancient Mysteries and the artistic dominance of Ionia have in their time been accepted as fundamental truths. We may laugh at these past follies, but they are also a warning to look for equal follies of our own.

Abbreviations

A (in description of a pot) = the front.

AA Archäologischer Anzeiger (supplement since 1889 to *JdI*, previously to *AZ*).

ABSA = BSA.

ABV J. D. Beazley, *Attic Black-figure Vase-painters.*

AC Archeologia Classica.

Act Arch Acta Archaeologica.

AD Antike Denkmäler.

A Delt 'Αρχαιολογικòν Δελτίον.

AdI = Ann. (1).

AE = EA.

AJA American Journal of Archaeology.

AM Mitteilungen des Deutschen Archäologischen Instituts, Athenische Abteilung (shortly *Athenische Mitteilungen*).

Ann (1) *Annali dell'Instituto di Corrispondenza Archeologica.* (2) = *ASA.*

Anz = AA.

ARV J. D. Beazley, *Attic Red-figure Vase-painters.*

ARV² J. D. Beazley, *Attic Red-figure Vase-painters* (ed. 2).

ASA Annuario della Scuola Archeologica di Atene.

Ath Mitt = AM.

AZ Archäologische Zeitung.

B (in description of a pot) = the back.

BCH Bulletin de la Correspondance Hellénique.

BdI Bullettino dell'Instituto di Corrispondenza Archeologica.

Bf black-figure.

Bg black-glazed (or black-painted).

BM British Museum.

BPW Berliner Philologische Wochenschrift.

BSA Annual of the British School at Athens.

BSR Papers of the British School at Rome.

BWP Programm zum Winckelmannsfeste der Archäologischen Gesellschaft zu Berlin (shortly *Berliner Winckelmannsprogramm*).

Bull (1) = *BdI.* (2) = *RM.*

Cl Rh Clara Rhodos.

CVA Corpus Vasorum Antiquorum.

Delt = *A Delt.*

EA = Ἐφημερὶς Ἀρχαιολογική, since 1910 Ἀρχαιολογικὴ Ἐφημερίς.

Eph = *EA.*

EVP J. D. Beazley, *Etruscan Vase-Painting.*

FA Fasti Archaeologici.

FR A. Furtwängler and K. Reichhold (and others) *Griechische Vasen-malerei.*

GGP J. N. Coldstream, *Greek Geometric Pottery.*

Hesp Hesperia.

I (in description of a cup) = the inside.

Jahreshefte = ÖJh.

Jb = JdI.

JdI Jahrbuch des Deutschen Archäologischen Instituts.

Jb = ÖJh.

JHS Journal of Hellenic Studies.

LCS A. D. Trendall, *The Red-figured Vases of Lucania, Campania and Sicily.*

MA Monumenti Antichi per cura della R. Accademia dei Lincei.

MdI (1) *Mitteilungen des Deutschen Archäologischen Instituts.* (2) = *Mon Ined.*

MEFR = *Mél.*

Mél Mélanges d'Archéologie et d'Histoire publiés per l'école française de Rome.

ML = *MA.*

MMS Metropolitan Museum Studies.

Mon Ant = *MA.*

Mon Ined Monumenti Inediti pubblicati dall'Instituto di Corrispondenza Archeologica.

Mon Inst = *Mon Ined.*

Mon Piot Fondation Eugéne Piot, Monuments et Mémoires.

MuZ E. Pfuhl, *Malerei und Zeichnung.*

NC H. G. G. Payne, *Necrocorinthia.*

NM National Museum.

NSc Notizie degli Scavi.

ÖJh Jahreshefte des Oesterreichischen Archäologischen Instituts.

PAE Πρακτικὰ τῆς ἐν Ἀθήναις ἀρχαιολογικῆς ἑταιρείας.

PBSR = BSR.

PGP V. R. d'A. Desborough, *Protogeometric Pottery.*

Praktika = *PAE.*

RA Revue Archéologique.

Rf red-figure

RM Mitteilungen des Deutschen Archäologischen Instituts, Römische Abteilung (shortly *Römische Mitteilungen*).

SA *Sovetskaya Archeologiya.*
SE *Studi Etruschi.*
Vroulia K. F. Kinch, *Fouilles de Vroulia.*
VS K. F. Johansen, *les Vases sicyoniens.*
Wg white-ground.

Bibliography

These lists are not complete. Where a good comprehensive study is available, references to earlier and more particular studies can be found there. I have added the ostensible date of publication, as a guide to what the writer could not have known. For abbreviations see pp. 328–30.

Chapter 1: Introduction

GENERAL STUDIES

[E.] A. LANE, *Greek Pottery* ed. 3. Excellent illustrations with a short and intelligent text. 1971.

E. BUSCHOR, *Griechische Vasen* ed. 2. Good illustrations and good, though rather mystical, account. 1969.

A. RUMPF, *Malerei und Zeichnung* (Handbuch der Archäologie VI. 4.1). A short and instructive account with bibliography. 1953.

E. PFUHL, *Malerei und Zeichnung der Griechen* [*MuZ*]. Generous but mediocre illustrations and very detailed classification and analysis. The text, obsolete almost before it was published, is useful for older references. 1923.

F. VILLARD, *les Vases grecs*. A useful summary. 1956.

MUSEUM CATALOGUES

Most museums of any importance have published catalogues of their more noteworthy exhibits. These catalogues vary greatly in the quality and number of their illustrations and in the accuracy and fullness of the commentaries.

Corpus Vasorum Antiquorum [*CVA*]. An international series, which has published about 170 fascicules each of about 50 large plates. The quality of text and illustrations is uneven, but generally the more recent fascicules are better. Methods of numbering and citing the plates vary: the most usual citation is by the code symbols at the top of each plate, the most convenient by the national serial at the bottom. There is a useful analysis of the contents of the first 74 fascicules in J. W. CROUS, *Konkordanz zum CVA* (1942). 1922–.

E. LANGLOTZ, *Griechische Vasen in Würzburg.* An exemplary catalogue of a well-balanced collection. 1932.

CURRENT WORK

JdI, Archäologische Bibliographie (especially III. D. 2 and III. E. 2). Annual list of studies, published in the next year but one.

FA, sections II. 2, III. 2 and IV. 1 under 'Pottery'. Annual list of studies, with summary of contents; published about three years later.

Révue des Études Grecques, Bulletin Archéologique-Céramique. Biennial list, selective but critical, published in the next year but one.

PHOTOGRAPHS

ALINARI, Via Nazionale 6, Florence.

GIRAUDON, 8 Rue des Beaux Arts, Paris VI.

These two firms have large collections of photographs for sale; the subjects are not only from Rome and Paris.

Chapter 2: The Protogeometric Style

1. GENERAL

V. R. d'A. DESBOROUGH, *Protogeometric Pottery* [*PGP*]. A comprehensive and detailed study. (His final Transitional stage is now classed as Geometric.) 1952.

V. R. d'A. DESBOROUGH, *the Last Mycenaeans and their Successors,* 258–70. Supplements and modifies *PGP.* 1964.

J. N. COLDSTREAM, *Greek Geometric Pottery* [*GGP*]. Includes some further additions and modifications. 1968.

2. ATHENS

W. KRAIKER and K. KÜBLER, *Kerameikos* 1, and K. KÜBLER, *Kerameikos* 4. Publication and analysis, perhaps too precise, of Attic Protogeometric. 1939 and 1943.

3. OUTSIDE ATTICA

J. K. BROCK, *Fortetsa.* For Cretan Protogeometric at Cnossus. 1957.

N. M. VERDELIS, ὁ Πρωτογεωμετρικὸς ʽΡυθμὸς τῆς Θεσσαλίας. A useful collection of Protogeometric in Thessaly. 1958.

NOTE ON MYCENAEAN

A. FURUMARK, *the Mycenaean Pottery: Analysis and Classification*, and *the Chronology of Mycenaean Pottery*. Fundamental and detailed, but too precise. 1941.

F. H. STUBBINGS, *BSA* 42, 1–75. Mycenaean in Attica. 1947.

F. H. STUBBINGS, *Mycenaean Pottery from the Levant*. On the Rhodian and Cypriot schools particularly. 1951.

V. R. d' A. DESBOROUGH, *the Last Mycenaeans and their Successors*, 1–28. Reconsiders the latest Mycenaean pottery. 1964.

Chapter 3: The Geometric Style

1. GENERAL

J. N. COLDSTREAM, *Greek Geometric Pottery* [*GGP*]. A fundamental, though not final, conspectus, which should be consulted when use is made of most of the special studies listed below. 1968.

2. ATHENS

K. KÜBLER, *Kerameikos* 5.1. Publication of an Attic Geometric cemetery and a detailed analysis of the style: the last phase is dated about twenty-five years earlier than seems likely to me. 1954.

R. S. YOUNG, *Hesp* Supplement 2. Contains much useful information about later Attic Geometric, but the chronology is improbably compressed. 1939.

E. T. H. BRANN, *Hesp* 1961, 93–146. A useful collection of Late Geometric from the Agora of Athens.

E. T. H. BRANN, *The Athenian Agora* 8. Complementary to the last item. 1962.

J. M. DAVISON, *Attic Geometric Workshops* (Yale Classical Studies 16). Useful for illustrations of the figure style. 1961.

J. M. COOK, *BSA* 42, 139–55. A neat review of progressive Late workshops. 1947.

CVA Louvre 11 (F. VILLARD), pls. 777–92. For illustrations of human figures. 1954.

3. THE ARGOLID

P. COURBIN, *la Céramique Géométrique de l'Argolide*. A detailed analysis. (See also pp. 29–34 for 'Argive Monochrome'.) 1966.

4. CORINTH

S. S. WEINBERG, *Corinth* 7.1, 9–32. For illustrations. 1943.

S. S. WEINBERG, *AJA* 1941, 30–44. A good analysis of the later phases, distinguishing the Thapsos class.

R. S. YOUNG in *Corinth* 13, 13–49. Adds useful material and contexts. 1964.

Note: Weinberg's names for Middle and Late Geometric are Late and Protocorinthian Geometric.

5. LACONIA

E. A. LANE, *BSA* 34, 101–7. A survey of the Late phase. 1936.

W. VON MASSOW, *AM* 1927, 46–53. Useful for finds from Amyklai.

J. P. DROOP in R. M. DAWKINS, *Artemis Orthia*, 54–68. Useful for finds from Sparta. 1929.

6. WESTERN GREECE

[C] M. ROBERTSON, *BSA* 43,60–113. A solid account of Ithacan, but including much Corinthian and too high in its dates. 1948.

S. BENTON, *BSA* 48, 255–358. Supplements and in part corrects ROBERTSON. 1953.

7. BOEOTIA

R. HAMPE, *Frühe griechische Sagenbilder*, 20–31. Useful for illustrations of Late Geometric and for references, but the classification is unsound (see E. KUNZE, *Göttingische Gelehrte Anzeigen* 1937, 285–88). 1936.

F. CANCIANI, *JdI* 1965, 18–75. Useful for Late Geometric.

8. EUBOEA

J. BOARDMAN, *BSA* 47, 1–13. Some useful notes on Late Geometric from Eretria. 1952.

J. BOARDMAN, *BSA* 52, 2–7. For fragments from Chalcis. 1957.

J. BOARDMAN, *Anatolian Studies* 1959, 163–9. For Greek cups apparently made at Al Mina.

9. THE CYCLADES

C. DUGAS and C. RHOMAIOS, *Délos* 15. For the Geometric from Delos and Rheneia; the classification is unreliable. 1934.

H. DRAGENDORFF, *Thera* **2**, 133–76. For Theran Geometric. 1903.

E. PFUHL, *AM* 1903, 98–121. For Theran Geometric.

E. BUSCHOR, *AM* 1929, 142–63. Illustrates some sherds from Paros and Naxos, and attempts to define local schools.

J. K. BROCK, *BSA* **44**, 33–45. On the finds from Siphnos; see also pp. 74–9 on general classification. 1949.

N. M. KONDOLEON, *EA* 1945–7, 1–21. Illustrates some elaborate pieces, but claims too much for Cycladic.

(On the classifications of these writers see the table on p. 343).

11. THE EAST GREEK CITIES

Rhodian

K. F. JOHANSEN, *Acta Archaeologica* 1957, 1–192. An admirable conspectus of later Geometric. (Sometimes cited as *Exochi*.)

Clara Rhodos **6/7** (G. JACOPI), 119–32, 189–203, 360–3. For illustrations and grave groups. 1933.

Clara Rhodos **3** (G. JACOPI), graves lvi–lxiv. Ditto. 1929.

C. DUGAS, *BCH* 1912, 495–522. Useful for illustrations.

Samian

Samos **5** (H. WALTER), nos. 15–300. Useful for illustrations (see J. N. COLDSTREAM, *JHS* 1971, 202–4). 1968.

Chiot

J. BOARDMAN, [*Excavations in Chios, 1952–1955:*] *Greek Emporio*, 101–47. A good presentation and classification of the finds. 1967.

Lesbian Grey ware (Bucchero)

W. LAMB, *BSA* **32**, 51–6. For finds at Antissa. 1934.

12. CRETE

J. K. BROCK, *Fortetsa*. Contains much information on Protogeometric B and Geometric at Cnossus. 1957.

J. BOARDMAN, *BSA* **62**, 57–75. On the Oriental connections of Protogeometric B. 1967.

H. G. G. PAYNE, *BSA* **29**, 224–98. Tombs at Cnossus and a general account; but Protogeometric B is not recognized. 1928.

M. HARTLEY, *BSA* **31**, 56–114. Illustrates material from various sites in Crete. 1933.

D. LEVI, *ASA* **10/12**. Finds from Arkades (Afrati). 1931.

J. D. S. PENDLEBURY, *Archaeology of Crete*, 316–26. Useful for list of sites. 1939.

13. ITALY

J. N. COLDSTREAM, *Greek Geometric Pottery* [*GGP*], 354–6, 370–5. Brief but important. 1968.

Å. ÅKERSTRÖM, *der Geometrische Stil in Italien*. An important attempt at a general survey; but the chronology is too low and the Greek parallels are hazardous. 1943.

G. VALLET and F. VILLARD, *Mégara Hyblaea* **2**, 139–57. A well illustrated account of the local Geometric of that site. 1964.

E. H. DOHAN, *Italic Tomb-Groups*. Contains much sound information on Geometric in Etruria. 1942.

G. MATTEUCIG, *Poggio Buco*, 12–18. Useful for technical classification of Etruscan. 1951.

F. VILLARD and G. VALLET, *Mél* 1956, 7–27. An important introduction to the classification of Geometric in Sicily.

T. J. DUNBABIN, *the Western Greeks*, 487–96. An invaluable bibliography which includes the Geometric finds; see also the index, *s.v.* 'Siculan pottery' and 'Lucanian pottery'. 1948.

Chapter 4: The Orientalizing and Black-figure Styles

There is no comprehensive term which describes all the schools of Greek vase-painting of this chapter. '*Archaic*' would be convenient, if it did not also include the early phase of the red-figure style. '*Orientalizing*', which implies dependence on Oriental models, may with caution be applied to the Animal style, but is improper for the human figures which are purely Greek. '*Black-figure*' conventionally defines the incising technique and the style based on that technique; it therefore excludes much Protoattic that is not Orientalizing either, while on the other hand such pieces as those of PLATE 11 can be described both as Orientalizing and black-figure.

1. GENERAL

J. BOARDMAN, *the Greeks Overseas*. A useful provisional survey of the relations between the Greeks and the East. 1964.

E. AKURGAL, *the Birth of Greek Art*. A helpful illustrated survey of much relevant Oriental art. 1968.

C. DECAMPS DE MERTZENFELD, *Inventaire commenté des ivoires phéniciens et apparentés découverts dans le Proche-Orient*. Convenient for illustrations. 1954.

R. D. BARNETT, *a Catalogue of the Nimrud Ivories*. A well-illustrated and informed account of a large collection of Oriental ivories. 1957.

2. CORINTH

K. F. JOHANSEN, *les Vases sicyoniens*. The fundamental study of Protocorinthian, though the dates are too early and the attribution to Sicyon has proved wrong. 1923.

H. G. G. PAYNE, *Necrocorinthia*. The fundamental study of Ripe Corinthian. 1931.

H. G. G. PAYNE, *Protokorinthische Vassenmalerei*. A good short sketch of Protocorinthian, though the dating is rather too early. 1933.

S. S. WEINBERG, *AJA* 1941, 30–44. Useful for the Early Protocorinthian period.

T. J. DUNBABIN and [C.] M. ROBERTSON, *BSA* 48, 172–81. An important analysis of Protocorinthian by painters. 1953.

J. L. BENSON, *die Geschichte der korinthischen Vasen*. A more disputable analysis, less complete for Protocorinthian but including Ripe Corinthian. 1953.

J. L. BENSON, *AJA* 1956, 219–30. Supplements and criticizes the last two items.

W. E. KLEINBAUER, *AJA* 1964, 355–70. One of several recent studies of particular Ripe Corinthian painters, but the last to give a list of earlier studies (on p. 355, n. 2).

R. J. HOPPER, *BSA* 44, 162–257. A useful commentary and supplement to PAYNE's *Necrocorinthia*. 1949.

D. A. AMYX, *Corinthian Vases* (Univ. of California Publications in Classical Archaeology 1, 207–40). For some detailed comments on the Animal style of the early sixth century. 1943.

S. S. WEINBERG, *Corinth* 7.1. Informative on Subgeometric and Linear wares. 1943.

Antike Denkmäler 1, pls. 7–8; 2, pls. 23–4, 29–30, 39–40. For illustrations of the plaques from Penteskouphia. 1886–1901.

M. T. CAMPBELL, *Hesp* 1938, 560–4. For illustrations of Corinthian imitation of Attic Bf.

H. PALMER in *Corinth* 13, 97–149. Instructive on late wares, including imitations of very late Attic Bf lekythoi. 1964.

E. G. PEMBERTON, *Hesp* 1970, 265–307. Useful comments on local styles of the later fifth century.

Ithaca

C. M. ROBERTSON, *BSA* **43**, 60–113. A careful publication of the material, but the dates are too high and some Corinthian is included. 1948.

S. BENTON, *BSA* **48**, 255–358. Supplements and occasionally corrects ROBERTSON. 1953.

A concordance of terms and dates for Protocorinthian may be helpful. I accept Coldstream.

Coldstream	*Weinberg*	*Payne*	*Johansen*
720 Early Proto-corinthian	725 Early Proto-corinthian	750 Early Proto-corinthian	800 époque des aryballes pansus: style de transition
690 Middle Proto-corinthian I	700 Middle Proto-corinthian I	700 Middle Proto-corinthian I: 1st Bf and Orientalizing styles	725 époque des aryballes ovoides: style archaïque A
670 Middle Proto-corinthian II	675 Middle Proto-corinthian II	675 Middle Proto-corinthian II: 2nd Bf and Orientalizing styles	690 époque des aryballes ovoides: style archaïque B
(650 Late Proto-corinthian)	650 Late Proto-corinthian	650 Late Proto-corinthian	650 époque des aryballes piriformes: style archaïque C

The periods of Protocorinthian are often abbreviated to EPC, MPC (I and II) and LPC. Similarly the periods of Ripe Corinthian, which is usually called simply 'Corinthian', are abbreviated to EC, MC, LC I (to 550 B.C.), and LC II (for the Ripe and other styles after 550 B.C.).

Some students now put the end of Early Ripe Corinthian at 590 or 585 B.C. with corresponding adjustments of the dates of other periods of Corinthian, but without valid reasons.

3. ATHENS

Protoattic

J. M. COOK, *BSA* **35**, 165–219. An excellent analysis of the Early and the Black and White phases, but sketchier for the later phase. 1938.

K. KÜBLER, *Altattische Malerei*. A good survey with representative illustrations, but stretches the chronology at both ends. 1950.

R. HAMPE, *ein frühattischer Grabfund*. Adds to understanding of the Early phase (see J. M. COOK, *JHS* 1961, 220–2). 1960.

CVA Berlin 1 (R. EILMANN and K. GEBAUER). A valuable publication of Early and of Black and White pottery from Aegina (see J. M. COOK, *JHS* 1939, 151–2). 1938.

S. PAPASPYRIDI-KAROUZOU [S. KAROUZOU], *EA* 1952, 149–66. On the Ram Jug painter.

S. PAPASPYRIDI-KAROUZOU [S. KAROUZOU],'Αγγεῖα τοῦ 'Αναγυροῦντος 1. A detailed and well-illustrated study of some Late Protoattic works. 1963.

J. D. BEAZLEY, *Attic Black-figure Vase-painters*, 1–7. Lists works of some painters whom J. M. COOK and I call late Protoattic. 1956.

R. S. YOUNG, *Hesp* Supplement 2. Contains useful information about Protoattic, but dates its beginning twenty years later than COOK. 1939.

E. T. H. BRANN, *the Athenian Agora* 8. An illuminating survey of finds in the Agora. 1962.

E. T. H. BRANN, *Hesp* 1961, 305–79. Supplements the last item.

K. KÜBLER, *Kerameikos* 6.2. A detailed publication of finds from the Ceramicus cemetery. 1970.

Cook (as adjusted by J. N. COLDSTREAM) divides Protoattic into Early (700–675 B.C.), Middle (675–630 B.C.) and Late (630 to a little before 600 B.C.). Beazley classes Cook's Late Protoattic (or most of it) as early black-figure. My division is nearer Cook's.

Attic Black-figure

J. D. BEAZLEY, *Attic Black-figure Vase-painters* [*ABV*]. A monumental catalogue by painters of 10,000 pieces. 1956.

J. D. BEAZLEY, *Paralipomena*. Supplements *ABV*. 1971.

J. D. BEAZLEY, *the Development of Attic Black-figure*. An admirable, concise account. 1951.

I. SCHEIBLER, *JdI* 1961, 1–47. A good study of the Gorgon painter.

S. PAPASPYRIDI-KARUSU [S. KAROUZOU], *AM* 1937, 111–35. An account and catalogue of Sophilos, with whom she incorporates the Gorgon painter.

A. GREIFENHAGEN, *eine attische schwarzfigurige Vasen-gattung*. A good account of the Comast cups. 1929.

H. G. G. PAYNE, *Necrocorinthia*, 190–202. Useful for Corinthianizing groups of the early sixth century. 1931.

A. FURTWÄNGLER and K. REICHHOLD, *Griechische Vasenmalerei*, pls. 1–3 and 11–13. Complete drawings of the François vase. 1900–1.

H. THIERSCH, '*Tyrrhenische' Amphoren*. Still a standard work on Tyrrhenian amphorae. 1899.

D. VON BOTHMER, *AJA* 1944, 161–70. Groups Tyrrhenian amphorae by painters.

J. D. BEAZLEY, *MMS* 5, 93–115. An account of the C painter (mainly Siana cups). 1934.

J. D. BEAZLEY, *JHS* 1932, 167–204. A lucid account and list of signed Lip cups and Band cups.

P. N. URE, *JHS* 1932, 55–71. A good account and list of Droop cups. (Supplemented in *Studies Presented to D. M. Robinson* 2, 45–54. 1953.)

A. RUMPF, *Sakonides*. A good and well-illustrated study of Lydos, Sakonides and their connections, whom RUMPF combines into one painter. 1937.

G. M. A. RICHTER, *MMS* 4, 169–78. An account of Lydos. 1933.

J. D. BEAZLEY, *JHS* 1931, 256–85. On the Amasis painter and the earlier Heidelberg group of Siana cups.

S. KAROUZOU, *the Amasis Painter*. A well-illustrated account of the Amasis painter. 1956.

D. VON BOTHMER, *Antike Kunst* 1960, 71–80. Further information on the Amasis painter.

K. SCHAUENBURG, *JdI* 1964, 109–41. Yet more on the Amasis painter.

D. VON BOTHMER, *RA* 1969, 3–15. A short study of 'Elbows Out' and comments on the Affecter.

W. TECHNAU, *Exekias*. A well-illustrated account of Exekias and his group. 1936.

J. D. BEAZLEY, *JHS* 1927, 63–92. A good account of the Antimenes painter.

C. H. E. HASPELS, *Attic Black-figured Lekythoi*. A detailed analysis of late black-figure painters. 1936.

J. D. BEAZLEY, *AJA* 1943, 441–65. Notes on Panathenaic amphorae by known painters.

K. PETERS, *Studien zu den panathenäischen Preisamphoren*. Notable for attributions to red-figure painters. 1942.

G. R. EDWARDS, *Hesp* 1957, 320–49. On Hellenistic and Roman Panathenaic amphorae. (See also H. A. THOMPSON, *Hesp* 1960, 366–7.)

4. THE ARGOLID

J. M. COOK, *BSA* **48**, 42–50 and 57. An intelligent summary of finds from Mycenae. 1953.

P. COURBIN, *BCH* 1955, 1–32. For illustrations of the Polyphemus krater from Argos.

5. LACONIA

E. A. LANE, *BSA* **34**, 99–189. An excellent account. 1936.

J. BOARDMAN, *BSA* **58**, 1–7. Revises Lane's chronology. 1963.

B. B. SHEFTON, *BSA* **49**, 299–310. A fuller list of figured pieces with an undemonstrated conflation of painters. 1954.

J. P. DROOP in R. M. DAWKINS, *Artemis Orthia*, 66–109. Useful for illustrations of finds from Sparta. 1929.

6. BOEOTIA

P. N. URE, *Boeotian Pottery of the Geometric and Archaic Styles*. Still valuable for references, but I do not entirely accept the classification (which Ure himself later modified) and reckon II. A. ii and iv as Orientalizing: II. B⁴ is Corinthian. 1927.

F. CANCIANI, *JdI* 1965, 18–75. Contains useful groupings of Subgeometric and earlier Orientalizing.

R. HAMPE, *Frühe griechische Sagenbilder*, 20–31. For illustrations of earlier Orientalizing, but the classification is unsound. 1936.

J. BOEHLAU, *JdI* 1888, 325–64. For illustrations only of Bird cup group.

A. D. and P. N. URE, *AA* 1933, 1–42. Bird cup group and black-figure in Bonn.

J. D. BEAZLEY, *Attic Black-figure Vase-painters*, 13–14, 22–3, 29–31, 680. Early black-figure. 1956.

A. D. URE, *MMS* **4**, 18–38. Early black-figure lekanai. 1932.

A. D. URE, *JHS* 1929, 160–71. Early silhouette black-figure.

G. BRUNS in P. WOLTERS, *das Kabirenheiligtum bei Theben* **1**, 95–128. A general study of Cabiran. 1940.

A. D. URE, *BSA* **41**, 22–8. Some late black-figure groups. 1946.

A. D. URE, *JHS* 1926, 54–62. Late black-figure cups of southern group.

A. D. URE, *Hesp* 1946, 27–37. Late black-figure cups of northern group.

7. EUBOEA

J. BOARDMAN, *BSA* **47**, 1–48. A comprehensive study of pottery from Eretria, supplemented in *BSA* **52**, 15–22. 1952 and 1957.

K. KURUNIOTIS, *EA* 1903, 1–38. For illustrations of Geometric and early Orientalizing from Eretria.

A. D. URE, *BSA* **55**, 211–17; **58**, 14–19; **65**, 265–70. For black-figure mainly of the fourth century. 1960, 1963, 1970.

8. THE CYCLADES (see Concordance on p. 343)

H. DRAGENDORFF, *Thera* **2**, 198–210. Linear Island. 1903.

E. PFUHL, *AM* 1903, 183–93. Linear Island.

I. STRØM, *Acta Archaeologica* 1962, 221–78. Useful but partly speculative examination of Orientalizing groups before 'Melian'.

C. DUGAS and C. RHOMAIOS, *Délos* **15** (Ab and Ad). 1934.

C. MUSTAKAS, *AM* 1954/5, 153–8. Publishes finds of Ad group from Kimolos.

C. DUGAS, *Délos* **17** (all pots classed as Cycladic and some classed as Rhodo-Ionian). The classification is unreliable. 1935.

C. DUGAS, *Délos* **10**, plates 1–8. 'Melian'.

A. CONZE, *Melische Thongefässe*. Coloured plates of large 'Melian' amphorae. 1862.

J. K. BROCK, *BSA* **44**, 33–49. Finds from Siphnos; see also pp. 74–80 on general classification. 1949.

H. G. G. PAYNE, *JHS* 1926, 203–12. On Leyden group and general classification.

E. BUSCHOR, *AM* 1929, 142–63. On general classification.

C. KARUSOS, *JdI* 1937, 166–97. Publishes an amphora from Naxos and comments on classification; he dates too early.

J. BOARDMAN, *BSA* **47**, 24–6. Useful comments on 'Melian'; other comments on Cycladic elsewhere in this paper. 1952.

9. THE EAST GREEK CITIES
General

Clara Rhodos **3, 4, 6/7** (G. JACOPI), **8** (L. LAURENZI). For grave groups from Camirus and Ialysus in Rhodes. 1929, 1931, 1933, 1936.

K. F. KINCH, *Fouilles de Vroulia*. For grave groups from Vroulia in Rhodes and illustrations of other Rhodian finds. 1914.

Samos **5** (H. WALTER), nos. 301–631. Illustrates finds from Samos and some comparanda. 1968.

Bird Bowls

J. N. COLDSTREAM, *Greek Geometric Pottery*, 298–301. A concise analysis of the development. 1968.

Concordance of Classifications of Cycladic

(*Note:* the equations are approximate)

	Délos xv, xvii & x	Brock	Board-man	Buschor	Payne	Dugas (*Céram-ique des Cyclades*)	Pfuhl	Strøm	Coldstream *Greek Geometric Pottery*
Geom. & Subgeom.)	*Aa*	*Parian Geom.*	*Parian (Geom.) n. 79*	*Parian I(–II)*	—	—	—	*Parian Geom.*	'Parian' Geom.
Geom.)	*Bb*	*Naxian (Geom.) n. 8*	*Naxian Geom.*	*Naxian*	—	—	—	*Naxian Geom.*	*Naxian Geom.*
Wheel grp	*Ab* ⟨1–7⟩	*Parian Trans.*	*Parian n. 49 & Theran n. 79*	*Parian (Trans. I to II)*	—	*Island Geom.*	*Euboean* 'Besondere Gruppe' *J. 14–18*	*Parian*	'Parian' Geom.
heran Geom.	—	*Theran*	*Theran Geom.*	*Theran Geom.*	—	*Theran Geom.*	*Theran*	*Theran Geom.*	*Theran Geom.*
inear Island	—	*Parian Or. I*	*Theran n. 79*	*Parian II*	*Linear Island Geom. & Or. I*	*Island Geom.*	*Euboean*	*Southern Cycladic*	—
eyden grp	—	*Parian Or. II*	—	—	*Linear Island Or. II*	—	—	*Southern Cycladic (late)*	—
d grp	*Ad*	*Ad*	—	*? Siph-nian II*	—	—	—	*Parian (preced-ing* 'Melian')	'Parian'
eraldic grp	*Ba*	*Naxian Or. I (Heraldic grp)*	*Naxian (Or.) p. 21*	*Löwen-wappen grp*	*Proto-Melian*	*Argivo-Cycladic Or. I*	—	*Naxian*	*Naxian*
rotome grp	*C* ⟨1–7, 9⟩	*Naxian Or. II (Protome grp)*	*Naxian Or. n. 94*	*Parian III*	*Linear Island Or. III*	*Argivo-Cycladic Or. IV*	—	*?*	—
rp D	*D*	*D*	—	*? Siph-nian III*	—	*Argivo-Cycladic Or. V*	—	—	—
elian'	*Island (Or.)*	*Melian*	'Melian'	*Melian*	*Melian*	*Island Or.*	*Melian*	'Melian' (*Parian*)	—

(Geom. = Geometric; Trans. = Transitional; Or. = Orientalizing)

Wild Goat Style

C. KARDARA, Ροδιακή 'Αγγειογραφία. A valuable and detailed study, but unequal (see R. M. COOK, *Gnomon* 1965, 502–7). 1963.

W. SCHIERING, *Werkstätten Orientalisierender Keramik auf Rhodes*. A valuable detailed study, but the classification into Camirus, Euphorbos and Vlastos groups does not convince me. 1957.

A. RUMPF, *JdI* 1933, 61–3 and 69–83. Exposition of 'Camirus' and 'Euphorbos' grouping, with useful lists.

Samos 5 (H. WALTER), nos. 502–631. Publishes the material from Samos (with some from elsewhere). 1968.

Clara Rhodos 6/7 (G. JACOPI), 475–543. Publishes the material from Nisyros. 1933.

J. BOEHLAU and K. SCHEFOLD, *Larisa am Hermos* 3. For Aeolian, but the classification is too precise and the chronology hazardous. 1942.

C. H. GREENWALT, *Univ. of California Studies in Classical Antiquity* 1968, 139–50 and 1970, 55–89. For some Lydian imitations.

Chiot

J. BOARDMAN, [*Excavations in Chios, 1952–1955*:] *Greek Emporio*, 102–53 and 156–75. A valuable survey. 1967.

E. R. PRICE, *JHS* 1924, 205–22. Useful illustrations.

J. BOARDMAN, *BSA* 51, 55–62. A partisan claim for manufacture in Naucratis with some useful general comments. 1956.

Ionian Little Master Cups

E. KUNZE, *AM* 1934, 81–122. A detailed study.

Fikellura

R. M. COOK, *BSA* 34, 1–98. Attempts a detailed analysis. 1936.

CVA British Museum 8 (R. M. COOK), pls. 568–81. For illustrations. 1954.

Clazomenian and other East Greek Black-figure

J. M. COOK, *BSA* 60, 114–42. A good account of various groups from Smyrna. 1965.

R. M. COOK, *BSA* 47, 123–52. A short provisional analysis of Clazomenian. 1952.

CVA British Museum 8, pls. 582–95. For illustrations of Clazomenian. 1954.

Clazomenian Sarcophagi

K. F. JOHANSEN, *Acta Archaeologica* 1942, 1–64. A good study of early sarcophagi.

CVA British Museum 8 (R. M. COOK), 45–56. Attempts a short general classification. 1954.

R. M. COOK, *Anatolia* 1966, 179–92. On the earliest sarcophagi.

Situlae

CVA British Museum 8 (R. M. COOK), 29–37 and pls. 596–605. For illustrations and a speculative account. 1954.

Vroulian

K. F. KINCH, *Fouilles de Vroulia*, 168–90. For illustrations. 1914.

East Greek Cups

F. VILLARD and G. VALLET, *Mél* 1955, 14–34. A useful general study, though too precise and claiming too much as East Greek.

J. HAYES in J. BOARDMAN and J. HAYES, *Excavations at Tocra, 1963–1965: the Archaic Deposits* I, 111–34. Corrects and refines the classification of VILLARD and VALLET. 1966.

(Bucchero *Grey ware*)

W. LAMB, *JHS* 1932, 1–12. For finds from Lesbos. (*Cf.* also *BSA* 32, 51–6. 1934.)

J. BOEHLAU and K. SCHEFOLD, *Larisa am Hermos* 3, 99–128. For finds from Larisa in Aeolis. 1942.

10. THASOS

Études Thasiennes 7 (L. GHALI-KAHIL). A selection of finds from Thasos. 1960.

11. CRETE

J. K. BROCK, *Fortetsa*. Contains much information on Orientalizing at Cnossus. 1957.

J. BOARDMAN, *BSA* 56, 78–80. Isolates the Fortetsa painter. 1961.

D. LEVI, *Hesp* 1945, 1–32. Useful for illustrations.

H. G. G. PAYNE, *BSA* 29, 277–98. Exaggerates the earliness and importance of Cretan. 1928.

D. LEVI, *ASA* 10/12. Material from Arkades (Afrati). 1931.

12. ITALY

Greek Colonial

G. VALLET and F. VILLARD, *Mégara Hyblaea* **2**, 137–99. An intelligent account of local pottery at Megara Hyblaea. 1964.

P. E. ARIAS, *BCH* 1936, 144–51. Publishes the Fusco kraters from Syracuse, but supposes them imported.

T. J. DUNBABIN, *the Western Greeks*, 261–4. References to colonial imitations generally. 1948.

Apulian and Lucanian

M. MAYER, *Apulien*. A general study, which needs revision. 1914.

CVA British Museum 7, pls. 456–67 (F. N. PRYCE). Useful illustrations and summary. 1932.

Italocorinthian

J. SIEVEKING and R. HACKL, *die k. Vasensammlung zu München*, nos. 610–795. A comprehensive set of illustrations. 1912.

J. G. SZILÁGYI, *AC* 1968, 1–23. A convenient summary of recent work on the Ripe style.

Etruscan Bucchero

N. H. RAMAGE, *BSR* **38**, 1–61. A careful survey of early groups. 1970.

P. MINGAZZINI, *Vasi della Coll. Castellani*, 1–60. Useful for parallels. 1930.

S. GSELL, *Fouilles dans la Nécropole de Vulci*. Useful for grave groups. 1891.

R. SUNKOWSKY, *ÖJh* **40**, 117–26. Explains technique of decoration in relief. 1953.

Etruscan Black-figure

T. DOHRN, *die schwarzfigurigen Etruskischen Vasen*. A detailed study till the early fifth century. 1937.

J. D. BEAZLEY, *la Raccolta B. Guglielmi* I, nos. 87–106, and *Etruscan Vase-painting*, 11–24. Enlarges and rearranges DOHRN's groups. 1939 and 1947.

J. SIEVEKING and R. HACKL, *die k. Vasensammlung zu München*, nos. 796–1014. A good series of illustrations. 1912.

P. DUCATI, *Pontische Vasen*. Good illustrations of Pontic. 1932.

'Chalcidian'

A. RUMPF, *Chalkidische Vasen*. A thorough and fully illustrated study. 1927.

H. R. W. SMITH, *the Origin of Chalcidian Ware* (Univ. of California Publications in Classical Archaeology 1, 85–149). Asserts against RUMPF its Etruscan manufacture. 1932.

G. VALLET, *Rhégion et Zancle*, 211–28. Puts the case for Rhegion. 1958.

Northampton Group

E. WALTER-KARYDI, *CVA München* 6, 42–3. For illustrations and references. 1968.

Campana Group

F. VILLARD, *Mon Piot* 43, 33–57. A good study, but assigns group to Rhodes. 1949.

R. M. COOK and J. M. HEMELRIJK, *Jahrbuch der Berliner Museum* 1963, 107–20. Modify Villard's account.

Caeretan Hydriai

J. M. HEMELRIJK, *de Caeretaanse Hydriae*. A good, detailed study. 1956.

CVA Louvre 9, pls. 609–20 (N. PLAOUTINE). For illustrations. 1938.

P. DEVAMBEZ, *Mon Piot* 41, 29–62. For illustrations. 1946.

M. SANTANGELO, *Mon Piot* 44, 1–43. For illustrations. 1950.

Campanian Black-figure

CVA Capua 3 (P. MINGAZZINI), pls. 1293–1303. Illustrations of earlier and later classes, with useful comments and references. 1958.

F. P. BADONI, *Ceramica Campana a Figure Nere*. A general study of the earlier class. 1968.

E. ROHDE, *Wissenschaftliche Zeitschrift der Universität Rostock,* Ges. und Spr. Reihe 7/8, 499–505. Useful comments on the earlier class. 1967.

13. THE EASTERN FRINGES

E. AKURGAL, *Phrygische Kunst*, 1–59. A pioneering study of Phrygian pottery. 1955.

A. DELLA SETA, *EA* 1937, 629–54. For illustrations of some of the finer pieces from Lemnos.

D. MUSTILLI, *ASA* 15/16. Useful for grave groups from Lemnos and for illustrations. 1942.

Chapter 5: The Red-figure Style

2. ATTICA

General Works

J. D. BEAZLEY, *Attic Red-figure Vase-painters* ed. 2 [*ARV²*]. The indispensable catalogue by painters of 21,000 red-figure and white-ground pieces. 1963.

J. D. BEAZLEY, *Paralipomena*. Supplements *ARV²*. 1971.

J. D. BEAZLEY, *Attic Red-figured Vases in American Museums* [*VA*]. Contains a lucid summary of the style till the end of the fifth century. 1918.

E. PFUHL, *Malerei und Zeichnung der Griechen* [*MuZ*]. A long and mainly reliable account, useful for the number of illustrations. 1923.

E. PFUHL (translated by J. D. BEAZLEY), *Masterpieces of Greek Drawing and Painting*. An abridged and amended version of the last item. 1926 (reprinted with revised bibliography 1955).

G. M. A. RICHTER, *Attic Red-figured Vases*. A rather statistical survey, based on BEAZLEY. 1958.

J. D. BEAZLEY, *Attic White Lekythoi* [*AWL*]. A short general account. 1938.

E. BUSCHOR, *Münchner Jahrbuch der bildenden Kunst* 1925, 167–99 ('Attische Lekythen der Parthenonzeit'). A detailed study of white-ground lekythoi.

W. RIEZLER, *Weissgrundige attische Lekythen*. Most useful for illustrations of white-ground lekythoi. 1914.

K. SCHEFOLD, *Kertscher Vasen*. A well-illustrated short account of the progressive late painters. 1930.

K. SCHEFOLD, *Untersuchungen zu den Kertscher Vasen*. A detailed, but not wholly reliable study of the progressive late painters. 1934.

L. TALCOTT and B. PHILIPPAKI, *Hesp* Supplement 10, 1–77. Valuable for the poorer red-figure of the fourth century. 1956.

L. D. CASKEY and J. D. BEAZLEY, *Attic Vase Painting in the Museum of Fine Arts, Boston* 1–3. A catalogue with excellent illustrations and commentary. 1931, 1954 and 1963.

A. FURTWÄNGLER and K. REICHHOLD (and others), *Griechische Vasenmalerei* 1–3. Contains accurate drawings and descriptions of many important pieces. 1900–32.

R. LULLIES, *Griechische Vasen der reifarchaischen Zeit*. Admirable photographs of some Archaic pieces. 1953.

P. E. ARIAS, M. HIRMER and B. B. SHEFTON, *a History of Greek Vase-painting*. Admirable photographs and erudite notes. 1962.

P. JACOBSTHAL, *Ornamente griechischer Vasen*. A detailed and well-illustrated study, mainly of red-figure ornaments. 1927.

H. BLOESCH, *Formen attischer Schalen*. A pioneer study of the shapes of red-figure cups till *c.* 450 B.C. 1940.

Special Studies

H. MARWITZ, *ÖJh* **46,** 73–104. An interesting examination of the Andocides painter. 1961–3.

A. BRUHN, *Oltos and Early Red-figure Vase Painting*. A well-illustrated survey. 1943.

H. R. W. SMITH, *New Aspects of the Menon Painter* (University of California Publications in Classical Archaeology 1, 1–64). A good account of the painter now identified as Psiax. 1929.

W. KRAIKER, *JdI* 1929, 141–97. A useful paper on Epictetus.

J. D. BEAZLEY, *der Kleophrades-Maler*. A lucid and well-illustrated estimate of the Cleophrades painter. 1933.

J. D. BEAZLEY, *der Berliner Maler*. A comparable study of the Berlin painter. 1930.

J. D. BEAZLEY, *der Pan-Maler*. A comparable study of the Pan painter. 1931.

F. P. JOHNSON, *AJA* 1945, 491–502. A useful study of Hermonax.

J. D. BEAZLEY, *RM* 1912, 286–97. A close analysis of the Villa Giulia painter.

T. B. L. WEBSTER, *der Niobiden-Maler*. A well-illustrated account of the Niobid painter. 1935.

H. DIEPOLDER, *BWP* **110.** A well-illustrated account of the Pistoxenos painter. 1954.

H. DIEPOLDER, *der Penthesilea-Maler*. A well-illustrated account of the Penthesilea painter, but conflating the Pistoxenos painter (pls. 1–8) with him. 1936.

H. R. W. SMITH, *der Lewis-Maler*. A well-illustrated analysis of the Lewis painter and his group. 1939.

J. D. BEAZLEY, *JHS* 1914, 179–226. A close analysis of the Achilles painter.

S. PAPASPYRIDI [S. KAROUZOU], *A Delt* 1923, 117–46. A good account of the Reed painter.

W. HAHLAND, *Vasen um Meidias*. A well-illustrated survey of painters of around the end of the fifth century. 1930.

F. P. JOHNSON in *Studies Presented to D. M. Robinson* **2**, 96–105. A useful study of owl-kotylai. 1953. (Supplemented in *AJA* 1955, 119–24.)

S. HOWARD and F. P. JOHNSON, *AJA* 1954, 191–208. A classification of the St Valentin group, consisting of small pots with simple ornaments and mostly of the second half of the fifth century.

M. CROSBY, *Hesp* 1955, 76–84. Publishes a late fifth-century group with polychrome comic figures.

3. CORINTH

P. E. CORBETT in T. J. DUNBABIN, *Perachora* **2**, 286–9. A provisional survey of Corinthian Rf. 1962.

A. D. URE, *JHS* 1949, 18–24. On the Haloa group, here wrongly assigned to Boeotia.

4. BOEOTIA

R. LULLIES, *AM* 1940, 1–27. A good account of fifth-century painters.

A. D. URE, *AJA* 1958, 389–95. On two painters of the later fifth century.

A. D. URE, *AJA* 1953, 245–9. On the group with women's heads.

5. ETRURIA

J. D. BEAZLEY, *Etruscan Vase-painting* [*EVP*]. A fundamental study and catalogue, though reticent about the dating of the later groups. 1947.

H. DRAGENDORFF, *JdI* 1928, 331–59. On the Praxias group.

C. ALBIZZATI, *RM* 1915, 129–60. On the school of (Clusium and) Volterra.

M. M. PASQUINUCCI, *le Kelebai Volterrane*. A well-illustrated catalogue of the (later) school of Volterra. 1968.

M. A. DEL CHIARD, *SE* 1970, 91–102. References for some minor late groups and tentative attributions to Caere and Tarquinia.

M. A. DEL CHIARO, *the Genucilia Group* (Univ. of California Publications in Classical Archaeology **3**, 243–372). On the Genucilia plates. 1957.

6. SOUTH ITALY

Red-figure

A. D. TRENDALL, *South Italian Vase Painting* (British Museum guide). A good short survey. 1966.

A. D. TRENDALL, *Frühitaliotische Vasen*. A short well-illustrated account of Early Lucanian and Apulian. 1938.

M. SCHMIDT, *der Dareiosmaler und sein Umkreis*. An account of a leading Apulian Ornate painter. 1960.

A. D. TRENDALL, *Jahrbuch der Berliner Museen*, 1970, 174–90. On the antecedents of the Darius painter.

A. CAMBITOGLOU and A. D. TRENDALL, *Apulian Red-figured Vase-painters of the Plain Style*. The standard study. 1961.

A. CAMBITOGLOU and A. D. TRENDALL, *AJA* 1969, 423–33. Addenda to the last item.

A. D. TRENDALL, *the Red-figured Vases of Lucania, Campania and Sicily*. A fundamental catalogue, critical and well illustrated, which assigns 5,000 pieces to their painters [*LCS*]. 1967.

A. D. TRENDALL, *ditto: First Supplement* (Bulletin of the Institute of Classical Studies of the University of London, Supplement **26**). Supplements *LCS*. 1970.

A. D. TRENDALL, *Paestan Pottery*. A comprehensive and well-illustrated study of Paestan. Supplemented and revised in *BSR* **20**, 1–53, **21**, 160–7, **27**, 1–37. 1936, 1952, 1953 and 1959.

E. GRECO, *il Pittore di Afrodite*. On an early Paestan painter of Apulian antecedents. 1970.

A. D. TRENDALL, *Phlyax Vases* ed. 2 (Bulletin of the Institute of Classical Studies of the University of London, Supplement **19**). A list with short introduction. 1967.

L. LACROIX, *la Faune Marine dans la décoration des Plats à Poissons*. Well illustrated; but on the text see A. D. TRENDALL, *JHS* 1937, 268–9. 1937.

K. ZIMMERMANN, *Wissenschaftliche Zeitschrift der Universität Rostock*, Ges. und Spr. Reihe 7/8, 561–70. Further comments on fish plates. 1967.

H. HOFFMANN, *Tarentine Rhyta*. A catalogue and study of South Italian rhyta. 1966.

H. SICHTERMANN, *Griechische Vasen in Unteritalion*. Excellent illustrations of Apulian. 1966.

Gnathian

L. FORTI, *la Ceramica di Gnathia*. A useful preliminary survey. 1965.

T. B. L. WEBSTER, *Bulletin of the Institute of Classical Studies of the University of London* 1968, 1–33. A more precise classification of Gnathian in Apulia.

J. R. GREEN, *ib.*, 34–50. Identifies some Gnathian painters.

CVA Naples 3 (A. ROCCO). A good set of illustrations. 1954.

M. BERNARDINI, *Vasi dello Stile di Gnathia; Vasi a Vernice Nera.* Another good set of illustrations. 1961.

MISCELLANEOUS

L. STEPHANI, *Compte-Rendu de la Commission Impériale Archéologique* 1874, 42–51. A clear account of some South Russian attempts at red-figure.

Chapter 6: Hellenistic Pottery with Painted Decoration

2. WEST SLOPE WARE

C. WATZINGER, *AM* 1901, 67–102. Still a useful analysis.

H. A. THOMPSON, *Hesp* 1934, 438–47. Supplements WATZINGER'S account.

3. THE LAGYNOS GROUP

G. LEROUX, *Lagynos*. A good study. 1913.

J. SCHÄFER, *Hellenistische Keramik aus Pergamon*, 101–15. Helpful comments based on finds at Pergamum. 1968.

4. HADRA WARE

R. PAGENSTECHER, *Expedition E. von Sieglin* 2.3, 32–52. A short analysis. 1913.

E. BRECCIA, *la Necropoli di Sciatbi*, 26–8 and 33–45. A shorter analysis. 1912.

L. GUERRINI, *Vasi di Hadra* (Studi Miscellanei 8). Classifies and illustrates the dark-painted group; the dating and connections are dubious (see B. F. COOK, *AJA* 1966, 205). 1964.

B. F. COOK, *Inscribed Hadra Vases in the Metropolitan Museum of Art.* Makes some good general points. 1966.

H. BRAUNERT, *JdI* 1950/1, 231–63. Corrects the dating of the hydriai inscribed with regnal years.

B. F. COOK, *Brooklyn Museum Annual* **10**, 115–38. Some additions and corrections to BRAUNERT. 1968/9.

5. CANOSA WARE

M. JATTA, *RM* 1914, 101–9 and 116–26. A brief but useful account.

6. CENTURIPAE WARE

G. LIBERTINI, *Centuripe*, 145–86. A useful collection of the material. 1926.

G. LIBERTINI, *Atti e Memorie della Società Magna Grecia* 1932, 187–212. Supplements the last item.

G. M. A. RICHTER, *MMS* **2**, 187–205, and **4**, 45–54. Contains good illustrations and technical notes. 1930 and 1932.

MISCELLANEOUS

T. N. KNIPOVITCH, *Sovetskaya Archeologiya* **7**, 140–51. A short account of a light-ground group from South Russia. 1941.

CVA Copenhagen **4**, pls. 185–6 (C. BLINKENBERG and K. F. JOHANSEN). Illustrations of Hellenistic pots from Rhodes. 1931.

F. MAIER, *JdI* 1963, 218–55. A provisional study of 'Galatian' light-ground ware.

M. JATTA, *RM* 1914, 110–15 and 123–4. Illustrates some Daunian pots.

CVA British Museum **7**, pls. 446–7 (F. N. PRYCE). Illustrations of Daunian and some sound notes. 1932.

E. POTTIER, *Mon Piot* **20**, 163–79. A short description of Carthaginian oinochoai. 1913.

Chapter 7: Black-painted and Relief Wares

B. A. SPARKES and L. TALCOTT, *The Athenian Agora* **12**. An excellent detailed account of Attic black-painted ware from the sixth to the fourth century. 1970.

A. D. URE, *JHS* 1936, 205–15 and 1944, 67–77. Lists Attic red-figure cups with impressed decoration.

G. KOPCKE, *AM* 1964, 22–84. A good study of fourth-century Attic black-painted ware with gilded decoration.

H. A. THOMPSON, *Hesp* 1934, 429–38. A provisional survey of Attic black-painted ware of the third and second centuries.

P. N. URE, *Black Glaze Pottery from Rhitsona*. A careful study of some Boeotian black-painted ware. 1913.

J.–P. MOREL, *Mél* 1963, 7–58 and 1969, 59–117. Provisional studies of Campanian black-painted wares.

H. COMFORT in PAULY–WISSOWA–KROLL, *Real-Encyclopädie* Supplementband 7, 1295–1352. Still a useful survey of Sigillata. 1940.

R. J. CHARLESTON, *Roman Pottery* ed. 2. A brief illustrated survey of the pottery of the Roman Empire. 1972.

F. COURBY, *les Vases grecs à Reliefs*. A comprehensive account of Greek relief wares, but needing much revision. 1922.

J. SCHÄFER, *Studien zu den griechischen Reliefpithoi des 8.–6. Jahrhunderts v. Chr. aus Kreta, Rhodos, Tenos and Boiotien*. A useful arrangement of the material. 1957.

N. M. KONDOLEON, *EA* 1969, 215–36. For early Cycladic relief ware.

C. A. CHRISTOU, *A Delt* 1964, 164–265. For early Laconian relief ware.

D. FEYTMANS, *BCH* 1950, 135–80 and 1952, 197–200. For Rhodian coarse amphorae with stamped decoration.

S. S. WEINBERG, *Hesp* 1954, 109–37. Collects earlier stamped and relief wares from Corinth.

E. A. ZERVOUDAKI, *AM* 1968, 1–88. A detailed study of polychrome Attic relief ware of the late fifth and fourth centuries.

W. SCHWABACHER, *AJA* 1941, 182–228. The fullest study of Attic 'Megarian' bowls.

G. R. EDWARDS, *Hesp* Supplement 10, 79–112. Some good observations on 'Megarian' bowls from Athens. 1956.

U. HAUSMANN, *Hellenistische Reliefbecher aus attischen und böotischen Werkstätten*. A detailed study of 'Megarian' bowls with Homeric scenes. 1959.

R. PAGENSTECHER, *JdI* Erganzungsheft 8. A detailed study of Calene, though in part wrong on its dates and relations. 1909.

G. M. A. RICHTER, *AJA* 1941, 383–9 and 1959, 241–9. Some corrections to Pagenstecher's account of Calene.

H. DRAGENDORFF and C. WATZINGER. *Arretinische Reliefkeramik*. The standard general account. 1948.

CVA Metropolitan Museum, New York 1 (C. ALEXANDER). Excellent illustrations for moulded Arretine. 1943.

V. R. GRACE, *Hesp* Supplement **10**, 113–89. A good entry into the study of unpainted amphorae with stamped handles. 1956.

Much useful material and criticism is included in the more conscientious reports of excavations, such as those of Labraunda, Olympia, Olynthus, Pergamum, Priene, Samaria, Sparta and Tarsus.

Chapter 8: Shapes

E. DIEHL, *die Hydria*, 49–64, 223–36. An account of the development of the hydria till Hellenistic. 1964.

B. PHILIPPAKI, *the Attic Stamnos*. A detailed study. 1967.

H. BLOESCH, *Formen attischer Schalen*. A meticulous and well-illustrated analysis of the shapes of Attic cups from *c.* 540 to *c.* 450 B.C. 1940.

G. LEROUX, *Lagynos*. A fair account of the lagynos. 1913.

G. M. A. RICHTER and M. J. MILNE, *Shapes and Names of Athenian Vases*. Gives evidence for conventional names, bibliography and illustrations of the principal Attic shapes from the mid sixth to the mid fourth century. 1935.

D. A. AMYX, *Hesp* 1958, 163–254. Contains some useful evidence on ancient nomenclature.

F. BROMMER, *Hermes* 1942, 356–73. A cautionary examination of the names of pots in Homer.

L. D. CASKEY, *Geometry of Greek Vases*. An excellent collection of measured drawings of Attic shapes of the later sixth and fifth centuries, and some fanciful theory. 1922.

D. K. HILL, *AJA* 1947, 248–56. A salutary, but exaggerated denial of the influence of metal on earthenware shapes.

Many special studies on particular schools or groups of vase-painting include a discussion of the relevant shapes.

Chapter 9: Technique

J. V. NOBLE, *the Techniques of Painted Attic Pottery*. A comprehensive and generally reliable compendium. 1966.

A. WINTER in *Technische Beiträge zur Archäologie*, 1–45. Useful particularly on the preparation of clay. 1959.

U. HOFMANN, *Angewandte Chemie* (International edition) 1962, 343–50. Adds some chemical explanations.

M. FARNSWORTH, *AJA* 1970, 9–20. Analyses of some Corinthian clays.

R. M. COOK, *BSA* **56**, 64–7. Contains a list of kilns excavated in Greece. 1961.

Chapter 10: Inscriptions

2. INSCRIPTIONS BEFORE FIRING

P. KRETSCHMER, *die griechischen Vaseninschriften*. The only comprehensive study, and still useful. 1894.

H. G. G. PAYNE, *Necrocorinthia*, 38–9 and 158–69. Lists and discusses inscriptions on Corinthian pots. 1931.

J. D. BEAZLEY, *Attic Black-figure Vase-painters*, 664–78 and 847–51. Lists signatures and καλός names in Attic black-figure. 1956.

J. D. BEAZLEY, *JHS* 1932, 167–204. Lists and discusses inscriptions on Attic Little Master cups.

J. C. HOPPIN, *a Handbook of Greek Black-figured Vases*. For signatures on black-figure other than Attic. 1924.

R. M. COOK and A. G. WOODHEAD, *BSA* **47**, 159–70. List and discuss inscriptions on Chiot pots. 1952.

A. RUMPF, *Chalkidische Vasen*, 40–53. Lists and discusses inscriptions on 'Chalcidian' pots. 1927.

J. D. BEAZLEY, *Attic Red-figure Vase-painters*, ed. 2, 1553–1616. Lists signatures and καλός names in Attic red-figure. 1963.

3. INSCRIPTIONS AFTER FIRING

H. BRAUNERT, *JdI* 1950/1, 231–63. Discusses the dated inscriptions on Hadra hydriai.

R. HACKL in *Münchener Archäologische Studien*, 1–106. A detailed and cautious study of commercial inscriptions. 1909.

D. A. AMYX, *an Amphora with a Price Inscription* (Univ. of California Publications in Classical Archaeology **1**: 179–206). Adds usefully to HACKL. 1941.

Many excavation reports include some inscriptions on pots. Generally the fewer that were found the more fully are they published. Captions are the first to be omitted, then dedications.

Epigraphically important inscriptions are examined in L. H. JEFFERY, *the Local Scripts of Archaic Greece*. 1961.

Chapter 11: Chronology

Most special studies of particular schools discuss the relevant evidence for their dating. The references listed below are for the material associated with the fixed absolute dates rather than for the interpretation of that material, which is usually done better in the special studies: of these J. N. COLDSTREAM's *Greek Geometric Pottery* may be singled out for its discussion of Tell Abu Hawam, Megiddo, Samaria and Hama (pp. 302–11), of Syracuse, Megara Hyblaea and Gela (pp. 324–6) and of the Bocchoris grave at Ischia (pp. 316–17). For the bracketing of Samaria with the Bocchoris grave and of Old Smyrna with Meṣad Ḥashavyahu see *BSA* **64,** 13–15.

Amarna. W. M. F. PETRIE, *Tell el Amarna*, 16–17. 1894.

Philistines. A. M. SNODGRASS, *the Dark Age of Greece*, 107–9. 1971.

Tell Abu Hawam. R. W. HAMILTON, *Quarterly of the Department of Antiquities in Palestine* 1935, 23–4 and 67–8; W. A. HEURTLEY, *ib.*, 181.

Megiddo. C. CLAIRMONT, *Bérytus* 1955, pl. 20. 1–2.

Samaria. J. W. CROWFOOT, *Samaria-Sebaste* **3,** 210–13. 1957.

Hama. K. F. JOHANSEN, *Acta Archaeologica* 1957, 107.

Syracuse. G. VALLET and F. VILLARD, *BCH* 1952, 329–35.

Megara Hyblaea. G. VALLET and F. VILLARD, *BCH* 1952, 335–40.

Ischia, Bocchoris grave. M. W. STOOP, *Antiquity and Survival* 1955, 265 fig. 17.

Tarsus. G. M. A. HANFMANN in H. GOLDMAN, *Excavations at Gözlü Kule, Tarsus* **3,** 19–20, etc. 1963. But see J. BOARDMAN, *JHS* 1965, 5–15.

Gela I. P. ORSI, *MA* **17.** 1906.

Aziris. J. BOARDMAN, *BSA* **61,** 150–2. 1966.

Selinus. G. VALLET and F. VILLARD, *BCH* 1958, 16–26 (for the earliest finds). E. GÀBRICI, *MA* **32,** 1927.

Old Smyrna. J. K. ANDERSON, *BSA* **53/54,** 143–8. 1958/9.

Meṣad Ḥashavyahu. J. NAVEH, *Israel Exploration Journal* 1960, 129–39; 1962, 27–32 and 89–113.

Scarabs. T. G. H. JAMES in T. J. DUNBABIN, *Perachora* **2,** 461–4. 1962.

Siphnian Treasury. E. LANGLOTZ, *zur Zeitbestimmung der strengrotfigurigen Vasenmalerei*, 17–23. 1920.

Tell Defenneh. *CVA British Museum* **8** (R. M. COOK), 57–60. 1954.

Marathon. V. STAIS, *AM* 1893, 46–63.

Athens, Persian sack. B. GRAEF, *die antiken Vasen von der Akropolis zu Athen.* 1909–33.

Camarina II. P. ORSI, *MA* **14**, 783–892. 1904.

Delos, purification. C. DUGAS, *Délos* **21**, 1952.

Thespiae, Polyandrion. R. LULLIES, *AM* 1940, 8–10.

Athens, grave of Lacedaemonians. J. D. BEAZLEY, *ARV²*, 1344. 1963.

Motya. (Material mostly unpublished.)

Olynthus. D. M. ROBINSON, *Excavations at Olynthus* **5** and **13**. 1933 and 1950.

Gela II. P. ORLANDINI, *AC* 1957, 44–75.

Chaeronea. (Material in Chaeronea Museum and National Museum, Athens.)

Alexandria. E. BRECCIA, *La Necropoli di Sciatbi.* 1912.

Alexander, representations. A. FURTWÄNGLER in FR **2**, 150–5. 1906.

Lipari. A. D. TRENDALL in *Meligunìs-Lipára* (L. BERNABÒ-BREA and M. CAVALIER) **2**, 269–89. 1965.

Koroni. E. VANDERPOOL, J. R. MCCREDIE and A. STEINBERG, *Hesp* 1962, 26–61 and 1964, 69–75.

8th and 7th centuries generally. T. J. DUNBABIN, *EA* 1953/4. **2**, 247–62. A valuable examination, though in parts questionable.

Scientific Aids. D. BROTHWELL and E. HIGGS, *Science in Archaeology* ed. 2, 46–57 (Radiocarbon, E. H. WILLIS), 76–87 (Thermoremanent Magnetism, R. M. COOK), 106–8 (Thermoluminescence, E. T. HALL). 1969. (See also M. J. AITKEN, *Philosophical Transactions of the Royal Society of London* **A.269**, 77–88. On Thermoremanent Magnetism and Thermoluminescence. 1970.)

Chapter 12: The Pottery Industry

J. D. BEAZLEY, *Potter and Painter in Ancient Athens.* Offers some shrewd comments on Attic workshops. 1946.

See also the Bibliography to Chapter 10.

Chapter 13: Uses for Other Studies

Most special studies of the schools of Greek pottery include sections on distribution and subjects.

R. M. COOK, *JdI* 1959, 114–23. A rather fuller statement on trade.

F. VILLARD, *la Céramique grecque de Marseille*, 72–161. The most rational, though not entirely convincing, attempt to make economic sense of Greek pottery. 1960.

F. BROMMER, *Vasenlisten zur griechischen Heldensage* ed.2. An invaluable catalogue of heroic subjects in Greek vase-painting. 1960.

H. METZGER, *les Représentations dans la Céramique attique du IV siècle* and *Recherches sur l'Imagerie athénienne.* A good study of the subjects of later Attic Rf. 1951 and 1965.

Chapter 15: The History of the Study of Vase-painting

This subject has been neglected. Even the writers of special studies usually do not go far back. The notable exceptions are for Geometric F. POULSEN, *die Dipylongräber und die Dipylonvasen* (1905), 50–71, and for 'Chalcidian' A. RUMPF, *Chalkidische Vasen* (1927), 1–6.

O. JAHN, *Beschreibung der Vasensammlung*, ix–lxxxv. Gives a brief account of the history of the study and early collections, and a fuller account of places of finding. (The introduction to the *Beschreibung* is sometimes cited as JAHN, *Einleitung*.) 1854.

C. B. STARK, *Handbuch der Archäologie der Kunst.* Useful for its short biographies. 1880.

Katalog der Bibliothek des deutschen archäologischen Instituts in Rom 2. 1, 560–732 and 809–23. Classifies by title most books and papers published from 1825 till 1925 and some earlier works. 1932.

Note on Museums

Most museums outside Greek lands, that is museums which have no local sites to fill them with Greek pottery, are much the same in their composition. That is because they have been formed in much the same way. Since the first and far the largest supplies came from Italy, there is a core of Corinthian, later Attic black-figure, Attic red-figure till the end of the fifth century, South Italian red-figure and Etruscan (especially bucchero). Part of this went originally to private collectors, but private collections generally end in public museums, large or small. A much scantier and less evenly spread contribution from Rhodes provides Rhodian Mycenaean and Geometric, Wild Goat style and Fikellura, as well as more Corinthian and Attic black-figure. Attic Geometric, which can still be obtained, is dispersed widely. There is also more than enough Cypriot pottery of the Early Iron Age. Besides these constituents, which since they come from graves consist mainly of whole pots, East Greek and Attic sherds from Naucratis, mostly of the sixth century, were widely distributed. Examples of other wares are comparatively rare; their possession depends on the luck or management of each museum. Of the largest collections the most varied are those in the British Museum and the Louvre, which were active in acquiring pottery at the time when opportunities were good.

In the regions where Greek pottery is unearthed the museums are no more complete in their range, since they contain local finds and little else. It is easy to guess the character of Italian museums, though not their quality. In Greece the standard of finds has been poorer, but since the free export of ancient pottery was prohibited before much had been discovered there are several schools and groups that are rarely or never to be seen elsewhere.

Generally the museums of Greece and Italy will continue to grow as long as excavation flourishes. Some of them are already badly overcrowded, but national and professional pride are not likely to allow the reasonable solution of selling off the surplus. In most other countries the supply of pots is short. There is some reshuffling of ownership, when the dwindling private collections come onto the market, but in recent years only the Russians have honoured the ancient custom of taking works of art as reparations of war, though they too soon weakened so far as to send them back. Selections of second-rate sherds are sometimes given to honest excavators and may fill some gaps in foreign collections. But fine or rare pieces are likely to be got only through the antique trade, and their nature depends on where at the time clandestine digging is being successful. The casuists might well consider the proper conduct of the director of a museum.

Most museums of any importance have published some sort of catalogue. In the nineteenth century these catalogues were usually fairly complete in their listing, but neither detailed nor illustrated; and even when their numbering is still retained they have little value except for the history of scholarship or of the collection. Later catalogues are often illustrated and sometimes learned, but more rarely comprehensive. In general the bigger and established museums are dilatory; Copenhagen is a notable exception. But some of the museums of middling size, especially when connected with a university, have produced good catalogues, of which Würzburg's is exemplary.

The list that follows is only a rough guide to the major collections. The principle of choosing varies from one country to another, or the Italian entry would be still longer. The citing of catalogues too is unjust, particularly for those museums which are stocked from excavations; for some excavators publish their pottery satisfactorily and it would be extravagant to do the job again.

I. Greece, Turkey and Italy

Museum	Principal Source	Illustrated Catalogue
GREECE		
Athens, N.M.	Greek mainland (and some Aegean islands)	*CVA*. M. COLLIGNON and L. COUVE, *Catalogue des vases peints* (1902–4). B. GRAEF, *die antiken Vasen von der Akropolis zu Athen* (1909–33)
Athens, Agora Mus.	Athens, Agora	*Hesp* (casually) and *the Athenian Agora* **8** (1962), **12** (1970)
Athens, Ceramicus Mus.	Athens, Ceramicus	*Kerameikos* **1, 4, 5, 6** (1939–)
Corinth	Corinth	*Corinth* **7.1** (1943) and **13** (1964), and casually in *Hesp*.
Aegina	Aegina	W. KRAIKER, *Aigina* (1951)
Heraklion	Crete	
Mykonos	Rheneia (Purification deposit)	*Délos* **15, 17, 21** (1934–)
Thera	Thera	H. DRAGENDORFF, *Thera* **2** (1903). E. PFUHL, *AM* 1903, 1–290
Rhodes	Rhodes, Nisyros	*Cl Rh* **3, 4, 6/7, 8** (1929–36)

Museum	*Principal Source*	*Illustrated Catalogue*
TURKEY		
Istanbul	Asia Minor and Rhodes	
Smyrna	Western Asia Minor (recent finds)	
ITALY		
Rome, Vatican	Etruria and S. Italy	*Vasi antichi dipinti del Vaticano* (1925–: C. ALBIZZATI; A. D. TRENDALL). J. D. BEAZLEY, *la Raccolta Benedetto Guglielmi* I (1939)
Rome, Villa Giulia	S. Etruria	*CVA*. P. MINGAZZINI, *Vasi della Collezione Castellani* (1930)
Florence, Mus. Arch. Etr.	N. Etruria; Rhodes	*CVA*
Bologna, Mus. Civ.	Emilia	*CVA*. G. PELLEGRINI, *Catalogo dei Vasi greci dipinti delle necropoli Felsinee* (1912)
Ferrara, Mus. di Spina	Spina	N. ALFIERI, P. E. ARIAS and M. HIRMER, *Spina* (1958)
Naples, N.M.	S. Italy	*CVA*
Taranto, N.M.	S. Apulia	*CVA*
Lecce, Mus. Prov. Castromediano	S.E. Apulia	*CVA*
Palermo, N.M.	Sicily	*CVA*
Syracuse, N.M.	E. Sicily	*CVA*

II. Other Lands

Museum	*Unusual Sources*	*Illustrated Catalogue*
AUSTRALIA		
Sydney, Nicholson Mus.		
AUSTRIA		
Vienna, Kunsthistorisches Mus. (incorporating former Oesterreichisches Mus.)		*CVA*. K. MASNER, *die Sammlung antiker Vasen und Terracotten im k. k. Oesterreichischen Museum* (1892)
BELGIUM		
Brussels, Mus. du Cinquantenaire		*CVA*
CANADA		
Toronto, Royal Ontario Mus.		D. M. ROBINSON, C. G. HARCUM, and J. H. ILIFFE, *a Catalogue of the Greek Vases* (1930)
DENMARK		
Copenhagen, N.M.		*CVA*

Museum	*Unusual Sources*	*Illustrated Catalogue*
FRANCE		
Paris, Louvre	Rhodes; Athens (Geometric)	*CVA*. E. POTTIER, *Vases antiques du Louvre* (1897-1922)
Paris, Bibliothèque Nationale		*CVA*. A. DE RIDDER. *Catalogue des vases peints* (1901-2)
GERMANY		
Munich, Mus. Antiker Kleinkunst		*CVA*. J. SIEVEKING and R. HACKL, *die k. Vasen-Sammlung* (1912)
Berlin (West), Ehemals Staatliche Museen (the major part of pre-war collection)	Rhodes; Aegina (Protoattic)	*CVA*. K. A. NEUGEBAUER, *Führer durch das Antiquarium* **2** (1932). U. GEHRIG, A. GREIFENHAGEN and N. KUNISCH, *Führer durch die Antikenabteilung*. 1968
Würzburg, Martin von Wagner Mus.		E. LANGLOTZ, *Griechische Vasen* (1932)
GREAT BRITAIN		
London, British Mus.	Rhodes; Naucratis; Tell Defenneh	*CVA*
Oxford, Ashmolean Mus.		*CVA*
Cambridge, Fitzwilliam Mus.		*CVA*
HOLLAND		
Leyden, Rijksmus. van Oudheden	Aegean	J. P. J. BRANTS, *Description of the Ancient Pottery* **2** (1930)
Amsterdam, Allard Pierson Mus.		*CVA Hague* (mostly now in Amsterdam)
POLAND		
Warsaw, N.M.		*CVA* (including fascicules on [formerly] Goluchow and Wilanow)
RUSSIA		
Leningrad, Hermitage	S. Russia	A. A. PEREDOLSKAYA, *Krasnofigurniye Atticheskiye Vaz y v Ermitazhe* (1967): for Attic Rf.
SPAIN		
Madrid, Mus. Arqueológico		*CVA*. G. LEROUX. *Vases grecs et italo-grecs* (1912)
UNITED STATES		
New York, Metropolitan Mus.		*CVA*. G. M. A. RICHTER and L. F. HALL, *Rf Athenian Vases in the Metr. Mus. of Art* (1936)

Museum	*Unusual Sources*	*Illustrated Catalogue*
Boston, Mus. of Fine Arts		A. FAIRBANKS, *Catalogue of Greek & Etruscan Vases* (1928). L. D. CASKEY and J. D. BEAZLEY, *Attic Vase Paintings in the M.F.A., Boston* (1931–63)
Philadelphia, University Mus.	Near East	E. H. DOHAN, *Italic Tomb-Groups* (1942)

Note on Sites

It would be useful if someone would compile a list of sites, noting in each instance what pottery has been found, where it is published, and which museum or museums now exhibit or conceal it. Lists which include many relevant publications up to 1925 are given in the second edition of the *Katalog der Bibliothek des deutschen archäologischen Instituts in Rom* (**1**, 83–600; **1** Supplt, 76–414; **2**, 579–84); studies on sites are tabulated in the *Bibliographie* appended to *JdI*; and since 1946 more information can be extracted from *FA*. But most excavations remain unpublished, in whole or in part. The fact is that too many excavators still prefer the thrill and glory of discovery to the drudgery of publishing their finds, and even those who are conscientious too often refuse to make their evidence available till they have at last elaborated a learned commentary on it. There are, of course, distinguished exceptions. But what is wanted is a strict code of excavation with heavy penalties for failure or delay in reporting what has been found. It is less easy to understand why so many reports forget to say where the finds have been deposited. A rough rule is that the greater part remains in the local museum, if there is one, and the finer pieces are taken to one of the more important and better-guarded museums; but as new museums are founded or old ones raised in status, even this rule may be misleading.

A Glossary of Terms not already explained

AEGIS. A sort of breast-plate worn by Athena, fringed with snakes and bearing the Gorgoneion on its front. [PLATES 21B and 38 show only back and side views.]

ANIMAL STYLE. A style in which animals are the principal subject of the decoration.

APOTROPAIC. A term used of objects that avert evil. Archaeologists are too fond of invoking this sort of magic.

ARCHAIC. The style and period between Geometric and Classical, conventionally 720–480 B.C.

ARGIVO-CYCLADIC. *Obsolete*. Used of an incompatible assortment of Cycladic Geometric and Orientalizing.

ATTIC-IONIC. *Obsolete*. A Panionist term for Attic pottery supposed to be influenced by East Greek or 'Chalcidian': it was used first as a replacement for Attic-Corinthian (see p. 317), and later as a complement to it.

BALLOON AMPHORA. *Rare*. A large amphora with very swelling body, especially of the SOS group.

BALSAMARIUM. Another fancy name for Fusiform Unguentarium.

BAROQUE. A term misapplied by some archaeologists to the late, full-blown phase of a style.

BARREL AMPHORA. In South Italian Rf an amphora with concave profile to the body.

BELLY AMPHORA. A one-piece amphora.

BILINGUAL. An unpleasant designation of those Attic pots on which one field is Bf and another Rf.

BLACK DIPYLON. *Obsolete*. Attic Geometric pottery largely covered with dark paint [e.g. PLATE 3A].

BOEOTIAN CYLIX GROUP. The Boeotian group of Bird cups.

BOMBYLIOS. *Obsolete*. Alabastron of Corinthian type [PLATE 10C]. The name is possibly justified.

BUCCHERO ITALICO. *Obsolete.* Impasto.

BUCCHERO PESANTE. *Obsolete.* Heavy, generally late, Etruscan bucchero.

BUCCHERO SOTTILE. *Obsolete.* Fine, generally early, Etruscan bucchero.

BUTTERFLY ORNAMENT. A variant for Opposed Triangles, when the decorative emphasis is lateral.

CADUCEUS. The herald's twining staff, often carried by Hermes. Examples appear on PLATES 34 and 53.

CAMIRAN. *Obsolete.* An alternative name for the Wild Goat style.

CARCHESION. *Rare.* A kind of footless kantharos. The name is possible.

CHITON. A fine sleeved dress [see PLATE 43, women].

CHLAMYS. A short cloak, worn especially by riders [see FIG. 31].

CHTHONIC. Connected with the underworld and its gods (as opposed to the gods above).

CLASSICAL. The style and period between Archaic and Hellenistic, conventionally 480–323 B.C. But in Attic Rf 'Classical' does not extend beyond 400 B.C.

COMAST. A participant in a comos or drunken dance.

CORINTHIAN-ATTIC. *Obsolete.* A short-lived variant for Attic-Corinthian.

COTHON. A conventional name for a large saucer with rim turned over inwards: this may have been a bowl for unguent or a lamp. The name belongs properly to some kind of drinking vessel.

DAUNIAN. The native school of northern Apulia.

DELIAN. A name sometimes ventured for this or that group of Cycladic.

DIPINTO. A painted inscription, especially one added after the firing of the pot.

DIPYLON. An overworked term used once for all Geometric, then for Attic Geometric, lastly for Attic Geometric with funerary scenes (see p. 301). In a still more restricted sense Dipylon is sometimes applied to the big Attic Geometric kraters with high stems and scenes of human figures. More reasonably it is confined to the Dipylon painter (see pp. 19–21) and his school.

DOUBLE AXE ORNAMENT. A variant for Opposed Triangle, objectionable because it suggests a connection with Minoan.

DÜMMLER'S GROUP. A German variant for Pontic.

EPICHYSIS. A small oinochoe, especially frequent in Apulian Rf, with narrow neck and a body shaped like a reel. The name was used of some sort of jug.

EPINETRON. A kind of thigh-guard, used in spinning.

ETRUSCO-CAMPANIAN. *Obsolete.* A class of Bg ware, mostly Campanian.

EUBOEAN. *Obsolete.* An early name for Linear Island. But there is also true Euboean.

EUBOEO-CYCLADIC. *Obsolete.* Another name for Linear Island.

EXERGUE. The segment of a circular field below the base-line of the main decoration. The term is borrowed from numismatics.

FENESTRATED. Used of pedestals with rectangular holes cut through the wall.

FIGURE STYLE. Often used of decoration with human figures, in contrast to Animal style.

FINE STYLE. In Attic Rf an alternative to 'Classical.'

FUSIFORM UNGUENTARIUM. A coarse little tubular pot, bulging in the middle; on Greek sites Hellenistic, but elsewhere once (and perhaps misleadingly) reported in a context as early as the seventh century.

GRAFFITO. An incised or scratched inscription.

GREEK KEY. An unarchaeological name for the key meander.

GUILLOCHE. Cable-pattern.

GUTTUS. Strictly a pot like a flat askos but with a single ring-handle to one side. But sometimes used for Askos.

HANDLE PLATE. A rectangular projection from the rim (especially of a column krater), meeting and covering the handle.

HEAD-VASE. A pot in the shape of a human head, with the lip or spout at the top.

HELLADIC. A term conveniently used to distinguish the Bronze Age from the Iron Age in Greece.

HELLENIC. The counterpart of Helladic.

HELLENISTIC. The style and period following Classical, conventionally dated 323–27 B.C.

HELMET ARYBALLOS. A small pot in the form of a helmeted head with a narrow mouth at the top. Most examples are East Greek of the early sixth century.

HERAEUM. A sanctuary of Hera.

HEROÖN. A sanctuary of a hero.

HIMATION. A heavy cloak or mantle [see PLATE 38, Heracles; and FIG. 34].

HOLKION. A name misused by some bucchero specialists for the handleless chalice.

HOMERIC BOWL. *Obsolete.* A Megarian bowl of the class, probably Boeotian, that is decorated with scenes from Homer.

HORROR VACUI. A psychological explanation, once fashionable, of the thick filling ornament of many Geometric and Orientalizing scenes.

HOURGLASS ORNAMENT. A variant for Opposed Triangles, when the decorative emphasis is vertical.

HYDRISKE. *Rare.* An unpleasant name for a miniature hydria.

IMPASTO. A native Italian ware, characterized by its coarse, poorly fired clay.

IONIAN BOWL. *Obsolete.* A generic name for East Greek Bird, Eye and Rosette bowls.

ITALO-PROTOCORINTHIAN. Italian, especially Etruscan, imitation of Protocorinthian.

KALATHOS. A pot shaped like a basket or inverted bell. The name was certainly used of wicker baskets.

KELEBE. *Obsolete.* A conventional name for a column krater.

KERCH. The usual name for the progressive school of Attic Rf around the middle of the fourth century: the first important finds were made at Kerch (Panticapaeum).

KEY MEANDER. The ordinary continuous meander, as on PLATE 3B.

KRATERISKOS. (1) A small krater. (2) A rare alternative for Lydion.

KYATHOS. (1) A kind of ladle, frequent in Mature and Late Bf: it resembles a tea-cup with very high handle: the name seems credible. (2) A confusing and unnecessary name for the small, footless kantharos (especially that of earlier Protocorinthian).

KYLICHNIS. *Rare.* An Attic name that was used of some pyxides.

LACRYMATERIUM. Another modern name for Fusiform Unguentarium.

LEKYTHOS-OINOCHOE. An aberrant name for the conical oinochoe.

LEPASTE. *Obsolete.* A conventional name for what is now called Lekanis.

LYDION. A conventional name for a small pot shaped like a krater with high foot, but without handles. It may have been used to hold ointment. Most lydia are of the sixth century: some are supposed to be Lydian, some are East Greek, some are Etruscan.

MASTOS. A cup in the shape of a woman's breast. The name is likely.

MERRYTHOUGHT HANDLE. A handle shaped like a wish-bone.

MESSAPIAN. The native school of southern Apulia.

METOPE DECORATION. A misleading name for the system of decoration of PLATE 6A.

MINOAN. The conventional name for the Bronze Age of Crete.

MYCENAEAN. A generic name for the Late Bronze Age in Greek lands. Mycenaean specialists prefer Late Helladic.

NECKING RING. A projecting ridge or moulding on a pot where the neck fits into the shoulder.

ONE-HANDLER. A low cup with one handle common in Attic Bg in the fifth and fourth centuries. One example is inscribed with a variant of the name 'kanastron'.

ONOS. Used, perhaps wrongly, as an alternative to Epinetron.

OPEN CABLE. A simple cable pattern in which the links do not join [as on PLATE 14B, behind the horses and before the lions' jaws].

OVERLAP CUP. A name for those Siana cups on which the row of figures extends across lip and handle frieze [as on PLATE 24B].

OXYBAPHON. An ancient name for some kind of small dish. Some students, misinterpreting a graffito, have identified it with the fish-plate.

PEPLOS. A heavy sleeveless garment [see PLATES 22 and 45, female figures].

PETASOS. A hat with a broad brim, especially for travelling [see FIG. 31, middle boy].

PEUCETIAN. The native school of central Apulia.

PHALERON. *Obsolete*. A name for small Protoattic pots, especially jugs and mugs, of the Early and Middle periods. So called from finds in graves at Phaleron, published in 1869.

PHOCAEAN. A name sometimes given to Grey ware found in Provence, on the unlikely plea that it was imported to Marseilles from Phocaea.

PHORMISKOS. A conventional name for a bulbous object of terracotta, pierced for hanging, that was common in Attic graves of the sixth century.

PINAX. (1) Plaque. (2) *Obsolete*. Plate.

PLASTIC VASE. A pot made in the shape of a human figure, animal or other natural object.

PLEMOCHOE. A low lidded bowl with wide shoulder and high foot.

POLOS. A pill-box hat.

POT-PAINTER. A painter of large pots in contrast to a cup-painter [*ARV*].

PREHELLENIC. A useful and proper definition of the cultures of Greece before the Hellenic (and Iron) Age.

PROCHOUS. A kind of jug. The name is ancient.

PROTHESIS. The lying in state of a corpse.

PROTO-. A prefix denoting the forerunner of a style that had previously been recognized and called by a simple name. So Protogeometric, Protocorinthian and Protoattic. Mercifully other formations of this sort have been stillborn.

PROTOME. The upper part of a human figure or the forepart of an animal.

PSYKTER. A rare pot, in Attic of mushroom shape. Presumably a cooler, and so reasonably named.

RESERVED. When a figure or detail is deliberately left unpainted within an area of dark paint, that figure or detail is said to be reserved. Examples of reservation are the light stripes on the lower part of the pot of PLATE IC, the inner markings of the animals of PLATE 31, and figures in the red-figure technique.

RHYTON. A cup in the shape of a horn [as on FIG. 22] or an animal's head. There is ancient authority for the name.

RUNNING DOG. Another name for Open Cable.

SACRED TREE. A vertical combination of volutes. The motive is derived from Oriental art, where it had some religious meaning.

SAKKOS. A kind of snood.

SAMIAN. (1) *Obsolete*. A name for Fikellura, since supposedly made in Samos. (2) A general term for Geometric and Orientalizing found and probably made in Samos. (3) An obsolescent name for Sigillata. (4) A name for a class of Sigillata, perhaps made in Samos.

SECOND WHITE. The whiter paint used for female flesh over the less white slip of many of the earlier white-ground lekythoi.

SEVERE STYLE. (1) In Geometric this term is often used of the early part of the Middle phase and conventionally dated 850–800 B.C. (2) In Attic Rf it is equivalent to Archaic.

SITULA. A name given conventionally and loosely to deep pots of rather cylindrical shape.

SIX'S TECHNIQUE. The application of colour over the dark paint to give the effect of the reservation of the true Rf technique; inner details are incised through the colour to the dark paint.

SLIP. In potter's parlance a slip is a roughly equal mixture of clay and water, but archaeologists usually mean by 'slip' a coating of clay different in colour and character from the clay of the pot it covers.

STEP MEANDER. A continuous form of the meander, popular especially in Late Argive Geometric. The name explains itself.

STIRRUP VASE. A pot with more or less globular body, and on the shoulder a narrow false spout in the middle, two thin handles joining the false spout, and a genuine spout forward of it. The shape is typically Mycenaean.

STRONG STYLE. A mistranslation of the German 'streng' = severe.

SUB-. A prefix denoting a degenerate extension or survival of a recognized style.

SYMPLEGMA. An interlocked group, usually erotic.

TERMINUS ANTE QUEM. A date *before* which something occurred or was made. So pottery which the Athenians put in their grave-mound at Marathon must have been made before the mound was constructed in 490 B.C.

TERMINUS POST QUEM. A date *after* which something occurred or was made. For example a scarab naming King Bocchoris must have been made after his accession about 718 B.C.

THERICLEAN. A class of vases celebrated in antiquity, perhaps including some Corinthian terracotta relief ware of around 400 B.C.

THYMIATERION. An incense-burner. The name is given, probably with justice, to some smallish bowls attached to high, elaborate pedestals.

TORZELLA. Another name for Nestoris.

TRIPOD-PYXIS. A pyxis supported by three feet.

UNGUENTARIUM. See Fusiform Unguentarium.

VILLANOVAN. A native Italian ware of the early Iron Age.

VOTIVE. Used loosely of all offerings at a sanctuary. A votive deposit is usually a heap of such offerings thrown out at some clearance of the sanctuary.

WASH. A term sometimes used by archaeologists for a thin slip.

WAVE PATTERN. A row of spiral hooks used as a border.

Index

Plates

A. Cup: ht. 14·7 cm. 10th cent. B.C.

B. 'Tea-cup': ht. 9·2 cm.
10th cent. B.C.

C. Lekythos: ht. 15·5 cm.
Early 10th cent. B.C.

D. Oinochoe: ht. 30 cm.
Late 10th cent. B.C.

I. ATTIC PROTOGEOMETRIC

Amphora: ht. 52·5 cm. 14th cent. B.C.

2A. MYCENAEAN

Amphora: ht. 46 cm. 10th cent. B.C.

2B. ATTIC PROTOGEOMETRIC

A. Amphora: ht. 72·2 cm. c. 875–50 B.C.

B. Amphora: ht. 77·5 cm.
Middle or later 9th cent. B.C.

3 . ATTIC GEOMETRIC

B. Oinochoe: ht. (with lid) 80 cm.
c. 750 B.C.

A. Amphora: ht. 155 cm.
c. 760 B.C.

4. ATTIC GEOMETRIC

Detail of Plate 4A

5 . ATTIC GEOMETRIC

Amphora: ht. 28 cm. c. 700 B.C.

6B. THERAN GEOMETRIC

Pyxis: ht. (with lid) 19·5 cm. c. 740 B.C.

6A. ATTIC GEOMETRIC

Hydria: ht. 27·7 cm. Later 9th cent. B.C.

7B. CRETAN PROTOGEOMETRIC B.

Oinochoe: ht. 21·9 cm. Late 8th–early 7th cent. B.C.

7A. RHODIAN GEOMETRIC

Oinochoe: ht. 33·4 cm. c. 720–690 B.C.

8C. PROTOCORINTHIAN

Cup: ht. 6·7 cm. Later 9th cent. B.C.

Kotyle: ht. 10·5 cm. c. 740–30 B.C.

8A, B. CORINTHIAN GEOMETRIC

A. Aryballos: ht. 7·5 cm.
c. 720–690 B.C.

9. PROTOCORINTHIAN

B. Aryballos: ht. of field 3 cm. c. 675 B.C.

C. Aryballos: ht. of field 2 cm. c. 650 B.C.

D. Aryballos: ht. 5·2 cm.
c. 675 B.C.

A. Kotyle: ht. 19 cm. *c.* 660 B.C.

B. Aryballos: ht. 7·8 cm.
c. 600 B.C.

C. Alabastron: ht. 9·7 cm.
c. 625–00 B.C.

10. PROTOCORINTHIAN AND RIPE CORINTHIAN

Olpe: ht. 27·5 cm.
c. 640–25 B.C.

IIA. TRANSITIONAL
CORINTHIAN

Oinochoe: ht. 38 cm.
c. 625–00 B.C.

IIB. RIPE CORINTHIAN

C. Column-krater: ht. 46 cm. c. 600 B.C.

12. RIPE CORINTHIAN

A. Kotyle: ht. of field 6 cm.
c. 580 B.C.

B. Kotyle: ht. of field c. 6·5 cm.
c. 580 B.C.

Column-krater: ht. of fields *c.* 20 cm. *c.* 570 B.C.

13. RIPE CORINTHIAN

B. Krater: ht. 39 cm. c. 690 B.C.

14. PROTOATTIC

A. Hydria: ht. 52·5 cm. c. 700 B.C.

B. Dinos? scale c. 1 : 1. c. 580–70 B.C.

A. Amphora: scale c. 1 : 4. c. 660–50 B.C.

15. PROTOATTIC AND ATTIC B.F.

Amphora: ht. 108·5 cm. *c.* 660 B.C.

16. PROTOATTIC

Amphora: ht. 122 cm. *c.* 615 B.C.

17. PROTOATTIC

Dinos and stand: total ht. 93 cm. *c.* 590 B.C.

18. ATTIC B.F.

A. Volute krater: ht. 66 cm. *c.* 570 B.C.

B. Detail: ht. of upper field 5·6 cm.

19. ATTIC B.F.

A. Hydria: ht. *c.* 25 cm. *c.* 600–570 B.C.

B. Amphora: ht. 38·8 cm. *c.* 570–60 B.C.

20. ATTIC B.F.

A. Amphora: ht. 54 cm. c. 600 B.C.

B. Panathenaic amphora: ht. 61·2 cm. c. 560 B.C.

21. ATTIC B.F.

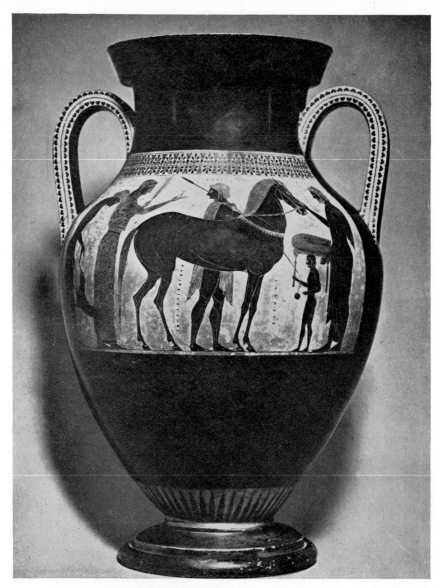

Amphora: ht. 80·5 cm. *c.* 530 B.C.

22. ATTIC B.F.

Amphora: ht. 33 cm. *c.* 530 B.C.

23. ATTIC B.F.

A. Comast cup: ht. 9·5 cm. *c.* 580–70 B.C.

B. Siana cup: ht. 13 cm. *c.* 570–60 B.C.

24. ATTIC B.F.

A. Lip cup: ht. 12·4 cm. *c.* 550–30 B.C.

B. Band cup: ht. 13·3 cm. *c.* 550–30 B.C.

25. ATTIC B.F.

A. Cup: diam. (without handles) *c.* 21 cm. Early 6th cent. B.C.

B. Cup: ht. 9·5 cm. Early 6th cent. B.C.

26. LACONIAN

A–B. Cup: diam. (without handles) 17·8 cm. *c.* 550–40 B.C.

27. LACONIAN

Amphora: ht. 75 cm.
c. 625–00 B.C.

28B. ERETRIAN

'Cup': ht. 21 cm. Mid 6th cent. B.C.

28A. BOEOTIAN

Details of Plate 29A

Cup: ht. 5 cm. c. 675-50 B.C.

29D. EAST GREEK: BIRD BOWL CLASS

Amphora: ht. 43·5 cm. Early 7th cent. B.C.

29A-C. CYCLADIC: LINEAR ISLAND GROUP

B. Oinochoe: ht. 36 cm. c. 625–00 B.C.

A. Oinochoe: ht. 30 cm. c. 630 B.C.

30. WILD GOAT STYLE

A. Oinochoe: ht. of field *c.* 6·5 cm.
c. 625 B.C.

C. Bowl: ht. of field 7·8 cm.
c. 615–00 B.C.

B. Krater: ht. of field *c.* 3·7 cm.
c. 600–575 B.C.

D. Sarcophagus: ht. of field *c.* 17 cm.
c. 515–00 B.C.

31. WILD GOAT STYLE (C CHIOT, D CLAZOMENIAN SARCOPHAGUS)

Amphora: ht. (as preserved) 31 cm. c. 540–30 B.C.

32B. CLAZOMENIAN B.F.

Amphora: ht. 30·5 cm. c. 540–20 B.C.

32A. FIKELLURA

Cup: diam. (without handles) 23·5 cm. *c*. 550 B.C.

33B. EAST GREEK B.F.

Situla: ht. (as restored) 47·6 cm. *c*. 575–50 B.C.

33A. EAST GREEK SITULA

Amphora: ht. 35·1 cm. *c.* 540 B.C.

34. ETRUSCAN B.F. (PONTIC)

Hydria: ht. 44 cm. *c.* 520–10 B.C.

35. CAERETAN HYDRIA

Column-krater: ht. 45·7 cm. *c.* 550–30 B.C.

36. 'CHALCIDIAN'

A. Amphora: scale *c.* 4 : 1. 500–490 B.C.

B. Bell-krater: scale *c.* 2 : 3. *c.* 440 B.C.

37. ATTIC R.F.

Amphora: ht. of field 18·1 cm. *c.* 520 B.C.

38. ATTIC R.F.

Amphora: ht. of field 24·2 cm. 510-00 B.C.

39. ATTIC R.F.

Cup: greatest length of fragment *c.* 18·7 cm. 500–490 B.C.

40. ATTIC R.F.

Amphora: ht. of figure 27 cm. *c.* 490 B.C.

41. ATTIC R.F.

Cup: diam. (without handles) 32·2 cm. 490–80 B.C.

43. ATTIC R.F.

Bell-krater: ht. 37·1 cm. *c.* 470 B.C.

44 . ATTIC R.F.

Pelike: ht. 41 cm. 460–50 B.C.

45. ATTIC R.F.

A. Amphora: ht. 58·1 cm. c. 440 B.C.

B. Lekythos: ht. 19·4 cm. 410–00 B.C.

46. ATTIC R.F.

Lekythos: ht. of field 9·2 cm. 430–20 B.C.

47. ATTIC R.F.

A. Bell-krater: ht. 31·5 cm. 420–10 B.C.

B. Bell-krater: ht. of second figure 15·4 cm. *c.* 440 B.C.

48. ATTIC R.F.

A. Lekythos: ht. 38·7 cm. 450–40 B.C.   B. Lekythos: ht. 31·5 cm. 420–10 B.C.

49 · ATTIC W.G.

Pelike: ht. (as made up) 28·7 cm. *c.* 380 B.C.

50. ATTIC R.F.

Pelike: ht. 42·5 cm. *c.* 350 B.C.

51. ATTIC R.F.

A. Volute-krater: combined ht. of fields *c.* 29 cm. 430–20 B.C.

B. Bell-krater: ht. of field *c.* 17 cm. 440–30 B.C.

52. EARLY SOUTH ITALIAN R.F.

Calyx-krater: ht. of field 28·5 cm. 360–50 B.C.

53. APULIAN R.F.

Amphora: ht. 81 cm. *c.* 340 B.C.

54. LUCANIAN R.F.

Kotyle: ht. 29·5 cm. *c.* 330 B.C.

55A. CAMPANIAN R.F.

Bell-krater: ht. of field 16·3 cm. *c.* 350 B.C.

55B. PAESTAN R.F.

Amphora: ht. 17·4 cm. First half of 2nd cent. B.C.

56A. WEST SLOPE

Bell-krater: ht. 22·2 cm. Second half of 4th cent. B.C.

56B. GNATHIAN